A HARD RAIN

A JIM LOCKE NOVEL

PF HUGHES

For Kelly-Ann, Arlo and Lula

A HARD RAIN

PART I

1

They say cities have ghosts. Mine is no different. They live in the walls, in the squares, in the warehouses. They gather around the rail tracks, sleep in the parks, chatter at night beneath the neon lights. You can feel the history when you walk the streets, and I'd done my share of that all right.

Before I made my way to the top of the multi-storey, I spent some time just walking. It was a bright day, but cold. A cold that would blow through your bones and make you feel like cracked glass. My eyes watered, my eardrums stung, but that was the least of my concerns. I didn't have any at that point. I'd been thinking about what it would feel like for weeks. Perhaps I wouldn't feel anything and I'd just blink out of existence before I hit the ground. I hoped it would be that way, but I couldn't be sure. And did it matter anyway? With any luck, if I timed it right, and followed my planned trajectory and velocity - if I got the speed right - it would be over quickly. I needn't worry about the mess afterwards. And besides, I'd given up on giving a shit long ago. Living on the streets can do that to a man.

I didn't walk far, just circled a few blocks. Gazed at my reflection in shop windows and saw a man I didn't recognise. I was aware of eyes upon me. Workers on their lunch break, the odd tourist. I suppose I must've been attracting attention, not that I cared. No one would disturb my last moments. I tried to remember when I was a kid, when things were all right, long before anything went wrong. I couldn't find it, couldn't connect, because I felt nothing. Nothing at all. When I tired of walking, and everything just went by in a blur, I willed myself to focus on the task at hand. I had one thing I needed to do before I climbed those stairs.

It was a pub that smelt of piss before you were even six steps from the gents. A hang out for rent boys and drop outs. There was horse racing on the T. V and betting slips and cigarette ends littering the carpet, sticky with spilled beer and worn down in patches at the bar. All eyes fell on me as I stepped up. Pulled a fiver from my coat pocket.

'Guinness. Cold.'

They were the first words I'd said to anyone in a week. Felt strange. Was only used to hearing my own voice in my head.

The barmaid poured. I caught her looking at me as the Guinness rested. Wondered what she was thinking. I remember thinking this would be the last human interaction I would have on this earth. It wasn't what I would've expected. I told her to keep the change as she placed my last pint down on the bar. Then I lifted it, took one sip to savour the taste, and threw the whole thing back. I almost brought it straight back up again. My stomach had been empty for days. I put the glass down, said my thanks, then left the pub to throw myself off the car park roof.

2

I found the door to the stairs down the side of the exit ramp. Choking on exhaust fumes, I took the first flight, then paused, looking up. Could I make it up six flights in my condition? Nothing would stop me. I couldn't give two fucks if it took all day. And when I reached the top, with my bones cracking and muscles aching, my broken heart pounding like a drum, I'd have myself one last smoke before I gathered my thoughts - or at least what I had left of them - and took the plunge.

I made it in less than five minutes, almost surprised to find myself running up the last few steps. I'd imagined that with each one, a memory would come, perhaps things that had once been important, and they did. But they didn't last long, didn't stop me. The hurt was too much. The bad stuff followed any morsel of good memories I had. It had all left me a wreck. A failed marriage, booted off the force, my daughter Nicole taken away into the custody of her mother. I couldn't go anywhere near either of them. I'd been fucked over by a justice system gone mad. Lost my wife and kid, lost

the house - repossessed thanks to the recession - and ulti-
mately lost my mind. Friendships, too. I could rely on no
one. It was as if my entire life had been swept aside by a
force of nature, blown away by a hurricane of bad luck and
broken promises. The last phone call I'd made to Karen had
ended with a dead tone. It was the final countdown as far as
I was concerned. The only thing I had in my head as I
reached the roof and stepped out into the freezing afternoon
was the photograph of us all on holiday in Spain. I think it
was the last time I was really happy. Now I was just tired.
Tired and fucked. There was only one answer.

I hadn't realised how out of breath I'd be but by the time
I was standing in the middle of the roof with my hands
clasped to my knees, gasping for air and almost choking on
it, I knew my recklessness had taken its toll. I was knackered. I'd lost weight, felt weak, had the shakes. I wasn't just a
shadow of my former self; I was shit scared of it. Kept
hearing voices in my head telling me to drop more pills than
I needed, or buy a rope from some hardware store and
throw it over a bridge with myself attached. Razor blade, slit
your own fucking throat. Handgun, a bullet in the soft,
pulpy matter of the brain, up through the mouth to make
sure. I wasn't even sure if the voice was mine, tell you the
truth. It sounded like my Dad, old bastard that he was.
Goading me, taking the piss, daring me. I blotted him out,
and it worked for a while. But it always came back. I'd had
enough.

I stood and took in the view. Manchester's landscape had
changed over the years, no doubt about it. I hardly recognised the place. Everywhere you looked, there were new
build apartments skirting the ship canal and out to Salford.
Castlefield had undergone another resurgence after the

boom in the nineties and there were new, high rise property developments going up down the bottom of Deansgate and beyond the Mancunian way. Not that any of that bothered me now. This was what I was leaving behind. I felt no part of it. I'd spent the last year living under canal bridges and back doors of office blocks, out of sight down the narrow back-streets. No one would miss me.

I walked to the edge and tried not to look down. It was hopeless. A tram went past below, on its way to Rochdale or Oldham or some other run down place on the outskirts. Looked like a kid's toy train. I must've been a hundred feet up. A decent enough height to get the job done. I thought about taking a running jump, so the momentum would carry me over the edge if I backed out at the last second. Or I could just dive off. I tried not to think about it. Tried not to think about anything.

I must've stood there a while, trying to summon up the courage to swing my leg over the rail and stand up on the ledge. The rail was at waist height and the ledge must've been only two feet until it dropped into empty space. Gave me the shits, big style. Tried - and failed - to think about something other than the mess I'd make when I hit the ground or whether I'd feel anything at all when my head bounced off the pavement. See, that's the thing about madness, you get all kinds of thoughts running through your mind at a hundred miles per hour, each one not lasting long enough to allow any focus. Then they just come back around again and it doesn't rest. I wasn't in my right mind. Something crazy had taken over. More than that. It was as if I was possessed.

I swung my leg over the rail so that one foot was on the ledge and the other on the roof, with the rail between my legs. Felt cold. I gripped tight, then swung my other leg over until I was facing the roof with that empty space, that deathly drop, behind me. I turned around, still clutching the rail behind my back. My fingers felt like icicles as the bitter wind bit into them. My knees jangled, my teeth chattered, and I think I might've pissed myself. Never had a head for heights. It was made even worse because, as soon as I'd summoned the balls to let go and fall forward, I would be dropping through the air and then splattered on the ground barely two seconds later. Kept telling myself that's all it would be. Two seconds. Forty years on earth, all that life and two seconds later, gone. Just like that. I looked out, glanced down. Saw people walking below, as small as toy soldiers on a kid's bedroom floor. Soon they'd get the shock of their lives. They'd get their smartphones out to film the blood pouring from my head like water from a tap. There'd be screams too, followed by the sirens and the car horns. And yet I didn't care for that because I'd be dead and the world would go on, they'd clean up in an hour or two, and I'd be nothing but a few column inches in the local rag.

'So, you going to jump, or what?'

I wasn't sure if it was another of those voices in my head, but then I heard her again.

'Just get it over with, if that's what you want. No point in hanging around, eh?'

It was coming from somewhere behind me, a girl's voice, youngish, caught on the wind. I mean, what the fuck?

'Just so you know, you'll plummet to the ground at sixty miles an hour, maybe more, and when you hit the pavement, your skull will smash and the shit inside it will just come leaking out like the inside of an egg. Imagine that. So what're you waiting for?'

'Leave me alone.'

'I'll leave you alone when you let go of that rail.'

'Just fuck off!'

My head and heart were pounding and I could feel my arms shaking as they gripped the rail tighter. My knees too. I caught a bit of the Stones' *Can't You Hear Me Knocking?* between my ears and I almost laughed. Maybe I did.

'I'll give you two choices,' she said. 'I can fuck off now, just as soon as you leap from this building to your gruesome death, or I can fuck off later on when you climb back here to me and we go down to the street. Your choice.'

This was all I needed. Fuck's sake, why me? And who was she anyway? 'What do you want? Can't you see what I'm trying to do here?'

'Can you not see what I'm trying to do?'

'Why the fuck would you care about me!?'

'I don't care about you! I care about them out there. You think anyone out there wants to see you smashed up all over the pavement like a fucking roadkill? You selfish cunt, you really are fucked up.'

'Oh, piss off!'

She laughed then. The bitch *laughed*. I clutched at the railing tighter, harder, my hands frozen and murdering me. I could feel my arms aching because they'd been stuck rigid for so long. And God knows how long I'd been standing on that ledge. Time is a funny thing when you're about to kill yourself, to leap into the unknown.

'There's a better way, you know. You could cut your wrists. Overdose. Heroin overdose, that'd be good. I could get you some. Let's see. Hanging, throw yourself in front of a train, poison yourself with an exhaust.'

'Will you shut up!'

'Hey, I could even get someone to do it for you! You know, like a hit. I could arrange that.'

'Jesus Christ...'

'Not going all religious on me, are you?'

'No.'

'I wonder what he'd say, you know, probably wouldn't be best pleased. They say suicides end up in limbo, don't they?'

It was just my luck to get saddled with some tart intent on talking me out of it. I'd come this far, I wasn't gonna back down. And then it occurred to me that the barmaid wasn't my last interaction with another human being, it was this silly cow.

'You got a light?'

I was aware of her beside me now, could hear her high heels clack clacking on the concrete behind until they scraped up not two yards away. As she leaned over the railing, I caught a glimpse of her from the corner of my eye. She was all red lipstick and peroxide blonde hair cut in a bob, a tacky leopard print fur coat wrapped around her.

'Do I look like I've got a light?'

'I know you're a smoker. Seen you around here before. Well, not *here*, but ... well, around, you know? You're on the streets, aren't you?'

'Not for long.'

I could hear her digging around in her pockets. 'Found one. You want one?'

I could murder one right now. I shook my head.

'Oh, come *on*. You can't top yourself without having a last smoke, eh? Just think. Do you really want to spend your last moments up here thinking about how much you want a fag but won't have one because if you did it would hurt your pride? Fuck's sake, you're worse than I thought. Maybe you are better off dead.'

'Don't say that.'

'Come again?'

'I said, don't say that!'

'Say what?'

'The things you're saying!'

'God, you're a sensitive type, aren't you?'

'Just...'

But I'd run out of things to say. I suppose she was right. It would be a shitty way to go out. I'd been haunted by these thoughts for weeks now, ever since I'd decided to throw it all away. And now, when it came to it, I was having my doubts.

'So tell me why. Why this?'

'Just because.'

'What's your name?'

'Why do you want to know?'

'Two things. So I can have a proper conversation with you, cause that's what two people do when they meet. And so I can find your next of kin and give them the awful news when you hit the ground.'

'Why are you doing this? Why would you care?'

'Because I don't want to see you kill yourself. It's that simple.'

'It's Jim.'

'Well now we're getting somewhere, Jim. I'm Angel. I'd shake your hand but it's stuck rigid to that rail and I don't want to distract you and make you fall. So come on. Why? Do you want to tell me about it?'

'No, I do not. My business.'

'Got kids?'

Shit. She knew how to put me on a guilt trip. I took a deep breath, struggled to get the air in. Felt like a kid again, emotionally drawn and gasping for breath.

'One,' I said. 'A daughter, Nicole.'

'And how do you think young Nicole would feel when

she finds out her Daddy didn't care about her and just jumped off a bloody car park?'

'I do care about her!'

'What's that?'

'I said I care about her. More than anything!'

'Doesn't look like it, Jim. Not from where I'm standing. So why don't you tell me what happened? Come back here and tell me all about it.'

'I can't,' I said. It takes tremendous effort. I'm scared that if I stutter, I'll lose my grip and fall.

'You can. You can.'

'I can't,' I said, shaking. 'I can't move.'

'Take a deep breath, Jim. Nice, big deep breaths.'

I did just that as she crept closer and breathed with me.

'Don't look down, it'll make you dizzy. Can you turn to me?'

But I couldn't. I was stuck. My head felt like it was trapped in a vice, all my muscles tense, the veins in my neck bulging. 'I can't.'

'Just take your time. Do you want to do this, Jim? Do you really want to let go?'

I didn't need any time to think. 'No.' I swallowed. Could taste copper in my mouth. 'No, I don't.'

'Good.' A gust of wind blew across the roof and my legs went to jelly. 'Now this is what we're gonna do. I'm gonna grab your arms and you're gonna let go of this rail. You got me?'

'I can't!'

'I've got you, Jim, you won't fall, I promise. Just loosen your fingers, I've got you, okay? Take your time, love.'

Easier said than done. All I wanted at that moment was to fall to my knees. I felt so weak, so useless. I thought that at any minute, I could just slip or another gust of wind would blow me out into space. Felt detached. Saw the faces of Karen and Nicole in my mind. Could hear the blood pumping in my temples.

'I can't let go, I can't let go.'

'I've got you, Jim.'

'I can't do it!'

And I felt her behind me, her hands stronger than I thought, gripping each elbow. I could feel her breath on my neck, could smell her perfume too. I knew just one step out would take me over the edge. I wanted a way out, but I didn't want that. Christ, I didn't want that. How the hell I got up here, I'll never know. I don't know what the scariest thing was. Knowing that I wasn't in my right mind, or knowing I could fall to my death any second if I didn't hang on for dear life.

'You *can* do it, Jim. Now trust me. There's just a few things you need to do. Take one hand off first and I've got you. You won't fall. Can you do that?'

I just focussed on loosening my fingers until my palm wasn't holding freezing metal anymore, and when my grip came free, she had me. All I could do was look straight ahead, fixed my eyes on the building opposite and tried not to scream. In my head, I was screaming the world down.

'Great! You did it. I've got you, haven't I? Now, can you turn towards me? Turn around, Jim.'

'I can't do that, Jesus, I can't do *that*.'

'Deep breaths again, Jim.'

We did those breaths together again. Tried to blot everything from my mind, but it was all too much. It was racing, like my heart.

'Nice and easy,' she said. 'I've got you. Now just turn to face me, nice and easy does it.'

I wondered how the fuck I'd got myself in this mess. I

mean, how in God's name did I find myself standing on a ledge a hundred feet up on a Manchester street? I didn't want to die! Things had turned to shit, big style, but I didn't want to *die*. And I didn't want to be responsible for my end.

'Nice and easy.'

I took her advice. Nice and easy. I didn't look at my feet as I shuffled them around, because I didn't want to look down and I couldn't move my neck. There were a few things I could've done with at that moment. A very stiff drink and a packet of smokes. But I kept on going, my nerves jangling and my legs quivering. She had a hold of me, I'm sure she did, but all I could do was just shuffle those feet one tiny inch at a time. I so wanted to close my eyes but knew that if I did, I'd be a goner. Shit, this was harder than I thought.

When I was close to her, and my back was facing the other way, I could smell her perfume strong. Could feel the soft fake fur of her coat on my face, her cold cheeks beside my own.

'You did it,' she whispered in my ear. 'You did it, Jim. Now just one more thing to do, love. I want you to lift your leg until it's over this railing here, right beside us. Can you do that, Jim?'

'I don't know...'

'Jim?'

It was the hardest thing in the world to say yes, but I did. I wanted to be off this ledge more than anything. I felt her arms go under mine and she had me in a bear hug. It was the best feeling I'd had in years. Her breath was in my ear as I lifted my shaking leg over the railing. I rested it there for the briefest of moments, but it felt like forever. When I could feel the bar under my crotch, the world almost fell out of me when I felt her drag me over the other side with the strength of a man, and we fell to the floor in a heap. I let out a cry of anguish and she held me in her arms, the warmest I've felt then or since, and I bawled like a baby as she rocked me and kissed my head, and stroked my hair up there on that roof.

'It's over, Jim,' she said. 'We did it, love. We made it.'

3

'So dig in. You must be starving. Like a dog without a bone.'

I felt it. We were sitting at the back table in a cafe just off Piccadilly. Outside, the rush hour was in full throe and the weather had taken a turn, the north wind coming in hard and the freezing rain streaming down the windows. Buses filled with commuters and the steam from the coffee machine hung like a cloud over the room. It was busy, a few students topping up on a cheap tea before hitting the bars, and a handful of shoppers nursing their coffees before braving the rain. I looked down at my double egg and chips and felt queasy. I pushed the food around my plate and broke a yolk, picturing my brain spilling out of my head on the pavement.

'You need to eat, Jim. I can tell you've not eaten in days. Won't do you any good, love.'

'I'm not hungry.' Truth was, I couldn't tell the difference between hunger and emptiness.

'Try.' She forked a handful of chips from her own plate and waved it at me. 'Please?'

I took a sip of tea and managed a few chips and a forkful of runny egg. It seemed to get easier with every mouthful, but I expected a long haul. I guess I *was* hungry, I just didn't have the motivation.

She called herself Angel, but that wasn't her proper name. She refused to tell me. Angel was her street name, the name she used for punters. She told me she was working later tonight. She was certainly dressed the part. Told me she'd be celebrating her thirtieth next Saturday night. Even invited me along. I said I was busy, which wasn't true. As I sat there, trying to eat, I wondered how long it would be before the black dog came again and I'd find another way.

'So come on. Do you want to talk about it?'

I didn't, not really. Not at all, in fact. 'There's nothing to say. I really don't know why you're interested.'

'It's not every day you see someone on a car park roof. I don't think you were up there for a laugh, do you?'

Every word was like a bullet through the heart. But she was right. I had my reasons, of course I did. I suppose it had been a while since anyone gave a shit about me. I must admit, I was pretty floored to find it coming from a working girl.

'Look, it's a long story, okay? Not really in the mood.'

'I'm all ears, Jim. When you're ready to talk about it, I'm here. Might even be a blowjob in it for you.'

It was the first thing to raise a smile out of me in months. 'Free, I hope.'

Now it was her turn to laugh. She sounded like a hyena. 'I suppose I can make allowances.'

We were silent for a few minutes, content to eat. Or rather, she was. I was struggling to put the food in my mouth. I couldn't help thinking about where my next drink would come from. And after what I'd been through, I wanted oblivion, nothing less.

'So, where're you gonna sleep tonight, love?'

I didn't know whether to laugh or cry. Would it be behind Ho's Chinese Bakery or somewhere under a bridge on the canal? 'Don't know, I'll find somewhere.'

She gave me eyebrows, chewed the last of her food and drained her tea. 'There's a room where I'm staying. You can have it. For a while, at least.'

'No,' I said. 'Look. Angel. You've done enough. I wouldn't expect anything more. So thanks for the food and...you know, the other stuff. Sorry to put you through that.'

She shook her head, wiped her mouth on a napkin. 'No, you're staying with me. I'm not letting you sleep on the streets tonight. Especially tonight. Just one night, okay? Come on, you know you need a decent bed. It's no bother at all. You could do with a bath.'

'Look, I'm not sure.'

'There's no not sure about it, Jimmy. Look, it's not my flat. I'm looking after it for someone for a while.'

'A client, is it?'

'Something like that, yeah,' she nodded. 'Look, I've been there three months and I'll probably be there another six at least, before he comes back. So it's cool. It's a nice place.'

'Comes back from where?'

'Hong Kong. Business stuff. I've not heard a peep from him in weeks, actually. Look, the offer's there. It's up to you. But I'd hate to see you sleep out here tonight. Especially after today. And I know you need a drink.'

I looked at her.

'Well, it's obvious. You need to get on the wagon, Jim. Looks like it's killing you. But if you want a drink, it's there.

No one will disturb you. I'm working tonight, anyway. You've got the place to yourself.'

'I can't believe you'd even trust me.'

She smiled, looked down at the table, looked back at me. 'I've got my eye on you. I don't think you're the stealing type. Besides, I won't be out late. You'll have probably knocked yourself out by the time I get back home.'

I didn't know what to say, so just pushed the cold remains of my food around. It had been a long time since I slept in a proper bed. There were one or two hostels, but I always hated those places. Preferred my own space, my own cold concrete under a bridge somewhere. Don't think I even remembered what a mattress felt like. I shivered. Wasn't sure if it was the cold or the blessing of good human nature. I looked at Angel, who was playing with her mobile phone, and felt like crying. Maybe I would too. But it wasn't the bed I was thinking about at that moment. It was the drink. A double whisky, a few pints of snakebite, a bottle of expensive red wine. I only hoped there wasn't a full drinks' cabinet as I was likely to drain it until I fell on my arse. She was an excellent judge of character.

'I've got to go soon. Get ready and stuff. You know. Anyway, the room's there. No funny business. Not sure you could even get it up, anyway.' She smiled. 'But if you change your mind, you can have my number.'

'I'll come,' I said. 'Just for tonight. I suppose I should try to get some proper sleep and stuff, you know.'

She put her finger to her lips to silence me. 'We'll get a taxi,' she said, tossing me one of her smokes. 'I'm paying. You can rest when we get back. You look knackered.'

We looked at each other. I wondered if she could read what was in my mind. Then we left, me following her as we weaved our way through the traffic, smoking, and into a taxi rank queue, which was quiet. Two minutes later, I was on my way to a flat I'd never seen with a woman I'd only just met. I didn't know why she was doing this, maybe it was just in her soul or something, but I didn't see the point in thinking about it. She linked her arm through mine and smiled as the cab pushed through the traffic towards the river. I looked out the window, wondering what in the world I'd gotten myself into.

4

The 'flat' was more like a high-class penthouse apartment. It overlooked the canal in an exclusive, gated section of Castlefield. It was enormous. There were three large double bedrooms, one of them with an en suite bathroom–the main bathroom was huge too, with marble flooring and top end facilities. She led me into a living room filled with expensive furniture, a stereo and entertainment system that looked brand new, a marble coffee table, parquet flooring throughout. The kitchen wouldn't look out of place in a top restaurant. There was a window the entire length of one wall, which opened out onto a garden roof terrace so green it looked like a personal jungle. I looked out at several moored barges at the canal side. The entire place sang money. I wondered exactly what this client of hers did for a living. Didn't bother asking.

She told me to sit down, brought me a bottle of beer from the kitchen. Japanese. She said she was going for a shower and to make myself at home. I sat there on a big leather couch and drank the beer while she freshened up.

Helped myself to a few smokes, too. Got restless and paced around the living room. Tried to step out onto the roof terrace, but the door was locked. Probably just as well. Sneaked a peek in the fridge, one of those big American ones with two doors. There were another seven beers sitting there on the top shelf. All the food was from M&S. It wasn't just food; it was M&S food. Not that I'd be eating any of it. Not in my condition. As I drained the beer, the shakes came again. Almost dropped the bottle on the tiled kitchen floor.

Caught a look at myself in the big mirror in the hallway. I looked a fucking mess. My coat was covered in shit. I looked like a pissed up Jesus. My hair was greasy and had grown down to my shoulders. My beard was thick and heavy, my eyes were circled with red blotches. My skin had a sickly pallor to it, like I'd been living on nothing but crack for several years. The telltale signs of a functioning alcoholic stared back at me. There was a black emptiness in those eyes. A sickness I couldn't define. I'd been having stomach cramps for several weeks now. Wasn't sure if the booze exacerbated it. Probably. When I drank, the pain went away. Trouble was, I had to keep on drinking to keep it at bay. I knew I was slowly killing myself. No wonder Karen left me. I'd leave me too.

When Angel came out of her room in a little black dress and covered in makeup, she threw a towel at me and told me to get a shower. I needed one.

'I'm going out,' she said, writing her number down on a pad by the phone in the hallway. 'Should be back by midnight. You'll find beer in the fridge and help yourself to anything you want food wise, if you're hungry. And try to get some sleep. You look like shit.'

She had a way with words.

'Phone me if you need me,' she said. I couldn't take my

eyes off her arse. 'You can change your clothes. He won't be needing them. And get a shave, it doesn't suit you.'

'Why are you doing this? There's really no need, you know, I can...'

'You can do nothing and just sort yourself out. God knows you need it.'

'Angel...'

'No excuses now. I'll let myself in. Tomorrow we think about how to get you on the straight and narrow. I'll see you later.'

Then she was out the door. I listened as her footsteps faded down the hallway, then took a deep breath. Caught myself in the mirror again. It was more than a strange feeling to find myself alone in a posh apartment. Nearest I got to something like this was in the pages of a Habitat catalogue. Life is strange. It occurred to me that I could be dead now. Instead, I headed to the bathroom and the shower that wouldn't look out of place in a Saudi Palace.

I must've been in there a good half hour. When I stepped out, the steam clouded everything. Had to give it ten minutes until I attempted a shave. Found a pair of scissors in the cabinet and set to trimming my beard before I lathered on the gel. It came off in thick clumps, which I dumped in a little bin beside the toilet. Another half hour later and my face was as smooth as a baby's arse. I hardly recognised myself.

I cut my hair too. Found a set of clippers in what must've been the owner's room. Shaved down to the bone in front of the hallway mirror with a towel on the floor to catch my greasy hair. The turnaround was amazing. I felt like I'd just rid myself of the weight of the world. Shit, I even looked handsome.

I found a pair of jeans that fit just right and a t-shirt with a stencilled skull on the front. The sunken cheekbones looked pretty much like my own. I put my own boots back on, with a fresh pair of socks. Drew the line at wearing another man's kecks. Went commando instead. Threw on a thick grey hoodie, unzipped.

Then I cracked open a beer and hovered around the stereo for ten minutes, trying to find something decent to drown out the silence. And to shut out those voices in my head. If Karen could see me now, she'd just about shit. Found *Sticky Fingers* and put it on. Felt like I hadn't heard proper music for years. I had a complete record collection in my head, but no means of playing it. When *Can You Hear Me Knocking?* kicked in, I almost burst into tears. I was instantly taken back to the events of the afternoon. I must be insane, I thought, to come so close to jumping. I swung the bottle back until it emptied, then went to grab another.

Took me ages to find the key that opened the door to the roof terrace. I'd moved onto *Exile On Main Street* by this time and just sat there in a big old garden chair, smoking and listening to the Stones as I looked blankly out into the night. Although the depression hung over me like a dead weight, I don't think I'd ever felt as content in years as I did then. I finished the last bottle and dozed off as the sound of the local bars echoed around me. Sleep had never been as blissful as this. I don't remember any dreams. Just a comforting blackness and a cold breeze.

I woke up shivering some time later to the sounds of the night. I'd become so familiar with those sounds. Traffic, laughing night owls, the odd siren blaring through the streets. The penthouse was so close to the bars down here that I could even hear chinking glasses and pumping bass leaking out over the water.

Angel said to help myself. I checked the fridge again, but all the beer had gone. The empty bottles lay on the side. I thought about warming up a tub of miso soup in the microwave, but I quickly knocked that idea on the head. Found a drinks cabinet in the living room. It was a dream come true and a living nightmare all at the same time.

I found an unopened bottle of Jim Beam in the cabinet and got stuck in. Didn't bother finding a glass at first, then filled a tumbler to the top. I caught the time on a digital clock on the cooker. 22:16.

I'd been thinking of phoning Karen for weeks, but since my last call, when I got a dead tone, I figured she'd changed her number. Tonight was the first opportunity in ages. I stared at the phone in the hallway, goading myself to pick it up and dial. It might be the last opportunity I had for a while. I knew that she'd been spending a lot of time at her parents' house, naturally assumed that was where she might be. Or maybe I was just telling myself that. To make myself believe that the dead tone was just an innocent mistake, and that she wanted to speak to me, of course she did. Who the fuck was I kidding? I picked it up, dialled the number to her mother's. Ringing. I just wanted to hear her voice, and Nicole's too. I guess I just wanted confirmation that someone could hear me, that I wasn't just out in the void somewhere. To confirm to myself, I guess, that I wasn't dead.

'Hello?'

Shit. Frank. Her Dad. As much as we got on during our marriage, Frank said he never wanted me to show my face again after the 'affair'. There was no affair, never was. I wouldn't know how to chat up another woman if I had the guidebook imprinted on my brain, let alone get her into bed. Karen had been convinced my late nights after work

were with the elusive woman copper I was supposedly shag-
ging, but they weren't. I was in the pub which was even
worse. I don't know who told her I was playing around.
Must've been a proper vindictive bastard to even consider it.
I don't remember ever getting in anyone's bad books. I
suppose the drink didn't help. Someone on the force was
out to fuck my life up. And they did. I had my suspicions. I
couldn't prove one way or another if anyone I used to work
with decided to spread malicious rumours about me, which
were all false. Had to be someone who knew both Karen
and me. Our marriage was fine until the drink came into my
life. Pressures of the job, though I must admit, I always had a
taste for it. It wasn't an affair that wrecked my marriage. It
was the booze.

'Hello?'

I almost said the words. Frank, it's Jim. But I couldn't do
it. Not this time. When I realised I was holding my breath, I
put the phone down. Spent the next half hour pacing. I
thought about pouring the rest of the bottle down the sink,
but decided on locking it in the cabinet instead. I couldn't
tear my eyes from it after that. Went out onto the roof
terrace again and chain-smoked as my past came back to
haunt me. Karen and me on our first date. Nicole's birth.
Our wedding day out in a Derbyshire hotel and the brilliant
time we all had. All gone now. Two years down the line after
a messy divorce case, no contact from Karen or my daughter–she'd be seven now–and a life on the streets going from
hostel to hostel. Kipping on friends' couches. They soon left
me high and dry. The repossession took everything out of
me. Out of *us*. In the end, there were only bitter goodbyes.
Last time I saw Karen, she'd moved into her friend Emma's
house. I gave up trying to contact her when she sent me a

text message saying she never wanted me anywhere near her or Nicole again. She said she was changing her number, and that was that. I've no idea where they are now. But I know someone who does. I kept telling myself I would call Frank again tomorrow. And if he or Maureen refused to talk, I'd go to their house and find out.

Yeah, that's what I kept telling myself.

I wondered that, if I did do it–kill myself–would they even give a shit? And even if I did, I'd never find out if they gave a shit or not. And I would leave my daughter without a Dad. As far as I knew, Karen could tell her all kinds of stuff about me. It killed me to think she would. But after everything, all the heartache, all the damage and pain, I wouldn't put it past her.

I was ashamed. Ashamed to have let the idea even cross my mind. But that's what I mean about not being in my right mind. I mean, how the fuck could I be? I felt like shit and I hated what I'd become, but doing myself in was no way to deal with it. I had to find another way. I didn't know what or how, but I had to find it. And I wondered why Angel had come into my life. She said she'd seen me on the streets. I suppose it's not unreasonable to have seen me around, walking around the city or out begging. A working girl would get to see a lot of familiar faces, no doubt. Still didn't fully explain why she wanted to help me. I didn't believe there were any good souls still out there. I guess I was wrong. I shook my head as I took in my surroundings. Could barely believe she'd even trust me to stay here alone. It occurred to me that I could just nick anything I wanted. She'd never see me again. But I liked her. And I couldn't do that. And I believed in honesty. I wouldn't have joined the force if I didn't. I might be fucked up, but I wasn't a thief. I might be a drunken arsehole, but at least I had some integrity.

I heard the front door slam–a big old heavy piece of work–followed by the click clacking of her high heels on the parquet floor. I turned from the roof terrace and stepped into the living room. She dropped a big brown bag on the floor when she saw me.

'Holy fuck!'

'What?'

'What?! Look at you!'

I suppose she meant my appearance, though it could be the fact that I was spaced out on bourbon.

'You look... great! God, you scrub up well. How did you...?'

I stroked my stubbled head. 'Found some clippers. Hope you don't mind?'

'Shit, no.' She picked up the paper bag. 'Course not. Look, I know you probably haven't got much of an appetite, but I got Chinese. Just in case.'

I shrugged. 'I suppose I could try it.'

'Believe me, once you've had Yan's chilli beef, you won't look back.'

She was right about the chilli beef. I managed half a plate. It was all my fragile insides could take. She offered me more booze–she had a few glasses of white wine–but something held me back. I knew I had to start somewhere. Kept repeating the mantra 'I don't need a drink' as I watched her guzzle it back with her prawn toast. Truth was, I needed it like I needed air. Said I was gonna get my head down. I wasn't tired. I just knew I needed to lie down in a dark room without the smell or sight of booze to tempt me into an oblivion I wanted badly.

In the early hours, as a pale blue dawn leaked through

the blinds, I felt her creep into bed beside me. Felt her soft, naked skin against my own. As her arm stroked my ribs and settled somewhere around my heart, I thought I was dreaming. I didn't last long, but she didn't mind. Kept telling me it was all right. I suppose it was.

5

I spent the next week with Angel in that penthouse. When I woke up in her arms on that Saturday morning - she was still sleeping - I had several thoughts in my mind. Could this really be the start of something new? If so, what the hell attracted her to a homeless drunk? And what was in it for her? Why did she live the life she did? Had she chosen it? And whose bed was I sleeping in? Who was this guy who owned the place, and why was he in Hong Kong?

We had breakfast looking out onto the roof terrace - or rather she did, while I sipped a strong coffee, my hands twitching. The rain came down hard. I thanked her for letting me stay. She told me to stop feeling sorry for myself. I thought about asking her how she came to live in this place, who Mr. Hong Kong was. Thought better of it. Maybe later. She was a girl with secrets, I could tell that much. I suppose she had to be, given her line of work, which made me wonder all the more why she put her trust in me.

We spent all day just sitting inside, talking. We had the

talk. I told her about Karen and losing the house and my job. She nodded in all the right places and made a few jokes about truncheons and handcuffs. I was beginning to like her more and more. But it was hard talking about it. I suppose it did me some good to let it all out. God knows I had locked it up in my head for a while. On the streets, you spend most of your energy just trying to survive. She said she understood. Had been on the streets herself, for a while. Before she started on the game. I wanted to ask her how it came about. It was clear she didn't want to go into detail. 'I just fell into it,' she said. Just like I fell into a bottle of whisky. I suppose there are some things in life you just can't choose.

The sex was good. She was a professional. But that's all it was, nothing more. I wasn't about to kid myself that there could be more to it. I'd had my fair share of delusions, but I wasn't that deluded. I knew this was nothing more than her taking pity on me, or something like that. And maybe it wasn't just that. Maybe she needed something from me too. She seemed somewhat fragile, in her own way. I got the impression that she didn't want to be doing what she did. Prostitution, I mean. I didn't think she enjoyed it. But I couldn't get her true thoughts out of her, and I didn't want to push it. It was better to just accept what was happening for what it was. Her being nice, me accepting it. It was the most human contact I'd had in years. To be honest, it floored me, but in a good way.

I think it was a Wednesday night when she said I should try to get off the streets for good. Said I could use this address to aid my job hunting. And if I found something, I could move on. She was happy for me to stay for as long as I wanted. But I didn't feel right doing that. I was grateful–who wouldn't be?–but I wasn't ready for that. And I didn't want to put her out. We didn't have much in common, anyway. She was a prostitute; I was an ex copper. I don't think she wanted anything to develop either. It was just a sex thing. An attraction, I suppose. A few years back, I would've been nicking her for soliciting. Now I was liable to get nicked myself for begging or sleeping in some department store's doorway. Funny how things change. And besides, it wouldn't work. We'd be the most unlikely couple you could ever meet. And I couldn't live with her job.

'You don't have to stay on the streets forever, Jim. What's happened has happened. You can make a new life for yourself. If you gave it a go.'

She was hanging around the oven, monitoring the pizza she'd stuck in ten minutes ago. She was on wine; I was on beer, at least for now. I didn't want to have this conversation. She was right, but I just couldn't see a way. Being booted off the force didn't bode well for finding a new job. And besides, I wasn't cut out for working, anyway. I had to be honest with myself. I was a drinker. The only thing I was fit for was getting pissed and feeling shit about it afterwards. I told her.

'But people get through it. With the right support. You're not a worthless man, Jim, but you seem to have convinced yourself otherwise.'

I nodded. She was right. I wasn't a bad person. It's just things went tits up and they've been going downhill ever since. She'd been trying to get me to call Frank. Even offered to go with me to their house. I said I didn't think that was a good idea. Like rubbing salt in the wounds, though there shouldn't have been any wounds to begin with. But she was right about calling him and Maureen. Nicole was my daughter, my flesh and blood, and I had every right to see her. I had never had my father-in-law down–my ex father-in-law–to take the moral high ground. Perhaps it was time, especially after lying low for a while–maybe a bit too low–to take the plunge and try to make contact. For Nicole's sake. For *my* sake. She told me to get off my arse and stop feeling sorry for myself. Pack in the drink and get back on track. Trouble was, with every beer I drank in that swanky penthouse, I felt more and more at home. Maybe I didn't have such a drink problem after all. Kept telling myself it was something I was just meant to be doing.

I knew I could lie to myself like that. Because it wasn't me talking.

Angel did kind of hint on what Mr. Hong Kong was doing there. She just mentioned something about 'the girls' and I knew she must've meant others like her. I knew he was a businessman, just didn't know what type of business he was in. But I could guess, because something wasn't right with this cosy set up. I think Angel knew it too. She tried not to let it slip too much, but I could tell by her demeanour - always changing the subject, however casually whenever I brought it up. He 'looked after her' was all she said. She claimed they were friends. One thing I was interested in was her other clients. Who were they? When I realised Angel wasn't an ordinary prostitute hanging around on street corners, but a 'high class' call girl earning big money, I kept a closer eye on her. She had some issues, that much was clear. She came across as this ultra confident young woman, but I knew inside she was falling to bits. Because she had her addictions, too. Takes one to know one, I suppose. I'd hear her snorting coke in the bathroom, then crying afterwards. I wasn't sure if this was because she knew she was caught in that spiral of addiction that I was so familiar with, or whether it was simply because she'd run out of stuff to put up her nose. Or both. I wondered who her dealer was. A client? Friend of a friend? I was tempted to join her, anything to escape, but she never once offered, never pulled out that bag of white powder. She probably wanted it all to herself. Didn't matter to me. It would be the last thing I needed.

'So, when are you gonna phone them? Or go round? I can still go with you.'

'I'll get round to it. It's not a good time at the moment.'

'You've probably been telling yourself that for years. Time to get real, Jim.'

That stung. Time to get real. She was right. I had been telling myself I'd get around to it as soon as I got off the drink. But I never got off the drink, I just grabbed another.

Right on cue, I drained the beer and flipped the cap off the next one. One down, seven more to go. I hated myself for it, but it was just too good to ignore. I knew I wasn't ready to give it up yet, although I knew it was making me ill, both physically and mentally. But I couldn't let go. I just couldn't.

'So, you never said.' She took the pizza out and flung it on the side. 'Are you gonna come or not?'

She'd asked me to go for drinks at some new bar in the Northern Quarter on Saturday to celebrate her thirtieth. Didn't really feel like it and, to be honest, didn't feel I warranted the opportunity to raise a glass to her birthday. I mean, I hardly knew her. I'd feel like a pea in a tin of beans. Hated feeling awkward in social situations. And I couldn't be arsed with all that faux celebratory stuff. Was wary of getting too pissed and making a fool of myself which, let's face it, was bound to happen.

'I don't think so. I wouldn't feel right. I mean, it's your

birthday and you want to be with your mates. I'd just get in the way.'

'Yeah, but you're a mate too.' She stepped towards me, wrapped her arms around my waist. 'I'd like you to come.'

'I don't know....'

'Oh, please...'

'Look, I just don't feel up to it. You know how it is. I'm hardly the life and soul of the party at the minute, am I? Look at me.'

She backed off, got to cutting up her rocket and parmesan with a pizza slice. Took a sip of white wine. I pulled hard on the beer and took it down halfway.

'Look, I just think it'll do you good,' she said. 'You know, change of scene, meet new people...'

'Oh, I can see how that's gonna go. "So what do you do for a living, Jim?"'

'Well, just lie. It won't be like that, anyway.'

'You sure about that?'

'You've not met my friends. Look, it's up to you. And I understand how you might not feel up to it, but... well, it's my birthday! And I'd like you to be there.'

'Angel, I'm still getting to grips with what's happened with us. You know, you letting me stay here. Taking pity on me. The sex...'

'I'm not taking pity on you!'

'Come on...'

'I just like you, that's all!'

I put the rest of the beer away while she turned away in a huff. Don't get me wrong. I was grateful for the invite. But like I said, I just didn't feel up to it. And I didn't trust myself. I went to the fridge, grabbed another, flicked the cap off, drank.

'I take it you've got no money.'

'You know I haven't. All I've got is the clothes on my back, and they're not even mine.'

'I'll lend you some.'

'Angel, no...'

'That's it, then. Get used to the idea. You're coming to play out.'

6

Saturday night came around quickly. Too quickly for my liking. In the days leading up to it, she was like a dog with two dicks. I benefited in small ways. While she was busy organising, getting giddy, on the phone to various friends, I parked myself on the roof terrace, chain smoking and going over my own shit in my head until I got tired of it. I emptied half the drinks cabinet, but Angel didn't seem to mind, let alone notice. Occasionally, she'd drag me to bed - when I wasn't three sheets to the wind and could get it up - but most of the time I paced the flat, trying to come up with a way out. Felt like I was climbing a mountain and I couldn't see the peak.

The day itself went by in a blur. Angel picked out some clothes of Mr. Hong Kong's—I'd learned by now that his name was Han Lan—a black pinstriped suit jacket sharper than a Chinese Cleaver, a fresh pair of Diesel jeans and a pair of Chelsea boots so polished I could see my reflection in them. I wore a plain white shirt underneath. The whole outfit smelt of serious business. I wasn't entirely comfortable wearing another man's clothes. It was as if I'd shed my own skin and replaced it with someone else's. I felt like a fraud. A smartly dressed fraud, but a fraud nonetheless. I was ready and waiting a good two hours before she was, pacing the flat and nursing a Woodford Reserve. I'd added a fair bit of water to dilute the alcohol. Didn't want to get too pissed before we'd even started. Splashed on some expensive after shave from his immaculate dressing table. I'd had a sneaky route through his things, which I'd been putting off all week. Mostly paperwork, bank statements, shit like that. The bourbon went down the wrong hole and I sneezed a mouthful of it all over his Persian rug when I read the balance on one of the bank statements. He had a grand total of seven hundred and sixty-eight thousand pounds in his current account alone. There were other accounts too, but I felt a twinge of anxiety and put the stuff back in his drawer before retreating from the room in a daze, my head pounding. Here I was with barely a spare sock to my name, and this cunt had nearly three quarters of a million quid offshore. Probably more. Angel staying here just got a great deal more interesting all of a sudden.

Now I was more than intrigued about what this guy did for a living. I wanted to ask her, pressure her into telling me, even. But I had an inkling that if I did, I'd fuck things up. I'd be out on the street by the end of the night and back up shit creek. I still felt down, disembodied from my soul somehow, but staying with her had helped ease it a bit. Back out there, I wouldn't last another day. I lived the fantasy while it lasted. I knew that eventually, things would take a turn for the worse. So I kept my mouth shut where Angel was concerned. Didn't stop me from asking a few questions once a few of her friends' tongues were loosened later on. If I could stay sober for that long.

I'd managed to line my stomach–Angel forced me to eat

a ready meal bolognese–so I was fairly confident I'd last the night. My constitution was a strong one. Good job too, as I was likely to put away twice as much as everyone else. Thought about trying to force down a bowl of bran flakes but thought that might be pushing it. Opted for a handful of Greek olives and a wedge of feta cheese instead. It was getting easier to eat, but I still didn't have an appetite. She'd been banging on at me so much that I became an expert at forcing food down without bringing it back up. Probably got through less than half the calories I needed, but the booze topped it up. Trouble was, I was shitting water most of the time.

I realised I needed a cover story. Who's gonna take any notice of a homeless drunk? I'd been thinking about what that could be. I wasn't the type to mingle anyway, but if asked; I had it down pat. I had now become the owner of a small paper manufacturing business which had fingers in Italy and Spain. I spent most of my time in London and was looking for a place in Manchester. More a bedsit in Gorton than a four bed penthouse, but I was hoping I wouldn't have to get that far. I'd have to wing it big style if I was to be convincing. And anyway, who the fuck's interested in paper? I reckon I could walk the walk and talk the talk if push came to shove. I once spent a weekend undercover back when I was a DS. Well before I hit the bottle. Reckoned I still had the skills to pay the bills. And what if they blew my cover? Ah, well. Fuck it. It wasn't as if I'd be seeing these people again.

'Here. Two hundred quid. Should see you through the night.'

'Two hundred? Jesus, where're we going?'

'Thai, then a few bars. I've booked a table. There'll be twenty of us.'

'And what do they serve the food on in this place? Jade plates? Have they got velvet napkins as well?'

She smiled, then touched up her lipstick. I drained the bourbon and finished my smoke, then flicked it into a mulberry bush when she wasn't looking. Standing here on the balcony, I was shivering. Wasn't sure if it was the shakes coming back or if it really was that cold. It was November. I pocketed the cash, still gob smacked she was doing this at all. I wondered that, if old Han Lan was one of her clients and he had that much cash in his bank account, how much was Angel charging for a mere hand job? Here I was getting banged like a sledgehammer on a building site–for free–and he was forking out a few hundred quid for a blow job. Probably. Brought a whole new meaning to the Chinese proverb 'may you live in interesting times'. I know I was.

7

We stepped out into the night. Had been a long time since I'd stepped out with a woman, let alone a beautiful one. Felt strange. We walked through the canal side in Castlefield, past bars that charged nearly six quid a pint and high-end restaurants occupied by solicitors and media types. Never felt at home in places like this. Give me a dirty pub with a dartboard, a pool table and a decent jukebox and I'm there. I suppose I looked the part but didn't feel it.

'So, which bars?' I asked, as we made our way to Deansgate, hoping it wouldn't be bars like the ones we were passing. 'Round here?'

'No. Though maybe later on if anybody comes back to the flat. The restaurant's in Chinatown, then we'll head down to the Northern Quarter. See what happens after that.'

God, I hope no one came back to the flat. I could do without a load of cokeheads clouding my alcohol infused delirium, all me me me. Plus, I didn't need the temptation to join in. Was bad enough keeping my boozing under control.

Last thing I needed was a bugle habit. I sparked up, blew smoke across the water. Felt the chill in my bones.

'Are you gonna be okay tonight? You're not gonna do anything stupid, are you?'

What the fuck did she take me for? 'What do you mean?'

'You know,' she said. 'You're not gonna run off or anything like that, are you?'

'You mean jump in front of a bus or something? Throw myself into the canal?'

'You know what I mean.'

'No,' I said. 'I don't. But no, I'm not gonna do anything stupid. If I don't feel like hanging around, I'll just cut off after the meal. That okay with you?'

'I suppose so. Though I would like you to come for drinks. Someone's got to keep an eye on you.'

I just kept my mouth shut. I suppose I should've been grateful for her concern, but I wasn't. Just felt crowded, like she was wrapping me in cotton wool. Was fucking dying for a drink after that. Really put me off my stride and brought all the nasty shit to the surface again. We didn't say much on the way to Chinatown. Well, I didn't. Angel went into a stream of consciousness rambling about how she couldn't believe she was thirty–her actual birthday tomorrow–and how I'd like this girl and that guy and I'd really get on with Sara. And the rest, which I forgot in a hurry. I suppose she was sweet, in an innocent way. And she was. I enjoyed being with her, but we mostly had nothing to talk about. I let her talk. I think she knew this as well. I suppose she was just one of these people who couldn't stand silence. Felt awkward in it. Especially being around an alky nut job like me.

We got to the restaurant within ten minutes. There were several girls outside, all of them dressed like it was eighty odd degrees, all short skirts and plunging necklines. I wasn't complaining. Angel made the introductions. I nodded and smiled, trying to be enthusiastic but struggling. Couldn't remember anyone's name. There was a Suzy, a Grace, and a Carol. She was much older than the others, early fifties. The rest is a blur. We stood outside for a while, smoking and making small talk while Angel waited for her other guests to arrive. Another three or four turned up, a couple of blokes this time too. Fella called Matt, who looked like he needed a good punch. Slapped me on the shoulder and called me 'bud'. Felt like decking him right there. Another one, Simon, built like a brick shit house but with manicured fingernails and a satin shirt. And was that eyeliner? Seemed too keen to strike up a conversation with me. Hoped I didn't have to spend the night with my back to the wall. Stood there a while, listening to Simon and Matt talking stocks and easy money and how they were planning a trip to Qatar to propose some shite business venture or something, thinking I could just about nail a decent Guinness right now, until we went to the table and waited for the others. Couldn't come quick enough. Wasn't sure how long I'd last with this bunch but dug my heels in and convinced myself to grin and bear it, for Angel's sake. I suppose I owed her. For some unfathomable reason, she wanted me here with her and I didn't know why. I couldn't spoil the girl's birthday. So I sat down, ordered a bottle of Tiger and pretended to be interested in Matt's investment banking exploits. I couldn't be sat with a bigger twat. Was eternally grateful when Angel buzzed in and introduced me to another of her girlfriends, a stunning young thing called Sherry. Even her name got me smiling. Soon got engrossed in a conversation about Greek islands and her forthcoming Christmas trip to Bali, and how much she just *loved* Thai food.

I came to realise quickly that virtually all of these people, bar one or two, were a mix of clients and prostitutes. I wondered if they'd all seen each other naked. Looked at Simon and wondered if he'd joined in too. Angel grinned at me from across the table, pleased that I was making the effort. I raised my half empty bottle and smiled back.

A tiny, four foot Thai girl turned up and asked me my order.

'I'll have another Tiger,' I said. 'And a gin and tonic.'

'And to eat?'

I looked to Sherry, bewildered. 'I'll have what she's having.'

She nodded and shuffled off to the other end of the table. The restaurant was loud and lively now, and all of her guests had turned up except for one. The food came and I did my best to keep up with everyone else. It tasted great, but I just couldn't find the strength to put it all away. I made small talk with several others, a couple of close friends of Angel who seemed keen to get to know me, and a bloke called Dang, another Chinese guy–I wondered if he knew Han Lan–who seemed to take a keen interest in my paper business. Had to wing it for a while there. Made my excuses several times and disappeared to the gents.

Soon after everyone finished, we settled the bill and then left, most of us waiting out on the street until the last of the party had finished powdering their nose. Angel led the way to some ultra cool bar in the Northern Quarter, her and her mates all giddy. It was a chilly night but town was busy now, all the pubs and bars filling up, the restaurants bustling. I was familiar with the sounds of the city, usually from inside a shop doorway or sitting on a cold concrete floor with a foam cup in front of me. So it felt strange to be walking with a group of people any passer-by would assume were my friends. I lingered around at the back and got stuck with two girls I didn't know and wouldn't attempt to speak to if we were the last people on earth. I saw a few pills pass between them and caught them whispering. Wondered if they were discussing offering me one. I would've refused if they did. They didn't. Wondered if Angel's friends could pick up on my true identity. What I really was. If they knew, would they even give me the time of day? I doubt it.

The first bar was Odd. Odd by name, odd by nature. It was heaving by the time we got there, just after nine. There were no seats, either up or down, and I soon found myself parked near the door with a bottle of Russian beer and a bourbon and coke. It was hot too, and the main door had been left open to let the cool air in. Just as well as I felt like I was burning up.

Couldn't wait to get out of there. Thought of my daughter and my ex wife and wondered where it all went wrong. I didn't have to look far. I knew I'd blown it. And the reason was in my hand and going down my throat every chance I got. Thought about phoning Frank again and tried to piece together what I would say next time he picked up the phone. Or Maureen. I'd had no contact with any of them since the day Karen walked out. Tried, but they cut me off. Never knew if Nicole got my birthday cards. I suspected all involved on Karen's side of the family had me down as a right evil bastard, and would mould Nicole into this way of thinking every chance they got. Really cut me up to think they would do this. My child, my daughter, my baby. I hadn't seen her face in two years. It was killing me.

'Jim, this is Sara,' Angel said. I could tell both girls were high on something. They each nursed mojitos with fancy straws. 'Sara, this is Jim. He's staying with me for a bit, aren't you, Jim?'

I nodded to Sara, shook her dainty hand. 'I am. For a while, at least. Until I get something lined up, you know. Trying to keep busy.'

Angel left us to talk, more out of interest of putting something up her nose than giving us space to get to know each other. I watched as she hustled through the crowd. Took a long drink of beer and turned to Sara, feeling awkward.

'So,' I said, thinking about asking the obvious question. 'How do you know Angel?'

She smiled, looked wary. 'Since we were kids,' she said, raising her voice over the noise. 'Went to school together, amongst other things.'

'Oh yeah? What other things?'

'Just, you know. We kind of ended up in some trouble a while back. Angel got involved in what she's doing now, you know. And I got shitfaced every night.'

I knew that feeling. Was intrigued to learn more. I raised my eyebrows, questioning.

'Got stuck in a bad thing. The two of us, really. All through that now.'

I took another long drink. 'So you were a drinker?'

She almost laughed, but I saw a twinge of restlessness there. She took a drink through her straw and waved the glass in front of my nose. 'Not anymore. Three years without so much as a glass of wine. Took some going, but I made it in the end.' She waved her glass towards the stairs, where it led to the ladies and Angel putting sixty quid of white line up her nose. 'She's got it bad, though. I didn't see her for years while I got off the booze, you know? Couldn't. She was hanging around with some proper dickheads. I knew if I carried on like that, I'd be dead before thirty. So I fucked off.'

I'd never met another drinker before, especially a recovering one. Blew my mind at how wrong I was about this girl. She looked at me.

'She told me. About the drink. How bad is it?'

It floored me. What else had she told her? Had she mentioned how we met? I downed the bourbon. 'It's not as bad as she's making out. I can handle it.'

'Yeah, that's what we all say, love.'

'It's true.' I downed the rest of the beer. 'I don't know what she's told you, but I'm no alcoholic. I like a drink, yeah, but it's not as if I wake up every morning needing a vodka. You want another?'

She didn't answer, just gave me a look like she'd seen and heard it all before.

I got her a coke.

8

W e ended up chatting alone in the corner for a while, just small talk, joking about some of the freaks on show. Had a few more beers until I was dragged out by Angel, insisting we go to the cocktail bar around the corner. Everyone else was, she said, so I should too. Cocktails. Probably the worst thing I could have. I went along. Told myself I was doing it for her, but I knew I wasn't. The prospect of some hard spirits was enough to get me through the door of the place. I think I was the first one in and was halfway through a sour mash whisky by the time the last of the party stumbled through. Found a seat near the back, a plush red leather couch. Got talking to Sara again–who was on a booze free mocktail–and tried to look interested when she got to talking about how she'd straightened herself out. I was interested, but not enough to think about jacking it in myself. I was on a roll with the cocktails and soon saw the cash Angel had lent me vanishing from my pocket like a magician's trick.

Sara was a nice girl, young and carefree, with a lot going for her. I liked her. She kind of let on that she knew I was sleeping with Angel, or rather Angel was sleeping with me. Made out that this was the kind of thing she liked to do. Got shacked up with someone new every couple of months until she got bored and kicked them out. She'd been doing it for years. But they were clients she'd either fallen for or wanted to use in some way. It was always a bonus when Han Lan wasn't around. She could play the lifestyle as much as she wanted. Sara said she wasn't living in the real world.

'Don't think you mean anything to her. Because you don't. I think she's just trying to help, that's all.'

'What exactly has she told you about me?'

She sipped her fruit punch and looked away before touching my arm. 'I know you're not who you say you are. And that you nearly killed yourself. And that you used to be a copper.'

'That's it?'

'Why, is there more?'

'I don't believe this. I can't believe she'd just...'

'Look, you think she cares? To her, you're just another story, another thing she can show off. Like, look at how kind and considerate I am, you know?'

'You sound like you don't get on much. Why bother with her at all?'

'I don't *hate* her, Jim. In reality, I'm the only friend she's got. None of these people give a fuck about her. They barely know her. They weren't there when she overdosed, they won't be there when she does it again.'

'She overdosed?'

She nodded, then shook her head as if she'd said too much. 'Do you fancy a smoke?'

I drained my sour mash and followed her out into a garden at the rear. She offered me one of hers. The night was cold. I needed a whisky to keep my blood warm.

'Look, don't tell her I told you this, but she's not... well, she's not very well. Mentally, I mean. She won't admit it, but it's the truth. She has these bouts of depression that can last months. Gets silly with it, you know? And then she just sort of snaps out of it and starts doing daft things, has these little schemes and stuff and thinks she can do anything. That's when the drug use kicks in. You must've noticed.'

'I know she's doing a lot of coke.'

'Yeah, and the rest.'

'Rest? Like what?'

'Oh, you know. Pills. Uppers. That kind of thing.'

'Smack?'

She shook her head. 'No. At least, I don't think so. Shit, that would be bad, wouldn't it?'

'Where does she get her gear? One of her clients?'

'I don't know. Maybe. Could be, I suppose.'

'So, this overdose. When was this?'

'A few years ago.' She took a final drag and crushed the butt in a coconut ashtray on a table decked out like an Honolulu garden party. 'Tramadol. She came to stay with me for a while afterwards. Then, when she thought she was all better, she found this guy Han Lan and moved into his flat soon after.'

'Was he a client?'

'Oh yeah, she was fucking him. Landed on her feet when he told her he had to go to Hong Kong and let her stay in his flat.'

'I bet.' I took another smoke and sparked up. Took that shit in deep. 'So what's the deal with this guy? I mean, what's the deal with Angel?'

'He pays for everything. Won't have it any other way, and Angel thinks it'll last forever, but it won't. When he comes back, she'll be out again. Knocking on my door and looking for a place to stay. And I'll be there for her when she does. Always have been.'

I wanted to get to the bottom of their relationship. Not Angel's and Han Lan's, but Angel's and Sara's. Or maybe both. No, definitely both.

'Look, I'm sorry if I hit a nerve earlier,' she said. 'About, you know. Your stuff. But if it's any consolation, I think I can empathise with your situation. I've been there too, remember. It's not nice, I know.'

'I just can't believe she told you anything.'

'She's not told me to be gossipy or anything. She's just trying to impress, in her own way. Like an attention seeking thing. She wants to show me she can do something good as well as be an enormous fuck up. Don't take it personally.'

'But I just don't understand why.'

'I don't think she knows herself. These people she's with are fucking vampires. They'll take everything from her soul and leave her to rot. Someone's gotta keep an eye on her, eh? And God knows I've been doing it all my life.'

Back inside, my eyes were drawn to Angel, who had several men around her, each anticipating her every word. Some I recognised, others I didn't. She was flirting with them all, perhaps toting for business, even on her birthday.

I felt drunk but able to manage one or two more. Who was gonna stop me? Sara came back from the ladies, gave me a hug, and took her phone out. Said she had to go. Her babysitter had phoned about her son, Charlie. They needed her at home.

'Everything okay?'

'Yeah, I think so. My sister said he's not stopped crying for his mum since I left the house. He's only three. Bloody typical. I'm gonna have to go. It was nice meeting you, Jim. What's your number? I'd like to get in touch to check on Angel, if that's all right?'

It was more than all right, but I didn't have a phone. I told her as much.

'I'll call the flat then. Tomorrow morning. But I'll give you my mobile, just in case.'

She took an eyeliner pencil from her handbag and wrote her number on the back of my hand. Karen was the last person to have ever done this. My heart skipped a beat, and I wondered if Sara had an ulterior motive other than an interest in Angel's welfare. I hoped so. I enjoyed her company and had forgotten all anxiety about being around Angel's friends.

'Phone me,' she said. 'And keep an eye on her.'

'I will.'

She kissed me on the cheek then went over to Angel, said her goodbyes. Angel didn't seem too disappointed she was going and turned back to some slimeball beside her as soon as Sara had left her side. I watched her leave, thinking I'd like to go with her, and she stopped at the door and waved before stepping out into the street.

One more for the road and I'd be following her lead. Was about to step up to the bar when Matt stopped me in my tracks with an exotic-looking cocktail in a tall glass.

'Here you go, bud. Saved you the bother.'

I took it, said thanks. Last thing I wanted was to get lumbered with this little smartarse. I said I was going for a smoke and he didn't follow. I went out in the garden, which was busy, and stood under a halogen lamp while I smoked not one, but two. Thought about what Sara had said regarding Angel and her mental health. I could see what she meant, could sense it myself. Wondered why it hadn't crossed my mind sooner. It didn't make any sense for her to let me stay in the flat. Perhaps I was just the latest in a long line of casualties she'd taken under her wing. I had no clue. But it was clear the girl had addictions. And secrets. I was keen to know more.

I drank the cocktail in three long swigs and decided to leave before I'd reached the bottom of the glass. I'm sure she meant well, but I'd never felt comfortable with the situation. I'd find a hostel tomorrow and see if I could get my life back on track.

I wanted out of there. Asked her for the keys, made my excuses. Truth was, I was shattered anyway. Felt what little energy I had being drained by the second in the company of her friends. Couldn't relate to them, and I'm sure they felt the same about me.

She was talking to an Asian guy as I approached, another finance type by the cut of him.

'Oh, don't go yet!' she protested. 'We're only just getting started.'

The Asian guy had his hand resting on her thigh, stroking like some kind of stage hypnotist. Seemed to work as she giggled like a two-year-old when he whispered in her ear.

She reached into her bag. 'Here,' she said, dangling the keys before me. 'Door code's on the chain. We'll try not to be too noisy when we get back.'

But I planned to knock myself out by that time.

I pocketed the keys, said my goodbyes to anyone that could be arsed to reciprocate. Told Angel to be careful. She just laughed and waved me off. I didn't hang around. Felt the chill would wake me up and the walk would do me good. Maybe have some time to think. I took one last look as I headed for the door. That hyena laugh of hers screeched through the room as she enjoyed a joke with the Asian guy and made her way to the ladies with him following behind like a dog on heat.

I didn't know it then, but things were about to get a lot worse.

I felt drunk, but that wasn't unusual. Surprising, really, given my constitution. Then again, I'd lost count of how much I'd put away. Tried to add it all up, but it was useless. Several beers, mixers, cocktails. Don't know how many I had, but it wasn't enough. I wanted more, *needed* more. I sparked up as I stumbled off down the street. It was late on a Saturday night. Busy. Loud. Everything suddenly became louder as I hit Oldham Street. I could hear a throbbing and pounding in my head, like a continuous drum n bass beat that just wouldn't stop. Maybe it was the sound of my own heartbeat, the blood pumping through my temples.

The streetlights were vivid. The howls and wails of punters cut through the night. With each bar I passed, the music flooded out, leaking across the pavement, and it all coalesced into some freakish, fantastic orchestra.

I felt hot, burning up, and I loosened my shirt. Felt fucking weird.

I passed a doorway and saw a guy I knew. Everyone knew him as Dogends, on account of him walking the streets looking for cigarette butts. He was hunched in a doorway, wrapped in a dirty blanket. There was a Moroccan lamp on the pavement before him, which I thought was odd, and when I approached, the blanket had become an old lady's black lace shawl. I stepped up to him, the neon lights whirling around me, voices splintering the night.

'Dogends?'

I leaned in, his long beard making him look like an ageing rocker. He was deathly thin, like he'd been in a concentration camp or something. He had his eyes closed, leaning against the doorway wall, urine spilling out onto the pavement at my feet. I reached out to touch his naked shoulder.

'Dogends?'

His head lolled towards my hand and his mouth opened, his tongue sticking out between his teeth like a grey, infected piece of meat.

His face melted.

'Oh, fuck...'

I fell back, struggled to stand still. A few people barged into me, sending me further off balance, and I fell to the pavement, smacking my forehead on the kerb. Heard several cries of horror before I felt a pair of arms beneath my own and I was brought to my feet. A tall black guy asked if I was okay, but I couldn't speak. Was as if my mouth didn't work. I could feel my tongue moving, but I couldn't make the sounds. Caught sight of my reflection in a window and saw my lips had swelled. Felt like the Elephant Man. Felt like I was melting too. Lost all control of my limbs and slumped to the deck.

Was moved against the wall somehow by several men, their faces bearing down on me like disapproving priests. They put me down on the concrete and told me to stay there. Tried to say I'd be all right–as if–until it all faded away from me and I was looking down a tunnel towards which a light I could not find. I closed my eyes. Breathed.

What the fuck was happening to me?

I don't know how long I'd stayed slumped against that wall, but I must've fallen asleep or something. When I opened my eyes, I could see again. Put a hand to my head and checked my fingers. They were slick with blood. I just couldn't make any sense of it. I craned my neck to the left, sure I would find Dogends just a few yards away. He wasn't. There was no one, and the puddle of urine was gone too. I got to my feet and leaned against the wall. The streets were quieter but still busy enough and no less weird looking. Across the road was an old woman with a shopping trolley. Surely not right at this time of night. I dug around in my pocket, trying to find the smokes I knew were there. There was no packet but a single one lurking at the bottom of my pocket. I pulled it out, sparked up. Tasted strange. Had a few drags, knew it was strong. When I focussed on what it was I was smoking, I nearly dropped it. The joint was long and thicker than my thumb. I mean, shit. Where did it come from? I threw it in the gutter and watched it burn like acid in the puddle of rainwater where it landed.

Acid.

Shit. I'd been spiked. Some cunt had spiked my drink.

I stumbled towards Piccadilly Gardens, all lit up like a football pitch. Was like wading through water. I felt soft, malleable, like a real life plasticine morph. Had no control over my limbs at all. Wherever I looked, objects rippled and swirled. Walls swam and bent, the concrete beneath my feet flexed. There were thousands of tiny bugs crawling the floor, onto my shoes, up my trouser leg. I fell to my knees to get a closer look. Got one in my hand. Its legs were made of copper wire and its back a shiny alien metal.

'Jesus,' I said, wondering how the fuck I was gonna get back to the flat. I didn't know the address, couldn't get a taxi. If this was LSD I'd been hit with, it could last all night.

I dropped the bug, struggled to my feet. Looked around. Had no clue of the time. Felt my face tingling, wondered what the fuck I looked like. I supposed I could find a doorway, maybe crash behind the back of Ho's Bakery. I knew I could be safe there. But if I could get to Chinatown, I'd be halfway back, anyway. I could chance it. I had to get out of this open space. There were too many people, a sea of faces moving in all directions. Made me want to throw up. Couldn't focus on anything for too long, otherwise it melted before I could look elsewhere. Took a breath and focused on putting one foot in front of the other. Gripped the railing beside the fountain for support. One step at a time.

I'd never felt these sensations before. Scared the living shit out of me. As I crossed the bus station, some sitting idle, one or two moving - had to be really fucking careful to not get run over - I saw Karen and Nicole standing outside Piccadilly Amusements, an all night gambler's haven. Used to sit out the front to shelter from the rain late at night. A bus went past, but I could just make them out through the blur of a passing window.

'Karen!'

Thought I saw her turn to the sound of my voice before they went inside, the flashing lights that were so alive illuminating their faces. Nicole was trailing her favourite teddy bear behind her, her pink pumps dirty from playing in Frank's back garden.

'Karen!'

No response. I watched them disappear into the depths of the arcade. Stood outside and peered in. The colours and flashing lights almost sent me spinning. Legs went to jelly again. I stumbled forward, leaned against an open door, shielded my eyes from the blinding lights to try to see. A fat man in a string vest turned to look at me, pushing coins in a slot on a one-armed bandit.

'Did you see them?' I said. 'Karen! Nicole!'

The noise was deafening. Coins clattered, waltz music rang around my ears, laser guns, shoot 'em ups, a fucking jack in the box that frightened the shit out of me.

The fat guy didn't speak English. He jumped off his stool and strode towards me, kebab stains down his vest, a hole in his shoe. I realised I was on my knees and when he reached my face, he jabbered in Pakistani. He was about three foot four. A dwarf. Shit, my head was in bits. All I wanted to do was sink into the carpet and fade away. I clasped my hands around my ears, but it was pointless. The dwarf helped me to my feet and I clung on for dear life. Inched my way around the arcade, a one-armed bandit at a time. Kept looking between the gaps in the machines for a glimpse of my wife and daughter. Ex wife and daughter. No sign.

When I reached the end of the aisle, a step or two away from the CHANGE booth, I turned and saw her standing there, her purse open as if looking for cash.

'Karen!' I said, over the din. 'Fuck's sake, Karen, it's me!'

Someone tapped her shoulder and she turned.

It wasn't Karen. My daughter turned as well, and it wasn't Nicole.

'Sorry. Shit, I'm sorry, I ... I thought you were someone...'

'Time to go, mate,' someone said. Felt my shoulders being drawn back. 'I don't know what you've been drinking but you've had enough, son.'

Three seconds later and I was on the pavement, a hard rain coming down. It seemed the noise got louder behind me, around me, the sounds going through me. Lifted my head from the floor and scanned around. The punters must've started leaving the bars and heading for the clubs. The bus station was busy. Toyed with the idea of jumping on one and pretending to be asleep, but thought it might do more harm than good.

I needed the backstreets instead. The quiet, dark narrow alleys where no fucker knows. I just needed to get the hell out of where I was. I got to my feet again, gradually felt some semblance of balance on my pins. There had to be more than LSD in my system, besides the booze. I'd felt nothing like it. This wasn't drunk. It was something else. I felt tranquilised, doped up. It was as if my whole nervous system was fucked. The messages from my brain weren't working. Had to focus so hard on the basics. Just walk, I kept thinking, just walk. But I couldn't, not really. Co-ordination had vanished. All sense had gone.

I found my way into Chinatown and slipped down a back alley straight out of Gotham. Half expected Batman to drop from the sky on a wire and rescue me. If only. Laughed hard against the wet Victorian bricks. Slumped down behind an industrial sized refuse bin and tried to catch my breath. It'd be funny if it wasn't so disturbing. I'd get the cunt, whoever did this. I still knew people on the force, could still get in contact. I had witnesses, evidence. I knew the system. I was lucky I hadn't been killed.

I sat there in the darkness, the cold air helping me to calm down, just the quiet stillness except for the kitchen noise from a nearby restaurant and the hum of the city beyond. I felt like I was in a cave. A fucking bat cave.

I sat and got my breath for a long time, smelling nothing but Crispy Peking Duck and thinking how fucked up tonight had become.

11

I got to Deansgate through the back streets without drawing attention to myself, though there was a queue of black cabs on Bridge Street that really put the shits up me when I staggered past. Felt sixteen pairs of eyes upon me, both drivers and punters alike. There must've been something seriously wrong with my face, or it could've been the way I walked that did it. Felt like I was trudging uphill all the time, arms outstretched to shimmy along the shop fronts beside me. Heard a lot of laughing as I crawled by and one or two flashes from smartphones. Seems I'd become a minor celebrity, just the latest circus freak for people to gawp at. Couldn't be arsed telling them to fuck right off and wasn't sure I even had the power of speech to do so, anyway.

My mind whirled in circles, so many thoughts running around my head that I couldn't keep up. It had been bad enough anyway these past few years, but now it was worse. Kept seeing Karen's face in my mind, especially now that I thought I saw her with Nicole. Could it have been them? I was utterly convinced of it. I had to wrestle with my emotions out there on the streets. Thought, naively, that it was something I'd left behind. Who the fuck was I kidding? And then the horror of what I'd almost done a week ago kicked in. Shit, if it wasn't for Angel, I'd be dead. I felt a fool. A useless, pissed up fool. I probably looked the part too.

I finally reached Deansgate Locks a half hour after the humiliation of trudging through the streets like Mr. Soft. Heard that old song by *Cockney Rebel* jingle jangle around my head like a fucking itch. The relative quiet of the Castle-field canals helped me to get some semblance of normality, though only a bit. The frost skirting the canal side sparkled like the milky way and I couldn't tear my eyes from it. Had the sense to stay well away from the water, though, and I was pleased that I could at last think straight. Got mesmerised by the illuminated steel and glass of Beetham Tower. I knew I just had to let the feeling pass, whatever was happening to me. I realised I was hallucinating. I knew it would go eventually if I just accepted it. If I could get to the flat in one piece, it would be a victory.

I stumbled on, knew I was close. When I saw the bar we passed earlier, I knew I was on the home straight. I didn't feel as bendy when I passed the bar–still open, still plenty of people inside–and I picked up pace after I tore myself away from the fountain outside the door. Jesus, the visuals on this thing were immense. Too much. I wanted nothing more than to get back to the flat and lie down in a dark room until it all passed. I knew I would need a stiff drink after all this, but not until it wore off. I hoped it would be soon.

Got to the front door of the building and pushed it. Locked. Fuck. I guessed I'd just have to crash somewhere on a bench in the gardens or something until I discovered I had a set of keys in my pocket. Found the door code written in black biro on the key ring. Punched it in several times and fell through when it buzzed a third time. Took me a while to realise I had to push on the buzz and not after. Funny how the little things can be so confusing when you're high as a fucking 747. I realised, as I climbed the stairs to the fourth floor–wondering why the hell I didn't take the lift–that whatever I'd been spiked with had an amphetamine base to it. Could've been all kinds of shit in that drink, from cocaine to speed to spice to fuck knows what else. I practically ran up the stairs, eager to be inside where I could curl up in a ball.

The drink. Was it a drink? Must've been. And the only person to get me one, just half an hour or so before this weird shit kicked in, was Matt. I knew the guy couldn't be trusted as soon as I'd laid eyes on him. The question was, what the hell did he want? Why did he want me drugged? What fucking game was he playing here?

I thought of Angel and the people she liked to associate herself with. Tried to piece together some things Sara had said, but it all got tangled up with the other junk in my head. All I knew, an instinct, and intuition if you like, was that something wasn't right. I cursed myself for even agreeing to go out for Angel's birthday. I mean, shit, I barely knew the girl. I *didn't* know the girl, not really, and yet I'd allowed myself to be around her and her friends for a night I wasn't ready for.

I reached the door, put the key in the lock. Struggled a bit before it opened and I let the door slam behind me. Fumbled around for a light switch and caught myself in the mirror in the hallway. There was a long cut above my left eye and drying blood down the right side of my face. A yellow bruise was forming around my jaw. Was gonna be a nasty one.

Threw my jacket off and left it on the living room floor. Spent ten minutes trying to wash the blood from my face.

The water was soothing. Found a pack of smokes in Angel's room and smoked several as I knocked back two pints of cold, cold water. Felt good. I could barely believe the ordeal I'd been put through, but it had happened. Yet it still wasn't over. The walls swam, and I kept thinking the parquet floor had miniature stairs in it. Had to remove several paintings from the walls. They were freaking me out so much.

When I'd finished smoking–not even considering going onto the roof garden in case I jumped off–I switched all the lights off, got into Han Lan's king sized bed, and hid under the duvet until I fell into a bottomless pit of absolute darkness.

12

I awoke to a chink of light leaking through the blinds. Felt light as a feather, as if I wasn't actually there. When I pushed the duvet off and got to my feet, I saw the bruises on my legs and arms, and one huge one down my right side. My head hurt, like I'd been hit with a medicine ball. Felt like shit. Caught my reflection in Han Lan's full-length mirror. Looked like I'd gone ten rounds with Ali. Something had hit me all right, but not with uppercuts or body blows. Whatever the drug was, it had knocked me for six. I could be dead. Felt it too. There was nothing more frightening than not being in your right mind. I knew this from experience. But last night was something else.

The memory of it came back in waves. Dogends, his face melting. Smacking my head on the pavement. The colours, the lights, the sounds. Karen and Nicole that weren't Karen and Nicole. Chinatown, the taxi rank, the humiliation.

I needed to wash this shit away. Showered quickly and dressed, putting on a pair of Han Lan's jeans and a tight fitting military style jumper. Went into the kitchen and got myself several glasses of that icy water from the tap on the fridge. Caught the time on the oven clock. It was just gone eleven thirty. Felt a pang of hunger but was certain that if I ate, I'd bring it right back up again.

Opened the fridge. There was a bottle of Japanese beer on the top shelf, but my eye was caught elsewhere. There were two bottles of expensive champagne, half a bottle of white wine, mixers galore. Wondered if Angel had stocked up then remembered she could've had people back. Didn't hear anyone, and I was in late. But I was fucked, out for the count. Could've slept through it all.

I flicked the cap off the beer and launched it down my throat. Felt good. Carried it through to the living room and stopped at the threshold. My first thought was that the flat had been robbed, turned over in a big way. Then I saw the girl on the couch, dress rising up her thighs, knickers up her arse. Asleep. I could only hope she was the only one.

Grabbed a smoke from a packet on the coffee table and stepped through the mess. There were empty bottles every-where, small plastic baggies with traces of coke and grass in them, a small bag of pills, a pile of MDMA sitting next to an overflowing ashtray. There was an open laptop, still on. Phones lying around, cash in twenties. This I pocketed and didn't feel a shred of guilt about it. Counted a hundred and twenty quid. It was mine now.

Opened the doors onto the roof terrace and stepped out into a bright, frosty morning. There was a man I didn't recognise asleep on the lounger. Felt like throwing a bucket of water over him but instead sat there with the beer, chain smoking and overlooking the canals and thinking about how I ended up in this mess.

I didn't stay there too long. Just long enough to drink the beer and get tempted by another, but I got fidgety. Wanted to know who else was back here last night. Plus, it was cold, and my head wasn't up to it. This come down was rough. Was convinced I had traces of whatever I'd been spiked with floating around my system. I felt detached from everything, in a lot of ways.

I stepped back inside. Tried to make a coffee but got restless and forgot about it. Tiptoed around the living room and the girl on the couch and inspected the damage. Be fucked if I was cleaning it up. I guessed Angel was in the flat somewhere, so I thought I'd check the other rooms. I turned the handle on the one next door to mine. Found a naked girl I didn't recognise beside the Chinese guy, Dang. Both were asleep. In the room across the hall, I assumed Angel would be in there either alone or, more likely, with a client. Crept up and turned the handle. Two women. Carol, the older woman, and Sherry. There was some stirring, but both were asleep. Great. I had a flat full of fucked up cokeheads and no sign of Angel. It must've been a hell of a party. But where the hell was she? I wondered if Sara knew, then remembered I had her number written on the back of my hand.

Shit. I'd washed it off. It was now nothing more than a black smudge.

Went out on to the roof terrace again. Started pacing. Went back inside, got another beer. Started pacing again. Halfway down the bottle, the guy on the lounger stirred from his sleep. Sat with his head in his hands for a few minutes while he came to. I watched him closely. I knew that whoever had spiked my drink could've been here last night. Or, whoever was here last night, including those that had gone–I assumed there were others given the state of the flat–knew who was dealing LSD, speed, Ketamine, any of that shit. They were probably all on one or more of those drugs last night. Someone must know who'd hit me with it. Someone must know why. I intended to find out.

The guy on the lounger looked familiar, but I didn't have a name. Was certain he was there in the Thai place, though. Don't remember being introduced. My guess was he was in finance, like all Angel's acquaintances seemed to be. He was well dressed, had money. The kind of bloke who plucked his own eyebrows and went for a regular manicure down at the salon to go with his ninety quid haircut. Expensive Rolex on his wrist. Three hundred pound alligator skin shoes. A face you wanted to punch.

'Woah, fuck,' he said, running a hand through his carefully waxed bed hair. 'Man, I'm mashed. Give us a light, will you, bro...?'

Southern. Londoner, probably. I tossed him a lighter. He lit up a Marlboro Light, blew smoke out into the chilly air.

'So, dude. You get any?'

Almost laughed at 'Dude'. 'Get any what?'

He laughed, shot me a grin. With his pristine teeth and chiselled jaw, he looked like he belonged on the cover of Twats Weekly. 'What do you think, bro? Pussy. You get any pussy to play with?'

'No. You?'

'No?! Fuck me, bro. You missed out, dude. That Sherry's something else. You should've said, I could've hooked you up with Angel, she'll go with anyone for the right price.'

'Is that right? So which lucky bastard ended up with her, then?'

He grinned, tossed his fag in an ashtray beside him. 'Matt. I guess she just can't resist the cash, eh?'

Then he went on laughing, stunned by the hilarity of his own observations. Was getting ready to ask more about this fucking Matt when the phone rang. It could wait. Left him on the roof terrace while I went inside to answer. Noticed the girl on the couch was stirring too.

I picked up on the fourth ring. 'Hello?'

'Hello, Jim?'

'Yeah?'

'Jim, it's Sara. From last night...'

'Sara. Yeah, I'm glad you phoned, I lost your number.'

'Party back at the flat, then?'

'Yeah, but not for me.'

'Too tired?'

'No, someone spiked my drink. In the cocktail bar. That's how I lost your number. Look, it's a long story...'

'Spiked it with what? God, you okay?'

'Acid, I think. And something else.'

'Well, did Angel not know? Is she there?'

'No. She's not. Don't know where she is. That wanker Matt became one of her clients, apparently. Look, I'm still getting my head together myself. I don't know what went on here last night, but it's a fucking mess.'

'Charlie?'

'Yeah, and the rest. If they're not gone within an hour, I'm kicking them out.'

'Yeah, well, not until I get there. I'll be there as soon as I can.'

She hung up before I could reply. Put the phone down and went back out on the roof terrace. On my way through the living room, the girl on the couch, knickers up her crack, tits spilling out, said 'Morning'. I ignored her and stepped outside.

'This Matt,' I said. 'And Angel. Any idea where they went?'

He looked up, tried to step through the door to the living room, but I stood in his way.

'Hey, easy, dude. Just getting a coffee if that's -'

'Where did they go?'

'Hey, bro, how the fuck should I know?'

'Sit the fuck down,' I said, grabbing him by his shirt and pushing him back towards the lounger. 'You're going fucking nowhere until I know where they are. Are we clear?'

'Fuck's sake, man, what the fuck's wrong -'

Gave him a slap, waved a finger in his face.

'See this face?' I said, pointing to the bruises I'd acquired. 'Thanks to your fucking mate, the little weasly cunt who spiked my drink, I spent the night trying to fucking walk back here with fucking goblins and wizards on my arse. Where did it come from?'

'What!?'

'The acid. Why did he spike my drink and where the fuck did it come from? And where did they go? Simple questions.'

'What? I don't fucking -'

But that was enough. Pulled him up, launched him headfirst over the roof terrace wall. Grabbed his jeans, pulled them tight up the crack of his arse until he squealed like a puppy caught in headlights.

'See that drop? Nasty fall, that. Could kill a man, smash your skull open like a cracked egg. Wouldn't want that, would we?'

'No!'

'Good. Now I'll ask you again, and I expect an honest answer. Where are they?'

'I don't know! Please -'

'Where could they be?'

'At the Hilton, they could be at the Hilton!'

'The hotel?'

'Yes! Please, just...'

'And where did he get the acid to spike my fucking drink?'

'I don't know! I know nothing about that!'

It was a long way down. I don't know what it was like for him, but for me it brought back the day I almost threw myself to my death. I couldn't stand it any longer, and if I dropped him I'd be more than fucked. I hauled him in, slung him back onto the lounger.

'Phone him. I want to know where Angel is.'

He was shaking, shitting himself. I suppose you would be after dangling over the edge of a very tall building.

'My...my phone's inside.'

'Which one?'

'The iPhone. Co...coffee table.'

He was hyperventilating. Guy looked like he could do with a drink. I went to fetch his phone while he sparked up. I suppose he couldn't get out of here quick enough, but he was going nowhere yet. The girl on the couch had found her way into the kitchen. She was pouring a glass of orange juice. No sign of the others yet. Sara knew them better than me, I suppose. I hoped she'd get here soon. I could see myself doing some damage if she didn't.

'Here,' I said, handing him the phone. 'Put it on loud-speaker.'

He took the phone, brought up Matt's number and pushed the call button. Ringing. We waited. It rang out. No answer.

'Call Angel.'

He did. Same conclusion. No answer.

'So what were you taking last night?'

'Just, you know, some coke, a pill. That's it.'

'And the others?'

'The same.'

'Was Angel on anything?'

'Yeah, coke and pills, like the rest of us.'

'Was Angel here last night?'

'Yeah, then she left with Matt.'

'What time?'

'I don't know. Early hours. Look, bro, I don't know anything about any acid, all right?'

'Has he been with her before?'

'What?'

'Matt. Has he been with her before?'

'Well... yeah. Yeah, I think so.'

'Have you?'

'Me? Nah, bro. No, she's not my type, I usually go for Sherry or one of the others...'

'How often do you lot get together?'

'Just when we're up in Manchester, bro. Look, I'm sorry if I'm not helping much, but I...'

I left him to it and retreated to the kitchen. Made a coffee and sipped it in silence while the whole thing buzzed about my head. Ten minutes later, the Intercom buzzed. Sara. Had to be.

Went to the Intercom and saw her standing there, arms wrapped around her. I buzzed her up. Heard someone turn the shower on as I went to open the front door. I wondered why Angel had left here last night. Thought she might've just stayed here instead of going out again. Why the hell would she bother going to his hotel room when there was a perfectly suitable bed here? It didn't make sense.

Left the girl with her orange juice in the kitchen and opened the door. Saw her emerge from a lift down the corridor. She had a phone pressed to her ear.

'Jim. What's going on? Do you know where she is?'

I told her about her apparently spending the night with Matt at the Hilton. She wasn't surprised–about the business–

but she was about her going to the hotel instead of staying here. She'd never done that before when she had a perfectly good room here. She spent her life in hotels, according to Sara. But had never spent a night with a client away from here when she didn't need to. Everything was always on her terms.

'I could murder a coffee,' she said.

We went to the kitchen and I brewed us both an instant Nescafe. The girl who liked to flaunt her chest said 'hi', as if it was perfectly normal to help yourself to stuff from the fridge in a strange flat. We nodded, let her pass. Asked Sara if she knew her. She said she'd never seen her before. Someone was still in the shower. Didn't know who, but I suspected Dang. Of the blokes I met last night, he was the least annoying. Sara commented on the mess and even started picking up empties from the floor. I told her not to bother, but she insisted.

I suppose it wasn't that unusual for a prostitute to go to a hotel room, but after what Sara had said, I couldn't see a reason why she would. It crossed my mind that something kinky was on offer. Or he'd paid her extra to do things his way. Or the promise of more drugs that weren't available here. Whatever the reasons, I supposed she'd be home soon, her work done. And I'd be speaking with her about this Matt character and what he'd done with my cocktail. If the cunt was still in the city.

Sara said the prick outside was called Luke. She'd never liked him, but he was a mate of Matt's so reckoned he was telling the truth about his whereabouts. She asked me about my ordeal last night, and if I was sure it was Matt who spiked my drink. I went through it all, from the very point she left the bar. I couldn't prove he was responsible for certain, but he was the only person to have bought me a drink last night. It had to be him. And he had to have had a reason.

'She's not answering her phone,' she said. 'It's not like her.'

'Maybe the battery's dead or something.'

'No, she's always careful like that.'

'Maybe she's had a late one. I mean, you've seen it here. They put enough away between them, and we don't know what else she's done since leaving here.'

'I want to wake these fucking idiots up. See what they know.'

'You can start with him out there. I'll speak to her in the living room.'

Found her rolling a joint on the couch. Jesus, this girl liked to start early. I was almost shocked at how she seemed to think she owned the place.

'Morning,' she said. 'I don't remember seeing you here last night. Fun party, though. Fancy a smoke?'

I sat down next to her, shook my head. Dived straight in.

'Where did Angel go last night?'

She laughed. 'Jealous, eh? You should've got in there first.'

I flicked the finished joint from her lips and tossed it aside. 'Look, I've no idea who you are, nor could I give a fuck. But I'm gonna ask you some questions, and I'd like a few answers. One. Where did she go?'

'Now just hang on a minute...'

I shook my head, showed her my teeth. 'Just answer me.'

'What do you mean? Why are you being such an arsehole?'

'Arsehole? It's my job. Now Matt spiked my drink with acid last night in the bar. I don't recall you being there yourself but I'd like to know a few things, like why he did it and where the fuck he went with Angel.'

'Look, I don't even know him. And I don't know anything about any acid, mate. So you're asking the wrong person.'

She was rattled. Looked like she was about to cry. 'You shagged him too?'

'What?!'

'Come on, love, do I look like I was born yesterday? I know your game. What's he like?'

'What the fuck are you on about? How *dare* you, what the *fuck*!'

'There's the door, you're welcome to leave.'

'Fucking gladly!'

She got up, grabbed her things–a handbag, her weed, cigarettes, phone–and stormed to the door, her high heels click clacking on the parquet floor.

'I didn't catch your name.'

She just turned round, gave me the finger, and walked out.

Sara didn't get much out of Luke either, other than a couple of surly grunts and denials. Was honestly wondering if we were gonna get anywhere and was there anywhere to get to begin with? I'd catch up with Matt eventually, but now it was Angel I was worried about. Should I be? I didn't know, but I had a strange feeling. I wouldn't have been spiked if he didn't want me out of the way somehow. Maybe he thought I was another potential client and he wanted to knock me out of the loop. Pretty fucking strange way of behaving, if that was his game.

Sara tried Angel's mobile several times. Got more worried with every dead call. She was biting her nails, chain smoking.

When Dang came out of the shower, I questioned him

too. Managed to calm myself down by then. Wouldn't be becoming if I dangled him over the roof in front of Sara. He denied all knowledge of where Angel and Matt were, claiming he didn't know Matt at all, having only met him last night. The girl he was in bed with wasn't worth bothering with. She was so high I thought they might have to peel her from the ceiling. Thought it best to leave her alone. For now.

They made their excuses and left. There were one or two looks exchanged between Luke and Dang that didn't go unnoticed. I made a mental note. I'd heard enough, anyway. Dave had spilled the Hilton. That was enough for me. I didn't have Dang down as the dodgy type. Just a late twenties Chinese guy with too much money and time on his hands. Sara seemed to think so too. Said she didn't know him, only met him once before. According to her, Angel would always have different clients every other weekend. The girls didn't change, always the same faces. I was interested to hear what Carol had to say.

'She's the madam,' Sara said. We were outside smoking. There was some movement from inside, the two girls remaining probably slapping a face on. 'Always around. I don't know whether she has clients too. Maybe. *Probably*. Maybe she specialises in the GILF department.'

'Gilf?'

'Granny I'd like to fuck,' she said, grinning. 'You'd be surprised.'

Was really tempted to grab a beer but forced myself to drink coffee instead. I think Sara noticed my craving. Was it the shakes or the cold? Both, probably.

'You eaten?'

'No. Not since last night.'

'You need to eat. Look, why don't we grab something

somewhere. If I don't hear from Angel soon, I'm gonna go looking for her. You may as well tag along and we can get something. Not much, if you don't feel like it. Just a sandwich or something. Up to you. You hungry?'

'Not really. But I can give it a go. What time is it?'

'Nearly one.'

'Okay. As soon as these two fuck off, we look for her. Wouldn't mind checking out the Hilton for you know who, to be honest with you.'

She asked me again how it was last night. Told her.

'I'm lucky I didn't jump in front of a bus. Not because I want to kill myself–which I don't–but because I was looking for the bat cave or something.'

'Bat cave?'

I laughed. Just. 'Long story.'

'Hello?'

We both turned. The woman I recognised as Carol was standing in the open doors, dressed in a business suit, mobile in her hand.

'I don't believe we were introduced,' she said. She was looking at me. We were introduced. She just didn't give a shit.

'Jim,' I said, taking her hand. 'Jim Locke. I was at the Thai place last night? You might not remember.'

She looked bewildered for a minute, then threw her head back, slapped her forehead. Not very ladylike.

'Of course! Hi Sara. Sorry. Sorry, Jim. I remember, it's just... well, been a long night. She's a lovely girl, isn't she?'

We both nodded.

'Yeah. We were just wondering where she'd got to. Some of the others here last night said she'd left with Matt. Do you know anything about that?'

'Matt? In trading,' she said, with a hint of a smirk, like

she'd seen his type before. 'Rich little bugger. I don't know if she left with him, but to be honest with you, I was pretty out of it. Getting too old for this.'

She could say that again. She was a well-spoken woman, wouldn't look out of place on the cover of Cheshire Today. Probably lived in a four or five bedroom detached out in Knutsford. She carried herself well and looked ready for a business meeting. Caught her eyes sliding up and down my front, as if scanning me for viruses. I let Sara do the talking.

'So could she have gone somewhere with him?'

'It's possible. I was a bit tied up at the time.'

'It's just that she's not answering her phone.'

'Unlike Angel. I'll call Matt, I think I have his number. Is there something wrong, do you think?'

'Nothing, really,' I said. 'It's just that she's supposed to be meeting us for dinner. Thought you might know her plans.'

'Oh, no one knows her plans,' she said, raising her phone to her ear. 'But I'm sure she'll be okay. Fiesty, that one.'

'Any joy?'

She still had her phone to her ear but shook her head. It rang out again. 'Afraid not.' She dug in her handbag and brought out a business card with her number on it. 'I'm sure she's just... working, or something. Call me if you hear from her. Or if you don't, for that matter.'

We went back inside just as Sherry came through from the bedroom. Carol asked if Sherry had heard where Angel had gone.

'The last I saw her she was leaving with Matt,' she said. 'Don't know where.'

'Hotel?' Sara said.

'Could be, I suppose. I think they might've gone to his hotel.'

'Is that common?' Sara said. 'You know, for you girls to go where they want? For the right price?'

There was a silence between them before Carol chirped up. 'It's really a matter for the girls to make their own decisions on where a client would like them to go. It's a mutual arrangement. I'm sure Angel would've agreed this prior to Matt's arrival last night.'

'So that's when he arrived?' I said.

'We assume so. But I'm sure Angel would be in total control. Matt's been escorted by one or two of our other girls and there have been no problems. The perfect gentleman, I'm led to believe.'

'Okay, well, sorry but I really need to get going,' Sherry said. 'It was nice to meet you, Jim. Bye, Sara.'

We smiled, nodded, did the decent thing and let them leave graciously. But something didn't feel right about Carol. I pocketed her business card as they opened the door. Sherry stopped at the threshold.

'It was a good party,' she said. 'Thanks for letting us stay. And I'm sure she'll be fine.'

'Yes,' Carol said. 'Thanks for the hospitality. And do let me know when she's back. We'll see you again.'

Not if I see you first, I thought.

Not if I see you first.

13

Sara cleared up while I put another coffee on and tried Angel's mobile. Told her not to, but it was like I was speaking Russian. When it came to cleaning, women were experts. Karen was the same, bordering on the obsessive. And there she was again, buzzing around my head like a fucking wasp. No matter how hard I tried, she always turned up, didn't matter what was happening. She'd always find a way in. Nicole, too.

Why did it always come back?

I went to the fridge, opened the last of the beer and drank it fast. Felt Sara's gaze on me as I swung the bottle back. Wouldn't be long before I was on the hard stuff. The vodka outside on the roof terrace seemed to be whispering to me. Calling me. *Provoking* me.

I didn't think Sara's gaze was a disapproving one. More concern. She had mentioned she'd been in this place, the place all drinkers know. It was the realm of self doubt and weakness. I didn't know how bad she'd had the sickness. Felt too intrusive just coming out and asking her. Wouldn't be right. I mean, we'd only just met. She didn't reveal much last night, and I wasn't expecting anything more soon.

'Try her again, will you?' she called from the living room. She was busy emptying ashtrays and bottles into a bin bag.

I tried again with Sara's mobile. Nothing. Just ringing out like before. I didn't know if we should be worried. Really worried. I mean, was this normal for her? Carol seemed to think so. Sara wasn't too sure. She didn't even have to say anything. I could see the look on her face.

She dumped the bin bag on the kitchen floor and leaned against the sink. Looked me in the eye and let out a long sigh. I drained the beer. Needed more.

'I don't like this. It's not like her to not answer her phone, Jim. Can we go out? Get some food and look for her?'

I didn't really want to go anywhere, but there was a hundred and twenty quid in my pocket and several pints of Guinness with my name on it. I nodded. 'I'll get my coat.'

'You've pulled.'

'Sorry?'

But she just smiled and looked away.

14

It was even colder down on the streets than it was on the roof terrace. I pulled Han Lan's jacket tight around me and dodged the ice that was forming beside the canal. It was the kind of cold you could almost see, hung over the water like a spectral mist. I felt light-headed. Not surprised given what I'd put in my body the last few weeks. I still felt a twinge of the drugs I'd been spiked with. Could feel a rush come on me as we walked. Tried to blot it out, but the only thing I could see was a pint of the black stuff standing cold on a bar top, the glass glistening with moisture, the creamy head like a miracle from God himself.

Sara linked me as we made our way towards Deansgate. I could see Beetham Tower looming. Wondered if Angel was in there with him, somewhere on the tenth floor. Wondered if she was asleep beside him or working her way through what he wanted. I had no actual proof it was him that spiked me. I didn't need it. I just wanted to put the smug cunt on his arse. Couldn't wait to see his face with my fist in it.

'Come on,' she said, grabbing my hand. 'They do a good cheese toastie in here.'

I was thinking more of a beer and burger type deal but didn't get a chance to make my suggestion. She had the door open and was dragging me through before I could even picture it in my mind.

I took a seat on a small table near the back window, both to be away from the group of students and their hangover cures, and to look out the window for any sign of Angel. Or Matt. The guy had a face like a politician. I knew I couldn't possibly miss it if he walked past.

Caught Sara smiling in my direction as she ordered two cappuccinos and a cheese toastie special each. Overheard the students–a couple of girls and three lads–recommending various cures after a heavy night. Wanted to chip in and tell them the best cure was to never stop drinking in the first place.

Sara put a coffee in front of me and sat down. Lifted her mobile to her ear again. Raised my eyebrows to ask if there was any joy, but she shook her head. Got busy with a text message as I helped myself to sugar.

'So what are you gonna do? If you see him?'

I took a sip of the cappuccino, hot and frothy. 'Give him a piece of my mind.'

'Do you really think it was him?'

'Who else could it be?'

She shrugged. 'The barman, maybe?'

'Nah. What would be the motive? There's only one person this entire thing points to.'

'But why him?'

'I don't know. I really don't, love. But don't you find it odd that he ends up with Angel? You know, the girl who decided she wanted to take me in, look after me? And I still can't get my head around that.'

'I told you,' she said. 'She's done this before. Blokes she takes pity on.'

'What, suicidal homeless guys? I was so close to jumping, Sara. I wouldn't be here if it wasn't for her.'

'You've got a soft spot for her, haven't you?'

I couldn't deny it. 'Yeah. I suppose I do.'

She reached out, grabbed my hand and squeezed as I lifted the coffee to my lips. Looked her in the eye.

'It will get easier, Jim. It takes time, a lot of time, but it will change. I promise.'

I hoped she was right. I needed to see my kid. I couldn't let this go on forever. I couldn't miss any more of her life than I already had. I told her so.

'Have you tried getting in touch?'

'Yeah.' But I knew I was lying to myself. I *had* tried, but I'd given up too easily. I knew in my heart I wasn't up to it. I was scared. And I don't know what I was scared of. Living on the streets had changed me. Made me harder. But it made me weak, too. I could barely remember my old life. It's the little things that have drifted away. The smell of the laundry on the kitchen side. Washing the car on a Sunday. Things like that. 'Yeah, I've tried.' I could tell she was cynical because she just smiled.

'Try harder,' she said. 'I'll help you. Look, I know it's hard to go back to your old life after all the mess, all the bloody hurt. But it can be done. I'm sure your daughter wants to see her Daddy.'

A girl in a black and white apron appeared beside us and put down two cheese toastie specials. Looked like someone had vomited between two pieces of bread. Made me feel queasy. I watched Sara lift hers and take a hungry bite before removing a blob of cheese on her lip. I realised I liked her more than I thought.

'Eat up, it's gorgeous.'

I watched her making noises of pleasure as she munched away. Felt my stomach rumble. I'd been telling myself I wasn't hungry, but it wasn't that. I was. I just didn't remember what it was like to eat something with another person sitting across the table.

I made the effort and took a bite. The cheese was hot, and the other stuff inside it-whatever it was–was good too. She was right. It was pretty special. It was hard going, but I made my way through it and finished the coffee too.

'Told you,' she said. 'I used to come here all the time.'

I looked at her phone. 'Anything?'

'No.' She picked it up and dialled again. I said I was going for a smoke and she nodded.

The cold was blistering. The road was quiet, just the odd couple on their way to the cinema in the old Great Northern warehouse behind us. Little traffic. I sparked up, took that shit in deep. Got my eye trained on the Hilton in the Beetham Tower up the road. Remembered there was supposed to be a bar in there on the twenty third floor. Cloud Twenty Three, something like that. Wondered if they could be in there. Even if they weren't, maybe there was someone in there who saw them. Even if there were no punters–no reason there wouldn't be at this time of the day, but you never knew–there would be staff around. It was a good place to start.

Finished my smoke and went back inside. There was a fresh coffee waiting for me. Got the impression Sara was trying to tell me something. But I'd had a taste for booze already this morning, and I needed something stronger. Sara knew. I suppose, being a non drinker herself now, she liked to avoid pubs. It had never occurred to me before. I threw my idea out there.

'Okay. I know you need a drink. We'll have a look.'

'Any joy?'

'Nothing.'

'Right. Finish your brew and we'll head down there. How do I look?'

'Like a homeless guy in expensive gear.'

'Seriously?'

'No, you look good. You look great, actually. Look, thanks for this.'

'Thanks for what?'

'Helping me look for her. I'm sure you can think of better things to do.'

'No. Not at all. I want to find her too. I want to find him, but I want to find her as well. Can't bear to see you like this.'

'Like what?'

'Worried.'

She was quiet for a while and drank her coffee. Drank mine too, a bit too eager to get it finished.

'She's vulnerable,' she said. 'So I do worry about her. Always have, I suppose.'

I wondered if Sara was telling me everything she knew about Angel. Probably not. Given her job, I wondered how she'd ended up in it. Wondered if Sara had been a working girl too. Thought it best not to ask, let her bring it up herself if she wanted to.

She drained her coffee and played with her spoon, deep in thought.

'Come on,' she said. 'We're not gonna get anywhere sitting here.'

15

'How do I look?'

'Fine. More than fine.'

'So, what's the plan?'

'I don't know. Not thought of that.'

'Well, you're the copper.'

'Ex copper. And that was a long time ago.'

'I bet you haven't lost it, though. You know, powers of persuasion and all that...'

It had been a while since I questioned anyone. I really didn't know if I still had it. And besides, I really wasn't a copper anymore. I couldn't go in there demanding answers. And anyway, why not just the truth? We were two concerned friends looking for a possibly vulnerable young woman. There was nothing hard about that.

'We be honest with them. With maybe just a little bit of persuasion if they fuck us about. Have you got a photo of her or anything?'

'On my phone,' she said, holding it up.

'Not returned your text yet?'

She shook her head, bit her lip.

'Come on. Let's see what we can come up with.'

We walked through the swing doors into a marbled entrance hall. There were a few guests milling about and two girls on the desk. Clocked a bespectacled and frustrated looking supervisor type hovering about near a computer at the far end of the check in terminal. Shuffling papers about like his life depended on it.

'Helen Shields,' she said, nudging me. 'That's her proper name, she would've checked in with that.'

'And Matt?'

'No idea. I suppose we could find out if push comes to...'

'Can I help you?'

We looked up to see a youngish check-out clerk with a heavenly rack on her. Almost choked.

'Sorry,' I said, trying hard to look her in the eye. 'Got a bit distracted there. Yeah, what it is, see, a friend of ours...'

'My sister.'

'Her sister. And a good friend of mine. We believe she might've checked in here last night and she's due to meet us today, only we can't get hold of her. Starting to get a bit worried, you know...'

'Okay,' she said. 'What's her name?'

'Helen Shields,' Sara said. 'She was probably with a guy called Matt.'

She didn't reply, just put her head down and tapped away on a keyboard. I tried to look anywhere else but at her tits. Sara obviously clocked me because she was grinning widely when I had to turn away.

'Yes, a Miss Helen Shields, room twenty-seven.'

'Can you call the room?'

She was already doing just that. We stood there and waited; me looking at the ceiling, her biting her lip. The clerk–her pin badge said her name was Maria–smiled and fluttered her eyelashes.

'Hmmm, no, there's no answer. She could've just gone out or something.'

'What time is she supposed to check out?' Sara said.

'Tomorrow morning. By ten.'

I suggested Sara show her the photo on her phone. Maria shook her head, said she hadn't seen her leave the hotel since she came on shift this morning.

'Do you think anyone else could have?' I said. 'Would you mind asking?'

She called another girl over. Cara. And the stressed out speccy guy, too. None had seen her. Cara said their team started at eight this morning, taking over from the night shift. It was possible someone from nights had seen her, but they'd all gone home.

'It's just out of character for her,' Sara said. 'She's not answering her phone and I'm getting worried.'

'Have you called the police?' Specs said. There was a bead of sweat rolling down his neck, despite the chill. 'Is it at that stage yet?'

'Not yet,' I said. But if she hadn't turned up by tonight, it could be. 'Is it possible you could check her room? Just so we know she's used it?'

'I'll check with Laura,' Maria said. 'If you'd like to take a seat and I'll see what we can do.'

We sat on a leather couch while Maria went into a back room to consult the boss, a blonde business type who looked so indifferent - as if she'd never been so inconvenienced in her life - that her face looked like she'd just eaten something sour. I bet she hadn't been shagged in years.

'They seem okay.'

'And so they should be. It's not as if we're holding a gun

to their head, is it? We're just looking for a friend, that's all. It's the least they can do.'

Maria came over then, and once again I had to focus on her face rather than what was just below it. She dangled a key card, smiled.

'I'm just gonna check for you,' she said. 'We wouldn't usually do this but considering the circumstances... I won't be long. Can I get you a coffee or something while you're waiting?'

Would prefer something stronger than a Starbucks. 'No, thanks. We'll just wait.'

We watched her head towards the lifts. Cara and the speccy guy were busy with a line of guests. Checked the digital clock high above the check-in desk. Was getting on for three o'clock. I shifted in my seat, felt myself get the shakes. I needed a beer or two to stave it off. Sara turned to me, as if she could read my mind.

'We'll get a drink soon. I'll just try her phone again.'

I sat and watched the comings and goings from the guests. No sign of Matt. And I'd know that face anywhere. Clenched my fists in anticipation of his smug grin coming into view. Felt my heart beat that bit faster. It was Angel we wanted, sure. And I'd like to ask that girl a few questions of my own once she turned up. But Matt was the type of bloke who was just asking for a good kicking. I relished it.

My thoughts turned to Han Lan. Why he'd let Angel use his pad while he was away on business. Had to be a reason for it. And I reckoned Carol was in the loop on that too. Couldn't put my finger on why, but I instinctively knew she wasn't right, somehow. Han Lan, too. I decided that, once Angel turned up, I'd head down to Chinatown, see what I could find on this guy. Anyone with an account with over three quarters of a million in it had to be a big cheese.

Either everyone in the Chinese community knew what he was about–he struck me as the kind who liked to flaunt it, even though I'd never met him–or no one knew shit. Could be one or the other. Could be the type to keep his cards close to his chest. I assumed he was well known around here. But I learned that assumptions could lead down blind alleys. Despite trusting my intuition when it came to investigating–and I'd done enough of that as a DS-you could never be too sure. Sometimes it paid off, sometimes it didn't. I had a feeling I had some work to do if I was to get to the bottom of this. And really, what did I have to investigate, anyway? It was perfectly legal to let someone use your gaff, even for six months. As long as all expenses were covered–which Angel had said they were–then all was fine. But something didn't sit right. I could feel the bug coming back, almost like it'd never gone away. I wasn't with the force anymore, but I suppose it never disappeared. Once a copper, always a copper.

'She's coming back.'

We stood, and I knew already there was no news. I suppose no news was good news, though it didn't feel like it. Saw Sara's spirits drop and it hit me in the heart. Shit, this girl really cared for Angel. They must've been through a lot together.

'Sorry,' Maria said. 'We checked the room. Nothing, I'm afraid.'

'Had it been used?' I said. 'I mean, did it look like it had been slept in? You know, crumpled sheets, toothpaste in the sink, that kind of thing.'

Maria did that thing people do when they don't want to let you down, biting her lip at the corner of her mouth. 'Sorry. Hard to tell, really. The bed was made, and the bathroom looked okay to me.'

'Were there any bags or anything?'

'Didn't see any.'

'But she hasn't checked out, right?'

'Not according to our records, no.'

I remembered that Matt was supposed to be staying here anyway, according to Luke. They could've gone to his room, assuming he had one. I mentioned it to Sara as Maria stood looking between the two of us.

'Don't know his surname,' Sara said. 'I suppose we could find out? Call Carol?'

I nodded. Asked Maria to call us if she spotted Angel or a smarmy looking twat in an Armani suit. We left her Sara's mobile and our names. The girl, I have to say, was more than accommodating.

'We might be back later,' I said. 'We just need to find some other details of the guy she was with.'

'Just call back whenever. I'm on until eight tonight. That's when the late shift comes on. You might have better luck with them. You could always check the bar upstairs. Cloud twenty three...?'

My thoughts exactly.

'We will,' Sara said. 'And thanks for your help, it was much appreciated.'

'You're very welcome. And I'm sure she'll turn up. Hope she's okay.'

We nodded our goodbyes and headed for the lift. Had strong visions of that Guinness going down my throat. I gave Sara Carol's business card, and she dialled. The number was a dead line.

'Try again.'

There wasn't even a dialling tone. The number didn't exist.

'That can't be right,' she said, as we made our way up to

the twenty third floor. 'Just read it out to me while I dial again.'

I did. Same story. Nothing.

We exchanged glances as the lift door opened onto the wall to wall glass of Cloud Twenty Three. We were greeted with panoramic views of the city. The lights were twinkling already, and the light was fading. I took in the view, wondering if Angel was out there somewhere.

Out there alone.

16

'Two Guinness. And a double whisky, no ice. Any will do.'

The whisky came first. Knocked it back in one, felt the burn in my throat and the warmth in my chest. It was a blended, and not a good one. Like I gave a shit. The barman - Colin, according to his badge - put down two pints. I watched impatiently as they settled, then took the first one. It was just as I'd imagined. Jet black, cold. A creamy head, beads of chilled moisture on the glass. Guinness is good for you, they said. They weren't wrong.

I drank the first one quickly, the other I would savour like it was my last pint on earth. First went down in three. I was thirsty. Plonked it on the bar, got a strange look from Colin.

'You'd better give me a bottle of orange.' Handed him the cash, nodded, got just over a fiver in change. I knew there was a reason I didn't come to these places.

Sara had found us a table over near the far window. Floor to ceiling so you could gaze out at the city. Got to say, it looked beautiful. I wasn't one for heights, so I didn't get too close. Thought again of standing on the ledge of that car park. Got a shiver down my spine.

Didn't like the vibe in here. Great view, but the booze didn't come cheap. Flicked through a cocktail menu. Put it back when all I got were flashbacks from last night. Sara poured her orange into an iced glass and took out her phone. She tried Carol's number again and shook her head. I drank my pint and scanned the room. No sign of Angel or Matt, but there were plenty of other business types. There was a group of men in suits hogging a leather couch at the back wall and a few young women hanging on their every word. Wondered if they could be working girls too. Thought about asking if they'd seen her. Brought it up with Sara.

'Worth a try. Let's drink this first, give us a chance to think a minute.'

'No luck?'

'Nothing. And that fucking bitch, Carol, has really got my back up. How the hell can she give us a dud number...?'

'Well, she obviously had her reasons. Something to hide, I would've thought. I'll be paying her a visit if Angel doesn't turn up.'

'I'm getting scared, Jim.'

'I know. But it's not an emergency yet. Wherever she is, I'm sure she'll be okay. She's not daft, is she?'

'You'd be surprised.'

'Why?'

'Like I said... she's vulnerable.'

'Is there something you're not telling me? About this vulnerability?'

'No, nothing like that. I'm not hiding anything from you, Jim, and why would I? It's just that she's an easy target, you know. In the wrong company, she's a sitting duck. I just hope nothing's happened.'

'And what possibly could happen to her, Sara? Has she been in any kind of trouble before? You know, beaten up... raped. Anything like that?'

'Not that I know of.' But I could tell she wasn't letting it all out. 'Well, there was this one bloke knocked her about. She told me he'd hit her a few times during... well, you know. When she was fucking him.'

I tried to picture it. Couldn't quite do it.

'What happened?'

'She just had these bruises,' she said. 'I asked her and she told me. Broke down, you know. But I reckon there were other bruises as well.'

'You think he raped her?'

She sighed. 'I don't know. I suppose it's possible.'

Seemed more than likely to me. I drained the Guinness and stood up. 'I'm getting another. I'll have a chat to the barman while you make some calls. She might've lost her phone or something. Why don't you phone the flat? She might've turned up.'

I left her to it while I hit the bar. Felt the pull of something stronger but told myself to rein it in. I could still feel a twinge of the drugs I'd been spiked with. Felt like I'd been bowled over by a truck or something. Tried not to let it show as I approached Colin. He didn't seem surprised to see me. Ordered two more drinks. When he came back, I went straight for the jugular.

'We're looking for someone. Well, two people actually, but a girl in particular. You might've seen her before. About my height, bleach blonde hair. She was wearing a leopard-skin coat.'

I could see him mulling it over.

'How old, roughly?'

'Thirty. She was with a guy. Southerner in a suit. Banking type, lots of cash. Calls himself Matt.'

'Rings a bell. When was she here?'

I took the head off the pint and leaned in. 'She checked in last night. And we've not heard from her since. Her sister's getting really worried. Thought you might've seen her.'

'There was a blonde girl in here late on,' he said. 'She was drunk.'

'With a bloke?'

He shook his head, thought about it. 'Don't remember seeing a guy. We sat her at that table on her own. I finished about one and left so I don't know if she stayed. Could be anyone, I suppose.'

'If I showed you a photo, would you be able to rule it out?'

'Could have a look.'

I signalled for Sara to come over. She said she'd had no luck with any of the phone calls.

'Show Colin the photo of Angel,' I said. 'He said there was a blonde girl here last night.'

She handed him her phone and he studied the pic. 'Hard to say. We get a lot of these types in here.'

'What types?' Sara said.

'You know, women on the pull. Always looking for men with money. There's no shortage of them.'

'Is she the girl you saw last night?'

'I really don't know. This girl's got short hair.'

'It was taken two years ago,' she said. 'It's grown a bit since then. She was wearing a leopard print coat. I suppose she could've taken it off.'

'Have you got any others?'

'Not on the phone, but I could come back with more.'

'I wish I could help you out. But I just can't be certain if this is the girl I saw in here last night. It was busy, you know, and I see so many people in one night. Busy shift and all that. You might have better luck with some of the guests.'

'Is there anyone in here now who was here last night?'

He made a quick scan of the room. 'Can't say. You'd be better off trying later. I'm sure there'll be a few people who might recognise her.'

This guy was getting on my tits, but I suppose he was right. We'd have better luck come night time when the place was full.

'Okay, cheers anyway, Colin. Give me another Guinness and we'll leave you alone.' He went to pour another one while I put my money down and turned to Sara. 'He could be right. Maybe hang around until it fills up a bit. Ask around. There's bound to be someone who's seen her. Or Matt.'

'Are we here for the long haul, then?'

'I'll hang around. Ask about. You get off if you want. I'm sure you've a kid at home needs his mum.'

'He's at my sister's. I could phone and ask her to have him for the night. I'll only be pacing the kitchen if I go home now. Would you mind if I stayed here with you? I need to know what's going on, Jim. The sooner the better.'

'I'll get you another drink. We won't go anywhere until someone's recognised her. And we take it from there.'

'Do you think she's all right, Jim?'

I wanted to say yes, she's fine. But I was beginning to doubt it myself. Instead, I said nothing.

17

We sat there for several hours. I went through three more pints while Sara got sick of orange and went on to coffee. We watched the rain come down heavy around five o'clock, sweeping across the city in a downpour that didn't let up for half an hour. All the time I was thinking about Angel and where she could be. It was cold and wet out there. It was dangerous. Could be really dangerous in the wrong company. But she was an adult, and I asked myself many times if I should be concerned at all. I mean, I hardly knew the girl. We'd slept together–which was a huge surprise for me, though I envisioned nothing happening there–so there was some closeness, some intimacy I felt for her. But she was just another woman, albeit a woman who'd taken me in to give me a bed and a roof over my head and a meal, even though I couldn't eat and had no appetite for it. But I felt that she cared. I don't know why, but she cared. And I was grateful for that. When I saw the anguish in Sara's eyes, it hit home. It was her I was concerned about more than the missing girl we both knew. To Sara, Angel really was like a sister. To me, she was just a young woman who'd taken pity on me. I'd enjoyed a week in her company, she'd insisted I celebrate her thirtieth with her friends. I could've walked away, but I didn't. I think I didn't because I didn't trust my state of mind. Still don't. It was as if she'd cast a spell on me, luring me into her realm, a high-class apartment owned by a Chinese businessman. The plush bed I slept in was a welcome change from the cold ground on the streets. I'd have been an idiot to leave. On the streets, you learn to take whatever gifts come your way and be thankful for them, because the next week they might be gone. Another chance might never come again.

We tried to avoid conversation about my circumstances. Or rather, I did. I knew Sara knew some things–from what Angel had told her–and I wasn't happy about that at all. But it was done now. Like Angel, Sara cared. She said she'd been there, would help me get back in touch with Karen and Jenny, if I wanted to. I wanted to. I just didn't feel ready for it. Didn't know what anyone in Karen's family would say if I told them I'd been sleeping behind Ho's Bakery for the last two years. Alcoholic, I'm sure they knew all about that. But a homeless drunk? Perish the thought.

'What's the matter?' she said. 'You look deep in thought.'

I suppose I was. There wasn't a day went by when I didn't think about Karen and Nicole. My past. It haunted my every moment.

'I'm okay. Just thinking, you know.'

'About what? Or do I really need to ask?'

'About what I'm gonna say when I finally grow a pair and phone Frank. Keep putting it off.'

'You need to do it, Jim. You need to make that step.'

I knew it. She was right. But it wasn't as easy as putting one foot in front of the other. Seemed like the Niagara Falls had gone under that bridge a hundred times over. I couldn't bring myself to do it. Many times I'd picked up the phone, half pissed, and dialled. Even waited while someone answered, sometimes Maureen, sometimes Frank, but every time it was like I'd gone mute. Just couldn't find the words. It was much easier to say nothing and go back to the bottle.

'Forget about phoning them,' she said. 'You need to just turn up at their door. I'll go with you...'

'No, Sara, there's no need.'

But she just put her finger on my lips and looked me in the eye. 'When you're ready. It's a promise.'

The bar filled up gradually and we made our way awkwardly around the tables, asking anyone who'd listen if they'd seen Angel. No one had. There were one or two who thought they might have seen her but couldn't be sure, much like our barman friend Colin. I suppose it was to be expected. The picture was two years old, taken in the summer when the light had caught her hair and made it look like it was glowing. Here we were at the arse end of November and everyone was miserable with the gloom that hung over the city like a cloud of shit. Maybe it was the way she was dressed or the way she carried herself that didn't register with people. Or maybe I was just clutching at straws and she was never here at all. We were wasting our time. After spending an hour wandering from table to table and the seats at the bar, we gave it up as a bad day at the office. I could tell Sara was getting more and more agitated. She must've phoned Angel's mobile a dozen times, to no avail. Always the same conclusion: a dead line. I only hoped there wasn't a dead body lying next to it.

'Let's just go,' she said. 'We're getting nowhere. And I'm tired. And you're drunk.'

'I'm not drunk,' I said, knowing I was nowhere near

where I wanted to be. 'But we start again tomorrow. She's probably still on the job. Switched her phone off or something, you know.'

'But she always lets me know she's okay. Always, without fail. It's just not like her, Jim.'

I didn't want to say it, but I was becoming more nervy by the hour. Tried to put on a reassuring face, but I could tell Sara knew I was thinking something different from the picture I painted. When the music went up a notch and we had to shout to be heard, it really was time to leave. I ushered her out through the main exit and called the lift. Felt more myself when we were standing out in the hallway.

'Do you mind if I stay with you tonight? I mean on the couch.'

'If you like. Technically, I'm squatting. You can have a bed of your own.'

'Are you sure that's okay? It's just... well, I'd like to be there when she turns up. If she turns up.'

'She will. And it's no problem. I understand completely.'

'I'll shout you a takeaway. Pizza. Even though I don't feel like eating.'

'You and me both.'

The lift came, and we were down in the main reception in seconds. The check in team had changed, so we asked if anyone had seen her. We got nowhere fast. I was beginning to wonder if she'd checked in at all, but Maria had said so and there was no reason to doubt. Everyone at the flat had reason to believe she was here, and I couldn't see why they'd lie. But Carol giving us a dud number got me thinking. I couldn't fathom why she'd done that, but she obviously had something to hide. If I could find out where she was–I assumed she had an office somewhere–then I'd be paying her a visit tomorrow, Angel or no Angel. One by one, I'd seek out her birthday guests and ask questions until I got straight answers. I wasn't gonna let this lie. And who the fuck was Han Lan?

The bitter cold had taken a turn for the worst. Nothing that a snifter wouldn't sort out. I was thankful I wasn't out in this tonight. I knew a few lads who'd been taken by the winter. If the frostbite didn't get them, the booze would. Or they'd take themselves. It always amazed me how anyone survived the winter in this city, but they did. Clung on for dear life, some of them, though fuck knows what for because it wasn't a life, it was an existence. The strange thing was, some poor fuckers had chosen it because they couldn't live with where they'd landed. I wouldn't put myself in that category, but I could understand it. Though it could be a living hell on the streets, there was freedom in it. You lived off the grid. Became a ghost, of sorts. Angel had said she'd been on the streets herself, and I made a mental note of asking Sara about that later, but I had my doubts. Was beginning to think the girl was an enigma. The puzzle was getting more complex, and I knew I'd have to dig deep if I were to crack the code.

It didn't take us long to get back. Sara was keen to check the flat's landline for any messages or missed calls. I was keen to jump into the bottle of vodka we left on the roof terrace. I knew I shouldn't, especially given the circumstances - a girl was missing, after all - but the compulsion was strong. At the same time, we wouldn't be finding anything if I was half pissed. I knew I had to rein it in.

'Nothing,' she said, putting the phone down.

'Could she have gone to her parent's or something? Any family?'

She almost laughed. 'Her mum's dead and her dad's a

total bastard. There's no one else. I'm the only family she's got.'

'Any other friends?'

'You saw her friends last night. I'm all she's got because they don't give a fuck. It's all about partying for these people, and that's the last thing Angel needs. I've seen where it takes her.'

I made us both a coffee - put a nip of whisky in mine, just to shake the cold off - and sparked up. Sara said she was phoning the police to report her missing and I couldn't blame her. At least it might feel like she was doing something. It was a waste of time, though. GMP couldn't find a missing person if they were standing right outside HQ. I'd never found any missing person when I was on the job. Well, alive, at least.

I took the coffees into the living room and shivered when a blast of icy air hit me from the door to the terrace. Saw Sara standing out there with a cigarette, the smoke curling like a pale blue spirit as she poured the rest of the vodka into a plant pot. She caught me watching.

'I'm sorry, but you've got to start somewhere.' She took a drag and flicked ash away. 'My ex did this one night when he came home to find me in my dressing gown and a bottle of gin on the coffee table. I've forgiven him now, but at the time I wanted to chop his cock off.'

'Nice.'

She laughed, stepped towards me with the empty bottle. 'You should've been there.'

I was thankful I wasn't. 'How bad was it?'

'He got away with a bust lip.'

'No, I meant... the drink. With you. How bad?'

She took her coffee and stepped away with the empty

bottle of Vladivar, dropped it in the kitchen bin. 'It was bad. Terrible. I should be dead.'

'Jesus.'

'Don't worry, I'm not born again. Not in a bible bashing, happy clappy way. But I've not touched a drop for a long time. I want it to stay that way.'

'For Charlie?'

'And me.'

She sipped her coffee and took to the couch, curling her legs beneath her. I caught a whiff of the brandy in my Nescafe and felt a touch of guilt, but only a touch. Took more than a sip. I suppose I should've been angry with her for throwing the booze away, but I wasn't. I know she was only trying to help. And anyway, there was more in the drinks cabinet. Hemmingway and Oliver Reed had nothing on this stash. I joined her.

'So what did they say?'

'Hmm?'

'The police. You reported her as missing, right?'

She nodded. 'Gave a description, last whereabouts, that kind of thing. Spoke to some woman PC who seemed nice enough, but I get the feeling they won't take it seriously. People go missing every day, don't they?'

She was right. I knew we'd have to kick on with the search ourselves if she hadn't turned up by tomorrow morning. But it could be too late by then. If she was lying in a ditch somewhere, or some back street den of sin in a pool of blood, it was way too late. I didn't say it. Didn't need to. I knew Sara was thinking the same. Angel's job brought risks. Significant risks. We'd be fools if we didn't think the worst. There had to be nut jobs and psychopaths out there who got some weird kicks out of banging prostitutes. I had Matt down as just the type.

'I'm just gonna go around the flat,' I said. 'See if I can find anything left behind by our guests last night.'

'They've probably taken all their shit with them.'

'You never know.'

She sighed. 'You know, I suppose there isn't much else we can do right now, is there?'

'You've reported her missing. It's a start. But we need contact numbers for all the people who were out last night. That might get things moving.'

'Shit! She's got her laptop here. Shit, why didn't I think of that before!'

'What do you mean?'

'Her e-mail.' She stood, put the coffee down, sparked up another.

'You know her address?'

'Yeah.'

'Password?'

'Fuck...'

'It's worth a try. You dig it out while I search the flat. We might just be getting somewhere.'

For the first time in hours, I believed it.

I started in Han Lan's bedroom. Checked under the bed we'd shared. Found nothing but a shoebox I initially thought had something other than a pair of creepers in it, judging by the weight of it. Turned out to be a heavy pair of walking boots. Put them to one side with the intention of nicking them immediately. Fuck it. A man with seven hundred and fifty grand in his account wouldn't miss them. I heard Sara shout that she'd found Angel's laptop in her bedroom, followed by her voice on the end of a call to the local pizza place. I suppose a recovering alcoholic needed her vices.

Han Lan's bank statement had never left my mind.

Decided to take as many of his papers as I could find, including a fan file I discovered at the bottom of his wardrobe. Wondered what other eye openers were lurking in there. What I was really after were mobile phones, diaries, anything with a phone number on it. Computers. Surely no high-flying businessman could do without a laptop or an iPad or whatever the fuck they were these days. Found nothing else in Han Lan's room and precious little in the next one. Decided to dive straight in to Angel's wardrobe and took all her clothes and bags out. Laid them on the bed, intending to rifle all pockets and purses. There had to be something there. I felt more like a thief than an ex copper. Voyeurism wasn't in my makeup. But I'd learned to listen to that inner voice. It was time to dig in.

I'd guessed that Angel would have kept a record of her clients' phone numbers. They were probably stored in her phone, but I could only hope she'd written them down. There were virtually no pockets on any of her clothes except for a pink rain mac and several pairs of jeans. All were empty. I checked the bedside drawers and her dressing table. Besides a few dildos, handcuffs and various other sex toys, there was nothing much in the way of a diary or notebook. I did a double take when a large box of Viagra caught my eye. Assumed she'd kept this for her more 'mature' clients. Thought about pocketing them, but put it down to a bad idea. I might be a drunk, but I had no problems with blood flow just yet.

I took an assortment of handbags and Han Lan's paperwork into the living room. Sara was sitting cross-legged on the couch, the laptop resting between her thighs. She was tapping away, wracking her brains for a password to Angel's e-mail. I went to the drinks cabinet and poured myself a large bourbon. Couldn't be arsed getting ice, so just knocked it back. Poured another, this time with ice and a splash of coke, but only a splash. Sparked up and paced.

'Any luck?'

'No, not yet.'

She drained her coffee and asked for another. Was beginning to think this girl was substituting the booze for caffeine. Flicked the kettle on just as the intercom buzzed. She leapt from the couch and lifted the receiver. False alarm. No Angel, just a large four seasons with extra mushrooms. I brewed her coffee and took it through to the living room. She was already tucking into a slice and handed me one. The only thing I wanted to put in my stomach was liquid fire, but she insisted I make the effort. I could only manage the one slice, and that was pushing it.

I sat on the floor and tried to put some order to the stuff I'd grabbed. Most of the handbags were empty, the rest had nothing but used make up in and a few scribbled scraps of paper. Some with numbers on, but no names. I put them to one side on the mantelpiece. Han Lan's papers were a mixed bag of bank statements, bills, invoices. There was a lot to decipher, and I didn't have the inclination to go number crunching. Was never a fan of numbers, always made me want to reach for a drink. But I knew there could be something here. Specifically, where was the money coming from? And it wouldn't be the first time Hong Kong had crossed my mind. What the fuck was this guy's game? There were no photos of him here, no family pics. I assumed he didn't have any. Suspected he didn't actually live here at all, which begged the question: what was he using the flat for and why was he allowing Angel to stay here? It didn't make sense.

The night wore on and it only occurred to me to check the time when I realised the tapping on the laptop had stopped. I'd been staring at statements and invoices, looking for something, anything that might point me in the right direction. Trouble was, I didn't know what direction I needed to go in. I'd know when it arrived. I looked up from the mess of paperwork and handbags and saw Sara slumped on the couch; the computer beginning to slide off her knees. Poor girl was asleep. She must've been shattered with worry.

I grabbed the duvet from Angel's room and gently covered her up, moving the laptop to the table. Was surprised she could sleep at all with all the coffee she'd had. Checked the time on the oven clock. Just gone midnight. I grabbed the brandy, didn't bother with a glass, and went out to the roof terrace. The city was laid out like a sparkling carpet. She was out there somewhere. I knew it. I smoked and finished what was left of the bottle. It was hard work keeping my own demons at bay. When I finally got under my covers, I was just about blitzed enough to blot out Karen. I knew she would come back, as sure as night follows day. And I'd drink some more. It was what I did. It was my saviour, my curse.

It owned me.

18

Felt like I'd only been asleep for five minutes when I heard a knock on the door. Flipped over, peered an eye over the duvet. There was bright light coming in from the blinds behind me. Another knock.

'Jim?'

Fuck sake, what time was it? 'Yeah...?'

'It's nearly half ten. Are you decent? Can I come in?'

'Just a minute.' Rubbed the sleep from my eyes, yawned, shook away the image of a bottle of Jean Cave Armagnac from a nightmare I was having about a dwarf prostitute and a hoard of nineteen eighties style yuppies brandishing filofaxes and Cuban cigars. My legs were tinged with sweat, despite the cold outside, and I felt like I'd gone ten rounds with Tyson. Probably looked like it too. My mouth felt like sandpaper and there was a pounding coming from somewhere in my neck that I couldn't quite pin down. I was halfway between alive and dead, more dead than alive. I couldn't face the day. Not today, not any day. 'Okay,' I said. 'Come in.'

The door opened. Sounded like an axe murderer was coming to chop me into little pieces. I would've welcomed it.

'Coffee. Thought you might've needed it. Sorry.'

'Has it got anything in it?'

'Just milk,' she said, stepping inside. She sat on the bed beside me. 'Do you take sugar?'

'I meant something a bit stronger.'

'Oh.' She put the mug on the bedside table. 'No. Bit early for that.'

I sat up, leaned back against the headrest. 'You sleep okay?'

She shook her head. 'Sore neck. You should've woke me up. Could've done with a proper bed.'

'You looked so peaceful, thought it best to leave you.'

She smiled. 'Want some breakfast? There's eggs in.'

'Nah, I'm okay.' I grabbed the mug, took a scalding sip. 'Jesus, that's hot.'

She was silent for a moment. I could tell the anxiety had returned. I was willing to bet she'd checked her phone for texts and missed calls. Suspected no news.

'Nothing?'

She shook her head, bit her lip. 'No. I'm terrified, Jim. What if...?'

'No "what ifs". She'll turn up.'

'But this is the second day now. I've a right to be concerned.'

'You have, and I am too. Look, I'll get a shower, change of clothes, then we can head out again. Pay some people a visit if I can find out where they are.'

'No, I've got to get back to Charlie. Laura's taken him to school this morning. I got the impression she wasn't too keen.'

'She's your sister?'

'Yep. Younger sis. She thinks I'm a pain in the arse.'

'Maybe you are,' I grinned. She hit me with a pillow.

'Cheeky bastard. But I've got to head back, just for a while. I want to pick up some photos of Angel. Recent ones.'

'We can get them blown up and photocopied. Take them to the police, they'll want to put out some posters. We can do some of our own.'

'That'll be a great help if you can come with me later to pin them up. Round town, you know.'

I nodded. Took another scalding sip of coffee. 'Jesus, what did you brew this with, lava?'

She laughed, bit her lip. I liked the way her hair flopped in her eyes when she giggled. 'I'll knock up some scrambled eggs,' she said, rising from the bed.

'Not too much for me.'

She stopped in the doorway. 'Nonsense. You'll need to keep your strength up if we're gonna find her.'

She was right. I smiled. 'You're the boss.'

19

I took a shower. Thought about having a shave. There was a week's growth covering my face, but I kind of liked it. And I also couldn't be arsed picking up a razor. Hated shaving at the best of times. Was even worse with a hangover, though these days my hangovers sort of melded into one long head fuck. Put another fresh set of Han Lan's clothes on and added the walking boots I'd found last night. I anticipated using them more, as I'd be pounding the streets soon enough. I was determined to get results today. She was out there somewhere. We'd find her.

Sara had made us both scrambled eggs on thick white toast. Forced it down. She seemed pleased that I'd made the effort. She was in yesterday's clothes and I suggested she take some of Angel's but she declined. Said it didn't feel right while she was still out there missing.

We arranged to meet up in Albert Square at three o'clock, which would give her time enough to see to her son and explain everything to Laura. She reckoned her kid sister would understand. Offered her a room for the night again. She said she'd see how it went today. She held my gaze for the briefest of moments before heading onto the roof terrace for a smoke. I cleared the pots away, then joined her.

'I'll be wearing a red carnation and a Panama hat.'

'What?' She blew smoke out into the bright but freezing day. A heavy grey cloud loomed somewhere over Salford.

'In Albert Square. Three o'clock, by the fountain.'

She laughed, shook her head. It was a shit attempt at humour, but she found it funny. I was glad. I'd try my best to take her mind off the situation. But I knew it couldn't work more than once. She was already pushing the dial button on her phone. I smoked and looked out over the canals as she waited. She sighed, pinched the bridge of her nose.

'Still nothing.'

Then her lips trembled and she let the tears come. I pulled her towards me and held her in my arms. Could smell the shampoo in her hair and the perfume on her neck. She gripped me tight, and I pulled her closer, stroked the back of her head. Her shoulders jumped up and down as she shivered against the day and let the tears come. I kissed her head.

'I promise you,' I said. 'Everything will work out. She'll turn up. She'll know you'll be worried.'

'I've got this terrible feeling!' she said, sobbing, sniffing snot back up her nose. 'It's horrible, Jim!'

'I know, I know.'

And I knew, because I had that feeling too. I couldn't show it. Not yet. Though I suspected Sara knew what I was feeling. It was in her eyes, the fragility in her voice. The shared eye contact. The inner knowing. Neither of us could say it, but we were both thinking it.

She broke away, wiped her eyes on her sleeve. 'I'm sorry.'

'Don't be silly, I'd be more worried if you weren't crying.'

She was quiet for a moment as she looked out over the

city. 'I'd better go. Phone me if you hear anything, or if she turns up...'

'Course I will.'

'Three o'clock.'

'Albert Square.'

'By the fountain.'

I nodded, tried a reassuring smile.

'I'll get you a cheap pay as you go,' she said. 'Might be better if we split up later, cover different areas. We'll need to keep in touch.'

'Good idea.'

She hesitated, then leaned in to kiss my stubbled cheek. 'I'll see you later.'

She was gone in ten seconds. The sound of the front door closing echoed through the flat. I stood and sparked up and tried to keep my mind from the drinks cabinet. I had to start somewhere but could barely face it. My head throbbed for a start. And I was beginning to think of Sara in a different light. Was I right to go there? I wasn't sure if she was flirting or just being friendly. I mean, surely she had more important things on her mind?

I looked back into the living room at Han Lan's paper-work scattered on the floor. My heart sank as I stepped back inside.

20

I brewed a coffee and paced up and down, convincing myself I was weighing up all I'd learned so far and piecing the puzzle together. But I didn't know shit, and what I was really doing was avoiding Han Lan's papers. I knew I had to get stuck in some time, I just couldn't face it. Took two Paracetamol and added a shot of brandy to the coffee. I needed a livener, and besides, it was cold out there.

I made a reluctant start, shifting everything off the coffee table and leaving only the paperwork spread out across the glass. I tried to put it in order, sorting the bills from the statements and the invoices from the receipts. Found the entire thing incredibly boring and couldn't focus. Smoked several fags and finished the coffee while I stared blankly into space until I snapped out of it and forced myself to focus. Although Angel was missing–and vulnerable, according to Sara–I instinctively felt there were answers right here in the flat.

The bills were irrelevant. I glanced at them and saw that all had been paid on time, without delay, from an account in the businessman's name. I put them to one side. It was the bank statements I was really interested in. There were several accounts, some with your regular high street banks, one or two with more obscure off seas institutions. And there were a lot of them, going right back to 2006. That's where I started. The account he held with Citi-group, which I found odd to begin with–who in the UK has an account with an American Bank?–raised eyebrows straight away. Every three months, always on the 26th, there was a standing order going from Han Lan's account to a Bank of China account under the name Xiang Hun International Settlements. It was a princely sum too. One hundred thousand pounds went over no problem from Han Lan's personal trove, it appeared. I found it odd that, over the space of twelve months, for the last six years, Han Lan had been shifting a hundred grand to an account I assumed was based in China. But for what? I suppose it could all be entirely innocent. Maybe he was into importing Tiger bones or some other shit for the Chinese market here in the UK. Maybe it was just innocent commerce, a regular delivery of woks and cleavers for the restaurants in Chinatown. But I doubted it. I could only assume this was still happening now. And by my calculations, four hundred grand a year for the last six years amounted to a rather cool two point four million quid. The guy was rolling in it. But why?

The account he held with HSBC was even more interesting. Twenty-five grand every month went into this account from a company called Fever Corp, who were based in the USA. It totalled one point eight million over the last six years. There was a signature tag attached to these transactions that had remained the same since it began in January 2006. The codeword of 'Golden Dawn Commerce' gave me shivers. What the fuck was this guy's game?

There was another account held under Coutts

International. It was under the name Han Lan Investments. There was almost two million quid in it. I felt sick. It was time for a drink. I headed to the drinks cabinet and pulled out a bottle of Smirnoff. Found a carton of orange juice at the back of the fridge and topped up the glass with it. Technically, it was still breakfast time.

Sat back down and shuffled through the paperwork. It was a complete head fuck. This guy had more money coming in than he had going out. And it was big money. Silly money. For what, I didn't know. There were statements from the Schroder Banking Corporation in the Cayman Islands. Almost flung the shit in front of me over the roof terrace wall when my eyes fell on the balance in this particular account. Twenty-eight million, give or take a few hundred grand. Han Lan was one rich little cunt, of that I was certain. So why the fuck was he letting Angel live here in this swanky little penthouse apartment?

Perhaps more importantly, why the hell was I here too?

Felt the shakes come, then pass when I downed the vodka and orange. Sparked up a smoke and went out onto the roof terrace. The clouds were rolling in and the air smelt of damp and cold. Wouldn't be long before the frost returned. I thought of Angel, wherever she was, and hoped she was okay. I doubted it. I knew something was wrong. Knew it like I knew I needed the oblivion of the demon drink.

I went back inside, threw Han Lan's jacket on. Caught sight of the scattered scraps of paper I'd left on the mantelpiece last night. Numbers. Counted the bits of paper and found seven. For all I knew, they could be reference numbers for some underwear she'd bought online or some other shit like that. But there were two that began with a zero. Mobile numbers, no names attached.

Sparked up again and stepped up to the phone in the hallway. Dialled the first number, which rang, but rang out. Pocketed it for later. Dialled the second one. It rang seven bells before cutting to voicemail.

'Hi, this is Simon. I'm afraid you've caught me at a bad time. Just leave your name and number and I promise I'll get back to you.'

He signed off with a kiss.

Simon. Brick shit house, manicured nails, eyeliner. I'd recognise that voice anywhere.

'We have our man,' I said, to no one but myself. Caught my reflection in the hallway mirror. Looked like a young Robert De Niro. You talking to me?

Pocketed Simon's number, intending to call him later. Grabbed the keys from the side, looked around, and left the building. I'd had enough of number crunching and it was making me want to vomit. I had three hours before I'd meet up with Sara again. I intended to make it count.

21

Standing out by the canal, I stared blankly into the water, wondering where to start. I supposed a quick visit back to the Hilton wouldn't do any harm. It was the most likely place she'd be, or at least would've been seen. Then I'd wander up to Chinatown, take a stroll, see what I could pick up before heading back to those bars we went to on Saturday night. The night of her disappearance. Thought of the cafe where she'd bought me egg and chips after... well, after she brought me down from that car park roof.

I hoped I hadn't given her any silly ideas. Couldn't live with it if she'd gone and done something stupid. But then, I didn't believe she had it in her. And she always seemed so stable. Highly strung, but stable.

I walked to the Hilton, thinking about Han Lan's vast amount of cash and where the hell it was coming from. And where it was going. The incomings, the outgoings. The regular as clockwork transactions. I guessed there were more statements hanging around somewhere. And I wondered if he had other property here in Manchester.

Probably. A man with the money he had no doubt had properties all over the place. Did he have people working for him? Yes, more than likely. I wasn't even sure he was a client of hers. Probably. Maybe. But I had a sneaky feeling there was something more to this relationship of theirs. It was far too cosy. He had to trust her with his life in that flat. Or maybe he was just rolling in it so much he just didn't give a fuck.

Passed the Knott Bar and got to the crossing before I walked through the door. I knew they sold decent beer in there. Absently checked the money in my pocket. I could feel a nice clump of notes I wanted to part with. Could picture a nice Bavarian beer going down my throat right now. When the crossing beeped and the green man flashed, I just marched on, trying to put all thoughts of the booze behind me. I couldn't chance looking back. That was the problem I had around here. Anywhere, actually. I couldn't walk past a boozer without picturing myself sitting inside. Especially on a day like this. It was bitterly cold and the sky was darkening. We'd reached the tail end of Autumn, and winter was about to kick in. It was fucking grim.

The Hilton didn't bring any good news other than a pleasant view of Maria's chest. She was as lovely as yesterday, but sadly didn't have any answers. No one had seen Angel. No one had seen Matt. She reassured me she would phone Sara should anything arise. I thanked her and left, resisting the urge to look back at her pretty face.

Smoked as I made the short walk to Chinatown. The streets were busy, mainly with workers on their way to grab some lunch. The buses jammed the roads, tourists hung around on street corners. Spent most of my time dodging the people traffic on the pavements. It was a city I loved, a city I knew. But sometimes it could get on your tits. Like any

city, really. I kept my head up and my eyes peeled, looking
for any sign of Angel or Matt, or any of her bloody mates for
that matter. I needed someone I recognised, otherwise I was
just wandering around aimlessly and pissing in the wind.

Thought about Karen and Nicole. Mainly Nicole. And
also, what I would say when I saw them again. What I would
say to Frank and Maureen when I turned up on their
doorstep. Sara was right. I needed to do it. Needed to take
that chance. I'd lain low long enough. Too low, actually. It
was time to come out of the woodwork. Nicole needed to
know her Dad. I was ashamed of where I'd ended up. It was
easy to fuck up in life. I knew this, lived it, got the t-shirt. I
had to do something right. I needed a purpose.

Got to Chinatown with no sign of anyone. I was
wondering if I was deluding myself. I mean, what the fuck
was I playing at? Who did I think I was? I wasn't a copper
anymore; I had no authority. But the instinct was there. The
need. It was like I was drawn to it. The search for answers. I
knew that if I could just get one tiny lead, it would all piece
together. The Chinese kept their ear to the ground.
Someone had to know who Han Lan was and what he was
up to.

I walked up Faulkner Street, hovering around the menus
that stood outside every restaurant on either side. I was
hoping to catch the odd conversation that might reveal a
nugget or two. Of the Chinese community, most were in the
restaurant industry. If you weren't a chef, you were behind
the bar or waiting tables. Then there were the traditional
medicine types. Herbalists, acupuncturists. There were
traditional bakeries - Ho's being the most familiar to me -
and betting shops. The Chinese were big gamblers. And of
course, Chinese massage. I didn't kid myself. Some of these
places were genuinely into traditional treatments. But I

knew there were others that were no more than knocking shops, with names like Tropical Palms and Cloud Nine. For thirty quid you could get yourself a beef chow mien and a blow job for dessert. That's what I called a meal deal.

Caught sight of a girl I recognised. She was tiny, with a slim figure and a timid walk. Took a second or two to place her, then it clicked. It was the Thai waitress who served us on Saturday night. I followed. Most of the restaurants were open for the lunchtime trade. I guessed she was on her way to work, her handbag slung over her shoulder, talking in Thai on her mobile phone. From behind, she looked about sixteen. I wanted to know if she'd seen Angel or recognised anyone from our meal the other night. It was a long shot, but there was a possibility one or two of Angel's "friends" were regulars. I was thinking of the men in particular. Dang sprung to mind. It was an opening, at least.

I fell in step just behind her. She was heading for the Thai Banana. I suppose I could pop in for a bowl of soup or something but wasn't hungry. I'd just catch her on the doorstep. Try not to behave like a pervert.

She stopped at the threshold and went to push the door open.

'Excuse me'. No response. Tapped her on the shoulder. 'Excuse me? Sorry...'

She turned, alert as a Cobra. 'Yes?'

'I was just wondering...'

'We are now open for you to lunch.'

'Yeah, I was just wanting to ask you something, if...'

'Ask?'

'Yeah,' I said, trying hard to maintain a distance. Didn't want this girl to think I was invading her space. She was pretty. Gorgeous, in fact, her mouth as delicate as a lotus flower, her eyes as blue as coral. 'Sorry to bother you, I was just wondering if... Well, I was wondering...' Shit, I was getting nowhere fast here. 'Do you remember me from Saturday night? I was here with a party of about twenty people or so?'

'Ah! Yes! Birthday party, yes?'

'Yeah! Yeah, that's it.'

'You the drunk man,' she said, cheekily pouting and shaking her head. She wagged a finger at me. 'This is no good.'

'Yeah, I know,' I laughed. 'Birthday party, you know? Yeah, that's right. Look, I know this is a bit of an odd question, but I was wondering if you'd seen any of the people I was with from that night. I know you might not remember.'

'Seen?'

'The people I was with? Anyone.'

She put a finger to her chin, raised her eyes skyward. She was thinking. I was thinking of something else right now. She was cuter than a newborn kitten in the snow.

'A man?'

'Yeah, anyone you might recognise.'

'Ah, let's see. Um... there is one man who come here all the time. Very big man. Like Lady-boy.' She laughed. I laughed too. Simon. Who else?

'Big guy?'

'Very big!' she said, puffing her cheeks. 'He like the food.'

We laughed. I was beginning to like this girl. 'Anyone else?' She did that finger on chin thing. 'Was he in here yesterday? The big Lady-boy guy?'

'Yes, I think, late at night.'

'Was he alone?'

'Nah, with expensive man.'

'Expensive?'

'Big businessman. Lots money.'

'English?'

'Huh?'

'Was he a white guy?'

'Oh! Nah, very expensive. Chinaman.'

Han Lan? I doubted it. Dang? Maybe, though he was with us on Saturday. She would've recognised him. The likelihood was it was someone else entirely. She hinted he came here often, so I supposed I'd catch him eventually. I had his number anyway. It was a start.

'You want dinner? Seven pound fifty for two order...'

'No thanks. Had too much already.'

She was confused for a minute, then laughed. She was doing a lot of laughing.

'But I'll come back,' I said. 'Maybe tomorrow.'

She just nodded and smiled, then turned into the restaurant. Was half tempted to follow, but something else was tempting me more. I waved her inside, then turned to face the Chinese arch and a bench in the little garden beyond.

I sat there for a while, smoking, taking in the sights. The smells too. There were plenty of suits around, and this part of town was a stone's throw away from the big high street banks on Mosely Street. I guessed they were on a lunch break or something. Or maybe going for a quick lap dance in one of the local strip clubs. Didn't know they were open at this time of day, but wouldn't surprise me. I looked around. Some of the neon lights were on for sure. There was probably some action going on in these places. I wouldn't be going anywhere near them unless I had questions to ask. Maybe I would, eventually. I'm sure I remember Angel telling me she was once a dancer. She never said what kind, but I could guess.

My thoughts returned to the missing girl. Was she really missing or had she just decided to disappear herself? After

Sara had reported her gone, the police would surely be looking for her. But I knew they didn't take any missing person enquiry seriously until at least seventy-two hours after the event. We were barely forty hours into this. And besides, people went missing every day. All ages too. Why the hell would they pull their finger out for a thirty-something prostitute who was probably on the job somewhere? I wouldn't have taken it seriously back in the day. I don't think any procedure had changed in the last few years.

I spent a while browsing the Chinese medicine stores. There were one or two dotted around. The first one offered nothing but a confused woman in her nineties who kept shaking her head and saying 'No English, no English.' Had her down as racist until I realised she meant she didn't speak the language. The next one I went in was called Fun Deng. I mooched about the aisles, smelling herbal remedies and ginseng and pretending to be interested in a weird black tea concoction that was apparently good for the organs. Spoke to a little guy with a bald head who looked about ninety-two. He took one look at me and pointed at my blotchy complexion, the bags under my eyes and the broken capillaries on the bridge of my nose. Diagnosed me as being a heavy drinker. He wasn't wrong there. Perhaps he could smell the booze on me or just saw I was dying for a pint. Wondered if it was really that obvious. I agreed to buy something to settle my stomach and keep away the demon drink if he gave me some information. He didn't need much persuading.

'Han Lan,' I said, for the third time. I suppose he didn't understand my accent because he kept shaking his head. Did he think it was some kind of herb? 'Han Lan. Businessman. Big money.'

'Han Han?'

'Han Lan.'

He shuffled off towards the counter, went behind it and rummaged around for something, the spiders' legs at the corner of his eyes creased up. He kept nodding his head and ushering me towards him. He looked like an extra from *Kung Fu*. It was clear I was getting nowhere. When he saw the frustration on my face, he held his palms up–wait there– and disappeared through a beaded curtain. A minute later, a young girl came out. Had to be in her twenties.

'Can I help you?' she said, in a perfect Mancunian accent. 'He says you want something to help with too much alcohol.'

'No, no, no. Well, yeah. I suppose it wouldn't do any harm. But I'm looking for someone. Someone you might have heard of.'

She looked interested. This was encouraging. She motioned for me to go on. The old guy came out with a dusty-looking box and pressed it into my hands, whispering in Chinese. I smiled, thanked him, and then he was off again into the back room.

'His name's Han Lan. A businessman, I think. I'm not sure what, but he's... well, he's...'

'Ah, Mr. Lan. And who are you, if you don't mind me asking?'

So she'd heard of him. This was good. But who was I? I had to think on my feet. I wasn't a copper anymore, so I knew I couldn't get away with saying I was if this backfired. 'My name's Jim,' I said. 'Jim Locke. I'm a private investigator. You might've heard of me.'

'No,' she said. 'I haven't.'

'Well, that's good, because I like to keep a low profile. So you know Mr. Lan?'

'Everybody knows Mr. Lan.'

'Really?'

'Oh yeah.'

'So how come I haven't heard of him?'

'Well, why would you? You're not Chinese.'

'So do you know what kind of business he's in?'

'He's in all kinds of stuff. He owns half of Chinatown. A lot of the restaurants. Some shops.'

'Clubs? You know, private rooms, that kind of stuff.'

She didn't answer, just took out a Marlboro Light and sparked up. 'How do I know you're a private investigator? You got any ID? You could be anyone.'

She was right. 'You're a student, aren't you?' It was a wild guess, but I had her down as some kind of maths prodigy.

'How do you know?'

'I can just tell. Must be hard making ends meet as a student these days.'

'So what do you want to know?'

I dug in my pocket, fished out a crumpled twenty and dropped it on the counter. 'For the black tea. You can keep the change. If you can tell me what else you know.'

She took a long drag, blew smoke into the shop. 'Look, I know nothing other than what I've told you already. He's loaded, everyone knows him around here. You'd be better off asking some of the older guys.'

'Want to mention any names?'

She sighed, ran a dainty hand through her perfectly straight black hair. 'There's a guy called Bo. Bo Wong. Runs one of the dancing clubs. It's a private space above the little Yang Heng across the street. Ask him.'

'He know him?'

She looked down at the Chinese paper on the counter and flicked ash.

'Look, a girl is missing. Angel. Blonde, about this big. I'm looking for her.'

She looked up, her brown eyes staring blankly. 'And what makes you think I can help?'

This time it was my turn to sigh. I shook my head. 'Doesn't matter. Thanks anyway.'

'I'll keep an eye out.' She grabbed the twenty off the counter and pushed it into a leather purse. I was already through the door when she called out. 'Mr. Locke?'

I turned, raised my eyebrows.

'You forgot your black tea. It's good for the liver.'

'Keep it. I prefer Yorkshire Tea.'

I saw a hint of a smile as I stepped out into the cold.

22

Needed a drink like a plant needs rain. Had no idea of the time, so asked a passing Goth. It was just gone half-past one. Killed two birds with one stone and headed off to the Northern Quarter and the bars we'd been to for Angel's birthday drinks. Felt the pull of the booze more than a thirst for answers. Walking through Piccadilly brought with it memories of Saturday night and my trip into the unknown. Felt the anger rise. Then Karen and Nicole came into my head again, like ghosts from the past. I was so convinced I saw them in the amusement arcade and was certain it was my chance to put right some wrongs. Felt a fool for even believing the unbelievable, but eyes didn't lie. It was just the acid that did.

Negotiated my way through the crowds and whipped down Thomas Street. Felt my pace quickening. Was only one thing on my mind and it wasn't a white wine spritzer. I needed beer and a chaser. Didn't matter what. Walked past the local Pakistani curry spots and almost got dragged into The Millstone. The smell of real ale was that tempting. But I pushed on that extra few yards and, for the sake of a few quid, it was worth it. If I'd find out anything about Angel, it would be here at Odd.

Let myself inside. It was like a fallen angel going back to heaven. Stepped up to the bar and ordered a pint of Estrella Damm and a straight Maker's Mark, no ice. The girl behind the bar - sleeves full of tattoos and a nose ring - asked if I wanted to order food. Looked around, saw a couple of students and a young guy in a flat cap having a beer and burger special. I knew I had to meet Sara and couldn't face it, anyway. Knocked it on the head and got straight to the point. Swallowed the bourbon and took the head off the beer.

'I'm looking for someone. Girl by the name of Angel. Blonde, pretty. Short skirt, long jacket. Leopard print. I was here with her on Saturday night.'

'I don't work Saturday nights,' she said. 'And besides, we get a lot of people in here. I doubt anyone would've seen her.'

She was right. This was madness and I knew it. I went on. 'It was her birthday. Thirtieth. There was a group of us. She went back to her flat and hasn't been seen since, when she left in the early hours with a guy called Matt. I don't suppose you know him?'

'What does he look like?'

'Southerner. Face you want to punch. Flash, you know?'

'Like I said, we get a lot of people in here. And I don't know any members of staff who'd waste their time memorising faces. Too busy for that. We have lives, you know.'

I nodded, plastered on a smile. 'Would it be okay if I put a picture up of her? If I come back later?'

'Don't see why not. Seven pound eighty five.'

I paid her and took my beer to a seat in the corner. I liked bars like this when they were quiet. Much better to sit and watch the world go by than squeezed into a corner of a Saturday night. I looked out the window. There was rain coming in and the day was darkening fast. The last of the Autumn leaves were clinging on for dear life and the cold north wind would soon blow a winter in. Winters were grim on the streets.

I went through what I knew already as I sat and drank, which wasn't much at all. I doubted Angel was still alive. Everything pointed to bad news. If she was alive, she'd be home by now. Something had happened to her. I could feel it the way I felt the booze in the pores of my skin. I only hoped Sara could cope with the inevitable. But if someone wanted her dead, it begged lots of questions. The main one being why? And after what I'd learned so far about Han Lan–I still couldn't believe I was wearing the man's clothes–there was a mystery here as to why she'd been living in his flat. Why was I spiked with acid? Who wanted me out of the way? And what the fuck was that bitch Carol hiding?

I sat and drank and tried to empty my mind. It was useless. Kept seeing the image of Frank and Maureen tearing into me when I turned up on their doorstep. Karen, Nicole, Angel. They were all hanging around my head like a fresh and banging hangover. If I could've emptied it right there, I would. But I couldn't. I was in it now. Strange how barely a week ago I was willing to let it all go and bow out in a mess of blood on the concrete. I was truly amazed at my stupidity. I knew my patience had worn thin and my fragile state of mind hadn't really gone away. But Angel and Sara were right. I'd be a fool if I didn't fight to see my kid. Suicide was a coward's way out. But when you can't see through to tomorrow, it's easy to make decisions of life and death on a whim.

I looked at the rest of my pint. One scoop and it'd be

gone. I knew that if I didn't leave now, I'd be here all day. It didn't look inviting outside, but I had a meeting with Sara to attend to. I intended to stick to it. Just as soon as I'd had another.

There was a bloke serving me this time. Mohawk hairdo, lumberjack shirt, torn jeans, a full tattooed sleeve on his right arm and those fucking ear piercings that wouldn't look out of place on a Masai warrior. I think I recognised him from Saturday night but couldn't be sure. All the bar staff looked the same in this place. Ultra cool and trendy, Phd's stacking up until they could be arsed getting a proper job.

'Yes, mate.'

'Another pint. And a few questions.'

'Oh yeah?' He flicked the tap on the pump.

'You were working Saturday, right?'

'Was on until midnight,' he nodded. Handed me the beer. I paid, got stuck in.

'Your friend there said she wasn't working, but I know you were because I recognise you. I'm looking for a girl. She went missing Saturday night. With a bloke. Cockney by the name of Matt.'

He nodded, squirted himself a lemonade. 'You got a picture of her?'

'Maybe later. But I was thinking. You must get your regulars in here. You know. Do you ever see the same faces?'

'God, yeah, all the time. They come from the apartments around here.'

'Anyone with a southern accent? Any Chinese guys?'

'Well, you get a mixed bag. It's not as if you notice, to be honest.'

'I expect not.' Took a long drink. 'Look, I'll be back with a picture. Might jog some memories.'

'Okay, but this girl. What's her name again?'

'Angel. Lots of friends. Mainly girls and guys with a fair bit of cash.'

'I'll ask around. But bring that photo in and we'll stick it up in the window. Hope she's okay, man. She your girlfriend or something?'

Drained the pint. 'Something like that,' I said, and left before I could order another.

Toyed with the cocktail bar across the road but thought better of it. It was getting on now, and the afternoon light was fading rapidly. There was a steady rain, and I'd never been one for worrying about getting wet, but there was a foreboding cloud lingering above that looked just about ready to piss. Didn't want to get drenched. The booze had just about taken the edge off and I felt a fuzziness I was comfortable with. It would be enough to keep me walking to Albert Square and Sara.

I was worried about that girl. I worried about her being worried. I knew that the longer this went on, it could only get worse for her. For both of us. Perhaps most of all, for Angel.

I struggled to understand the motivation, if she'd chosen to go missing herself. I doubted that was the case. She gave no signs during our week together. Addiction aside - the coke snorting in the bathroom, followed by the tears - she gave no indication she was feeling the pressure. Maybe the addiction was enough. Addicts are good at masking problems. I knew that from experience. And besides, I could've been too wrapped up in my own affairs to notice. Her choosing to go missing herself just didn't make sense, although I knew it was common to want to just vanish and live off the grid. I'd done it myself. There were all kinds of reasons, and maybe she was hiding something. A terrible secret she couldn't live with. I guessed Sara would know. At least I hoped she did.

I took shelter in a Sainsbury's local during a downpour, which passed within minutes. When I finally walked into Albert Square, I spotted her standing by the fountain with her umbrella still up, though the rain had stopped. She had a rucksack on her back and was carrying a canvas shopping bag stuffed with papers.

She turned and smiled when I tapped her on the shoulder. Gave me a hug and I reciprocated. It felt good seeing her again. She seemed happy to see me too.

'The police phoned me,' she said, brushing a wet lock of hair from her face. 'They've put her on their missing person's website. They wanted some more information. Nothing I haven't told them already, but...'

'That's good. Did they say anything about stepping up patrols?'

'No.'

'Thought not. So, what've we got here?'

She held up the shopping bag. 'Posters. Well, just a load of A4 paper, really. Took me ages to print out. I photocopied a load at the library. Laura helped.'

She handed me one and I took a look. It was a recent picture. A very recent picture. 'When did you take this?'

'Saturday night. I got it off my phone.'

'Great.'

'Which reminds me.' She shook her rucksack off and dug into one of the outer pockets. Handed me a Nokia. 'Cheap pay as you go. I've taped your number to the back. Already put it in my contacts.'

'Thanks. Any news?' I nodded to her mobile.

She shook her head. 'Nothing. You?'

I filled her in on what I'd found out about our friend Han Lan. His money, his offshore accounts, particularly the one in the Cayman Islands and the massive transactions that were going in and out of it. Also updated her on my afternoon's activities, and my intention to revisit the Thai Banana and perhaps become a member of the dance club above the Yang Heng. Told her about this guy Bo Wong and our fat friend Simon. It wasn't much to go on, but it sounded promising. It was better than anything the police had come up with. She told me they'd made provisional enquiries about her last whereabouts. I assumed they'd been to the Hilton though, if they had, the beautiful Maria hadn't mentioned it. Yet.

'Sounds like you've been busy.'

'It's a start. Something to go on, at least. You sort Charlie out?'

'Yeah, Laura's having him again. She said she understood. She's as worried as me. She's known Angel for years too.'

I wanted to run a few things by her before we set off to put the posters up. Mainly what I'd been thinking on my way here, about the possibility Angel had chosen to go missing herself. Plenty of girls did, and I wanted to know if Sara had those thoughts too.

'I don't think so,' she said. 'She wouldn't. She wouldn't just... disappear like that. Not without saying goodbye.'

'Is there any possibility? Anyone who could help her? You said yourself she was unhappy. You know, doing what she does... Would that be enough for her to walk away from her friends and start again?'

'She wasn't trapped, Jim. She chose this life. She enjoyed it. There were parts of it she didn't like, yeah, but overall she was happy enough. I think.'

'You sound doubtful.'

She sighed, raised her eyes to the heavens and ran a hand through her hair. 'I don't know what to think. Right now I just want to find her.'

Now it was my turn to sigh. 'Okay, let's get these up before the rain comes again. Anywhere that'll take them.'

She nodded. 'We'll split up.'

Sara took everywhere south of Albert Square while I headed back the way I came. She said she'd try the Hilton again, joking that at this rate we'd be checking in ourselves before long. Didn't sound like a bad idea. I was becoming increasingly uncomfortable with staying in that flat. We agreed to meet again in two hours. It would give me enough time to whiz around and grab a pint before we met again. She said she'd phone me when she was done and if anything turned up. I said I'd do the same.

I kept my eyes peeled on my way back through China-town. Dropped several posters in every restaurant that would have them. None disagreed. The girl from the Thai Banana waved and smiled as I left a poster on the bar. Had a quick look out for Simon, but got no joy. Went back into the Chinese medicine store. The student girl had gone–probably to spend my twenty quid down some four bottles for a quid night at the student union–but the old geezer obliged with the poster, pinning it up in his window. I don't think he understood what it was for, but he seemed happy enough to see me again, slapping me on the back on the way out.

Headed back to Odd and the girl from earlier served me another beer while I put several posters up–two in the window, one in the gents, one in the ladies. Asked a few punters if they'd seen her anywhere. No one had. Drank the beer and had several smokes before moving on to the cock-tail bar across the road. Didn't have a drink in there, though

I was tempted. Didn't want to risk another spiked cocktail. Call me paranoid.

I must've gone in ten bars and pubs and left posters at every turn. Her face would be plastered all over town within the hour. Even pinned one to every bus stop I passed and pushed a few into the hands of a grease-ball serving behind the counter of the cafe where she'd bought me egg and chips. He was the only guy who recognised her. She must've used the cafe quite a lot. He didn't recall seeing her since she was with the 'smelly homeless man' the last time she was in. Didn't let on that was me.

On my way back through Piccadilly Gardens, my gaze was drawn to the advertising screen above the hotel across the bus terminus. The police used it sometimes to display their missing persons images. Saw a twenty foot portrait of the girl who'd taken me in and given me food, money and a lot more besides. There she was, her bleach blonde hair illuminating the greying sky. I realised that shit just got real. Helen Shields, aka Angel, it said. Call the missing persons helpline. Somehow, I had the feeling it wouldn't be needed. She was dead and I knew it.

I think Sara knew it too.

23

W e spent the next week doing pretty much the same. The days went slowly, especially for Sara. For me, too. I focused on Angel's whereabouts rather than the reasons for her disappearance, but Han Lan never left my mind. Nor Matt, or Carol, or Simon. Nor any of the others. I took photographs of Han Lan's bank statements with Sara's digital camera. Photocopies, too. I guessed the escort agency wouldn't be hard to find if we did some digging. Laura remembered it was called Provoke. Classy. A simple Google search brought us to where we wanted to be. Found a picture of Sherry in skimpy underwear on the main page. I found it a shame. I liked that girl. I could tell she was just an innocent little kid, really, albeit one who'd gotten carried away with the more glamorous lifestyle of high-class prostitution. Toyed with the idea of making a booking, but it could wait. We had other priorities.

There had been no sign of Angel. Sara was at her wits' end. Felt for the girl in a big way. On the Tuesday night an article appeared in the Evening Chronicle. It was on page six, easily dismissed, a small one hundred word column beside the much bigger story of a footballer crashing his car. You could say I wasn't surprised. Missing persons were ten-a-penny these days. There were a lot of them. Some had good reason to disappear. If you weren't connected to them, you wouldn't likely give a shit. There were no calls from any of her friends or acquaintances. Not even a single word of support. The silence was deafening. I wanted to know why.

We spent several days walking the streets, re-visiting places Sara knew she hung out. Bars, cafes, the lot. There was no sign of her. We knew we had to keep her image visible across the city if we were to stand any chance of finding her. Someone out there would've seen her. We worked with the police as best we could–well, Sara and her sister Laura did–while I kept a safe distance. I didn't want anyone on the force to know how far I'd fallen.

She never checked out of the Hilton. That alone set the alarm bells ringing. The police checked the CCTV footage from the main foyer. She was last seen leaving through the main entrance with Matt at 02:33am on the Sunday. A strange time to be leaving a hotel. They were arm in arm. From what Sara told me, Angel looked happy enough on the footage. She was practically beaming, she said, though my guess was that was probably the coke she had floating around in her bloodstream.

On the Thursday, Sara offered to put me up. She was aware I wasn't comfortable staying in Han Lan's flat. And I definitely wasn't. When I wasn't out looking for Angel, I was cooped up inside drinking and pacing around and looking out the window for any sign of a Chinese guy in an expensive suit. Spent most of my time sitting out on the roof terrace, as cold as it was, chain smoking and running things through my mind. It was usually frazzled. With her help and concern, I ate three times a day. She practically forced me to finish whatever was on my plate. I got to know her sister Laura a little bit–four years younger than Sara, pretty and curvaceous with a cheeky glint in her eye–but mainly thinking about our next move, if there was to be one. My money, or rather the money I'd been given or nicked, was running out rapidly. So when Sara offered to keep me fed and offered me a roof over my head, I obliged. Much like Angel had done, she said I could hang around until I got back on my feet, however long it took. I don't know whether it was my face or the fact that we were searching for her friend together. We'd quickly become mates. The fact that we were on this mission together helped cement our friendship pretty quickly, and besides, I think she saw something in me she recognised in herself. She said she wanted me to help her find Angel, whatever had happened to her. It was the least I could do. Being an ex copper, I knew she trusted me. It was in her eyes.

I packed a bin bag full of Han Lan's clothes–emptied him out, actually–and it was like I'd won the lottery. Some of his gear was worth hundreds. I'd be the best dressed homeless drunk in the entire world. I got copies of his flat keys and wrote down the access code for the gated entrance. Somehow, I had a feeling I'd be coming back. We emptied the fridge and his drinks cabinet and re-stocked it all in Sara's kitchen. I had to examine my conscience a bit. I didn't believe in theft. I'd investigated enough of that in the past. But I guessed he wouldn't miss it, and it would be a shame to let it go to waste. But I suspected he was somehow involved in Angel's disappearance, despite him being thousands of miles away in Hong Kong, so I didn't suffer too much with guilt. There was no certainty he was in Hong Kong, though I had no reason to believe Angel was lying. There was something dodgy about the guy. I would make a point of hanging around Chinatown to find out what he was really into soon enough. Pay a visit to this Bo Wong.

We drove through a bright but chilly morning on the Friday in Sara's knackered old Fiat Punto. I wasn't sorry about leaving Han Lan's pad behind. Her place was in a rundown part of North Manchester. As we left the traffic of the city and eased into the suburbs up north, I felt like I needed a drink. The place had let itself go in a big way. Urban disintegration wasn't the correct description, but it wasn't far off. It was worse than that. Felt my mood drop as she drove us through the main high street. All the shops were boarded up, and I half expected to see a tumbleweed roll past as we waited at the lights. The place was barren. The only life besides us was a hunched over eighty-year-old woman dragging a shopping trolley and a stray dog scratching his balls beside the old Co-op. It was a charming place. The recession had hit hard here. I wondered about the employment levels. Sara guessed what was on my mind and said half the people were out of work and virtually all the local youth had nothing better to do than kick doors in and start fires. I wasn't shocked. Half the country was on its arse. It was places like this that really felt it hardest.

Her house was a standard two up two down just off the high street. At least there were new trees lining the pavements on either side. Wondered how long it would be before some bright young spark tried chopping them down.

She showed me to my room. It looked out onto a selection of backyards, each one with piles of shit dumped in them, as if the refuse never got collected around here. The house across the way had its back bedroom window smashed in, with just a sheet of damp plywood covering up the gap. Glass glistened on the kitchen roof in the morning light.

But the bedroom was neat and tidy and clean, which was way more than I was used to. It was a modest house, but Sara's home. I respected that, and the fact she'd offered me a bed. Food, too. Felt humbled she'd invited me into her space. She said she knew it wasn't much, but it was all she could afford to rent. No one could afford to buy around here. Despite the drabness of the surroundings, she knew the area and still had one or two friends close by.

'Tea?'

I would've preferred something stronger, but nodded. 'No sugar.'

I joined her in the kitchen, sparked up by the back door.

'Charlie can get in with me. He's only three, so he's not at the age where he desperately needs his own room yet. And anyway, I was planning on giving it a lick of paint first.'

'Well, I can do that for you. Give it a once over. It's the least I can do. Shouldn't cost too much and I'll have it done in a few days.'

She brewed the tea, pinging the mug with a spoon. 'Would you? Would be great if you could. I'm no good at climbing ladders, I get vertigo.'

'Not a problem. We'll get the paint when you're ready.'

She smiled, left her eyes on mine for a second or two. 'It'll be nice to have a man about the house for a change.'

'It's nice to have some company for once. I'm not used to it. Feel blessed.'

24

I unpacked some things and piled them up on a chair in the corner of the bedroom. Got to looking through Han Lan's paperwork again–the photocopied ones–and shook my head in disbelief. Not for the first time.

Sara was downstairs doing household stuff–washing, ironing–and she'd been quiet for most of the day. We'd had a chat about the Angel situation. Tried to convince her that no news was good news. I could see it wasn't sinking in. I wasn't surprised. Heard her on the phone to the police half an hour ago. She got a bit exasperated with whom I assumed was a liaison officer on the other end. The girl was getting rattled. I couldn't blame her.

I hung around downstairs while Sara prepared us some tea–she'd gone all out for steak and chips–and smoked while I thought about what I was going to do tonight. Checked my cash flow. Had enough to get a few beers in town and see if I could chance my arm at the dancing spot above the Yang Heng. I was more than intrigued at what the student medicine girl had said about Bo Wong. Guessed he must be some kind of player in Chinatown. I supposed he knew people. Running a strip club no doubt meant you needed certain connections. Just what kind of connections, I needed to find out. If he knew Han Lan, he could give me some answers, but it'd have to be handled carefully. Discreetly. And I wasn't going to get anywhere scratching my arse here.

'I'm gonna go out later,' I said. 'See what I can find down Chinatown. Would you mind?'

'Of course not. Do you want to take my car?'

'Can't risk it,' I said. 'I'm not insured, am I? Besides, I couldn't do that. It's your car and I don't trust myself.'

She turned from peeling the spuds. 'It's no problem, I can get you sorted out online in no time... Oh. You want a drink, don't you?'

I didn't need to say anything. She sighed, nodded, said she understood. And she did. She'd been there. I felt a twinge of guilt at all the booze we'd–or rather I'd–nicked from Han Lan's pad. It was sitting there on the sideboard, asking to be drunk. I looked down, felt the shakes coming on.

She put the peeler down and took a tumbler from the cupboard. Screwed the cap off a bottle of gin and poured. Handed it to me. I took it.

'I'm sorry. It's just...'

'I know. I understand.' She reached out, put her hand across my cheek. I thought she was going to kiss me, and I would've let her. 'We'll get through this together, Jim. You can do it. I know you can. If I can, so can you.'

Felt a wave of emotion shudder through me like an earthquake. I wanted to cry, to let it all out, but instead I put the glass to my lips and drank to the bottom. Took a deep breath, felt the burn and bitterness of pure, dry gin seep down into my chest. She pulled me to her and hugged me tight. And then the tears came.

'What am I gonna do, Sara?'

'Shh,' she whispered. I could feel her breath in my ear. She kissed my neck and squeezed before letting me go. 'One day at a time.'

We shared the briefest of moments before the doorbell went. She went to answer while I tried to stop myself from picking the Hendrick's up again. A little boy came running into the living room, followed by auntie Laura. He was swinging a stuffed Spiderman and stomping his feet in a pair of Star Wars wellies.

'Meet Charlie,' Sara said, picking up and squeezing him until he giggled. 'He's a handful.'

I nodded my hello to Laura, who plonked herself down on the couch while Charlie clung to his mum's jeans. The kid was cuter than a basket of cockles. I crouched down and held out my hand. 'Hello, Charlie. Spiderman's cool, isn't he?'

'It's not Spiderman,' he said. 'His name's Peter Parker.'

I liked him already.

25

I left the house less than two hours later. Put away the steak and chips and had an in-depth conversation with Charlie about Spiderman, the Green Goblin and Ironman, though I think it was lost on him as much as me. He was in his pyjamas soon after tea and dosing in front of *Toy Story* while Sara and Laura talked quietly on the couch with a cup of tea. I had a long gin and tonic and left with Sara's words of caution ringing in my ears. Told her I'd be back by midnight. She gave me a spare key and asked me to text her later in the night, especially if I dug anything up about Angel.

Found the nearest bus stop a mere two-minute walk away and waited for a bus into town which, at this time in the evening, was every half hour. I felt anxious and I didn't know why. Found myself chain smoking until a battered old single decker arrived. Almost choked when the driver said the fare would be two fifty. I opted for the night saver and gave him a fiver, getting less than a pound in change. Sat halfway down the bus, a good distance from a couple of pensioners at the front and an overweight single mother giving verbals to her young son. There was a group of youths at the back, only fifteen or sixteen, but their bravado echoed down the bus and I could hear them making jokes about the other passengers. I turned and glared at one, a spotty kid with his hood up and a cut price necklace from Argos dangling from his neck. Kid fancied himself as a gangster. He tried staring me out, but I held his gaze until he looked away and they got to talking about how much weed they smoked and how many girls they'd fingered. I'd hazard a bet the nearest any of them got to pussy was when they opened a pouch of Whiskas for the family cat. Which was a far cry from where I was going.

I got off at Piccadilly with the memory of my bad trip fogging my thoughts. Made the brief walk to Chinatown and hung around under the arch for ten minutes while I clocked who was going in and out of the little side door beside the Yang Heng. I guessed it led to a set of stairs and the private club above. Wondered if I'd get in, but figured there'd be no harm in trying. They were mostly suits. Bankers, probably. Solicitors, maybe. Coppers. Local councillors. I'd heard it was an exclusive place, not at all like your average back street establishment that attracted the usual suspects. No, this was high end. Private members, invitation only. Wondered how I'd blag myself in. I was dressed for the occasion in one of Han Lan's designer suits and alligator skin shoes but never felt so out of place. I'd have to be in character if I stood any chance.

Then I saw my excuse waddle before my very eyes. Councillor Bob Thornton, responsible for Didsbury Ward. He stepped up to the side door like a man on a mission, his weasly eyes stealing a glance either side of the pavement and his jowls jiggling under the neon facade of the Yang Heng restaurant before he stepped in. I had my man.

Finished my smoke and flung it into the gutter before stepping across the street. There was a set of stairs leading up from a narrow corridor, lit up in neon blue. There was a small desk before the stairs with a waif like Chinese girl, no older than twenty, standing behind it.

'Can I help you, sir?'

'I'm with Mr. Thornton. He should have a table booked?'

'And you are?'

'Mr. Roper. There should be a party of us...?'

She checked the list, shook her head. 'No Mr. Roper. But go up, if you like.'

'He is expecting me.'

She nodded, said 'I'm sure', then went back to sipping her green tea. I took her invite and headed up the stairs, gripping the banister to steady myself on the way up. I reached a narrow door, solid wood. Pushed it open to find myself in another corridor, with more blue neon and music coming from my left. Stepped towards the end and turned the corner into a wide and spacious room with booths lining the velvet walls. The booths were horseshoe shaped, black leather and granite tables, with the smell of cigars and brandy and sex surrounding every one. And something else, too. The stench of corruption.

I stepped up to the bar at the centre of the room. There was a Chinese guy in a tuxedo polishing glasses. Looked a bit like Jackie Chan. There was a girl at the far end serving a customer who fit the dirty old man stereotype. Looked about seventy, dressed in a long raincoat. He caught my eye, then looked away as she served him a tall glass with ice in it.

'Yes?'

Jackie Chan appeared before me like a ghost. Thought about ordering what the old perv had just gotten, then

thought twice. Could be a twenty quid cocktail or something. 'Brandy. Large one, something regular.'

He nodded and turned to the top shelf, brought down a
bottle of Hennessey. He poured me a measure while I
scanned the room. Most of the booths were occupied, and I
saw a few smoking fat Cubans too. Saw one or two eyes
hover in my direction. Spotted an empty booth in the far
corner and decided to take it. He placed the brandy on the
bar and I gave him a fiver, told him to keep the change.

'I'm looking for Mr. Wong. He around?'

'Ahh, Mr. Wong not here,' he said. Saw him glance to a
booth behind me and the group of Chinese businessman
sitting around it like a group of fat, pissed up Buddhas. 'He
out on business.'

Dug in my pocket, brought out twenty quid. I didn't
know whether I was fooling myself or anyone else, but it
worked on the student in the medicine store. It might work
on him too. Placed it on the counter before us as I downed
the brandy. 'Give me another.' Saw his expression change.
'Keep the rest. Tell Mr. Wong I'll be sitting over there. Can I
smoke in here?'

'Kind of unwritten rule.' Handed me an ashtray and said
he'd do what he could. I nodded and left the bar.

I took the booth in the corner, which was in a good spot
as I could see across the rest of the room. The seats were
plush and comfortable. Sparked up and watched the blue
smoke curl across the table. Took to sipping the brandy and
tried to remain as inconspicuous as possible. Was proving a
problem. I felt all eyes upon me. Was half expecting the
music to stop and a silence to descend like thick fog. No
chance of that now that the girls were out. There were three
rather curvaceous Chinese girls - young, no more than
thirty - circling the room in bikinis. If I wasn't careful, I'd be

easily distracted. Wondered if the medicine girl had been tempted to take on such a job, to supplement her income as a student. I doubted it.

I watched as the girls toted for business. There was some cheesy nineteen eighties poodle perm rock coming from speakers somewhere above the bar. Clocked Jackie Chan cast a look in my direction. He nodded as he stepped over to the booth with the drunken Buddhas and took a glance back as he pointed in my direction. A fat Chinese guy with a loose tie and braces, his belly hanging over his trousers like a plump Peking Duck, looked in my direction. I raised the brandy glass and tipped it. Took a quick nip. He said something to Jackie Chan, then the barman went back to mixing cocktails. Moments later, Wong was sliding himself into the seat beside me, a bottle of Hennessey and two crystal glasses between us. Guy knew how to treat a guest, I suppose. He handed me a thick cigar. I declined, sparked up another smoke. He lit up the Cuban, his fingers as thick as the smoke itself. Took a long drag before blowing a cloud above us.

'So.' I expected a Chinese accent but got pure Mancunian. 'What can I do for you, Mr. Roper...?'

'Actually, it's Locke.'I reached out and helped myself to the Hennessey. Poured him two fingers too. 'Jim Locke. I'm interested in what you may or may not know about a Mr. Lan. Han Lan. Know him?'

'Mr. Lan is an old friend of mine. He owns this place. Well, the building. The club is mine. The restaurant's his. He's an honourable man.'

'Know where he is?'

'Yeah.' Took a sniff of the brandy before sipping. 'But why should I tell you, Mr. Locke? And why do you want to know?'

'Well,' I said, taking a glossy photo of Angel from my

inside jacket pocket. Han Lan's jacket pocket. I wondered if Wong noticed I was wearing his clothes. 'A girl's gone missing. Friend of mine. She was living in Mr. Lan's pad in Castlefield. Until last Sunday. She left in the early hours with a man named Matt. Financial type. Kind of guy who might come to this place. At approximately two thirty-three a.m., the CCTV at the Hilton caught her leaving with the same guy. She's not been seen since. Recognise her?'

I slid the photo across the table and took a drink while he scanned it. It was one Sara had given me before I left. She'd got it printed out from her phone. It was taken the Saturday she had her birthday drinks, so it was very recent.

'I don't think so...'

'Look again,' I said, eyeballing him. 'Closer.'

'Are you threatening me, Mr. Locke?'

'Not at all. It's just Angel here is quite a well-known girl around these parts. Frequently has a different man on her arm, if you get my drift...?'

'So she's a prostitute?'

'Not just any prostitute. A very expensive one. Seems Han Lan knew it too. He seemed happy enough to put her up rent free. I'm just wondering why that was. I thought you might have some idea, seeing as you're acquainted so well.'

A nervous laugh, a long drag, a deft sip of the brandy as his eyes wandered the room. A girl with a 34DD chest appeared beside me, her slender arm resting upon my shoulder. Wong waved her away with his cigar like an irritated Dad might wave away his kid.

'I don't know what it is you're getting at, Mr. Locke, but I don't think there's anything illegal in Mr. Lan enjoying the company of such a woman and putting her up in his apartment.'

'Some might have different opinions on that.'

'Oh?'

'Like some of the clientele in here right now,' I said. 'Coppers. Solicitors.'

'Please...'

'Don't think I don't know what kind of operation you're running here, Mr. Wong. You may have friends here,' I said, glancing around at some of the occupied booths. 'But it could be bad publicity in the wrong hands. They're not all corrupt little scumbags. Just the worst ones. I recognise a few.'

'That's bullshit, Locke.'

'No.' I was really winging it now, wading through the muddy waters, completely out of my depth. Any time now I'd be desperately trying to drag myself out of the quick-sand. I didn't know shit. It was all a bluff, playing the game. It wouldn't surprise me at all if there was dodgy stuff going on here. But I had to sound like I knew for sure. I eyeballed him again, did my best to put the shits up him. He was a caricature and he knew it. 'Don't bank on it. You'd be surprised how many people know.'

'Know what?'

Eyeballed him again, took a sip of brandy, savoured it before swallowing and took several drags on the smoke. 'So, you seen her?'

'I might've done.'

'Yes or no?'

'Yeah. I think. Maybe. I don't know.'

'When? Where?'

'In the restaurant. With one or two men.'

'At the same time?'

'No, different times. Look, I hope you find her, but I honestly don't know anything about her or why she was staying with Han Lan or who this other guy is.'

'Matt.'

'Matt. But maybe you should ask one of them,' he said, nodding to the booth at the back. It was clearly occupied by off duty coppers. There was no one I recognised, but I could smell a pig a mile off.

'They're already involved. But I thank you for your time, Mr. Wong. Just one last question, though.'

He raised his eyebrows, puffed on his cigar.

'When's he back?'

'Who?'

'Han Lan. When's he back from Hong Kong?'

'So you do know where he is? Why ask?'

'Just to see if you'd spill. And you didn't. I reckon you must be loyal. I'll come back one night. Maybe speak to those guys over there, like you said.'

'You're welcome to do so, Mr. Locke. We have nothing to hide here.'

I nodded, nudged out from my seat. 'I'll be seeing you.'

'Please, Mr. Locke. Stay a while. I'll get you a girl. Have a brandy or two on me.'

Have to say I was tempted. But I knew he'd only want me here to keep an eye on me and pretend he was a guy I needed to be friendly with. Could do without that bullshit.

'No,' I said. 'Got things to do, but thanks all the same.'

'Here.' He dipped into his breast pocket, pulled out a long cigar. 'On me. I would hate to get off on the wrong foot.'

I shook my head. 'No thanks. Reminds me of Jimmy Savile and I never liked him. Always gave me the creeps. Keep it.'

I drained the brandy and left, nodding to Jackie Chan on the way out.

Felt sick as I stepped outside. Wasn't sure if it was the booze or the general feeling of disgust from upstairs. Sparked up and gagged. Checked the time on the mobile Sara had given me. It was still early, just gone eight thirty. I had a taste for Brandy, but it would have to wait. I had other stuff to do.

Fished out Simon's number from the shred of paper in my pocket. Decided to walk back up to the Northern Quarter. I was feeling queasy with the brandy rolling around in my gut, and the smell of cigars lingering on my clothes. I needed air, and a moment to gather my thoughts.

I put Simon's number in my phone, along with the other one I'd found. The one that just rang out. I wondered who this number could belong to and decided to try it again, but first I needed a place to sit and drink and think about the next move. My gut feeling was telling me something was wrong about Wong's dancing club. The clientele in there was enough to give me doubts. I never got out of Wong exactly what line of business–or businesses–Han Lan was in. But I would return. The pieces were coming together, slowly, but it was all jumbled up. I needed answers. I felt time was running out for Angel–if it hadn't already–and someone, somewhere, would know something. I got the feeling there were things being hidden. Wasn't even sure I could trust the police on this one.

My thoughts went back to Matt as I walked the city streets. I was heading in a vague general direction but had no idea of a destination. I'd just see where my feet took me. I thought about our first–and only–meeting, the night of Angel's birthday meal at the Thai Banana. My first impressions were rarely wrong. I didn't like the vibes with the guy. I wondered how Angel knew him. He'd obviously been a client of hers before–and I remember Carol and Sherry saying he was a known customer of the escort agency. I'd need to speak to her again, especially as she'd given us a dodgy mobile number. The address of the office, according to the website, was on Bridge Street. Had to be a discreet affair given the service, so I reckoned it was a quiet space above a shop or something like that. I would check it out, perhaps make a booking for a date via the site. I wanted Sherry. Somehow felt that girl could tell me something.

Walked down Oldham Street until I came to The Castle. It was busy, but I wasn't going to let that put me off. Got a pint of ale and wandered through to the back garden, which wasn't really a garden, more a couple of chairs and a picnic table. Sparked up and sat down on a damp bench. Took my phone out and hovered my thumb over Simon's number. Put it off for several minutes while I took the head off the beer. A girl came out in a red woolly hat, made small talk about the weather before she put her fag out and went back inside. She had the right idea. It was getting chilly out here, and there was a frost forming on the back wall.

Pushed 'call' on the number and put the phone to my ear. It rang several times before he picked up.

'Hello?'

'Hello, Simon,' I said. 'It is Simon, isn't it?'

'Yes, love. Who's this?'

'Well, you might not remember me, but I was out for Angel's birthday. It's Jim. Jim Locke.'

'Jim?' I could almost hear the cogs turning in his massive head. 'Oh! The paper guy?'

'That's me. So you do remember me. Look, I know you might think it a bit odd that I'm calling you out of the blue like this, but I need to speak to you. It's about Angel.'

'Oh my God, what's happened?'

'Nothing, yet. You are aware she's missing?'

'Yeah, of course.'

'Okay. Thing is, I'm trying to find out why. I found your number in her diary. Hope you don't mind me ringing you out of the blue like this.'

'No,' he said, but I detected some irritability. 'So what can I do for you?'

'I need you to come and meet me.'

'What, now?'

'Tonight, yeah. I'm in The Castle. You know it?'

'Yeah, but... look, what's this all about?'

'Private meeting, Simon. This is important. And if you value your friendship with Angel, you'll come right now.'

'Okay, okay,' he said. 'I'm a bit tied up at the minute, but I could be there in an hour.'

'Perfect. I'll be in the back room.'

I hung up before he could change his mind.

Went back inside, got another pint, and found a seat in the corner of the back room. It surprised me at how easy it was to get him to come and meet me. It promised to be an interesting conversation. I wanted to know more about the people we were out with for Angel's birthday, particularly Matt.

Got a few looks from the younger student types. Perhaps it was my age, but they were looking at me like I was from Mars or something. With any luck, they'd leave soon enough. Already, one or two tables had been made vacant, which was just as well. I wanted this conversation with Simon to be as private as possible.

I sat down and sipped my pint, resisting the urge to down it. The jukebox ran through The Stone Roses to Led Zep to Springsteen, and I was more than content to sit and listen as I waited for Simon to turn up. Felt like I hadn't listened to decent music in years. Wondered what our fat friend would make of it all. Had him down as a Steps and Christina Aguilera man. Could easily see him throwing some shapes down the Gay Village of a Saturday night. Planned to ask him how he came to know Angel. Wondered what circles he mixed in. According to the girl from the Thai Banana, he'd been out with a big cheese Chinese guy. Lots of money, she said. I doubted he was into importing woks and cleavers. Make up, maybe, judging by the black nail varnish. But my guess was that his cosy meals in that place meant something else entirely. It had crossed my mind that he was an escort too, of the more exclusive kind. Perhaps he offered something the girls couldn't reach. Like a cross between Christopher Biggins and Gok Wan. Or maybe there was something else he was involved in. Shifting coke and pills? Some kind of go-between? I planned to ask him. Wouldn't surprise me if he was involved with dealing something. It was the innocent-looking ones you had to look out for. The guy had a face like a baby, but there had to be a dark side considering the people he seemed friendly with.

Matt never left his side that night. It was enough evidence for me. Had I been making assumptions? Maybe, but my instincts never let me down. I wasn't about to start doubting them.

Soon got myself involved in a session I could do without. Put it down to a combination of the music and happy memories. Memories that turned sour within the space of a few years. Was on my third pint in here when, just as I was leaving the bar, a face I recognised appeared on my shoulder like a demon haunting my dreams. I'd forgotten how big he was. Got him a gin and slim before we made our way to the back room. Took an empty table beside a travelling couple from somewhere Scandinavian. Kept it quiet for a moment or two until he'd settled down and the small talk was done with. The guy was trembling like a fat bird on a treadmill. I wondered why. He obviously had something to hide.

'So,' I said. 'We meet again.'

He was sheepish, sipped his G and T. Tried a smile. 'Didn't expect to hear from you.'

'How so?'

'Well, it's not as if we know each other, is it?'

'No, but the woman we both know is missing. Except you know her better than me. Better than most, I bet. Any ideas?'

'Ideas about what?'

'Where she is, you silly cunt.'

'I beg your pardon? I don't have to listen to this.'

He went to down his drink but I grabbed it, spilled some down his frilly Yamamoto jumper. Handed it back.

'Steady on. Let's try to be civil, eh?'

'No need to call me a cunt.'

'I can think of worse things.'

Took a long drink, dying for a smoke. Weighed up the look on his face, the secrets he kept behind it. 'So when did you meet her?'

'What?'

'Where do you know her from?'

His eyes wandered the room, shifted in his seat, coughed, swallowed.

'Met her two years ago.'

'Go on.'

'At a party.'

'Whose party?'

'Don't know. Some guy.'

'Some guy? Who?'

'We met him in The White Lion. Castlefield way. Don't ask me what we were doing there but...'

'Who's we?'

'Just me and a friend of mine. James. Anwen too, but she'd left by then.'

'By when?'

'All right, fuck's sake, give me a chance!'

Felt like shoving his gin n tonic down his throat, opted for another portion of ale, willing the annoying shit to tell me more. Needed a smoke.

'She'd left by ten. Anwen. It was a Halloween do. You know, everyone dressed up. So Anwen left, and it was just me and James. We were gonna move on, but then this group of girls came in and they were up for a party. Thank God. It was dying on its arse at that point. There was about eight of them, gave the pub some life, you know. So we got talking to a few and Angel - Helen - was one of them.'

'And that's how you met?'

'Yeah.'

'So what about this party?'

He shifted in his seat, looked about, finished his drink. 'I'll get us another.'

I watched him hover at the bar. Knew this wasn't his kind of environment. Guy stood out like a Skinhead at a Bar Mitzvah. Had no reason to believe he was lying - yet.

Drained my pint as he weaved his way back through the tables. Another group of students had come in and were sitting too close within earshot for my liking. Thought it a good time to move into the back for a smoke. Put the fear of God in him when I suggested we step outside. He stopped sweating when I waved my packet of fags. Plucked himself a Marlboro Light from his top pocket. No surprise there. Found us a small table below a heat lamp and sparked up.

'You were saying. About the party.'

He took a long drag, blew a cloud of smoke above his head. Got a picture in my mind of him applying that black nail varnish. Tried to picture him without the mascara.

'It was just a party. Nothing special. We just got talking - James and me - to Angel and her friends. The guy who invited us back was just some random guy who was joining in with the banter, you know. So we all ended up going back to his.'

'Yet you didn't know him.'

'I wanted to get to know him better, if you know what I mean?'

'Seen him since?'

'No, unfortunately.'

I nodded, took a drink. 'So who were her friends? Recall any names?'

He looked away for a moment, then down at the table. 'Why do you need to know all this? I mean, what's the point?'

'Just trying to piece some things together. Who she

knew, the things she did. That kind of thing. And I must admit, I find it a bit odd how no one's been in touch with her friend Sara - her oldest friend - let alone the police. I'm sure they'd be interested in finding out a bit more about what she was up to the night she disappeared. Who she was with. So any way you can help would be good, 'cause I know how you and the others care so much about her.'

I could almost see the sweat prickling his neck, despite the cold. Eyeballed him, urged him to go on.

'I can hardly remember,' he said. 'There was a lot of people. It was two years ago.'

'Jog your memory,' I said, and took a mouthful of beer. 'Must've been a fun night. Or were you all so high these parties end up blending into one?'

He didn't like that and showed it. Clocked him grinding his teeth.

'I met most of Angel's friends there. Mainly girls.'

'From the agency? Provoke, am I right?'

He nodded. 'Yeah. They're a good bunch.'

'Like a laugh?'

'Yeah.'

'That Carol's a bit funny though, don't you think? She gave me her mobile number the morning Angel went missing. And when I tried phoning her, it was a dead number. Any idea why that might be?'

He shrugged, brought the G&T to his lips. 'She must've given you the wrong number.'

'Simple mistake to make, I suppose. Must be a busy woman. Funny how no one seems to know anything about Angel's disappearance, though. You all seemed so close, I would've thought you'd be out there looking for her. I mean, she was a valued member of the Provoke team, so I'm led to believe.'

'I don't know anything about where she is,' he said. 'Angel is an independent woman. She doesn't have to tell her friends where she is all the time.'

'But she always told one friend everything. Sara. Her oldest friend, actually.'

He tried to look like he didn't know who Sara was, had never heard of her or met her in his life. Epic fail.

'She was out for her birthday drinks? Nice-looking girl, you know?'

Tried to look like he was putting a name to a face. 'Oh yeah...,' he said. 'I think I know who you mean.'

'Good. Because that's the girl who knows Angel - Helen - best. And she says her going missing is totally out of character. She might spend a few nights with the same client, working and all that, but she always showed up or let Sara know where she was. They go way back, you see. Old mates. Like sisters, really.'

He nodded, tried to look like he cared.

'And I know Sara's at her wits' end. Well, I suppose you would be, wouldn't you?'

He tried a smile, took on a look of concern, another epic fail. Said he needed the gents and left me there, outside under the heat lamp. Went into his jacket pocket, took his phone. Had a quick scan at his text messages, but there wasn't enough time to rifle through them. Pocketed the iPhone before he had the chance to catch me out. I wasn't gonna let the opportunity slip by.

When he came back, he swung his coat on and downed the gin. Said he had to go. Urged me to get in touch should Angel turn up.

'Just one more thing,' I said, nodding at the seat in front. He sat down. 'Won't take long and I don't want to keep you.'

He sparked up a Marlboro light and we shared the

flame.

'This guy, Matt. Mate of yours, isn't he?'

'Well, I wouldn't say that, but...'

'Only he was the last person seen with her,' I went on. 'One of her clients, apparently. Police pulled CCTV from the Hilton about two thirty a.m. on the Sunday she went missing. It's the last known image of her - and him - since she disappeared. Just found it odd, that's all. Wondered if you'd heard from him. Banker, isn't he?'

Now he really was sweating. Could've been the heat lamp, but I doubted it. I could see the tiny beads forming on his forehead.

'No,' he said, as innocently as he could manage. 'I've not heard a thing from him. But I doubt he's got anything to do with her going missing. I mean, he wouldn't be the type to...'

'To what?'

'Well, I don't know. Anything... stupid. I know he's a client of hers.'

'Fucked her a few times, has he?'

'Well, I don't know, he's never really talked about her.'

'Yeah.' I took a long drag, blew a cloud above us. 'I suppose he wouldn't discuss his sex life with you, eh?'

'Suppose not. Look, if I hear any news I'll be in touch.'

'Course you will.'

He nodded, gathered his cigarettes and lighter. 'It's been a pleasure,' he said, standing. 'But I really do have to go now.'

'Yeah, don't want to keep you. Gonna finish this and get going myself. The pleasure's all mine, Simon. Thanks for coming out.'

He tried a smile, then left, mincing his way towards the front door. I watched him go. He didn't look back. Wouldn't dare.

27

I finished my pint and left before he realised his phone was missing. It was edging towards ten thirty. I'd have to make my way back now if I had any chance of staying relatively sober. Besides, I didn't want to keep Sara waiting all night. Although no news was good news, I could picture her sitting there on the couch, her thoughts blank and elsewhere, little Charlie in bed dreaming of Spider-Man and Star Wars, the urge for a glass of red giving her a headache. I guess it never really went. The pull of the booze. Although she'd been dry a few hard years, I knew she was struggling. Every day was a battle, I knew that only too well. I was fucking annoyed with myself for allowing her to be around booze. My booze for my pain. I was a fuck up. I was only good for the bottle. I deserved everything I'd gotten in this shitty little fucked up existence of mine. It was my curse. I knew I'd drag her back down with me, Angel or no Angel. And yet I realised she was the first woman I'd wanted since Karen. I had to get back to her.

Just as I reached my bus stop, I felt a buzzing in my pants. Took out the mobile she'd given me. Answered and pressed it hard against my ear to drown out the noise. Even then it was hard to make out the words because she was barely coherent. More than that. She was hysterical. But I didn't need to hear it. Could feel her agony down the phone, rushing through me on the airwaves.

'They found her, Jim,' she said. 'They found her. She's dead, Jim. She's gone.'

28

They found her at approximately 21:23pm, after an anonymous call to Greater Manchester Police Headquarters around thirty minutes earlier. They found her lying face down, her hair frozen, on the sloping bank of Bridgewater Canal, in the shadow of a new build apartment complex, under a Victorian arch bridge littered with detritus, dumped rubbish and dog shit. She was naked from the waist down and her breasts were covered in dirt, her bra pulled up over her chest, her lips blue. She'd been raped. A hole the size of a golf ball dented her scalp, probably caused by a hammer blow, and the bruises around her anus, her thighs, her vagina, her throat, were black and purple and pulpy. Her nose had been broken and there were deep, six-inch lacerations to her lower back, her abdomen, her left cheek. Her blood stained knickers and her leopard print coat were found nearby. Her tongue had swelled to three times its normal size, protruding from her lips like a fat rat. Semen and bloods were found in her vagina, her anus, her mouth. She'd been lying dead for two weeks and her bodily fluids had leaked into the ground beneath her.

She'd been discarded like all the other shite around her, left to rot there among the broken bottles, the jumbled junk, the supermarket shopping trolley, the piss, the condoms, the used needles and burnt brickwork on either wall. Her throat had been cut. Her eye sockets crushed. She'd been tortured. She was partially decomposed. She was dead, dead, dead.

29

I found Sara slumped on the couch, a bottle of vodka on the coffee table before her. It was half full. I grabbed it, unscrewed the cap, swung it back. Sparked up and sat down beside her. Ran a hand through her matted hair, wiped the running mascara from her cheeks with my sleeve, and let her cry in my arms forever.

30

I could barely get a word out of her. She just sat shaking her head, pouring glass after glass. She needed it to take the pain away, to obliterate the entire world. I could understand that. Went upstairs and found Laura and Charlie both asleep in the same bed. It was late. A hard rain rattled on the bedroom window and I covered them both with an extra thick blanket I found at the foot of the bed.

I needed that oblivion too. I sat across from Sara on the couch and drank until the early hours. She didn't want to talk, not yet. There was nothing to say, anyway. She finally drifted off around four a.m. I covered her up with a duvet from the spare room - the room I was supposed to be sleeping in - and watched her as she slept. I hoped she would sleep long into the day, but I knew young Charlie would be up in a few hours. The silence in the house was deafening. We all needed it, but I tried to avoid the quiet. Brought back the memories like ghosts. I needed noise to help drown out my thoughts, but now wasn't the time. So I sat in that living room, drinking and smoking while Sara slept, and let them come back to haunt me.

PART II

31

I stood in the doorway, bursting for a piss and fumbling
for the keys in my jeans pocket. Karen and Nicole
would be in bed by now, both of them well off to sleep.
Couldn't find the fucking things. I stumbled around the
back, unzipped my fly and pissed into the drain beside the
kitchen wall. I knew it was late. When I finished, I went back
to the front door, found my keys and tried to put it in the
Yale lock. Banged my head on the door.

'Shit.'

I tried again, this time managing to fit the key, and
turned. The door clicked and I pushed it open, banging my
hip on the doorframe.

'Bollocks.'

I fell against the wall, and then the door rolled away
from me, slamming. Fuck it. I tip toed into the kitchen and
found my bottle of Bowmore in the cupboard beside the
breakfast bar. Grabbed a glass from the drainer and twisted
the cap. Poured two good measures and left the bottle on the
side. Fuck it.

Swung it back.
Felt the burn.
Felt the pain.

32

I managed two hours on the armchair before I woke up. Sara was still sleeping. I made a coffee and drank quietly in the kitchen, watching her and listening for any sign of Charlie making a stir. Wrote a note before leaving quietly and headed back to the bus stop.

Took a bus back to town and another out towards where the body was found. It was seven thirty-three a.m. by the time I reached the cordon. I'd had to walk out towards Regent Road, just on the edge of Salford. Stood on a foot-bridge over the Bridgewater Canal and watched the forensics and SOCA take her away in a plastic body bag. Shit didn't make any sense.

It was pissing down. Smoked a few coffin nails before anyone clocked me watching. A PC came over and asked me to move on. Asked him who the Senior Investigating Officer was.

'You got a pen?'

He nodded.

'Tell him to contact Jim Locke. Former DS. Tell him I've got information he might want to know about.'

'Mr. Locke. Sir. This is a murder inquiry and with all due respect, you're no longer a member of the force. Best to stay away, eh?'

'Just tell him he can contact me on this number, anytime.' I showed him my mobile with the number taped to the back. He wrote it down. 'And I know this is a murder inquiry, son. I've seen enough of them to smell the blood in my nose and picture the piss stains on my eyelids when I go to sleep at night. And being a good PC, you'll know not to ignore any information presented to you, especially from an officer above your rank.'

'Ex officer, sir. With respect.'

That stung. 'I'll leave that in your capable hands.'

Jumped up little smartarse.

Walked away towards Hulme with the rain on my back and a million thoughts crowding my head. I mean, what the fuck did I think I was doing? Did I really think I had anything more to offer this case? Perhaps I should just leave it to the police. It was their job, after all. I couldn't bring her back. It was done now. She was dead.

As I walked back towards town, feeling the cravings come and the chill rain in my bones, my phone buzzed in my pocket. Dropped into a shop doorway and answered.

'Jim?'

'Sara. You okay?'

Stupid question. Of course she wasn't. I could hear her sniff down the phone and knew she'd been crying. Of course she had. She'd just lost her best friend.

'Come back. Don't leave me today. I need you here.'

'Sara...'

'Please, Jim, I don't want to be on my own.'

I couldn't deal with this but knew I had to. 'I'll be back in an hour.'

She hung up.

33

Town was busy as I passed through. Silly season had begun already with Christmas looming, and it seemed the whole city was out in force, even at this ungodly hour. Couldn't wait until the whole thing was over, not just because of the rampant commercialism, but knowing that my little girl would be seeing another one without her Dad. I felt like a complete shit for knowing what I was about to do on that car park roof. Angel's face came back to me again and again as I trudged through the rain at Piccadilly. She could've let me go. I'd be dead now if it wasn't for her. I owed her big time.

Dropped into the cafe she brought me to afterwards and ordered tea and toast. It was called Leo's. Managed half a slice and left the rest. I still couldn't manage much food, even when I felt hungry. Just sometimes felt overwhelmed with nausea, and the image of her being carried away from that place in a body bag didn't ease it. I felt sick and it showed. The greaseball who failed to recognise me from when I was first in here with Angel came over and asked if I was all right. Offered me a glass of water and I took it and drank. I knew I smelt of booze. Seemed to seep from my pores like sweat.

There was an early edition of the Evening Chronicle on the table in front. I grabbed it and skimmed through. There was nothing on the murder, but I had a feeling it wouldn't be long before the vultures were circling. I guessed the police would put out a press conference soon enough. No doubt Sara would want answers too, but I wasn't so sure she could handle this shit in her condition. I had to get back to the girl before she did another bottle in. This was exactly what could take an ex drinker over the edge. I felt like a complete dick for bringing Han Lan's booze back to her place. It was like holding a loaded gun to her head. Poor girl didn't need that. I knew I had to put a stop to it, sharpish.

I sat and sipped the tea, leaving half a cup remaining in the pot. Took out both my own phone and the one I'd nicked from Simon's jacket pocket. Wanted to see what this guy was hiding. I didn't trust the big man and felt sure there could be answers in this thing. I held it in my hand, stroked its glossy screen with my finger. It was already switched on, but I couldn't unlock the screen. Bastard thing was asking for a code I kept getting wrong. Looked at the back, saw it was an iPhone, probably the latest one, but I didn't have a clue. Realised I was getting nowhere and put it away before I slung it across the cafe. I just hoped Laura knew what to do with it. She seemed a tech savvy type. My own shitty little thing was a breeze compared to this.

I finished the tea in my cup and left, nodding to grease-ball on the way out. Stood waiting for a bus nearby, going over everything in my head. Needed a drink but was determined to lay off it. Tried to piece the bits together. Everything from my first meeting with Angel to Han Lan's pad to my conversation with Bo Wong in his little dancing establishment. The bad trip on her birthday and all the shit in between. All the money in Han Lan's bank accounts. The dodgy business card from Carol. Matt. The vision, the absolute certainty that I saw Karen and Nicole in that amusement arcade. All the booze running around my system like the blood in my veins.

The journey back to Sara's passed in a blur. A blanket of dirty grey washed over the city and brought a heavy downpour with it like the rain on my black heart and the storm in my soul. I wasn't looking forward to whatever the day brought with it. It had occurred to me, more than once, that I could just walk away from the whole thing. I had no ties, nothing to keep me around. Had no affiliations other than the fact that Sara and I both knew Angel - Helen Shields - the dead girl. She was her best friend, I'd shared her company - and her bed. I never let on to Sara that anything had happened between Angel and me, but I reckon she knew, anyway. Got the impression Angel wasn't too good at keeping secrets.

Which brought my thoughts back to the dead girl. She must've been good at keeping some secrets. There had to be a reason she was staying in Han Lan's flat. And someone - some sick fuck - wanted her dead. It wasn't some weird sex game gone wrong. It wasn't an accident. She'd been taken from this fucked up world in cold blood and I wanted to know why. More than that. I had to know. I had to catch the bastard. I had to get down to work.

34

Got piss wet through as I walked the grey streets back to Sara's house. Wanted nothing more than to get into bed and fall into oblivion. Felt like I could sleep forever and was sure I would one day. Death came to us all. Seemed to hover around me like a fucking rain cloud. I was sure that, if I carried on like this - if I couldn't rid myself of the booze - then one night I would fall asleep and not wake up. Wasn't sure if that would be a blessing, tell you the truth. But then Nicole's little face kept coming back to me. Her mother, too. One of the last things Angel had said to me was to at least try and make contact, even offered to go with me to face Frank and Maureen. Sara, too. I knew they were right. I had to kick this shit, even if it put me so close to death's door I could push it open with one hand. I owed it to my daughter. I knew I owed it to myself more.

It wasn't what I expected when I walked through that door. Sara was standing at the sink, pouring a full bottle of Russian Standard down the drain. She was crying. I reached out to grab her, to stop her from this madness, but I slipped on the broken glass, the Lino sticky with booze. Saw that her hands were bleeding badly. Went to grab the bottle from her, but it slipped and went crashing into the sink.

'Sara, fucking hell!'

'Stop it!'

I grabbed her by the waist and wrestled her through into the living room, pulling her across the carpet as we both fell backwards. The kitchen was a fucking mess. Her hands were leaking crimson. Jesus, it was worse than I thought.

I spun her round, kept her down. Looked at my own hands, down my front, and saw I was covered in blood. Did a double take for a split second until I realised it was hers. Then she stopped fighting back. Her eyes rolled back in her head, went white. I'm sure I did too at that point. She flopped back in my arms and I let her go to the carpet where the blood was saturating, making a pool.

Oh fuck, she'd done her wrists.

Didn't have time to think. Nothing registered. I went on autopilot, my fucking heart pounding and my legs going from under me. Yanked the door open and stumbled into the street, shouting. Hammered on next door until I heard movement inside. Opened the letter box, screamed 'fucking move it!' until a doddery old woman in a pink dressing gown came down the hallway on legs so thin you could snap them.

Banged again and again, shouting 'Help!' so loud the pigeons on the pavement scattered. Fuck's sake, this was all I needed.

Ran back inside, ripped my jacket off and attempted to stifle the flow. She was losing colour quickly. Pulled my phone out, dialled 999. Got flustered when trying to make sense to the operator - she's done her wrists, she's fucking dying here! - until a bloke with a barrel chest came in, grabbed the phone and took over. Whoever he was, he turned up just on time. I looked up from Sara's pale, glassy face and saw the old dear from next door clutching her handkerchief, her mouth a perfect round 'O'.

'Fucking do something!'

The big guy dropped to his knees, took his t-shirt off - I saw it was covered in dirt, plaster, some shit like that - and joined me in pressing hard on the wounds.

'Fuck's sake, Sara, come on! Come on! Don't you fucking die on me, Jesus!'

'They're on the way, mate,' he said. 'Nice and easy.'

Was glad he was calmer than me. I'd seen plenty of blood in my time, but usually when I expected it. The shock of coming back to this had knocked me sideways. One thing was certain. I'd be having a stiff one after this.

I tried my best to keep her awake, kept talking to her, talking shit. The old dear was on her knees, stroking Sara's hair with liver-spotted hands. Had to tell her to watch for the ambulance whilst me and the big guy tried to keep the blood from spilling out. Wherever she'd cut, and what with - a broken bottle was my guess - she'd done a damn good job.

Heard pounding feet coming through the living room and I had to be dragged off by a woman in a green and yellow coat seconds later.

I stood back and watched as they got to work, and fuck knows what they were doing. I only knew I was glad it was happening. I'd never felt more relieved yet bewildered as I watched them address the wounds, tourniquet her arms, shove an oxygen mask over face, get her on a stretcher and get her in the ambulance.

It all happened so fast I didn't have time to breathe. They asked if I was coming and I said I'd follow. When the ambulance tore off out the street I went back inside, dazed out of my fucking mind, and poured a very large whisky. At least that was one bottle she hadn't gotten around to pouring down the drain. Smoked about ten fags as I paced the house, wondering where Laura was and what she'd say. Wondering what little Charlie would do when he found out Mummy was in hospital. Wondering if the girl would pull through or if that was it. Wondering why the hell I'd gotten involved at all.

Found her mobile on the mantelpiece and phoned Laura as I sat out on the step. The big guy -Alan, I think he said his name was - was helping himself to a whisky too. Turned out he was working in a house up the street, re-plastering. At least I think that's what he said.

Laura was hysterical. Tried to calm her down, but I might as well have been speaking Chinese. She hung up, said she'd get back to me.

I didn't know what else to do. I pocketed Sara's phone to join my own and Simon's, thanked Alan and the old dear and locked up. They offered words of support, but I wasn't listening. Alan offered me a lift, but I declined. At least get a taxi, he said. It pulled up before I could turn the corner and they both sat me in the back, told the driver where to drop me off.

And it was pissing down again. Got mesmerised by the tiny rolling rivulets of water on the window beside me. It was only when he pulled up outside North Manchester General's A&E that I came back to life. Fumbled in my pocket and threw him a tenner, slamming the door behind me.

As I wandered, dazed, through the foyer and triage, I looked down and saw I had blood on my hands. Caught sight of the time on a digital clock high on the wall. It was just 10:32am, but it felt like the dark night had fallen.

'Jim? What are you doing? Jim!'

I was sitting on the couch, the bottle of Bowmore on the coffee table, the whisky tumbler about to fall from my fingers. There was a wet patch in my crotch, my arse soaked. And the smell, too. Fuck, the smell.

'Come to bed, Jim. Come to bed.'

I felt her take the tumbler from my fingers before it fell, heard her take the bottle too and launch it into the bin. Good job it was empty.

I didn't remember anything else after that. Felt nothing other than the darkness surrounding me.

'I'm looking for Sara,' I said. 'Sorry, I don't know her surname.' Fuck! Why didn't I know her surname? 'She came in not long ago, cut her wrists...'

'I'm sorry sir, I can't help you unless -'

'Is her sister here? Laura...'

'Sir, I'm afraid I can't help you unless you're a relative or -'

'Forget it.'

I dragged myself over to the coffee machine, eyes peeled for the paramedics who must've brought her in. Went to put change in the slot and saw the blood on my hands, down my front. Found the Gents and washed it away in a frenzy, almost threw up when I caught sight of myself in the mirror.

Went back to the coffee machine, paid for a shite, mud coloured drink that felt like it had been warmed up over a candle flame and sat down. Things had gone pear-shaped in a big way. Thought about just walking out and running. Thought better of it. Sat and drank the shit coffee, wishing it was something stronger, and tried to wake up from this fucking nightmare. Got zombied out by fucking Flog It! and felt a dozen pairs of eyes on me as I sat there trying not to fidget. Noticed there were several empty seats beside me. People were keeping their distance. Couldn't blame them.

Paced up and down out the front, chain smoking and wishing I wasn't me, wishing I was somewhere far, far away.

It wasn't long before I turned and saw Laura running towards the entrance. She didn't see me at first, and I had to grab her to get her attention. The anxiety written all over face almost melted my heart. She could barely get the words out.

'Where is she -?'

'Just try to ca-'

'Where the fuck is she, Jim?!'

I took her by the elbow over to the reception desk. 'This is her sister, Laura.'

'Jackson.'

'Sara Jackson,' I said. 'She came in not long ago, cut her wrists. Can you just find us a fucking doctor?!'

'Please, take a seat, sir. I'll just see what I can do.'

'Please,' Laura said. 'She's my sister... please.'

The receptionist came around the desk, took Laura by the elbow like I'd just done, sat her down and whispered promises that she'd find someone. I took the seat beside her, ran my hands over my face, sighed. Told Laura I was going for a smoke and went back to pacing outside, keeping one eye on the fragile thing in there and the sight of a reassuring doctor. Somehow, given the amount of blood she'd lost - it must've been a lot - I didn't expect that doctor any time soon.

I was wrong. As soon as I finished my second smoke, I saw a nurse in a white uniform take Laura and lead her away from the reception area. I caught up before they could disappear through a set of double doors.

'How bad is it?' I said.

Laura turned, wiped her eyes, told the nurse it was ok, that I was with her.

'She's lost a lot of blood,' the nurse said. 'But she's stabilised. She's lucky this time.'

'This time? You mean she's done it before?'

'Not now,' Laura said. 'I'll explain later, let's just see her first.'

'She's asleep,' the nurse said. Clocked her badge as Nurse Simister. 'But you can see her, put your mind at rest. She's heavily sedated and not very well. I'm sure you understand.'

She led us down a brightly lit corridor. Through the long bank of windows beside us, I could see the rain hammering down into a garden I assumed was tended by patients. Child scrawls of nurses and doctors and hospital beds adorned the glass. I realised my heart was racing as Laura clung onto my arm.

Nurse Simister led us through another corridor before we turned a corner into a ward and Sara in a bed at the far wall.

'Doctor Rishi will be with you soon. I'll bring you another chair.'

We nodded and she left. Laura took the chair beside her sister while I stood at the foot of the bed. She was bandaged up, but that was the worst of it. At least there were no tubes, no drip, no blood transfusion - yet. Hoped it would stay that way. She looked peaceful and at rest. I felt a sense of relief that she was in the right place. Might be for the best if they kept her sedated. The last thing she needed was to remember her best friend had been murdered.

'Here you go,' she said. I turned to see Nurse Simister

plonk a chair on the other side of the bed. 'You look like you could do with taking the weight off your feet.'

I took the chair and smiled. Laura asked again if her sister would be okay.

'She's over the worst of it,' the nurse said. 'But she'll come through fine. We'll keep her in for a few days and she'll have to be assessed.'

'Assessed?' I said. 'What for?'

'We'll get a duty psychiatrist to talk to her tomorrow. For now, she needs to recover.'

'Psychiatrist? Oh, for God's sake...'

'I don't think she cut her wrists for nothing, do you?' Laura looked from Sara to me to nurse Simister. 'And we know it's not the first time, either. It's nothing to worry about. Just normal procedure in these cases. Doctor Rishi will explain further.'

She left to tend to another patient across the ward.

'A Shrink?'

Laura shook her head, looked back at her sister and took her hand. I wasn't surprised that Sara was feeling pretty shit about the whole Angel thing, but this? And after what Nurse Simister said - it's not the first time - I was beginning to wonder if there was more to Sara's past than just a drink problem. I suppose I shouldn't be surprised. She seemed a fragile woman. Maybe I should've seen this coming.

'Laura?'

'Not now. Can you give us a minute?'

I nodded. 'Yeah. I'll get us a coffee.'

'Not for me, thanks.'

'Look, Laura, this has got nothing to do with me. If I'd known she was gonna do anything like this...'

'Not now, Jim. I just need to get my head together. That okay?'

I nodded, got up from my chair and left the ward. Nurse Simister smiled on the way out. I thought about asking her more about what she meant, but guessed she wouldn't spill. I wasn't on a need to know basis. But I was more than intrigued. I didn't want to press Laura too much just yet, but I would when I felt it was the right time. If she'd done it before, how often? It was pretty clear Laura didn't want to talk about the Shrink thing. I wondered if Sara had been having trouble lately, before all this Angel business. Maybe she had. Maybe I was putting two and two together and making five. I'd learned not to make assumptions over the years. But I wondered if Angel dying had sent her over the edge. If she'd done this before–a suicide attempt–and let's face it, that's what it was, then how ill was she? How much worse was this going to get? And could anyone blame her?

I gave the coffee machine a miss this time and instead got a proper filter one from the WRVS before parking myself on a bench outside the main entrance. I guessed if Laura needed me, she'd know where I'd be. Sparked up and took that shit in deep. Tried to piece things together, but the more I thought the less it made any sense. Angel was dead, probably lying in a morgue right now. Han Lan, I assumed, was in Hong Kong raking in another million from whatever he was selling. Matt had disappeared off the face of the Earth, or so it seemed. I had Simon's phone without a means of discovering what was inside it–yet. Had to be a way of digging into it. I rolled it in my hand, trying to come up with a code to unlock it.

Then there was Karen and Nicole, not to mention Frank and Maureen. I hovered my thumb over the digits on my phone. I knew their number off heart, and I knew I'd have to deal with this shit soon, for my peace of mind. Nicole's too.

It made me feel sick to think what kind of lies they'd been telling my kid.

But a phone call wasn't enough. They could hang up, change their number, go ex-directory. It wouldn't be so easy if I turned up on their doorstep. Finished up and went back inside. Didn't realise quite how cold it was until I got back in and the warmth hit me. I didn't get as far as the Gents before my phone went off.

I pulled it out right there under the lights of reception and checked the caller. Private number. Took a moment to decide if I was in the right mind to speak then thought, fuck it, I can always hang up.

'Hello?'

There was a pause, then a cough, then a husky, gravelly voice I'd recognise anywhere.

'Locke.'

I thought about hanging up again and almost did when the past came back at me in waves. Scrap that. It was a fucking tsunami.

'Locke? Jim?'

Crashing through the doors with a sledgehammer on a drug bust when Phil got knocked out by a flying coffee table. Getting a bollocking the next day from DCI Woods whilst Phil had two bits of foam stuck up each nostril.

'Jim? Hello?'

Feeling Phil's enormous hand grab my collar and haul me out of the punch up before I got my arse kicked.

Caught my breath and answered. 'Phil. Been a while, eh?'

Detective Constable Phil Young, the guy I used to drive around with before the shit hit the fan. The only bloke I could call an ally after the force shipped me out. I thought he'd stay in touch, but even he didn't. I didn't know whether top brass had gotten to him, bent his ear, turned him against me like they'd managed to with all the other arse lickers. Or maybe he'd just kept a low profile when it came to hanging around with yours truly, DS Fuck Up.

'Fuck, it *is* you.'

'Nice to hear from you too, mate.'

'Nah, didn't mean that, Jimbo. Just that... well, you know. Lot of water under the bridge and all that. A few of us thought you were...'

'Dead?'

'Something like that, I suppose. Anyway, how's things?'

Well, I'm standing in A&E waiting to find out if a woman I barely know is gonna be okay after cutting her wrists, since her best mate has been murdered in brutal circumstances and I've taken it on myself to find out why, because in my tiny, drunken, fucked up mind, I'm still a copper.

'Well, you know, keeping busy. But I'm guessing this isn't a social call, Phil. Haven't heard a dickie bird out of you since they made me walk. Wouldn't have anything to do with that, would you?'

'Me? Shit, no. What do you take me for, Jim?'

'Just found it convenient that I didn't hear from you as soon as I left. Thanks for that.'

'It was a difficult time, Jim. You know that.'

'Oh, don't I fucking know it.'

'Look, I'm sorry, mate. Wasn't easy for me.'

'They told you to steer clear of the pisshead, didn't they? If you still wanted a career with the force...'

'It wasn't like that, but...'

'Convenient though, eh? What rank are you now? Must be a DS by now. Just like I was.'

'I had nothing to do with them having you marked down, Jim. You gotta trust me on that.'

'Yeah, well, like you say, it's in the past. And God knows I've been trying to put it behind me.'

'I'm sorry, Jim.'

Had to laugh at that one. 'Yeah, me too.'

There was a silence for a minute whilst I waited for him to get to the point. Looked down through the double doors and saw Nurse Simister doing the rounds beyond. No sign of Laura yet.

'Couldn't believe it when I saw your name written down,' he said. 'And why. Thought I'd better give you a heads up.'

'On what?'

'I'm working the Helen Shields case. Apparently, you know a bit about that?'

'Not much. Just some stuff about where she'd been living. One or two of her contacts. Don't tell me you're the SIO?'

'Not me. DI Robertson.'

'Robertson? What, Rob Robertson? DS Robertson?'

'Got made DI six months after you were...you know, after you left.'

'I bet he fucking did. Fuck's sake.'

I needed a drink all of a sudden. A strong one.

'Just thought you should know, given that you have some information, according to the PC you spoke to this morning.'

This morning felt like a fucking week ago. 'So what difference does it make? I've got info, the police should fucking deal with it.'

'Well, it's just that,' he said. 'I don't think he will.'

'And what makes you say that, Phil?'

'Doesn't trust you, I suppose.'

'And you?'

'What?'

'You trust me? I mean, why the fuck would I be arseing around with any of this if I didn't think any of it was relevant?'

'He thinks you want to fuck him over.'

'Oh, I do. And the rest. I never thought that'd include you, Phil, but you live and learn, I suppose.'

'Me? What've I done, Jim? You know I had nothing to do with all that shite. I'm your mate...'

'That's what I thought.'

'Come on, man.'

'Made sure you kept your nose clean, didn't you?'

'Jim, come on. You know I couldn't afford to lose anything. I had Chez and a new mouth to feed. I had to keep my nose clean. I knew you weren't bent, Jim. You just had a few...'

'Issues. That's a good word for it, isn't it? Uncomfortable to be around. A bit of a lia-fucking-bility.'

Silence again. Uncomfortable one at that.

'I'm sorry, Jim, I really am. But I mean it. How are you, mate? I mean, really?'

Fitness fanatic, brand new life. Feel fucking great. 'I'm okay. Things are looking up.'

'Good. Great. So. About this information.'

'Ah, it's nothing. Not relevant, really.'

'You just said it was, Jim. You know we can't ignore it.'

'Robertson seems to think so.'

'Yeah, but I don't.'

'Well, tough. You're not the SIO. It was him I asked for.'

'Jim.' I could almost see him on the other end of the line. 'Come on, man. It's a murder inquiry. I'm sure you'll want to make sure the poor girl gets justice.'

Saw Laura walking towards me with her head bowed,

mascara running down her face. Wondered what we were gonna tell young Charlie.

'Look, I've gotta go. Some things to deal with.'

'Okay, but what would you say to a drink? You know, have a proper catch up. My shout.'

I always thought that if anyone from the force had asked me this ever again, I'd give them a big 'fuck you' and hang up. But I didn't need to think twice on this one. As much as Phil had pissed me right off, I had to admit that I liked the fat bastard, even if he was a traitorous twat.

'Where?'

'Marble? I come off duty at five. Make it six?'

'See you there. And you fucking owe me one.'

I hung up and went to meet Laura, who fell into my arms, tears rolling down her cheeks. Shit, was it worse than we thought?

'Thanks, Jim,' she said, sobbing. 'The Doctor said you did enough to stop her from bleeding to death.'

'Fucking hell...'

'Yeah,' she said, shoulders bouncing up and down. I wasn't sure if they were tears of relief or something else. 'I need to go. I need to get Charlie.'

'What are you gonna tell him?'

'I don't know.'

'I'll come with you.'

'You've done enough, it's okay.'

'No, I'm coming, I can't stay here, it'll drive me nuts. And the coffee's shite.'

She managed a half smile, then nodded. 'Okay. Come on.'

'So what did the doc say? She gonna be okay?'

'I'll tell you all about it on the way.'

I woke up when the light peeled through the blinds at the back patio. Felt like shit, with a banging head and my mouth so dry it was like I'd swallowed a bucket of sand. It took me a moment to feel the wetness beneath me, but when I got to a sitting position, I knew it was bad.

I stood up, went into the kitchen, saw the Bowmore sticking out of the metal bin near the door. Sparked up and peeled the damp jeans off. Went to put them in the washer but it was full so I opened the back door and smoked while I stared into the freezing morning. Must've been early. I checked the clock on the kitchen wall. Seven thirty four. Flicked the smoke into the drain, the drain I pissed in, and trailed myself and my damp jeans upstairs to the shower.

When I reached the top, I gently pushed the door to our bedroom so I didn't wake her, but she was awake already, clutching the duvet right up to her neck.

'Morning.'

She said nothing and turned over.

'So, what's the prognosis?'

'They're keeping her in for a few days at least. They just want to sort her blood sugar and make sure the wounds are well dressed. It's not that they're worried about, though.'

'The Shrink?'

She nodded, took it down into second as we approached the lights on green and swung a left onto Victoria Avenue towards the school. 'They're worried about her mental health. The Doctor was asking me all sorts of stuff, you know? They want me there tomorrow, to speak to this psychiatrist.'

'Want me to come?'

She shook her head. 'No point. But thanks. For being there, I mean.'

'There's a bit of a mess. I'll clean up if you want?'

'Thanks, but...'

'No, I think I should. Charlie can't see that. It's not nice.'

'Is it that bad?'

I said nothing. She understood.

'Look, we'll pick him up. Then you can drop me off. I'll clean up while you take him for a burger or something and talk to the kid. No point frightening the lad any more than we have to.'

She nodded and focussed on the road. I suppose she knew it made sense. I had assumed she was bringing him back home and not taking him to her flat.

'You're probably right. I'll get him some dinner and break the news.'

'You're not gonna tell him everything, though?'

'Course not. Mummy's fallen over, but she's okay. Something like that.'

'And what about the Shrink? What if..?'

'What, if she's sectioned?'

'Well, I suppose it's a possibility.'

'I know. Might be the best thing. She has just lost her best mate and tried to fucking join her.'

'Don't want her to try again before getting some help first.'

'I know.'

'Look, I couldn't help... well, I couldn't help thinking about it. What the nurse said, you know. She's done it before, it's not the first time, all that. That true?'

Massive sigh. We pulled into St Claire's and she found a space, cut the engine. 'A long time ago. Fifteen years, nearly.'

'She's got the scars then?'

'You could say that, yeah. Then there's the overdose.'

'Fuck's sake. You're kidding me...'

'I wish I was, but no.'

'She's been there before, hasn't she? You know, mental ward...'

'She's not a bloody lunatic, Jim.'

'I never said she was. Look, she's in the right place, I

suppose. I guess we'll find out when she's ready to talk about it.'

'Well, that's just it. She's not a good talker. But maybe you're right. Right now, she needs to rest. We'll take it from there.'

She went to open the door and I put a hand on her shoulder. 'She's gonna be okay. I promise. Everything's gonna be all right.'

'I hope you're right,' she said, then stepped out and walked towards the main entrance. I watched her, thinking, I hope to God I'm right too.

39

A fter she dropped me off, I cleaned up as best I could without making it worse. Binned all the glass, mopped the floors, vacuumed, covered up the drying blood with a rug I found in her bedroom. Charlie, bless him, was busy playing with his Spiderman figure as we drove back to Sara's gaff. I made a special point of getting the kid something to take his mind off things as soon as I could. We exchanged glances several times as he asked where Mummy was and why he'd come home from school early. But I knew Laura would do a good job with the kid. He loved her to death.

When I finished, I spotted the almost full bottle of Jameson's sitting on the side. One bottle she didn't get around to. But there was something odd about it. I unscrewed the cap and took the piece of paper out that was sitting in the bottle's neck. Poured myself a stiff one before looking at it. I'd already guessed what it was. I suppose she wanted me to find it and knew where I'd go first.

I took a sip and let the burn carry me away for a moment. Sparked up and unrolled the note.

Jim.

I'm sorry I have to do this, but it's for the best. Thank you for being you and for wanting the truth. Hope you don't find this as hard as I do. Take care. The car is yours.

Love

Sara

Xx

40

I re-read it several times. Made a coffee, topped it up with whiskey, then read it again. I didn't doubt that she meant to go all the way with it. But several questions remained. Sure, she'd had bad news, enough to send anyone's mental health plummeting. But suicide? Really? If so, there had to be more than the untimely death of her friend. I knew she had secrets, secrets that I might never get to know or understand.

I stood in the kitchen, going over these thoughts and trying to blank them from my mind at the same time. When I couldn't think anymore, I went into the front living room and took her car keys from the rack. It had been a while since I got behind the wheel.

Laura turned up with Charlie just as I was about to try the car. The little man seemed unaffected by the fact his Mum was in hospital. I asked Laura if she'd come clean.

'She's got a bad tummy,' she said. 'Like the time he had to be sent home from school. He's fine.'

'Good. And what about you?'

She tried a smile. 'Okay, I suppose.'

'Suppose?'

'As much as I can be. Not looking forward to tomorrow.'

'I know, but it'll be okay. I meant what I said. I can come with you if you want.'

She stepped around the living room and I showed her the bloodstains when the little man was out of sight and engrossed in CBeebies. Didn't want to, but she insisted, wanted to see for herself how bad it had been.

'I'll be fine. I just hope she is.'

'She will be.' But I only half believed it.

We made small talk, both tip toeing around the events of the day so far, and it was still only early afternoon. I mentioned the phone call with Phil Young and the fact that I was meeting him later on. Didn't mention that Sara had left a note. Could only guess if she'd left Laura a note at all. I guessed she'd find out.

'You mind if I go out? Could be important, you know.'

I'd forgotten how Laura had known Angel, too. Forgotten how all this could be affecting her. I asked her as much.

'I knew her,' she said. 'But not like Sara. They were like sisters, I suppose. I just knew her to say hello to. Shared a drink or two with her once. She was nice. She'll be missed. It's terrible, what happened.'

I made her a tea while she kept Charlie busy. She knew I was looking into the case, but I supposed she didn't know the full details. I didn't know the half of what Sara had told her and thought it best to keep my mouth shut. Not that I didn't want the girl to know - far from it - but I didn't know if it was right discussing any of this without Sara knowing about it too. I knew I needed to speak to the girl as soon as she woke up. Also knew it maybe wasn't the best circumstances. But I had her trust and she had mine, I hoped. I let

Laura know I'd like to speak with her sister as soon as it was right. She said she understood.

'I don't want you to think I'm not grateful, Jim, because I am. She could be dead by now.'

We were standing in the kitchen. Charlie was through in the living room, munching on a peanut butter sandwich his favourite auntie had knocked up to keep him quiet. Watched the little man eating and wondered how the hell Sara could leave the kid behind. She clearly wasn't in her right mind. Laura knew it too by the look on her face.

'Look,' I said. 'I'm gonna take her car. See what I can find out. She said I could anytime. I suppose if I'm gonna get anywhere, I need transport. You know how shit the buses are. You mind?'

She shrugged her shoulders. 'It's her car, I suppose. Just don't crash it. And are you sure you should be driving in your condition?'

'Am I that bad?' I was only half joking.

'Sober up first. And get a shower.'

I didn't need to be told twice. I did as she suggested. Showered, changed my clothes, and even fell asleep on the couch for a few hours. Told myself it was the whiskey, but I knew it was just my body catching up. Early mornings and late nights had taken their toll. I was exhausted.

She woke me with a brew and a ham sandwich at five o'clock. Charlie had eaten his tea - potato faces and spaghetti - but Laura said she wasn't hungry. I didn't have much of an appetite either, but managed the sandwich before getting my shit together. My thoughts turned to Phil Young and our meeting at the Marble. I supposed I'd need to part with at least some information, but I wasn't entirely sure how much. I didn't want to give too many details at this stage of the game. Still wasn't sure I could trust him with what I had and whether he'd go squealing to Robertson. That man was likely to fuck up any inroads I'd made already. With my mind foggy over Sara, and Angel still to undergo an autopsy - as far as I was aware - I thought it best to err on the side of caution. The more I could get out of Phil, the better.

I said my goodbyes to Laura as she was getting Charlie ready for a bath. She asked I keep in touch in case anything came up, and I likewise, especially where Sara was concerned. Then I grabbed my jacket and got in Sara's old Punto. It was better than nothing, and at least it had a stereo.

I was nervy about getting behind the wheel again, but it was just like riding a bike. You never lost it. An hour driving this old thing and it'd be like I was on traffic duty all over again.

Needed something to keep the real world at bay as I drove and checked the glove box for CDs. I never had the girl down as much of a rocker, but besides the Beyonce and the Scissor Sisters, there were a few gems. Joy Division and The Smiths for that Mancunian vibe. Iron Maiden, Metallica, Nirvana, Foo Fighters and AC/DC. I realized this girl had some eclectic taste. Couldn't honestly see her in tight jeans and a vest, but you learn something new every day. I mixed them up, closed my eyes, and picked one at random. Joy Division. At least it would get the blood pumping. If I was going to get stuck into this Private Investigation business, I might as well do it properly.

I was ready. Sparked up and popped the disc in. Atmosphere kicked in as I started her up and pulled out towards Rochdale Road and my meeting with Phil at the Marble.

41

I wasn't looking forward to seeing Phil. Too much had happened in the two years since I'd last laid eyes on him, most of it bad. On my part, at least. I wasn't sure exactly how much he knew about the breakdown of my marriage, but I reckoned word went round after they booted me out. There was the drink, sure. Everyone knew that. But I knew I wasn't the first copper to fall by the wayside when it came to booze, and I wouldn't be the last. The job could take its toll. He knew that as much as anyone. I didn't believe he had anything to do with the demise of my career, but now I wasn't so sure. I mean, why else would he cut off contact? I naively thought he was a mate beyond the job itself, that he'd be there when I needed him the most. Betrayal is a powerful word, but I felt it. Not just from him, either. So I would keep my cards close to my chest. For all I knew, he'd been given orders to get under my skin by that slime ball Robertson himself. Wouldn't put it past him. The guy was lower than a snake's belly.

Found a parking space in a little spot on Thompson Street, just beside the Smithfield Detox Unit. The very word brought me out in a cold sweat. As I walked past, on the way to the Marble beyond, a lone ambulance stood idle outside the front entrance and a couple of paramedics brought out a sixty odd year old geezer with a serious dose of the shakes. I guessed it must have been worse than the poor guy had been through before. There was a look in his eyes, pale yellow like nicotine, like he could see death itself. Or maybe he was just looking at me, back into his own past. There were bloodstains on his shirt and his mottled skin looked like it had been painted on. I could almost see myself in him.

It all brought back the events of the morning like an avalanche, and my thoughts briefly turned to Sara as I watched them wheel the gurney into the back. Poor bastard. Ironic that the last time I was in the Marble, they had a beer on called Delerium Tremens. Ten percent, or thereabouts. I felt I could do with one right now, just to take the edge off. I knew it wasn't wise to be mixing booze with the wheel, but I could leave the car where it was, if need be. Driving that death trap might be a small motivation for reining it in a bit. I supposed I'd find out.

Checked the time on my phone as I stood outside for a final smoke. It was just gone quarter to six. He was either in there already or on his way. Flicked the butt in the gutter and went through the arch and into the old Victorian interior. It was quiet inside but for a group of postal workers and an old fella reading the Evening Chronicle by the fire. No sign of Phil. Forgot about the sloping floor and got a bit dizzy as I approached the bar. A Weird Al Yankovic looka-like with a handlebar moustache served me a fresh pint of Lagonda, and I took a seat close to the door in the corner by the window. Would give me a good view of the whole pub. Something told me I might need it.

I'd barely got two fingers down on the pint before the doors opened and in he walked. He was wearing the same green coat he always wore. Some things never changed. I was immediately transported back to Christmas two years back, just a few months before I got the push. He was wearing the same clobber on our division night out in The Pev. I watched as he approached the bar and waited for him to spot me. I didn't have to wait long. Perhaps he could feel my eyes boring into the back of his head because he turned and picked me out pretty much straight away. There was a nod, as if we'd never parted company. We both knew it was a game. I decided to be civil, at least. Rise above the bullshit like I knew I ought to.

'Jim,' he said. We both nodded. He held out his hand and I took it. He sat on the stool opposite and took the head off his bitter. 'Been a long time. Good to see you.'

'Yeah.' Briefly thought that if things could've been different, there wouldn't be this awkwardness. 'You've not changed much.'

'Few grey hairs. The job, you know.'

I tried a smile, took a sip of beer, felt my palms getting sticky. Get the small talk out of the way before we got down to business. 'So. How's the job?'

'Oh, you know. Usual. Busy. Been putting the overtime in since this Helen Shields thing. Pain in the arse if you ask me, but I'm thankful for the money, you know. Yourself?'

I could tell he wasn't interested, didn't want to see my last two years in detail. Didn't want to face the guilt of not being a mate when it mattered most. I could either make shit up or give him the full and frank truth. Trouble was, I was hiding from it myself, keeping it at bay where it felt easier to deal with. It was my business, but if it meant Phil could see the reality instead of having his head up his arse, so be it. I wanted him to feel ashamed.

'It's been shit,' I said. 'The whole fucking mess. Karen left, she took my kid, I lost the house, ended up on the streets. Lost my job, as I'm sure you're all very aware. Other than that, it's been fucking hunky dory.'

'Jim, look -'

'Don't fucking bother.'

'Look mate, I'm sorry. We all are. If there was anything I could've done, I would've done it.'

'There was everything you could've done, Phil. But you didn't. None of you did. You did fuck all.'

That stung. I let it sink in while I necked half the beer. There was something very uncomfortable about saying it out loud, as if it had become more real and wasn't just in my head. Uncomfortable, but cathartic. I guess I needed to say it, as much to myself as to anyone else.

'You weren't there for me, Phil. You of all people.'

He looked down, shifted in his seat. Took a drink while I drained mine and returned to the bar. I knew this would be hard, and I don't think I'd ever drunk a pint so fast. Got two more beers and a whisky, which I downed before returning to my seat. Put a fresh bitter in front of him. Enjoyed watching him squirm.

'I didn't want to see you go, Jim. No one did.'

'That's bollocks and you know it. They could've put me on the sick, gardening leave, whatever. But no. Easier to let me fall apart in front of my colleagues, the people I trusted. I must've been fucking stupid to trust you bunch of cunts.'

'Yeah, well, you didn't do yourself any favours, Jim. Did you? You said so yourself. You were a liability. You'd turn up for work pissed, lost your rag with everyone. Is it any fucking wonder you got the push?'

'Thanks for that, Phil. Mate.'

I got up to step out for a smoke and he put his arm out, tried to stop me. 'Jim, don't. Let me...'

'I'm going for a bloody smoke, Phil. You can't get rid of me that easily.'

Stood outside, feeling sick. He was right. In a way. I just wish he could've told me that two bloody years ago when I needed to hear it. But it was easier for him and the rest to let it slide, to not confront me, to watch me become a shadow of my former self. It was easier to not get involved. It was easier to let me sink into the abyss.

Sparked up and tried to fight back the tears. Paced up and down while I tried to think of a good come back, knowing I was being a dick for doing so. Rise above it, I'd told myself. Yeah, as if.

When I got back in, he was browsing a food menu. Had hardly touched his beer. I got stuck into mine before my arse touched leather.

'I'm sorry,' he said. 'That was out of order. You're right. I should've been there when you needed me, Jim. Not just me, I know.'

'I wish you'd have said it years ago.'

He said nothing, just nodded, pretended to look at the menu. 'Listen, I'm starving. You want something?'

I shook my head. 'Liquid tea for me.'

He took a swig and went to order. I watched him go, thinking back to a time that felt in the distant past. Working the South Division, drinks after duty. Me, him, Lennox, Mags. And not a DI or DCI in sight. Good times, before I got too acquainted with the pub. Karen and me were planning the wedding and trying for a kid. Everything was good. Funny how things change.

He put another Lagonda in front of me. At this rate, I'd be half cut before seven.

'Thought you might appreciate another.'

He sat down, finally took his coat off and slung it on the seat beside me. I could feel it coming. The questions. He was getting into copper mode. I knew that look.

'So,' he said. 'About this case. You said you had info.'

'Nothing, really. You probably won't find it of any use.'

'Let us be the judge of that, Jim.'

I almost laughed but kept it in. 'What do you want to know?'

'What've you got?'

What did I have? Nothing I wanted to share with him, given that Robertson was the SIO. I kept it low key. 'She was living in a flat owned by the businessman Han Lan. Been there a while, as far as I know.'

'What kind of business?'

'I'd have thought you'd have had this covered? Ruthless Rob Robertson being on the job and all that?'

He shrugged, took a drink. 'I'm sure he's looking into it.'

'Bollocks, Phil. You've got fuck all and you know it. Has she been on the slab yet?'

'As far as I know.'

'Come on, Phil.'

'All right. Yes, she has. But that has no relevance to your information, Jim. Like I said, let the police deal with it. If you have something to help with our enquiries, spill it. Is that it, then?'

'She was a prostitute. High class.'

'You don't say.'

'So have you looked at her clients? You don't even know where she works, do you?'

'I never said that.'

'Phil, you're forgetting I know how this works. You can't kid a kidder. You learnt everything from me.'

Massive sigh. Must admit, I felt a bit smug. But just for a moment. I supposed I should've expected what was coming next.

'So. Exactly how do you know this, Jim? Care to elaborate?'

Dropped myself in it there. I didn't want to give him the full truth. Wasn't entirely sure what he'd do with it. I certainly didn't want anyone to know that I'd been intimate with her, or that she'd let me kip in Han Lan's flat. I especially didn't want him to know that she'd stopped me from plunging to my death. So what could I tell him? Not much. I had to do a bit of quick thinking on the spot. I had to wing it. Took a long pull on the beer and stepped up.

'I was approached by a friend of hers. After she went missing. She said you lot were fucking useless, so she decided to hire a private investigator.'

'What, you?'

'Me.'

'A private investigator? Fuck's sake, Jim. It's not Magnum fucking PI.'

'Well, what else was I gonna do? Not much else I'm qualified for.'

'How long?'

'Come again?'

'How long have you been... a private investigator?'

'Couple of months,' I lied. 'Look, she came to me. I had nothing else to do, so I looked into it. Besides, I needed the money, and it made sense. She just wanted me to find her, that's all. Then she turned up dead.'

'So that's it, then. For you. Case closed.'

'I don't think so. Now she wants to know why. She's paying me to look into it.'

'That's what we're here for.'

'And not doing a very good job of it, according to her. Can't exactly turn the money down, can I?'

'Jim, this is ridiculous.'

'Ridiculous? Why? There's nothing illegal about being a private investigator.'

'I don't think Robertson will feel the same way.'

'Well, tough. I have a duty to Helen Shield's friend. I'm not backing out.'

'Could do a lot of harm.'

'I don't think you lot are qualified to talk about harm. If you'd have bothered looking for her, she'd still be alive.'

'That's shite, Jim. We looked for her.'

'Checking the CCTV footage from the Hilton doesn't exactly constitute looking for her. You had a missing person, now you've got a murder case. If it wasn't for you dozy eyed fuckwits, she wouldn't have come to any harm.'

'You don't know that. The PM suggests she died shortly after she was last seen at the Hilton. Poor girl didn't stand a chance. And interfering in a murder inquiry could do more harm than good, Jim. Not just for the case, but for you.'

Was that a veiled threat? Not just for the case, but for me as well? Probably.

'I'm interfering in nothing. I came to you with information, don't forget. It's not as if I'm banging on your door looking for handouts. So take it or leave it. I'll do my thing, you lot do yours.'

'So why bother coming to us with the information at all if you think we're gonna do nothing with it?'

Got to admit, he had a point. 'The enemy of my enemy is my friend.'

'And what's that supposed to mean?'

'We're both after the same thing, right?'

'Except you're unlikely to get a conviction in court. And you know it. Not with your background.'

'With my background? What the fuck's that supposed to mean, Phil?'

But he didn't get a chance to answer. And by the look on his face, he was glad about it too. It could wait. The Weird Al Yankovic lookalike appeared beside us like a ghost, a bowl of shepherd's pie and a chip butty in his arms. He put them down on the table, asked if we wanted any condiments. Phil mumbled some shit or other while I was glaring at him.

'Got you a chip butty. Look like you could do with some food.'

'Not for me, thanks.'

'Come on, Jim, you look like you haven't eaten in days.'

'Yeah, and you look like you've overstayed your welcome.'

His smirk was quickly hidden by the forkful of shepherd's pie and pickled cabbage he shoved in the gap in his face. Phil had changed. For the worse. Seemed the guy had forgotten his manners, and his morals. I supposed working under Rob Robertson could do that to a man, copper or not. I felt sorry for him. For a brief moment.

'So, what do you mean? With my background?'

He didn't look up. 'I would've thought that was obvious.'

'No, Phil, it isn't.'

'Come on, Jim. Any daft cunt can see you're an alky. You think you've got any fucking credibility left? You must be a fucking -'

But he didn't get a chance to finish. I had him by the neck before he could get another mouthful of that shepherd's fucking pie down his fat, lying throat. The beer and food went flying and it was as if my whole life was happening in slow motion. The past, the present, the uncertain future. Got him up against the wall, forced the treasonous cunt against the glass partition behind him. Felt a sharp dig in my mouth and actually almost laughed when a raincoat fell on top of his bald head. Then there were two pairs of arms pulling me off. Postmen. Not just two put a group of them. They dragged be back into the belly of the pub as Phil fumbled to his feet, shepherd's pie down his front, his pint down his trousers.

'What the fuck was that for?!'

'Alky, am I?! Fucking Alky?!'

Then he barrelled forward, tried to swing an arm towards my nose. I backed off, got pushed on my arse by a couple of posties who, fair play to them, stood between me and the law.

'Come on then, Jim,' he said, spittle flying, teeth bared. 'Fucking truth hurts, does it? Truth fucking hurts, eh?'

'Fuck off, Phil.' The pub was silent, all eyes on us except for the old fella by the fire. I wiped blood from my lip. 'Just fuck right off, you thick..... stupid cunt.'

'Stay out of this, Jim,' he said, pointing. A couple of posties were trying to shuffle him out the door. 'You fucking stay out of this, Jim Locke. You hear me? You fucking hear me?!'

'Get fucked, Phil.'

'Once a piss head, always a piss head.'

He was still shouting shit for several minutes when he was long gone outside. There was a loud crack on one of the side windows as I was getting myself a double scotch. I thought about going out there to finish the job, my heart pounding, but there was a line of posties near the door. Something told me I wasn't going anywhere, not just yet.

They made room for me at the bar and I was given a seat by
the fire with the old guy and his *Evening Chronicle*, just while
I calmed down. Just while I gathered my thoughts.

Stared into the fire, wondering where it all went wrong.
Wondering where I fucked up first. I knew it, though. I knew
it all. Knew it like the blood in my veins and the blues in my
soul.

Karen. Karen...

Got swept away by Karen...by the coppers...by Angel...

The paper slammed down on the little table between me
and the old fella, followed by a pint. I looked at the whisky
in my nosing glass, took a sip, looked up.

The old guy was standing there, hands stuffed into his
brown cords. Looking down. Looking down at me.

'Made a mess of that, didn't we?'

I was quiet for a minute. 'Don't think so.'

'Gotta say I disagree, son. Could've handled it better.'

'Yeah, well, I'm not in the mood for it. He deserved it.'

'Probably,' he said, nodding. He took a seat in front of
me. His seat. Nodded at the pint. 'It's yours.'

'Thanks.'

'No bother.'

I drained the whisky, leaned forward and took the pint
to my lips. Caught him looking at me. Held up the pint pot
to show my appreciation. 'Cheers.'

'Cheers.' He took his own and swallowed a mouthful.
'Don't remember me, do you?'

'I'm sorry?'

'Thought not. I said you don't remember me.'

I took a closer look. The brown cords, the velvet waist-
coat, the expensive woollen blazer. The guy had a face that
had seen a lot of things. The lines, the ridges, the wrinkles.
He was well turned out, cleanly shaven, with hands that

looked like they hadn't done a decent days' work in their life. Eyes that knew things. A life well trodden. He looked vaguely familiar, but it was just that. Vague. Very vague.

'No, I'm sorry, I don't. I don't recall...'

'I'm surprised at that, Jim,' he said. 'Wasn't that long ago when you lot were ringing my office all hours, trying to stop us from going to press on Operation Silver. Remember that? The Chief was determined to keep our mouths shut, but the freedom of the press doesn't work like that. They were only too keen for us to give you lot a ringing endorsement when the gangs were behind bars though, eh? I suppose we have our uses. When it suits GMP, that is.'

Bob Turner, Chief Crime Correspondent at the *Manchester Evening Chronicle*. A real ball ache to the top brass at GMP back in the day, when Operation Silver–getting the gang ring leaders behind bars–was at its height. He was known as Bob Piles around HQ, because he was a pain in the arse. Journalists usually are. Anything for a story. Except in Bob's case, he was probably one of the more genuine ones. He wouldn't run a story unless it had solid truth to it. He'd been in the firing line a fair bit over the years for going out on a limb on a story involving the Assistant Chief Constable's wife. Now ex-wife. He was a hack, but a hack with morals. A rarity.

'Bob Turner. Isn't it?'

He smiled. Raised an eyebrow. 'I knew it'd come back to you, son. Been a while, eh? So, what was all that about?'

I tried for a stern look. Not giving the game away. 'Not gonna put it on the front page, are you?'

'God, no. Those days are long gone. I'm retired now, thankfully. No more hanging around police stations and crime scenes for me. I believe you're no longer with the force yourself?'

'Funny how news travels.'

'It was common knowledge, son.' I wished he'd stop calling me that. 'Not much gets past the press, Mr. Locke. You should know that. A lot of us thought it wasn't right at the time.'

I nodded, took another drink, rummaged in my pocket for a smoke. He offered me a cigar, which I declined, before indicating the back door to the little beer garden and smoking shelter. Was a good job there was a shelter out there. It was pissing down. I was under no illusions that this wasn't just a social chat. We were hardly friends. I wouldn't have recognised him at all if he hadn't have broken the ice. I guess kicking off with Phil gave him the excuse to poke around, perhaps put a fatherly hand on my shoulder.

We parked ourselves on a bench beneath the Perspex shelter and sparked up. I'd never liked the smell of cigars. Gave me the creeps. We were silent for a moment while we took the air in. A hard rain hammered on the pavement beyond. My thoughts went back to some of the guys I'd left on the streets and in the shelters. Wouldn't want to be out in this. It was too cold, too damp. It was the kind of night that could make you wish you were dead. The city was dirty and grey out there. The back streets of Piccadilly the perfect habitat for a rat or two.

'You were a good copper, Jim. Young and ambitious. Honest, too. And that's a hard thing for a copper. Honesty, I mean. If you're not careful, they can drain that honesty away until you forget what you went into the job for in the first place.'

'You were never a copper, Bob.'

'No, but I knew a lot of coppers, Jim. Lot of bent ones as well.'

'You must've seen a few in your time.'

'Oh, aye, part and parcel of the job. To be bent, I mean. I've been writing for the *Evening Chronicle* for well over fifty years, son. Never struggled to find anything to write about when it came to top brass. The corruption. The back handers. The politics.'

'You must've had some crimes to write about as well.'

He laughed, took a drag on his Montecristo, blew thick smoke between us. 'Oh, aye. You name it, I've seen it, written about it, got the t-shirt. Murder. Fraud. Drugs and gangs, gangs and thugs. And bent bastards. Was never a shortage of those.'

'Someone I should know about?'

'Well, that depends. One or two names would no doubt prick your ears up.'

'Care to tell me about them?'

He laughed. 'Not a chance, son. Not a chance. No, these secrets stay with me and me only. Would do too much damage if I let slip. With great power comes great responsibility.'

'That's what Spiderman said. So you're not thinking of being a friendly neighbourhood journalist, then?'

He shifted in his seat. 'Never was. I don't intend to start now. And anyway, like I say. I'm retired now. The only writing I'll be doing is my will. And my little book about the Peterloo Massacre. Helps move the days along nicely now I'm not up to my head in shite.'

I nodded, took a drink and smoked. I was waiting for the real reason he was being all friendly. I didn't have to wait too long.

'So, what was all that about? If you don't mind me asking?'

Truth was, it was none of his business. And yet I wondered if he might come in useful. He knew his way around these things just as much as I did. And I knew he had contacts in the media too. If I needed someone to sniff around, especially given my little argument with Phil, he could be the right man for the job. Retired, too. I bet he was getting sick of Homes Under The Hammer and the wife. Could do him good to make some enquiries. Keep his ear to the ground.

'I'm a private investigator now. Hired to look into why a Miss Helen Shields went missing two weeks ago. Except she turned up dead and my client wants to know why.'

'I know that much, son. Couldn't help but overhear what you were both talking about. I meant what was the fisticuffs about?'

'Personal. I don't take kindly to insults.'

He nodded, took a sip of beer. 'So I see. So go on. What of this woman. You say she turned up dead.'

'Yeah. Under an arch beside the Bridgewater Canal. In a very bad way.'

'How bad are we talking?'

'Raped, beaten, stabbed. Hit on the head with a hammer. Doesn't get much worse than that.'

'And what does he have to do with all this?'

'Who?'

'Bloke you had by the throat.'

'That was Phil,' I said. 'You don't remember him? Copper.'

'One of Robertson's boys?'

'So you know about him, then?'

'Like I said, I know all the bent bastards.'

'Is it that obvious?'

'Bent as they come, that one. His Dad was the same.'

'His Dad?'

'Oh, aye, he was in the force back in the day. Early seventies. Was a total prick.'

'Like father like son.'

'You could say that, yeah. Anyway, let me guess. They're investigating and you're in the way?'

'They wanted some information I had. I needed to find a way to get under their skin, find out what they knew. Which turns out to be nothing much.'

'I wouldn't bet on that, son.'

'No?'

'No.' He stood, took one more drag on the Montecristo and stubbed it out under his foot. 'Sly bastards, this lot. As you well know. It's a knocking bet they know more than they're letting on.'

'You seem to forget I was a copper as well. I know how they work.'

'But do you? You got the push, didn't you? Tell me I'm not wrong, son. My guess is it wasn't just because you liked a drink either.'

Wasn't sure where he was going with this. Whatever he was implying, his face told me to lay off it.

'Come on, it's still early. You can tell me all about it. My shout.'

I watched him go back inside then finished my smoke, wondering if I should come clean on the lot, or at least the more interesting bits I was digging up, and put my trust in him. But I knew I needed allies too. And he had connections. Given that the police weren't gonna give me anything, especially now they knew I was investigating myself, I knew he could be someone I could align myself with. The enemy of my enemy is my friend.

I stepped back inside.

42

We took a seat by the fire again. The pub had gotten busier with locals from the flats down the side of Ludgate Hill. Bob was holding his hands over the flames while I got us another couple of beers. Tell me all about it, he'd said. I wasn't exactly sure how much there was to tell, to be honest. But I guessed I should come clean on the bits I knew nothing about, at least. I was thinking of Han Lan and his business interests. And what went on in Bo Wong's dancing club. Bob struck me as the type who might even frequent such a place, and it would be interesting to see what he had to say.

I sat down and he joined me. The noise level had increased a notch, and soon all the tables were filled, leaving a line of punters blocking the aisle all the way to the front door. I could feel the heat from the fire beside us. Took my jacket off to settle in. Told myself it could be a long chat.

'So. What's going on? Do you know who murdered her?'

'No. She was last seen with one of her clients.'

'Clients?'

I nodded. 'She was an escort girl. High-class prostitute.

She was last seen with him at the Hilton. There's CCTV footage of her leaving with him around two thirty a.m.'

'And after that?'

'Nothing. Nothing until she turned up dead, that is.'

He looked away, sipped his pint. Thoughtful. 'So, you're investigating. Found anything?'

'A few things, though not much. Was wondering if you could help with that, actually.'

'Me?'

'Yeah. Maybe you can shed some light on one or two people I've managed to dig up.'

He raised his eyebrows. 'Go on.'

I told him what I knew.

Told him about Han Lan but steered clear of how I ended up in his apartment. Told him about Simon and how I had his phone but couldn't unlock the damn thing. About the agency, Provoke, that Angel had worked for. Carol, Sherry, Matt, the guy called Luke who I hung over Han Lan's roof terrace by his pants. How they were all characters in a game I was trying to figure out. Told him about Bo Wong and his dancing club. Told him about Sara's suicide attempt and how she was currently laid up at North Manchester General. I wondered how she was and thought about calling Laura. Something told me tomorrow would be a long day.

But it was Bo Wong he was most interested in. Bo Wong and the East Asian immigrants he had lap dancing in his club. It was how they were paid that most sparked my interest.

'We've known about it a long time. What goes on in that place. More importantly, what goes on off premises.'

'I'm intrigued.'

'You should be.'

'So go on then. Spill it.'

'It'll be more than just words that'll be spilt if this gets out, Jim. So it goes no further.'

Jesus, how big was this? 'You can trust me, Bob. But if it relates to my investigation, it'd be helpful if you could at least let me in on the secret.'

He smiled. 'Oh, it's a secret all right. One of the biggest. But it's hard to say if it relates in any way to your murdered girl. I'm not sure I should be telling. And even I don't know the full story. But I do know it goes deep, Jim. That rabbit hole goes very deep indeed.'

He took a mouthful of beer and edged his seat around the table to get that bit closer. Even looked about so that no one was within earshot.

'The girls are brought in from all over East Asia and the far east. China. Korea, Vietnam, Thailand, Laos. The Philipines. Those kinds of places. From anywhere really, as long as their face fits and they're willing to dance to his tune.'

'His tune being?'

'Play by my rules.'

'Which are?'

'I'll come to that in a minute. Anyway, they're brought in all legal and above board. Genuine passports and working visas. All that.'

'What, to lap dance? Visas?'

He shook his head. 'Some get kitted out with long-term holiday visas, others are here to work. Officially in the Asian and Chinese shops and markets and stuff. Restaurants, casinos, kitchens. You name it.'

'Strip clubs?'

'Oh, aye.' He drained his pint and I followed. 'But not just to dance, Jim. No, that wouldn't be quite enough.'

'Where is this heading?'

'I told you, this rabbit hole goes very deep indeed. It's my round.'

I scanned the pub as he stepped up to the bar. It was busy. A popular place, with several occupied tables tucking into cheeseboards and hamburgers and winter stews. Felt a pang of hunger, which was odd for me. I almost wished I'd had a go at the chip butty Phil had bought. Almost.

'Gonna make this my last one, Jim,' he said, putting the beers down. 'Body can't take it anymore. I'm getting too old for this game.'

I nodded. 'Fair enough. So you were saying...'

He swallowed a mouthful, looked me in the eye. 'Like I say, it goes deep.'

'So let me get this straight,' I said. 'The girls are brought in to work in the club, yeah? But they work in other places as a cover or something?'

'Something like that, yeah. But not just to dance, Jim. I'm sure you understand.'

I'm sure I did. 'So they get paid for sex, then?'

'You'll make a detective one day, son.'

'But I'm guessing most of the takings go to Bo Wong... and maybe others.'

'You're getting warmer. Which others do you have in mind?'

'Well, Han Lan, for a start. Something dodgy about his business interests.'

'Oh, aye?'

'What do you know about him?'

'Not much, except I know he has a lot of fingers in a lot of pies.'

'You can say that again.'

He raised his eyebrows. 'You dug something up I should know about?'

'Not really.' I was thinking about the copies of his bank statements and the millions he had floating around the globe. 'Only that he has a lot of money, but no one seems to know why. And strangely, Angel–Helen Shields–just happened to be living in his apartment while he was away in Hong Kong. He's still in China as far as I'm aware.'

I could tell by his expression that he thought Angel living in his flat was bizarre too. A strange coincidence and an unlikely place for an escort girl to be living.

'It does seem odd,' he said. 'So I take it you think he's got something to do with her death?'

'Her murder? Yeah. Yeah, I do. But I'm fucked if I know what the hell it is.'

He swallowed more beer. 'I wonder if he knows. About her murder?'

'Well, if he's got anything to do with it, I reckon he knew before any of us.'

'You think he might have ordered a hit? Something like that?'

'Gotta say, it has crossed my mind.'

'But why would he do that?'

'You tell me, Bob,' I said. 'You tell me.'

We went back out for a smoke, not just because we needed the nicotine but because it was that bit quieter too. We sat down and sparked up. The hard rain from earlier had eased a little, but the air was cold and damp. There was a heavy mist forming too, hanging in the air like spectral fog. I could almost hear the ghosts whispering on the wind.

'As far as I'm aware, he keeps them happy with his product. Though whether it comes from him is anyone's guess.'

'What kind of product?'

'A favourite of the Chinese in the seventeenth century.

I'm not too big on Chinese history, Jim, but I know enough to see the damage it can cause.'

'Opium?'

He took a long, thoughtful drag on his Montecristo. 'Aye. Or rather, the more common derivative.'

'Smack?'

'Got it one, son. Heroin. But you've not heard that from me.'

'Fuck me.' I smoked hard for several minutes whilst I let what he told me sink in. 'So what about the police? They know about this?'

He almost laughed. 'Oh, they know about it, all right.'

'I can sense a but coming.'

'And you'd be right,' he said. 'The thing is, it's rumoured–heavily in my circles, I might add–that they turn a blind eye to it. It's too big. And, apparently, there are certain sections of the force that like it just the way it is, if you get my meaning.'

'No, Bob, I'm not sure I do.'

'Well, let me put it this way. It's what they can get out of it that keeps Bo Wong sweet.'

'Sex on a plate?'

I thought I saw the beginnings of a smile at the corner of his mouth. It could've been a grin. 'Like I said, son. You'll make a good detective one day.'

'Been there, done that. No thanks.'

'You never heard of this when you were with GMP?'

I shook my head, took a final drag and tossed the smoke aside. 'Not a dickie bird. Should I have?'

'Well, I suppose you have to be a member of a very exclusive club.' He turned and wagged a finger. 'Of which I know nothing about, you understand?'

'Bob. What kind of 'exclusive club' are we talking about?'

'The kind that corrupts, son. Though I reckon you know that anyway, don't you? Deep down?'

I thought about what he was saying. It all seemed far-fetched. But having said that... I just didn't know. Could it be? He said he knew a lot of bent bastards. If what he was saying was true, he wasn't far wrong. Question was: how bent were we talking? From what I could make of his tale, Bo Wong was plying the dancing girls with heroin to keep them happy–and perhaps compliant–and the police, or certain members of the force, were getting their fix of what was on offer in exchange for silence. They were effectively giving a green light to people smuggling, class A drug supply and use, and exploitation of vulnerable women for sex. I didn't know what scared me most. And I knew that some of those women were very young indeed. Perhaps one or two weren't yet women at all. Fuck me, if this was true, it was one enormous rabbit hole.

'Bob, if what you're saying is true, why haven't you gone public with this? Chief Crime Correspondent of the *Manchester Evening Chronicle* and all that? You could blow this thing wide open, man.'

He blew smoke out and sighed. 'Oh, I'd like too. Almost did once, until the threats came.'

'Threats?! Fuck's sake, Bob...'

'Guarded threats, Jim. But threats all the same. I'm not gonna take that risk, lad. I've got grandkids now and a nice retirement to look forward to.'

'Threats from who, Bob? And what kind of threats?'

'I can't say any more, son, and I've said too much already. I'll keep my ear to the ground on this Miss Shields thing, though I wouldn't expect much.'

He got up and made his way back inside. I quickly followed, but he had his raincoat on before I could suggest one for the road. I grabbed his arm before he could step away from the coat hanger.

'Bob, you can't keep this to yourself. If you went public with this... fuck, it'd be massive.'

'That it might be.' He put a hand on my shoulder. 'But it's really not worth it, lad. Believe me. And you'd do well to steer clear of it, too. If you know what's good for you. Give me a call if you need a favour. But don't expect miracles.'

He grabbed my hand and gripped it tight, placing a piece of paper in my sweaty palm. Then he put a black Fedora on his head, nodded, and turned to the door.

43

I watched him leave, then drained my pint. Thought briefly about getting that last one for the road, then thought better of it. After our conversation, and the earlier encounter with Phil, I needed air and a quiet place to just... breathe. I unfolded the piece of paper he'd placed in my hand. There were two numbers written on it in red ink. The colour of blood. I saved them into the contacts on my mobile and pocketed the slip, just in case.

There was a lot going through my mind, a jumbled mess of junk like a pile of old shit in a skip. But somewhere in there, somewhere deep down beneath all the shite, I knew there lurked a gem. It was just a case of digging it out. But I couldn't think in here, no matter how much I felt at home. It was too noisy. The very sight of beer and optics and wine glasses, the smell of the boozer, would only tempt me more, and I knew that if I overstayed my welcome, the top shelf would entice me in like a pot of gold at the end of the rainbow, except there would be no riches there. Just memories and fading dreams. It was a sobering thought.

I left the pub in an almost blind panic, with the face of

the old guy on the gurney from outside the Smithfield Detox Unit almost flashing on my very eyeballs. Don't end up like him, I told myself. But something else told me I might not have a choice.

I knew I was over the limit to drive, so I left Sara's car where it was and walked into town. There was a little pub I knew just off Deansgate that I knew would be quiet, and I'd have a better chance of flagging a black cab down after I had that final pint. I knew I was kidding myself if I believed it would be my last. But that's what I kept telling myself. Just one Guinness. That was all.

The streets were quiet. I cut through the Northern Quarter, past the bars and the all-night cafes, the events of the evening running through my mind. I thought about Phil and what he'd said. Felt betrayed by a man I once considered a good friend. Was Phil a part of this 'exclusive club' Bob had talked about? I doubted it. Did he even know it existed, if indeed it existed at all? Probably not. Would he be the type to smell corruption on his very doorstep? No. At least I didn't think so–unless he'd changed. And I knew Phil was the type of man the top brass could mould. He was predictable, easily manipulated. If they'd got to him–and others–when did it happen? Before I got the push? After? And what Bob had said–'I'm guessing it wasn't just the drink'–what did he mean by that?

Too many questions, so few answers. Felt like I was pacing around some maze in my brain, reaching dead ends and finding no way out. Then there was Sara and her cut wrists, the psychiatric assessment tomorrow. And the reason she'd done such a thing, lying in some mortuary freezer at Force HQ. It was a brutal murder. Whoever was responsible wanted to make sure she was dead. But why? What had she done? What did she know?

And Karen. Nicole. The mess I'd made of our marriage and my career.

I tried to block it all out, let it slip away as I put one foot in front of the other, head down. There was a fine rain in the air and the mist was getting heavier, becoming a fog with every step. I could barely see twenty yards ahead. Sparked up as I turned onto Cross Street. There were a few late hours office workers about, a full rank of taxis, the chain restaurants busy enough with families and birthday parties. When I got to Albert Square, the action was in full swing with the construction of this year's Christmas markets, wooden cabins going up at breakneck speed, entire gangs of market traders getting their stock ready for the grand opening on Friday morning. Christmas again. I knew there would be more than a few people who wouldn't be looking forward to the festive period; myself included. I thought of Sara, and little Charlie. Karen and Nicole. God, Nicole. My daughter, my flesh and blood. I'd missed two Christmases with her already, and now she was at an age when she'd really be able to understand it all. She'd be getting excited now. I wondered if she thought of me and wished for me to come home this year. I tried to picture her face, then tried to blot it out with all the other stuff. I reminded myself that I must see Frank and Maureen. I mean, what the fuck was I doing chasing this dead end when my kid needed me? I knew I had to sort my priorities out before long. Tomorrow. Tomorrow would be the day. I promised myself I would take that step.

I cut down John Dalton Street and took Dalton Alley, a little cut through that would bring me out onto Lincoln Square and The Rising Sun. I felt claustrophobic; the walls seeming to get narrower and narrower as I got closer to the end. Wouldn't be long before I could -

I heard heavy boots running behind me and before I could turn around I felt a smack on the back of my neck. I fell to the deck, the cold stone pressed against my face. I must've hit my head on the wall because I almost blacked out. Felt a hard dig - a boot - in my ribs and I doubled over, my breath taken out of me. Couldn't get a chance to roll onto my back and the kicks kept on coming. I didn't know if there was more than one. It felt like it. Took a hard blow to my shoulder, then felt a fist smash into my teeth. I couldn't see. I must've been bleeding from my head because I could feel the blood dripping into my eyes, warm and wet and coppery. I went dizzy, tried to get to my feet but there was another hard, sharp dig to my shin. I fucking yelped in agony, took a blind swing and hit nothing but a brick wall. I screamed, spat blood, fell to the deck again. Kicked out, blinded, at nothing but air, and the boots were running off, echoing through the alley. Tried to get a look, but it was too dark. Even the wall lamps weren't enough. The figure had disappeared into the fog before I could get to my knees.

Bastard. Bastard, bastard, bastard.

I sank back against the wall and tried to catch my breath. I was shaking. I was fucking lucky I hadn't been kicked to death. Jesus.

I spat blood, sure I'd lost at least one tooth. Pulled my phone out to check the time, but all I saw was a blur. I quickly checked my pockets. I hadn't been robbed, just took a good kicking. For a reason I didn't know. But there had to be one. Whoever it was wanted to hurt me - and they did. Thought about phoning the police and decided against it. It's not as if they could do anything.

My belongings, what little I carried, were all intact as far as I could tell. Which was more than could be said for me. I examined my bruised fingers in the dead neon. They were dirty and bloody. My head fucking murdered.

I closed my eyes, let darkness wash over me. Felt the pain in my head and heard the blood pumping through my temples. Took long breaths and felt the fog close in, could smell the vapour making its way down the alley. Finally, I rolled onto my side, let my face touch the stone cold floor, and drifted.

I got in bed and she turned away, moved toward the edge as if she couldn't bear to be near me. I lay there, half drunk, trying to catch my breath as I stared at the ceiling. I didn't know the time, but it was light outside and the birds were singing so I guessed it must have been morning some time. My guts were churning and I needed a piss. I was cold, even though it looked warm and bright through the gap in the blinds.

'How many times?'

'It won't happen again. I promise.'

She said nothing.

I could feel something on my face. Someone slapping it. Felt his fingers near my mouth, could smell the alcohol and the piss on him as he tried to wake me up.

'Are you all right?'

'What?'

I couldn't think straight, couldn't think at all.

'What happened?'

What happened? Shit, what exactly did happen? I sat up, felt my head, looked at the blood on my palm. There was a bruise the size of an egg above my right eye, and I found I could stick my tongue between two molars on the left side of my mouth. I spat out more blood and realised I must've bitten my tongue because it bloody hurt big time. Winced when the old tramp helped me to my feet. I must've taken a good kicking to the ribs there. Felt a nasty pain shoot through me as I stood.

'Can you spare us any change for a cup of tea?'

Irish. The kind with a heroic constitution. I couldn't see this guy drinking tea any time soon. Another reminder of what I could become stared back at me in that alley. I dug in my pocket and handed him a handful of change.

'Give me some of that shit you're drinking.'

He handed me the plastic bottle of chemical cider, the kind you could use as paint stripper, and I took a long drink until he grabbed it back off me. I wasn't ready to wrestle him for it, but it was maybe just enough to dull the pain.

'Thanks, God bless,' he said, then wandered off, stumbling in the narrow alley. 'I'd get to a hospital if I were you.'

I dug out a smoke and sparked up. Took that shit in deep. Looked around, left and right down either end. Nothing but misty white. I remembered I was on the way to the Rising Sun and stepped to my left. I came out onto Lincoln Square, the statue of the great man looking down at me. The pub was closed, but Deansgate was just a few steps away. Thought about what the old Irish guy had said–get to hospital–but was it really that bad? I stumbled on, feeling dizzy, which I thought was probably a mild concussion. My head still felt damp with blood. Caught a look of myself in a car wing mirror. I looked a fucking mess. There was a big lump above my right eye, and when I opened my mouth, it was red.

'Fuck.' A spray of blood sparkled on the wing mirror.

I stumbled my way down to Deansgate, dizzy but awake enough to know where I was. The fog was thick now, and it was hard to make out the orange glow of a vacant taxi. Perhaps there were none around. I stumbled on, not entirely sure which direction I was heading in, dying for a drink and spitting blood every few yards. Finally heard a diesel engine as a black cab pulled up and a big black guy stepped out. He caught me before I fell over on my face and dragged me into the back of the cab.

'Shit, man,' he kept saying.

I lay there on the back seat as he put his foot down. Drifting again. Just heard the engine turn over and the roll of the wheels beneath me. Could smell the air and the fog as it blew through the window and it felt good on my face. I needed water. Better than that, I needed a drink. Oh, how I needed a drink.

'Shit, man. What happened, man?'

Opened my eyes and watched the lights drift past. The cab rolled at a constant speed, never slowing, even on bends and corners. He stopped once or twice at the lights, cursing.

Moments later–or I could've drifted again, I don't know–the cab door opened and I was being dragged out by my feet. I slumped in his arms, the bright white of the corridor surrounding me, enveloping me, until I was dropped onto a stretcher and there was a doctor or a nurse or someone shining a fucking torch in my eyes.

'Shit, man.' Again and again and again. I wished he'd stop fucking saying that. 'Shit, man.'

I tried to speak, tried to say thanks but I've got no change for you, tried to say cheers. But all that came out was a moan and more blood.

46

I came round to the smell of disinfectant. That was the first thing. When I opened my eyes, Bob Turner was sitting there staring at me.

'He's alive.'

'What?'

'Took a bad kicking, lad. They phoned me.'

Who phoned him? Where the fuck?

'You're in hospital, Jim. Concussion. Huge gash on the back of your head. A few teeth missing. They tell me your ribs are bruised.'

'Who?'

'What do you mean, 'who'?'

'Who phoned you?'

'The bloody hospital, lad. Found my number in your jeans pocket.'

'Shit.'

It was all I could say. All the energy I had.

'What happened?' He stepped from the foot of the bed to right beside me. 'You remember anything?'

I couldn't remember much, other than the taxi driver

and his somewhat limited vocabulary. 'Not much. I got jumped. Don't know who. I couldn't see them.'

He nodded. 'I'll get you something to drink.'

'Whisky.'

'Yeah, likely.'

I drifted again until sometime later I felt a tap on my shoulder and looked up to see Bob standing there with two teas in foam cups. He helped me to sit up, propped my pillows. A nurse came and took my blood pressure and checked my stitches. Apparently, I'd had twenty-three sutures in the back of my head and they'd strapped up my ribs. They'd had to shave my hair to deal with the wound. I felt wrapped up in cotton wool. Bob said I was on some powerful painkillers.

'Good job you were pissed. In a way. You wouldn't have felt much when you came in. Apparently, a cabbie brought you in.'

'I remember.'

'Who was it?'

'Not that, the cabbie. Black guy. That's about it.'

'Remember anything else?'

'Nothing.'

'Maybe it'll come back to you, give it a few days.'

But I didn't feel there was anything to remember. I'd been jumped, by whom I didn't know. But I could hazard a few guesses. 'What time is it?'

He glanced at the clock on the wall across the ward. 'Just gone half eight. The doctor wants to see you before they think about discharging.'

'Well, he better get a fucking move on.'

'She.'

'Whatever. Look, I feel fine. They can't keep me in here.'

'Let Doctor Coates be the judge of that.'

'I'll be the judge. And how long have you been here?'

'All bloody night, son. They phoned me just as I was getting my head down at half one this morning. Said they couldn't get anybody else.'

'There is no one else.'

'You were lucky, Jim. Could've been a lot worse.'

'You got any ideas? After our conversation, I mean.'

'Not a bloody clue, lad.'

'Come on, Bob. You said you'd had threats before. I find it odd that I'm the one gets battered so soon after you tell me about this exclusive club stuff.'

'It could've been anyone. Could be someone related to your investigation. More than likely, if you ask me.'

He was right. Shit, he really was. But the question begged: who? I lay there, trying to think of who might want to do me in, thought of all the people I'd nobbled over the past week. There was Simon, but I couldn't see him starting a fight in a pink leotard and a diamond tiara. He surely knew I'd nabbed his phone and perhaps got someone to get it back. I got Bob to check my belongings. The iPhone was in my jacket pocket. Asked Bob if he could unlock the thing, but he just shrugged and said he couldn't even handle a digital radio.

Then there was Bo Wong, and given that I'd stepped on his toes, implied I knew stuff about his operation when I actually knew fuck all, might've given him the impetus to get me to back off. I suppose it wouldn't have been impossible for him to send some heavies in my direction. And after what Bob had told me–the corruption, the threats–I supposed it wouldn't be all that unlikely to suggest someone might want to warn me off. Had someone been listening to our conversation in the Marble? Perhaps. Maybe. And if that had been the case, my attacker could've followed me all the way down to Dalton Alley, the perfect spot for a kicking, and took his chance. I was clearly a target.

And Phil. Our little bust up could've hit him hard, wound him up. He'd warned me to steer clear of the investigation. Could I really see my old mate losing it like that and just jumping me? The coward's way out? Unless he had gotten someone else to do it. Or had been ordered to get someone else to do it. Robertson. I wouldn't put it past that little shithead. He was the kind of copper to let power go to his head. The kind who could be corrupted and corrupt others. Whoever it was, they wanted me to steer clear. But they had me all wrong.

I wasn't fucking likely to steer clear after this.

'What day is it, Bob?'

'Tuesday. You sure you're feeling all right?'

'Just losing track, that's all.' I took a sip of tea. Tasted like piss. 'Pass me my phone, will you?'

He handed me the mobile Sara had bought me. I was keenly aware that she was in hospital too, and today could be a nightmare for the girl. I found Laura's number and pushed the call button. Ringing.

'Which hospital are we in, Bob?'

'MRI.'

Which would give me an hour at least to pick the car up and get over to North Manchester General. As soon as I discharged myself, that is.

'Hello?'

'Laura. It's Jim.'

'Jim, you've been out all night. I thought you'd ring.'

'I would've done.' I could hear a lot of noise in the background, and wind blowing through the phone. 'Except I got a bit laid up. Where are you?'

'Just dropping Charlie off at school,' she said. 'I'm

heading over to see Sara as soon as I can get away from here. Ward round's at ten.'

'I'll come over,' I said. 'I'll be there as soon as I can.'

'There's no need.'

'I'm coming. I'll see you soon.'

She tried to argue, but I cut her off. Took another sip of tea and spat it back in the cup. Put it on the side, then flung the sheets off.

'Jim, take it easy.'

'I'm fine. I need to get over to hospital.'

'You're in hospital, son.'

'The other one. For Sara's assessment, remember? Pass me my jeans.'

He slung my clothes across the bed and I whipped my jeans on. Felt a sharp pain in my ribs as I lifted my t-shirt over my head. A nurse came over and tried to get me back in.

'I'm going, love,' I said. 'Thanks for everything.'

'Mr. Locke, I don't think that's a good idea. At least let Doctor Coates examine you before you even think about going. You've got a nasty head wound.'

I started to peel the bandage off my head, but she reached out to stop me.

'Get her here, then. I've got shit to deal with.'

Ten minutes later and Doctor Coates, a fifty odd year old Carol Carpenter lookalike, was shining another bloody torch in my face as I sat on the edge of the bed.

'How many fingers am I holding up?'

'Four.'

'Who's the Prime Minister?'

'Cunto The Clown.'

'Okay, Mr. Locke, you're free to go.'

She handed me a prescription for some heavy duty

painkillers and warned me to stay off the drink. Apparently, my liver was like pate.

Bob picked up the script while I parked myself on a bench outside the main entrance and sparked up. Checked the time on my phone and thought about a swift half in the Grafton, but it wouldn't be open yet. Felt fuzzy but could still feel my head throbbing. The Doc had insisted I keep the bandage on, but I felt like a right prick. Couldn't wait to get a pair of scissors to it. I felt the wound around the back, the spiky little sutures sticking out. It was tender, as was the lump above my right eye. At least the bleeding in my mouth had stopped.

Bob handed me a bottle of water and two more pills. 'Here, get this down you. Come on. I'll give you a lift back to town.'

The traffic was busy as we headed away from the MRI in Bob's Volvo, and there was a hard rain on the horizon. Told him to put his foot down and he obliged, weaving in and out of the bus lanes on Oxford Road. My head was banging. Wasn't sure I was fit to drive. The painkillers explicitly advised me not to, but I'd never been one for following rules. I supposed I'd find out if I could handle the wheel. Besides, given the amount I'd drunk in the past seven days, I was probably over the limit, anyway.

'So what are you doing with your time, Bob? Now that you're retired?'

'Not much,' he said, concentrating hard on the road. 'Bit of gardening. Bit of shopping. Trying to write my book on the Peterloo Massacre.'

'Plenty of free time, then?'

He glanced at me before taking a right onto Princess Street. 'Where exactly is this going, Jim?'

Where was I going? I didn't know, just putting the feelers

out. But I'd been thinking about how handy he could be, before I got my head kicked in, that is.

'Well, I was wondering. You know. Seeing as you're not doing much...'

'No.'

'You haven't even heard what I've got to say yet.'

'It's not a good idea, son.'

'Just listen,' I said. 'It's not as if I want you to climb the Himalayas or anything. Just do what you're best at.'

'That being?'

'Snooping. You know... asking questions.'

'Of whom, might I ask?'

'Bo Wong.'

'Oh no, not a chance.'

'Come on, man.'

'Have you forgotten what I said last night?'

'Well...'

'Because you have had a severe kick to the head. Must be playing havoc with any sense you might've had before. Which I don't think was much.'

'I'm not asking much.'

'But you're asking enough. They know that I know about all this stuff. If I show up in Chinatown asking questions, they'll think I'm finally ready to go to press on this. Which I'm not. Not that stupid, son. And I haven't got a death wish.'

'Okay then, no questions. Just...you know, keep your ear to the ground.'

'This isn't some L.A. Noir novel, Jim, this is real life. My mere presence around there is bound to raise eyebrows. And like I say, I've got grandkids I want to be spending time with, not hanging around Chinatown in a bloody raincoat.'

'I'm not asking you to hang around, just... I don't know. Go for some food or something, have a drink in a bar or two,

see if you can find anything out about Angel. And Han Lan.
Especially him.'

'Why him?'

'His business interests are many, from what I can gather.
And I want to know why Angel was living in his apartment.
Anyone with the money he's got has got to be into some-
thing dodgy. I just don't trust the guy.'

'It seems odd that she was living there,' he nodded.
'More than odd, actually.'

We were quiet for a while as he drove, Five Live on the radio.
We did a right at Princess Street, then on up through Piccadilly
basin, down under the railway bridge and onto Great Ancoats
Street. The rain was sweeping in. He flipped on the wipers.

'Anyway,' I said. 'I want to know more about this exclusive club you were on about last night.'

He looked uncomfortable. 'I can't say any more about it,
Jim. Not that I know that much, anyway.'

'But you received threats?'

'Not directly, no. Just implied.'

'From who?'

'That would be too much information, lad. Look, all you
need to know is that yes, not all is as it seems in Chinatown.
And GMP... well, you know about them.'

'Not entirely, no. But I'm beginning to believe it.'

'Secrets, Jim.' He glanced at me as we drove. 'Secrets and
lies. Cover-ups. Been going on since the sixties, at least.'

'But I still don't understand that, if you journos had all
this information, why not go to press on it?'

'It's not as simple as that.'

'No?'

'You know it, lad.' He manoeuvred into the right-hand
lane and we joined a queue for the right turn onto Oldham

Road. 'Blowing it wide open would've meant the end of many careers, mine included. And it wouldn't have just been careers that ended.'

'Are you seriously saying you fear for your life, Bob?'

He said nothing, pulled off as the lights went green. 'Once, yeah. But I'm clear of all that now. Now that I'm retired. And I intend to keep it that way, which is why I don't want any involvement in this.'

'But you're not involved in anything. All I'm asking is that you just creep around. You know, just go about your business and see what crops up. Maybe speak to some of your colleagues and stuff.'

'Ex colleagues, son. We don't mix business with pleasure.'

'But you must keep in touch with one or two.'

He said nothing as we swung onto Oldham Road and eased off the gas as we approached the next junction. Took a left and pulled up down Thompson Street. The Punto was still there. Killed the engine and reached into his jacket pocket to pull out his wallet. Rummaged inside. Peeled off five twenty pound notes.

'It'll keep you going. For a few days at least.'

'Shit, Bob, what do you take me for?'

'Skint, that's what.'

'Is it that obvious?'

He laughed. 'Come on, Jim. We all know you've been sleeping rough, hanging about in shelters and doss houses. You're hardly bloody Rockefeller, are you?'

I took the money. Felt a bit of a twat for doing so, but needs must. 'Cheers, Bob. I promise I'll pay you back.'

'Don't let this become a habit, Jim. And here.' He handed me the painkillers. 'Don't forget them.'

I pocketed them and got out. 'So what do you think? Just a favour, that's all...'

He looked straight ahead, sighed, lit up a Montecristo. 'Don't expect much, son. At my age I'm getting tired of playing silly buggers.'

'But an innocent woman is dead, Bob. You know that. What if it was your daughter?'

'Don't even try it, Jim.'

'Try what?'

'Emotional bloody blackmail. Look, I'll see what I can find out. If I hear anything, I'll let you know. And do me a favour. Stay out of trouble.'

I nodded. 'I will.'

'Good. Because I can't watch your back, son.'

He started her up again and did a U turn before driving off. I watched him leave the road, then got in Sara's Punto and drove in the opposite direction, Joy Division ringing in my ears.

47

I drove out of town, up Rochdale Road towards North Manchester General. I was feeling fuzzy and struggled to keep my arms from shaking as I gripped the wheel. The clock on the dash said 09:32. I knew that parking could be a pain in the arse down there and just hoped I'd make it in time. I knew I wasn't really needed, and Laura would probably be there already, but I felt Sara needed all the support she could get. If they were gonna section her - and I had no reason to believe that they wouldn't, she'd tried to kill herself after all - I wanted to be there to fight her corner. Besides, I wanted to hear what she had to say for herself. And I needed to find out more about her past - and Angel's - if I was to get anywhere.

Felt like I was up shit creek without a paddle. Mentally swimming against an unstoppable tide. The jigsaw was slowly piecing together, except I had no clue who was responsible for her death. It scared me, not knowing. I needed more to go on. I'd already been spiked, then beaten up. Had to wonder if I was next.

I took a shortcut down beside the woods and an industrial estate, up around the back entrance. Had to put the wipers on full as the rain came down hard and cold. Found my way up through the winding Victorian back road, the looming edifice of the old infirmary darkening my route like some old workhouse. Put a chill down my spine. Found a parking space in the shadow of a giant oak and sat for a moment while I got my shit together. Looked at myself in the rear-view mirror. Looked as bad as I felt, like I'd been run over. My cheekbones were coming out in jaundiced yellow bruises and my eyes were bloodshot. Felt like I'd just been dug up.

I left the car and walked around to the main entrance, trying to get Laura on the phone. No answer. I checked at reception and spoke to the same woman I'd spoken to the last time. She checked her computer and pointed me down the corridor to the same ward. I wondered if Sara would be awake this time. I guessed she'd have to be. Hoped I'd catch another view of Nurse Simister. I needed something to brighten my mood.

Weaved through the traffic on the corridor and found the ward. Sara was sitting up in bed, her wrists still bandaged, hospital gown dangling off her like a funeral veil. She looked about ten years older. I suppose doing something like this would age a person overnight. Laura was sitting beside her drinking one of those shit coffees from a paper cup.

'Jesus,' Sara said. 'What happened?'

'Could say the same about you, love. It's nothing to worry yourself over. How are you feeling?'

She looked down, ashamed, and held her arms up. 'I feel stupid.'

'Well, you're not,' I said, though I was thinking the exact opposite. Given her circumstances, though, I couldn't blame her. But I never had her down for this. Did she really mean it or was it just a cry for help? 'You could've spoken to us. We would've got you some help.'

Her sister was nodding. 'He's right.'

'I don't know what came over me, I just... I just lost it.'

And then the tears came. I went to reach out, but Laura shook her head and hugged her tight, kissed her hair. She gave me a look, and I knew she wanted to be alone with her sister for a moment before the Doc turned up. I suggested I get us a brew and made myself scarce. I got the feeling that Sara was a bit spaced out. They'd doped her up on something.

Found my way back to WRVS and got three teas off a woman with a blue rinse. Got some funny looks too. I put it down to the bandage on my head. I must've looked like Mr. Bump.

When I got back, there was a middle-aged bloke in a suit sitting on the edge of the bed. I approached warily, assuming he was the shrink, and placed the teas down on the side. He asked who I was and I told him I was a concerned friend. He had an inch thick file on his lap with Sara's name on it. Tried to get a glimpse of what it said, but he kept his cards close to his chest. I glanced at Laura and she looked back at the Doc, Dr. Jefferson, according to the ID draped around his neck. Sara looked like she'd just seen a ghost, her face as pale as the walls as she knitted her fingers.

'When did you stop taking your medication, Sara?'

Medication? Exactly what kind of medication?

'I can't remember, about six weeks ago, I think.'

'That long?'

'I'm sorry, I just... they don't agree with me. Make me feel worse somehow.'

He was nodding. 'The thing is, Sara, you've been stable on them for a long, long time. And after you stop, you deteriorate. We've been here before, haven't we?'

'I'm sorry.'

'If you take your meds, you can live pretty safely and normally in the community. You're able to live with your illness and function very well.'

Illness? What kind of illness?

'I know, it's just... well, it's hard. You know. They're always there.'

'The voices?'

'Yes.'

He was nodding again. 'But when you stop your medication, they get worse, yes?'

'Yes. Please, Doctor, I'll start taking them again. I promise I won't do this again, I promise.'

'Well, I'm glad you've decided that, Sara. I really am. But I would like to keep you in for a little while so we can stabilise you again.'

'How long is a little while?' Laura said.

That's what I wanted to know, too. I was aware of sobbing beside me and took Sara's hand.

The Doctor sighed. 'This is not something we take lightly, believe me. And I wouldn't be doing my job if I allowed Sara home just yet.'

'Are you sectioning her?'

'I would like to, yes. And I know this isn't easy to hear, but it really is in her best interests, in my professional opinion. I'd like to come back sometime later with a Duty Social Worker and have the papers drawn up. In the meantime, I must find her a bed.'

'How long?' Sara said. 'How fucking long?'

'Section 2, Sara. Twenty-Eight days. After that, we'll

review you and decide whether you're fit for discharge. Which I expect you will be.'

'She can't be in this shithole for Christmas,' Laura said. 'What about her son?'

'We'll do our best to get her mental health up to scratch, I promise. Bur for now, I really must act on my judgement as her psychiatrist. I can't allow her to put herself at risk any further.'

Psychiatrist, illness, meds. Voices. Wondered just how bad Sara's condition was. Gotta admit, it scared the shit out of me.

'Okay,' Laura said, wiping her eyes. 'If you think this is the right thing.'

'I think it is, and I know this is difficult for everyone, but it'll be more difficult if I allow her to leave and she relapses again. You've seen how much of a danger to herself she's become. This is absolutely the right thing. I'll be in touch.' He nodded at me too. 'And Sara. Sara, listen to me.'

'I don't want to fucking listen.'

'I'll be back later this afternoon with another doctor and a social worker. We'll have this under control soon enough.'

I hoped so. For her sake, I hoped so.

48

We stayed with Sara a while, but given what she'd just heard I didn't feel it was an appropriate time to be asking her about her past or Angel's. She didn't ask me anything about what I'd dug up so far, and I wasn't about to fill her in on the details. After what Dr. Jefferson had said–about her meds, about the voices–I was sure that telling her about the immigrant dancing girls, the heroin Bo Wong appeared to be supplying, the police silence and even complicity, and the fact that I'd had my head kicked in wouldn't exactly help her mental state. If she really was that ill, and I guessed she was and had had an extensive history of it given the thickness of her file, Angel's death must have been the catalyst to send her over the edge. If the woman was living with delusions on a daily basis with her meds, how deluded had she been when I first met her, when she wasn't taking them? Was what she had to say–about anything–the truth? In short, could I believe a word she said?

It sent my head to bits, and I felt like it had been

smashed to a million pieces already. If I ever needed a drink, it was now. I had to get out. I told Laura I'd wait for her outside and kissed Sara on her pretty head. Said I would be back to visit, but she just looked away. I took one of the teas and made my way through the corridor, feeling bewildered and pissed off. Fuck's sake, this world. Does it ever get any better?

I passed Nurse Simister on the way out. She smiled, then disappeared into an office down the corridor. If only I'd been blessed with a different kind of life.

Sat on the same bloody bench again and sparked up. Looked out over the hustle and bustle of the entrance approach. Seemed like there were a million cars out there, all vying for the same parking spot. I watched patients on crutches and a bloke in a wheelchair with an oxygen mask on his face trying to light a fag. I'd really think about giving up if I were him. They just kept coming and going, patients and visitors, Doctors and Nurses, the frail, the weak, the young, the old. I suppose I was one of them too. Jesus. Was it any wonder people ended up like Sara? The world itself was fucking insane, and how anybody coped with it without something to cling on to was beyond me.

'Come on,' Laura said, suddenly appearing at my shoulder. 'I don't want to hang around here. Place gives me the creeps.'

I couldn't disagree. Laura's car was parked out on Delauney's Road. She said she wanted to talk, to tell me all about it over a brew.

'Meet you at the boathouse in the Clough? You know it?'

'I think so.'

'See you in twenty minutes. I'll get us breakfast. And what the hell happened to you?'

'I'll explain later.'

Drove back up Rochdale Road and took a left onto Charlestown. The rain had eased, but the pain in my head hadn't. I was feeling very drowsy suddenly and thought it might be best if I get my head down somewhere for a few hours. I swallowed two more painkillers dry and zoned out as I drove. Gunned it up the hill, the Punto choking all the way. When I pulled into the park, away from the traffic, the peace surrounded me. Didn't realise how much I needed it. Got a few funny looks off a couple of cyclists and a gang of women pushing prams. Was getting used to this now. Couldn't wait to get this bloody bandage off.

I found a space and walked up towards the lake and the boathouse. Got my head pecked by a gaggle of geese and one tried to bite my hand as I shooed it away. Sparked up again, looking out over the water, and waited for Laura. Didn't have to wait long.

She crept up behind me, smelling of bacon. 'Got us some breakfast. Cafe's open if you fancy a coffee?'

'Is it good coffee?'

'Doubt it for a quid.'

She linked me and I took a seat outside the boathouse while she went inside for the drinks. Sat down, feeling foggy, and tucked into the bacon butty. Didn't realise how starving I was and realised the fuzziness could also be down to lack of food as well as a kick to the skull. It tasted good, but she'd made the mistake of putting ketchup on it instead of HP.

'So,' she said, sitting down. 'You first.'

I raised my eyebrows.

'Hate to point out the obvious, but you've got a big bloody bandage on your head and you look like shit.'

'Thanks.'

'So what happened?'

Couldn't be arsed going over it, but I told her what I knew. That I'd got jumped and didn't have a clue who was responsible for my yellowing face. I left out my theories about who might have knocked my teeth out. Didn't want to worry her anymore than necessary and didn't expect her to be interested given her own circumstances and, more importantly, her sister's.

'Oh, God. Are you okay?'

'Bit of a headache, but I'll live.'

'And you've had stitches?'

I nodded. Took a bite out of the bacon butty. 'Twenty three.'

'Jesus. They should've kept you in. Especially with a head injury like that.'

'Doc said I was okay to go, but I do feel a bit stoned on these painkillers.'

'You should get some rest. You know, I don't think you've slept in that bed at Sara's yet. Why don't you go back, get a shower and some kip? It'll do you the world of good.'

Talk of Sara had changed the mood somewhat, and we were quiet for a moment as Laura ate her breakfast and I forced down the coffee. It tasted like mud, but at least it was hot. Was beginning to feel myself again now that the painkillers were kicking in. Thank God they were fast acting.

'So,' I said, knowing we had to have this conversation. 'What do you think?'

She sighed, put her butty down, looked out across the lake. A young mother went past pushing a pram. 'Like the shrink said, we've been here before.'

'How often? If you don't mind me asking?'

She smiled, touched my arm. 'Often enough. But this is the worst. No one saw it coming.'

'You didn't know she'd come off her meds?'

She shook her head. 'No. It usually takes a few weeks for her to deteriorate, but she seems to have hidden it well this time. The voices are always there, but without her meds they get worse. They tell her to do things. Command hallucinations, they call them.'

'What, like cut her own wrists?'

'Yeah. Take all your tablets, throw yourself in front of a bus, take your pick.'

'Has she ever done this before? You know, what the voices say?'

'She overdosed about two weeks after her eighteenth birthday,' she said. 'I was fifteen. Mum and Dad were away for the weekend and I brought my boyfriend back to the house, you know. I found her on the kitchen floor. When they finally stabilised her in hospital, we found out she'd taken a load of strong painkillers my dad kept for his sciatica with half a litre of vodka. All she could manage. They assessed her, and she was sectioned. It tore us all apart.'

'Fucking hell.'

'Yeah.' She sparked up and I joined her. 'That was the first time. That was a section two. It took them a while to diagnose her problem. She wasn't just depressed, and we all knew it. She was frightened to death. When we found out she was hearing voices and having these delusions - she'd think the radio and the telly was talking to her, and that the entire world was a puzzle she had to solve and that black angels were watching her every move - well, they said she had schizophrenia and put her on this really strong medication.'

'Antipsychotics?'

'Yeah. She stuck to them for a while, but then we found she was flushing them down the toilet. By then everyone realized she was getting ill again, except herself. When they took her back into hospital, they kept her in for nearly two years. That's when she met Angel.'

'What, when she came out?'

'No, Angel was in there too. They met on the ward. Angel had already been in for three years.'

'Jesus. Was she the same?'

'No. Not her. She was different. She had bi-polar disorder. Incredibly manic highs, thought she could do anything and everything all at once. And crushing lows.'

'Exactly how high are we talking?'

'She thought she was invincible, but she wasn't. She'd do crazy things. Full of these grandiose ideas, you know. She wanted to be an actress and believed she'd be a Hollywood superstar one day. She'd go around telling everyone she had a record deal, and that she was a model and stuff. Tried to set up a fashion business, even flew to Monaco and Paris and Milan.'

'How could she afford that?'

'She couldn't. She convinced the bank to borrow her thirty grand, then went partying until the money ran out. She even bought a fucking motorbike and had it painted up to look like a horse. Can you believe that? She couldn't even ride it. She ended up getting nicked when she tried to ride it down Kingsway in the wrong direction.'

'Fucking hell...'

'Yeah. But she was invincible, you see. She believed, and probably still did right up to the day she died, that nothing could touch her. She wasn't crazy, Jim. Just Ill.'

I thought about Angel and the week I'd spent with her

in Han Lan's apartment. There wasn't a great deal about her behaviour that raised suspicions, at least at the time. But then I remembered her coke habit and the crying in the bathroom. And her job, of course. How did she get into her line of work? I suppose believing you were invincible, that you were destined for greatness, could make a person vulnerable. Easily exploited. Question was, exactly who had exploited her and for what reasons? Han Lan? Carol? Bo Wong? Perhaps all three. One thing I did know: this whole thing just got that little bit more strange.

'You see,' she went on. 'They became friends. Great mates. I suppose they were mutually supportive of each other in some way, but we knew she was dangerous. A total loose cannon.'

'So how did this affect Sara?'

'It was good for her, at first. Angel came out of hospital long before Sara did, and she'd visit her every week, you know. Built a friendship, I suppose. And she was good for her, for a while. Then when Angel got manic again, she dragged Sara along with her. She hit the bottle to cope with the voices and stuff, and then that became a big problem. This was all in the nineties. A long time ago, really. When she got off the drink–which was no walk in the park, let me tell you–she saw less and less of Angel. I was glad. We all were. She kept in contact, though. I suppose she cared about her. Well, I knew she did. Still does. Well, not anymore, you know...'

'Did she ever tell you about what they did in the nineties? You know, any stories? Any incidents that come to mind?'

She gazed out across the lake and drank her coffee. By now, her bacon butty had gone cold. 'Well, I found out about Angel selling herself. Sara was quite open about that with me.'

'Was there ever... well, was there ever a time when Sara got involved in that?'

'What, prostitution? Nah. I can never be sure, I suppose, but... well, she was very guarded about herself. If I'd asked her, she wouldn't have told me. Especially if it was true. But by this time, she was well again. Very stable on the meds and she has been ever since. Until now.'

I nodded, took a final drag and stubbed it in the little foil ashtray between us. 'Why do you think she stopped taking them?'

She shrugged. 'Who knows? I only hope they can sort her out again. Because she'd been doing so well, Jim. Really well, living pretty much a normal life. She met a guy–Steve– and had Charlie. Amazing, for her. And he's a great kid. The relationship ended after a year, but she got a son from it and Steve's still involved. They get on. She's a good person. It's the illness that messes her up. That reminds me. I must get in touch with Steve. He can take Charlie off my hands for a bit and it'd be good for him to see his Dad.'

'Yeah,' I said, thinking about Nicole. 'It would. Good for Steve too, I expect.'

We were silent for a few moments. I thought about all Laura had told me, tried to visualise Angel and Sara together on that ward, and afterwards. I wondered what conversations they'd had, what went on behind closed doors when they were together. Laura got lost in her thoughts too, staring out across the lake, her head full of memories and 'what ifs'. Talking about all this must have been hard for her too.

'Sorry to ask about all this,' I said. 'I didn't mean to go on.'

'No, don't be daft. It helps. It's good. But I'm bloody freezing now.'

'You and me both.'

'Let's go. You need some sleep. You look terrible.'

I felt it. And I knew I could sleep for a thousand years.

49

I did sleep. I passed out on the bed in the back room about half an hour after getting in. I took two more of the painkillers with a shot of whisky and let myself fall into darkness as the rain battered the windows. Sara and Angel were flitting in and out of my head as I dozed and felt heavier and heavier. Then the madness came, weird shit, faces from the past as I raced away on a runaway train of dreams. Intense dreams, too. I woke up sweating, the light gone from the day, then turned over and went right back to sleep. Laura woke me around six. If she hadn't had done, I probably would've slept through the night.

'How's your head?'

'Seen better days,' I said, but I didn't actually feel too bad. It was my bloody shin that was murdering.

'Can I get you anything?'

She looked nice standing there in the doorway, but I put those thoughts away quickly. 'Could do with a drink.'

'Tea?'

'No.' I sat up. I was still dressed. I must've passed out

quickly. I checked the bruise on my shin. It was an ominous shade of purple. 'Maybe a vodka?'

'All gone, remember?'

Of course it was. Sara had poured everything down the sink. 'Whisky, then.'

She left me to come round. I sparked up and went over to the little desk in the corner. Han Lan's photocopied papers were sitting there and I had a quick look through, shaking my head in disbelief. This guy had it good. Too good, in fact. I wondered if he was responsible for supplying the heroin. Which got me thinking. How were they taking it? Injecting? If so, there'd be half of Chinatown with needle marks in their arms. Smoking? Seemed more likely. And if he was importing it, how the fuck was he getting past customs? Were they in on it too? It didn't make sense. And how long had this been going on? Bob had talked about secrets and lies and exclusive clubs. How exclusive were we talking? If the police knew about all this and had covered it up because they were complicit in it, how long had they been getting away with it? But what got me was the fact that Angel was dead, murdered in such a brutal fashion, and they didn't seem to have a clue about why. Or maybe they did. Maybe they knew exactly who'd killed her but had to keep it quiet because it would put them in the frame. The secrets, the lies. All of it. The rabbit hole goes deep, Bob had said. He wasn't fucking wrong.

Han Lan's paperwork was giving me a headache, so I went downstairs to find Laura making sandwiches in the kitchen. Charlie was sitting on the couch in his pyjamas.

'You need to eat. You've been sleeping all day. Roast beef do you?'

'Great.' Though I didn't feel like eating. I downed the whisky on the side.

'Doctor Jefferson called. They found her a bed. In Wythenshawe.'

'Wythenshawe?'

She nodded. 'No room at the inn at Park House.'

'Fuck. She gone over there, then?'

'They're taking her over tomorrow. She's gonna hate every minute.'

'I'm sure.' Our conversation from this morning came back to me then. Tried to imagine what Laura and her family had gone through over the years as Sara deteriorated, became someone else. It must've been terrible for her. And now she was reliving it all over again. Looked at little Charlie on the couch with his Spiderman toy. Obviously, the kid didn't know about his mum's illness. Perhaps one day he'd find out. 'What have you told Charlie?'

'The same. Nasty tummy bug. Don't know what I'm gonna do about visiting. Can't really take him with me, can I?'

'Not on the ward, I expect. Maybe they'll have a separate room.'

'Hope so.'

'So, is she gonna be in for a month?'

'That's what he said. Twenty-eight days. I don't think they'll let her out before then.'

'What about Christmas?'

'The section runs out the day before Christmas Eve. If she gets back on her feet before then, they could discharge her earlier. At least that's what I keep telling myself. It's up to her now. I don't believe she wanted to do any of this, Jim. So she has to get stabilised on her meds, then we'll see.'

'You sound like you really have been through this before.'

'Oh yeah.' She went to the fridge, cracked open a beer.

Handed me one. I liked how this girl operated. She took a long drink. 'I've seen it all with Sara. She'll get better. She always does.'

'The Angel situation sent her over the edge, didn't it?'

'You could say that, but she's always been close to it. If it hadn't have been Angel, it would've been something else. This day was always gonna come, to be honest with you.'

50

I got a shower and changed while Laura read a book to Charlie. When I came out, feeling better than when I went in, the kid was falling asleep in his Auntie Laura's arms. I went upstairs, changed clothes. Thought about taking a pair of scissors to the bandage on my head, but when I felt around the back, where the stitches were, it didn't bode well. I felt and looked like a complete twat. I had to do something to ease the embarrassment if I was to step out that door again. I had to keep on the case. Keep looking, keep asking questions, keep crawling down that rabbit hole, however deep it went.

Laura found me an old red woolly winter hat in the boot of her car. It was better than nothing. When I put it on, especially with my beard, I looked like a young Springsteen circa 1975. Laura said she quite liked it, and we shared a look for a moment before she went back to flicking through the channels on Sky.

'You going out?'

'Yeah, though I don't know where. I'd bring you along, but I suppose you've got your hands full.'

'Not sure I could be seen with a man in a red woolly hat.'

'Can't say I blame you.' I remembered Simon's iPhone and handed it to her. 'What do you make of this? Can you unlock it?'

'Where did you get this?'

I told her. She asked me how old Simon was. Said I hadn't a clue, but probably in his thirties. She nodded, played around with it. Asked me to wait a few minutes while she tried to figure it out. I grabbed us both another beer. Had a smoke and stepped around the living room. There was a photograph of Sara and Charlie on the mantelpiece. Must've been taken when he was just born. Couldn't have been more than a few days old. Sara looked good. Great, in fact. Looking at her, you wouldn't believe she had a mental illness. But I suppose that was the thing. It wasn't something you could see.

'There we go. Easy. Battery could do with charging, though.'

I turned. 'You've done it?'

'No worries.'

'Not just a pretty face, are you?'

'I try my best.'

She handed me the phone and gave me a few pointers on how to use the thing. I clicked on the message app and found a few hundred texts just waiting to be perused. Went into his contacts and found an extensive list of people. I quickly scrolled through, keeping an eye out for names that seemed familiar. Carol was in there. And Sherry. And the cream of the crop, Matt. He had a double-barreled surname. Matthew Brooks-Wilkes. What a twat. I pocketed it, intending to dig in properly later.

'So how did you do it?'

'Year of birth. That's what mine is. Just four digits and

hey presto. Nineteen eighty-six. Just remember that. The screen will lock itself after a few minutes.'

'You're a genius.'

She smiled. 'Thanks.'

'Looks like it's his bedtime,' I said, nodding to Charlie on the couch.

'Yeah, I'm gonna take him up soon. You back late?'

'I don't plan to be. Not after last night.'

'I'm not sure I'm happy about you going out like that.'

'Do I look that bad?'

'With your head injury. Just be careful, Jim. I don't like the way you were just jumped like that. Someone's obviously got their eye on you.'

'I'll be okay. I'll be careful.'

'Make sure you are. And phone me. I don't want to be up worrying all night.'

'I will.'

'You promise?'

'Of course. There's no need to worry. I'm a big boy.'

She smiled. 'I noticed. At least eat that sandwich before you go.'

51

I parked up four cars down on the opposite side from the house and waited. I just wanted to see, that was all. Hillroyd Road hadn't changed much since I was last here. The trees had grown, and one or two doors had gotten a lick of paint, but other than that, the same. The lamp-post beside me illuminated the Punto, and I had a good view. I was sure nobody would recognise me. It had been a long time, and I never had a beard like I did now. I reckoned I was pretty inconspicuous. I had a paper resting against the steering wheel and I pretended to be absorbed in the iPhone. And maybe I would be once I got started on the secrets lay hidden within it. But for now, I tried to look like I was waiting for someone. And I was. But they weren't expecting me.

Frank had a Ford Focus the last time I saw him. I could assume he still drove it, but it wasn't parked outside. Unless they'd gone out to Tesco or something. The usual. I don't recall them ever going out on a Tuesday evening. They were probably at home. The curtains were drawn and the glow from Maureen's favourite lamp—she was a lamp obsessive—

made the home look inviting. The lawn was immaculately trimmed, the rose bushes at the front pruned to perfection. She always was a keen gardener, though I suspect Frank took the burden of mowing. He usually made it a regular Saturday morning job, like washing his car and sweeping the front. Proud of their home. Protective, even. Protective of their daughter, too.

I wondered if Karen and my own daughter were home, Nicole doodling in her colouring book, Karen on the phone to a friend. Perhaps Maureen was busy in the kitchen with a homemade shepherd's pie and Frank was catching up with the news. A normal family home. A normal family routine.

I sparked up and let the window down. It was cold and there was a developing frost glinting on the pavements. Saw a bloke I didn't recognise walking a dog along the pavement on my side, wrapped up to beat back the wintry chill. He stopped a few yards away to let the Lab sniff around. I looked down at the phone, just a guy waiting in a car. He glanced at me as he passed, and I nodded.

I opened Simon's messages and scrolled through. He had e-mail too, and this was even better. And when I saw I could access his photographs, it was the cherry on top. There could be some serious evidence in here, and it was in my possession. It was the photographs I went to first. I sat and smoked while I scrolled through pictures of homemade curries and pasta, photos of people I didn't recognise and some that I did. Simon with the Chinese guy, Dang. Simon with Luke, the guy I'd hung over Han Lan's roof terrace wall. A few photographs from the night of Angel's birthday drinks. I stopped when I came to one of myself, standing in the corner with Sara. I had a bottle of Russian beer in my hand and I knew instantly the moment this was taken. I hadn't a clue I was in his sights, for whatever reason. Could all be innocent, but it just looked like a bloody surveillance pic. And I'd seen plenty of those. Scrolled on. Found several of Angel–with Carol, all smiles; with Matt, his hand clearly resting on her arse; with Dang, pulling faces. And here were three more. Simon and Bo Wong sitting in a booth at his dancing club. Simon and another Chinese guy I didn't recognise, laughing it up. A guy in leather bondage gear made up like Freddie Mercury or the bloke from the Village People.

Heard an engine roll up beside me and I turned to see an Audi pull into a space just beyond the house. It was a nice car, a brand new A6 in metallic silver. Nifty little beast. Must admit, I felt a pang of jealousy sat there in Sara's battered Punto. I watched as the engine died and the tail lights blinked out. The driver's door opened, and a smartly dressed guy got out. Sharp suit, expensive shoes, no doubt. Then the passenger door and Karen. Fucking Karen! She had a different haircut, looked slimmer. But it was her. I caught my breath and instinctively dropped down. Both doors clunked shut before they turned back towards Frank and Maureen's. Shit, it was really her. I hadn't seen her face in two years. I could barely remember the last time we shared a bed.

I watched as they stepped through the front garden path, arm in arm, his hand on the small of her back, her brown hair flowing and shimmering in the lamplit gloom. Watched her take a key from her purse, put it to the Yale lock. A turn, a click, the hallway light blinking on and Maureen there to greet my ex wife and her new man. There was a hug, a kiss, then Maureen's arms went to the guy's cheeks and the door shut the rest of the world out.

I sparked up. Thought about my daughter in there. It was the only place she could be. Wondered if she called the new guy 'Dad'. I waited, lost track of how long I was sitting there. Flicked my smoke out the window where it crashed in a miniature firework. Wound the window back up. Took the keys from the ignition, pulled the door handle and pushed it open. I stepped out into the cold night. Shut the door behind me. Gazed across at the house opposite.

Stepped off the curb and walked across the street. Felt the frost beneath my feet and the chill breeze nip around my ankles. My head felt like a bubble. My hands balled into fists. Gritted my teeth, flexed my jaw, put one foot in front of the other and reached the gate, unhooked it, stepped onto the path, let the gate swing open, felt ice forming on my fingertips, marched down the path and heard my shoes click clacking in the empty, silent street.

I reached the front door. The security light fixed to the wall blinked on and I stood there, expecting the curtain to twitch. I reached out, lifted the knocker and felt the cold bronze in my fingertips. Saw my breath fogging the air. They were behind that door. Karen, my daughter, Frank and Maureen.

The new guy.

I took a deep breath. Lifted the knocker higher.

And stopped.

Waited.

Tried to get my shit together.

The security light winked out, and I was in darkness again. I knew that now wasn't the time. But I would come back. I gently eased the knocker back to the door and let out a breath. Took a step back. Let out another breath and took another step back. Glanced at the window, just in case.

Then my phone went off in my pocket.

'Fuck.'

I nearly slipped on the path and went head first into

Maureen's rose bushes as it trilled, too close to their front door for my liking. I don't quite know how it happened, but I skipped and did a triple jump or something through the front gate and nearly slammed into the car parked outside. I ran across the street and quickly got in the Punto. Slammed it shut just as the lights came on and Frank appeared at the door, his breath fogging the air now that I'd left that space behind. I fumbled with the phone, couldn't find the hang-up button in the dark, and ended up sitting on it. I ducked down, just enough to peer my eyes over the bottom of the windscreen, the bloody gearstick digging into my ribs, the mobile vibrating up my arse.

'Frank,' I said, my breathing heavy, my heart heavier.

I watched as he turned right, then left, stepped out into the street and stood at the front gate, hands resting on his hips. Gazing deep into the darkness. He hadn't changed, maybe put on a bit of weight, still had the handlebar moustache like he was trapped in nineteen seventy-seven.

Saw his eyes fall upon the car. He took a step forward, thought better of it. He was standing there in his white shirt; the sleeves rolled up to his elbows. Scratched his head, sucked his teeth, then turned and went back inside. I allowed myself to rise a bit further now that his back was to the car and watched him step over the threshold. The vintage door clunked behind him and the hallway light went off.

Darkness again. Silence. The phone had stopped ringing, and I sat up behind the wheel. Went to light up another smoke and jumped when the text message beeped just as I pulled the phone from beneath me.

It was lit up in green. I didn't recognise the number. But I recognised the tone. I could almost smell the cigar smoke.

Can you meet me at 8:00? Midland Hotel. I'll be in the bar.

Midland Hotel? In this clobber?

I didn't need a second invitation. Messaged him back a quick response, then started her up. Wound the window down and let the cold hit me. Pulled out of Hillroyd Road, almost glad to see the back of it. Caught sight of their front door in the rear-view mirror, knowing that I would return another day, knowing that my daughter was in there, knowing that I would see their faces again.

My old life was a long way behind me, but oh so close. I gritted my teeth as I drove, blowing smoke out into the crystal air.

52

I parked her up at the NCP on Oxford Road and walked up towards St. Peter's Square. Central Library was lit up like a sparkling jewel, the new facade all clean lines and glass. A tram whispered past on its way to Altrincham before I crossed and stepped on towards The Midland Hotel. The grand, Edwardian Baroque red brick building was illuminated from top to bottom, clothed in regal opulence, decorated in Victorian grandeur. It was just the kind of place you might see Bob Turner hanging around.

I trod on, feeling somewhat out of place. Approached the main entrance, all marbled steps and red carpet. A handful of guests skipped down through the foyer with rolling cases, helped along the way by the Concierge, an old guy with silver sideburns and a top hat, like a mysterious magician in a heavy topcoat. I almost wanted him to dip into his inside pocket and reveal a rabbit, then point to the rabbit hole I was about to go down. The rabbit hole Bob had told me about.

I lingered on the edge of the front steps and sparked up. Checked the time on my mobile. I was five minutes early. I stood and watched the traffic, keeping one eye on the entrance for any sign of Bob. The evening clouds had cleared and I looked to the sky, saw Venus flickering high up. It crossed my mind that I wouldn't mind being on another planet entirely, away from the madness and the hurt and the pain. Would be nice to start afresh in a place where no one knew me and I didn't know them. I wondered how different my life would be if I'd never married Karen. Never met her, for that matter.

I scrolled through the e-mail on Simon's phone. Opened a lot of nonsense. Spam from credit agencies and clothing stores, paperless bills from his provider, random notifications from Facebook and Twitter, and some other social network I'd never heard of. Struggled to find anything incriminating in there. The guy had probably deleted most of the juicy stuff.

I moved into his text message folder, went to his inbox. There was too much here. A bit of mooching around told me he had over 240 messages. There was a lot to get through. The ones I found intriguing were the ones from Matthew Brooks-Wilkes, the guy I could only assume was Matt. Carol, too. There were a fair few in there from a guy–assumed it was a guy–calling himself 'Sun Yan'. Had to be Chinese, perhaps the bloke in the photograph I didn't recognise. Others. A lot of messages from 'Sean' and 'Carl'. Names I'd never heard from him. And I guess that, being a popular guy–and he was, I could see that from the moment I met him–he had a lot of friends. Maybe one or two of them were in high places too.

I put the phone away, reminding myself I would make time to study every message stored in there, including the ones he'd sent himself. Especially the ones he'd sent. My gut instinct told me there was stuff in here I'd find useful, but I needed to find a charger for it before the bloody thing died. Just remember nineteen eighty-six, Laura had said. It was embedded on my skull.

I fastened up the jacket as a north easterly whipped through the street. Han Lan's jacket. The chill was bitter, and it reminded me of that day when Angel dragged me back from certain death. I was reminded, once again, that I wouldn't even be standing here if it wasn't for her. I at least owed her justice.

Finished the smoke and crushed it under my boot, then headed up the stairs and into the main foyer. The Concierge smiled a greeting and led me towards a set of swing doors. I found myself in the grandest of halls, the outside chill gone in an instant and replaced by a pleasant warmth. I could hear jazz piano coming from a room beyond. I asked a member of staff–a smart-looking hotel porter–where the bar was, and he pointed me in the direction of the music.

Stepped into a well lit room, the pianist parked over in the corner playing a Baby Grand. The chords danced through the air and I set foot onto a plush carpet and headed towards the bar. I was aware of eyes upon me, and I guessed it must've been the Springsteen hat. I kept it on, knowing that what was beneath it was hardly becoming for the environment either. There were a lot of very well-dressed men in here, most of whom had a stunner on their arm except a few who were propping up the bar, a long and polished solid beech wood number. If he was in here, he was making himself hard to find. I stepped up, ordered myself a large house brandy, and looked around. My eyes fell on Bob just as I raised the warm brandy bowl to my lips. He was sitting in a leather booth over at the opposite end. Our eyes met and he beckoned me over.

'So what brings us here? Hardly a spit and sawdust place, is it?'

'I thought you'd like it. Music's great, isn't it?'

I couldn't deny it, though it hardly had the balls my mood required after this evening's events. 'You've got impeccable taste, Bob.'

'I like to think so.'

I grabbed a seat on the soft Chesterfield opposite and took a nip. I couldn't quite place his expression. 'So. Why drag me down here? You got news?'

'I wouldn't say news, as such. More gossip. And what've you got on your head? You'll draw attention to yourself.'

I pulled off the hat to reveal my bandage. 'Thought I looked much better with it covered up, you know.'

He nodded. 'Fair enough. How's the head?'

'Sore.'

'Been taking those painkillers?'

'Yeah. They're effective enough–for a while. I'm feeling a bit ropey now, though.' I took two more from my pocket and swallowed with a mouthful of the good stuff. 'Keeping me tired, as well. Not sure I'll last the distance tonight.'

'Good, because I haven't dragged you out for a session in a place like this. Not wise to be drinking on those things either, son.'

I knew he was right. 'So what's this gossip?'

He smiled, took a sip of bourbon loaded with ice and coke. 'Behind you. Don't look just yet. But over there, just beyond the piano, is a table full of ex coppers. Former Chief of GMP, Sir David Howe. His right-hand man, the former Assistant Chief Constable Phillip Browning; Bryn Llewellyn, former Chief of North Wales Police; and former Chief of West Yorkshire, Sir Michael Robert Fletcher.'

'Like pigs at the trough.'

'Very observant, Jim. But there's more. The Chinese guy they're with is Mr. Chen Longwei. Owns a couple of restaurants and is known to be good friends with...'

'Bo Wong?'

'You should put yourself forward for one of those teatime quiz shows, Jim.'

I took another drink. I wanted to turn and see for myself, waited for Bob to give me the nod.

'Go ahead. You and me are an irrelevance to those five men, son.'

I turned and watched them for a moment, once important men out on the town. A slap on the back here, a chink of crystal there. Waiter service with a tray of expensive red wine. I watched as they poured from two bottles and laughed it up. The night was theirs.

Turned back to Bob. 'So how did you find them?'

He leaned forward. 'Overheard the Concierge–Graham, likeable bloke, not at all what you'd expect in here, likes a pint in the Nag's on his night off–talking about Sir David Howe having a room. Joking about how when the cat's away and all that...'

'So you came in?'

'Slipped him a tenner and asked when he was checking in. He told me he was already here in the bar with a few other coppers. That's how he put it. So naturally, I bought the guy a drink and he sent me here.'

'He know you're a journalist?'

'Oh yeah. At least he knew I was once. Let's not forget I'm retired now, lad. What the hell would I want with a story?'

I sat back, took the weight off my feet. He asked me about Sara's assessment, and I told him the outcome. He also recommended I get some sleep and let my head wound rest. I told him that wasn't likely.

'Anyway. What about them?'

'Unusual to have so many coppers sat around a table with a Chinese restaurateur. Don't you think?'

'Coppers go for drinks all the time after duty. It's not unusual.'

'Maybe, but these are ex coppers, Jim. And high ranking too, not your average little arseholes. That bunch over there are nobility. Top brass, son. And I think you might remember what I said about the top brass.'

I did. Corrupt bastards, he'd said. I took another look. They certainly looked the type. 'So what do you think?'

He smiled. 'Well, on the face of it, they're just a bunch of blokes on a night out. But I've a feeling they won't be here for much longer once that wine's polished off.'

'Why so?'

'Chen Longwei, for a start. They'll either be heading to one of his restaurants or somewhere else entirely, if you get my drift.'

'You think they'll head to Bo Wong's?'

'It's not unlikely. They've been spotted in there before.'

I took it in. Whatever they had lined up for the evening, they certainly looked like they were looking forward to it. A spot of lap dancing, maybe, or something more. And given what Bob had said about the dancing girls in that place, I wouldn't put it past them if they thought they could get away with it.

'Would be the icing on the cake if Robertson was with them. You got anything on this lot? Anything you can't print?'

'There's a lot I can't put into print, son. But yeah. There are rumours. More than rumours, actually.'

'That they're involved in covering this thing up?'

'You could say that, yeah.'

'Evidence?'

'Enough of it.'

'Enough to stand up in court?'

'Now that's a dangerous game, Jim. All I'll say is that if you dig deep enough, the shit rises to the top. And there's a lot of shit.'

'Interesting analogy.'

'But it's true.' He took a sip of bourbon. 'It's dangerous shit, as well. But there's something else I want to tell you.'

'Go on.'

He reached into his pocket and pulled out a brown envelope, unsealed. He opened it up, took out the photograph and slid it across the table between us. 'This is Chi Phuong. She was found floating in the River Irwell back in two thousand and three. GMP investigated, of course, but it was recorded as inconclusive. A suicide, possibly. But the funny thing was...'

'She was one of Wong's girls.'

He nodded. 'So they say. Take a good look at her, son. They never found her next of kin, probably didn't even try. She was quickly forgotten about, even in Chinatown. Especially in Chinatown.'

'You think they might've put the shits up people? In case anyone wanted to speak out?'

'Who knows?'

'Seems likely to me.'

'Well then, you've just answered your own question, son.'

I took the photograph. She was pretty. Youngish looking. 'How old?'

'Reckon she was twenty-three.'

'Where did you get this?'

'Evening Chronicle stock photograph. It got me thinking. About your girl, Angel. I wondered if there had been any others, in recent years especially. Found in or near canals, I mean.'

'Were there any injuries on this girl?'

'We don't know. The police kept it all very quiet. As far as anyone knows, she was just found floating in the river. Fell in, they said. Accidental death. Which it could be. But there was at least one witness who came forward, confirmed she worked both at Wong's and a casino on George Street. Can you guess what happened to that witness?'

'Turned up dead?'

'As good as. Just days after going to the police to confirm Phuong's identity, she went missing. And she's not been seen since.'

'Fuck.'

'Exactly. And my guess is there'll be more. Missing girls, I mean. Strange disappearances. One minute they're there, the next–vanished into thin air. According to missing person reports, there have been nearly thirty women of East Asian origin disappeared since two thousand. So the question is: where are they?'

Shit, the rabbit hole did go deep. If I went any deeper, I'd be in danger of being buried alive. And I wasn't entirely certain I was thinking metaphorically either. How bad could this get? Was Angel just the latest in a long line? Was she killed because of what she knew? Undoubtedly. I was as certain of that as I was Sunday follows Saturday. All of a sudden, Matt became less of a suspect and the finger appeared to be pointing in Bo Wong's direction. Were the Triads involved? I knew Han Lan was all powerful. I wanted to know what Bob knew about him, other than the obvious.

I told him of his finances. He didn't look surprised, and if he was, he didn't show it.

'Mr. Big,' he said. 'You're not far wrong.'

'What do you know?'

'Not much. He's hardly ever in the same hemisphere, let alone the same country as you and I, son. But he's a very rich man, of that there is no doubt.'

'Is he the top man, you reckon?'

'Of what, exactly?'

'Gangs. Triads. They must have something to do with all of this. Women–East Asian women–don't go missing for no reason. You think that could be it?'

'It's a strong possibility. And even it is the Triads, GMP won't touch it. There are gangs, and there are gangs, Jim. Then there are the Triads. Not to be fucked with.'

'So they're basically a law unto themselves?'

'You're not wrong. Look, who knows who's responsible for Angel's murder. Could be anyone. But I agree, the finger most definitely points toward Chinatown and the secrets within it. My advice to you is to back off, son. Keep a very discreet distance, at least. I don't want to find out you're dead in tomorrow's paper.'

'I'll be okay.'

'I'm serious, Jim. This is no game, son. There are some serious hard cases about this city. You know that yourself, you don't need me to point out the obvious. So play the game.'

'You think that's what they do?' I nodded to the top brass behind us. 'Play the game?'

'Who holds the power in this city, Jim? Think about it. Her Majesty's police? Or the gangs?'

'You reckon there are backhanders? You know, to keep quiet?'

'I don't reckon it, son, I bloody well know it. Aye aye.'

I turned, saw Sir David Howe leave the table and head towards the back of the room. I got up to follow, just to get a closer look, just to get a feel for the corruption that walked among us. Bob reached out to stop me.

'Be discreet. You may have been a lowly DS once, but shit sticks, son.'

'He won't know me.'

'Maybe not, but just to be on the safe side, eh? Keep your distance, Jim.'

He took the photograph back as I left the table and weaved my way through the bar towards a set of double doors and a marbled area behind it. My boots clacked on the floor, and I pushed my way into the gents. They were spacious and polished, so clean you could eat your dinner off a toilet seat. Howe was having a piss in the urinal on the far left, and I took one a few places down. He was tall and thin, grey hair and smooth features. Well dressed, with a Rolex on his left wrist. Whistling, like a regular bloke in a good mood.

'God, that's better.' His voice echoed against the porcelain as his piss hit. 'Bloody cold out there, eh?'

'Could say that,' I said, trying to force one out. 'Be nice to get in bed with a good woman right about now. It's making me hungry, as well. Nice Chinese would go down a treat.'

He said nothing, pretended to laugh, shook the droplets off his dick. Zipped up. I watched him go over to the sink and wash his hands. He didn't hang around with the dryer. I was halfway through when he walked out and Bryn Llewellyn walked in. Said something about how they were leaving in ten minutes. Llewellyn sidled up at the urinal to my right. Fat, with baggy jowls and a grey goatee. Armani suit and a thick sovereign and gold bracelet on his wrist. He forced a fart out.

'Better out than in, that's what I always say,' he said, his thick Welsh accent booming through the room. 'That's a lovely hat you've got there, my friend.'

'Thanks.' Had to look away as he brought up a gob of green phlegm and spat it hard into the urinal. 'Off anywhere else tonight, then?'

'Oh, you know,' he said, zipping up. 'Just a few drinks with the lads and a Chinese. Nothing special.'

I nodded, zipped up myself and headed to the sink. 'Have a good one. I'm sure you will.'

'Right you are.' He made a half arsed effort of washing his hands, then left. He didn't know I'd be right behind him.

53

When I got back to my seat, Bob handed me a bottle of Heineken. I kept one eye on the copper's table and downed it when I saw they were all getting up and pulling overcoats on.

'Where are you going, Jim?'

'Where do you think? Following them.'

He sighed. Threw back the beer. 'Shit, Jim. Not on your own. I'm coming with you.'

'Oh no you're not.'

'Don't be silly. After what happened to you last night? No chance.'

'You're too old for any of this, Bob. You said so yourself.'

'Tough. If you don't let me come with you, I'll just follow you as you follow them.'

'I thought you valued your life. Grandkids and all that.'

He nodded, finished the beer. 'I do. But I've got nowt better to do, have I?'

'You could stay here, take in the ambience. Rumour has it Charlie Parker's up next. Be right up your street.'

'I'll give you Charlie bloody Parker. Come on,' he said, pointing at the coppers. 'They're leaving.'

He slung his own overcoat on and we stepped through the bar, careful to keep a casual twenty yards behind. They seemed keen on leaving the hotel pretty quickly. We followed them through the grand, marbled foyer, their laughter echoing off the mosaic walls.

'Nice and casual,' I said. 'We're just off to another bar, that's all.'

'You're looking at an expert, son. They used to call me the invisible man.'

'Yeah, well, you know how you're not welcome at GMP. I'm sure if you're spotted they'll think you're onto them. And they'd be right.'

'Nonsense, they won't have a bloody clue. Too busy thinking about what's in their pants than what's behind them.'

'Let's just keep it low key.'

They left through the swing doors and skipped down the steps, turning left onto Peter Street. We hung back, Bob casually checking his watch as they stepped out into the traffic and crossed over to Mount Street behind the Central Library. We guessed they were heading up to Chinatown via Albert Square and crossed to follow before they were out of sight. We got a move on.

'This is a good distance,' he said, his gaze fixed on the five of them up ahead. He stopped to light a Montecristo. 'What's the betting they'll cut up through the backstreets?'

'Nailed on.'

'You driving tonight?'

'Parked up at the NCP. You?'

'Same. So have you thought about what you'll do when they arrive at their destination?

'Don't know, maybe get a window seat in a nearby bar and watch the action.'

'You could be there all bloody night, depending on where they'll end up.'

'You get off, Bob. No point you tagging along, really.'

'You trying to get rid of me?'

I shook my head. 'You not got a wife to get home to?'

'Spend half my time trying to get away from the bloody woman. I'm in no rush.'

I sparked up as we walked on. The night was getting bloody cold, and I pulled the coat around me. When we reached Albert Square, the Christmas Markets were nearly built, but the Square was cordoned off. There were traders all over the place, bringing in stock and unpacking in the illuminated huts. The sound of electricity generators filled the air, along with the smell of frying onions and steam rising from food vans. A handful of workers in high visibility jackets huddled around in the cold drinking tea. A week from now the Square would be full of Christmas shoppers, half of them pissed up on German beer and bratwurst and mulled wine. Would be nice to drop in. I hadn't been to the markets since before I married Karen. It all felt such a long time ago.

We walked around the perimeter, keeping our eyes peeled on the five men in front. They seemed to be in a hurry. Then they stopped. I clocked the Assistant Chief Phillip Browning, face like a smacked arse, answer his mobile, beckoning to the others to wait while he dealt with the call. His head turned in our direction. The cunt was looking straight at us.

'Keep walking,' I said. 'We'll cross at the lights and head down towards Cross Street.'

'Shit, they know. Fucked this up, son.'

'We haven't. Just act normal. When we get to the corner, we split up. I'll shake your hand, then you head up Princess Street. It won't look obvious.'

'I'm not so sure, son. Look at the brass necked little shit. Who's on the phone, you reckon?'

'Not a clue,' I said, though I had my theories. Whoever had given me a good kicking was pretty high on the list. 'There's Sir David on his now, as well.'

'Bollocks.'

Which was just what I was thinking. 'Don't look at them.' We reached the crossing and waited for the little green man. 'Do me a favour. Take your phone out and pretend to answer it. We're gonna stop on the other side of the street while we wait for you to finish your call.'

'That'll make it bloody worse, son.'

I shook my head. 'It won't. We're just meeting up with that mate of ours, that's all. All normal, Bob.'

He took his phone out, pretended to answer. 'I feel like a right bloody twat. Look at me speaking into this sodding phone to no bloody soul.'

'That's good, Bob. Keep it up.' We crossed as the green man beeped and reached the other side. I stopped. 'Right, wait here.'

We stood there, Bob talking bollocks to nobody, taking in the view. I glanced across the street at the five men and smoked. Took my phone out to check the time. Nearly nine o'clock. It was still early. When I put it away, Bryn Llewellyn was pointing at me. Fuck's sake, this was all I needed. I turned to face Bob, flicked the smoke into the gutter, put my hands in my pockets, all casual. 'You ready?'

'Yeah.'

'Right, we walk to the corner, I shake your hand, you go up Princess Street.'

'So you said.'

'Let's walk.'

We walked. Bob went back to his Montecristo. When we reached the corner, we shook on it.

'Where shall I meet you?'

'Phone me in ten minutes. We'll take it from there.'

'Are we gonna lose them?'

'Not if I can help it. Okay, I'll see you later. Don't worry if you lose them, I'm on it.' I took a quick glance over his shoulder. They were crossing Princess Street. I'd bet any money they'd take a dark street beyond the lights. 'And they're off. Get yourself up to Chinatown. Wait by the arch.'

'I'll phone you in ten.'

I nodded, then turned towards Cross Street. I waited at another crossing and met Chen Longwei's eyes before they disappeared into the darkness. It was obvious we were following them, and I cursed that I'd let Bob tag along. Wondered who was on the phone to Browning and Howe. It begged the question if I was being followed myself. I looked around to see if there was anyone on my case. Perhaps I was being paranoid, a side effect of the bloody painkillers I was taking. But I wouldn't be surprised.

I walked down Cross Street for a while, keeping my eyes peeled for anyone lurking behind me. Cut through Chapel Walks and round the back of the high street banks before crossing Mosely Street and into Chinatown. The streets were dark and not very well lit. Wasn't sure if that was a help or a hindrance. I kept my pace regular, not wishing to seem too eager to get anywhere in case anyone was watching. A black Mercedes rolled up beside me and purred at a slow crawl, as if the driver was lost. Found it odd and kept on walking. I caught a glimpse of two darkened figures behind the privacy glass before it changed gear and moved off.

Could be anyone and anything, but it piqued my interest. I knew I had to be on my toes tonight.

I cut down beside the Art Gallery and into Chinatown, wondering if I'd glimpse the coppers. Strolled up George Street, in the glare of the neon, past restaurant fronts and health salons. The street wasn't busy, just a few people dotted around. Spotted the black Merc again as I made my way towards the arch. It was idling in a parking space, the rear taillights on, engine rumbling. Decided to drop into a food store I approached on the left. Kim's Thai Food was warm and inviting, the smell of Thai basil and galangal and incense circling through the air. There was an elderly Thai woman behind the counter, watching something loud and bizarre being beamed in from the other side of the world. She nodded as I smiled on entering, keeping one eye on whoever was behind me.

I browsed the aisles, picked up a bunch of coriander, peered into the freezer at the emperor prawns. Strolled round the back towards the noodles and the pastes. I was pretending to look at a jar of shrimp paste when a Chinese-looking guy in a sharp black suit walked in. He looked handy, with cheekbones like they'd been chiselled out of his face, like a young Bruce Lee. If he was half as hard as he was, I wouldn't have liked to be on the end of a roundhouse. Crossed my mind if we hadn't met already, back in Dalton Alley where my head got kicked in. He said something to the woman in Thai and started to do just what I was doing– pretending to shop. Our eyes met briefly. The guy didn't flinch. We both looked away together, and I put the jar down and moved on to the vegetables before quickly heading out through the steps, leaving him behind. I half expected another fist to the back of my head, but none came. I stepped out into the cold, the black Merc still turning over in the parking spot. Almost bumped into a guy wheeling a trolley of Coca-Cola bottles down the pavement.

I pressed on, picked up pace. Didn't like to think who could be sitting behind the wheel of that Merc. Didn't like to think Bruce Lee could be right behind me. Didn't like to think I could be bundled in the back any minute. I resisted the urge to look back, just put my head down and kept walking. When I looked up, I spotted the first appearance of Sir David Howe and Chen Longwei emerge from around the corner ahead. Shit, fuck, bollocks.

I dropped into a doorway on my left and pressed up against the wall. Hoped to fuck they hadn't walked this street as well. Would give the game away too much if I was spotted. Kept tight against the wall and took a peek as I heard several pairs of feet clopping on the concrete. They were heading away in the opposite direction, towards Faulkner Street was my guess. Just as well.

Then my phone trilled in my pocket. For fuck's sake. Had to be Bob. I pulled it out and answered.

'Where are you?'

'Hiding in a fucking doorway. They've just gone past. And there's a bloody Merc hanging about.'

'Black?'

'How do you know?'

'Been following me as well. Listen, I don't like the vibes here, son. Can you get here?'

'You at the arch?'

'Yeah.'

'Get over to Long Legs. I'll be there in two minutes.'

'Long Legs?'

'Long Legs. I can see the Merc from here and I reckon the driver's looking right at me as we speak. Not to mention Bruce bloody Lee.'

'You what?'

'Never mind. Just get the beers in. And act fucking normal.'

I hung up, stepped away from the doorway. Pulled the Springsteen hat over my brow and sparked up before marching towards Long Legs beyond the arch and garden. Had to make a sterling effort in not looking back. I must've lunged that smoke in fifteen seconds flat.

Inside, Bob was waiting for me at the bar, looking nervous. The place was quiet, with just a couple of punters lounging on a few tables against the wall. No music, just the sound of chinking glasses and muffled laughter. The carpet was sticky, with what I didn't want to know. The far wall was adorned with a blue neon model of a chick kicking her legs, can-can style. A haggard-looking woman in her mid-fifties handed Bob two bottles of Staropramen and a free bowl of salted peanuts. She said the dancers wouldn't be out until at least ten o'clock. Bob nodded, tried a smile, handed her a tenner and swung his beer back. I joined him. It tasted good, almost like relief. But I was keenly aware of what could be outside if the last half an hour was anything to go by. I kept one eye on the door and suggested we find a table nearby, just in case we needed to make a quick exit.

We sat down. Bob exhaled long and hard, looked me in the eye.

'So what now?'

I shrugged. 'You tell me.'

'What do you mean, 'you tell me'?'

'You brought me here, Bob.'

'I brought you to the Midland, son. It was your idea to follow them.'

'And it was your idea to come along. In fact, I think I remember telling you to go home to the wife.'

Another sigh. 'Yeah, well, I couldn't leave you on your own, could I?'

'It's a free country, Bob.'

'Why do I feel like I'm getting dragged into something I don't want to be involved in?'

'You're not getting dragged into anything. I just asked you to sniff around a bit, that's all. And you've come up with the goods. Four high ranking ex-coppers is good enough for me.'

'That kick to your head has really messed with your fucking sense, son. Do you have any idea of the shit we could be getting involved in?'

'Do you?'

'Oh, aye.' He took a long pull on the beer. I was beginning to think Bob was getting on edge. 'That bloody Merc has turned up on every sodding corner since I walked up here. Blacked-out windows, the lot.'

'It's putting the shits up you, isn't it?'

'Is it not putting the shits up yourself, son?'

I shrugged. 'Maybe.' But I was thinking something different. It was putting the shits up me all right. I glanced at the door, convinced there were a couple of Triads out there with a sword. Figured I had to keep Bob from freaking out before he gave the game away. Maybe we were both feeling paranoid. Kept telling myself it could all be nothing, just a result of the brandy and the painkillers, but I couldn't get Sir David Howe's face from my mind. Nor that fat cunt Bryn Llewellyn. Were they really watching us? And if they were, who was on the phone to them? Could it be Robertson? One of the Chinese? And who had seen fit to give me twenty-three stitches in the back of my head?

In short, who was out to fuck me up?

Bob jumped when the music kicked in. I didn't know

what it was, some R'n'B shite most probably, but it was loud. The door opened, and a group of blokes walked in. Tuesday nights weren't known for their stag parties and I'd be surprised if the place got more than a hundred in, especially on a bitter night like tonight. They couldn't have been older than twenty-one, giggling like a gang of hyenas round a kill. Saw Bob roll his eyes and he said something, but I couldn't hear him over the music.

'What's that?'

'I said 'Let's go'.'

I looked at him, took a long drink. 'To where, exactly?'

'There's a restaurant on Faulkner Street I know. We'll grab some Dim Sum and a few more beers. Away from the goggle-eyed masses.'

'Steady on, the women will be out any minute at this rate.'

'You think it might've gone?'

'What, the Merc?'

He nodded.

'Don't know. But what's the worst that can happen?'

He was slumped in the chair, fidgeting with a Montecristo. 'I'm going for a piss. Wait here and don't leave before I'm back.'

I gave him a salute and drained the beer, resisting the urge to grab another. The door opened as I was watching the bar and I turned to see three Chinese walk in, two in suits flanked by one in regular jeans and shirt. The kid was obviously younger than the others suited up, but he looked hard as nails, like he could handle himself in a big way. They stepped up to the bar and ordered. Clocked one of them, a suited up guy who looked mid forties, clocking me. There was a fag sticking out of his mouth like he didn't give two fucks. I looked away and swallowed, just minding my own business. Peered from the corner of my eye and knew they were watching me. Took a breath and willed Bob to hurry up before it went pear shaped.

Saw him coming back looking sheepish, and I said we were going before he sat down. He didn't argue, just gave me a look. I knew he'd clocked them too. We left the table and didn't look back as we exited.

'That Dim Sum doesn't sound too appetising now you mention it.'

He didn't reply, just kept his head down and picked up pace. He'd gone pale, the colour of lumpy porridge. I could understand why. I didn't want to take a glance back, didn't want to turn and see all three of them standing there, but I turned anyway. There was no one. From here I could see that the Merc had gone too. Were they the ones occupying it? It was impossible to know. The blacked out glass was so dark you could barely see a shadow inside.

'This is getting silly,' he said. 'Why the hell I even agreed to any of this, I don't know.'

'Bob, none of this is your fault.'

'I know it isn't.'

'Look, I don't know who they are. I'm just as freaked out as you are.'

'You think it's got anything to do with the coppers?'

'Probably. Though we could just be being paranoid, Bob.'

'I'm not being paranoid, son, I know I'm being watched.'

'They'll be much more interested in me.'

He just shook his head as we walked and lit up his cigar. There was no sign of the Merc still, but no sign of the coppers either. I could only assume they were in Wong's. I wanted to be sure.

'Bob, I want to be clear they're in there. The coppers. What's this restaurant you mentioned?'

'Oh no. I've had enough of this. I'm going home.'

I stopped him. He dragged hard on the cigar. The chill wind whipped around us, and he turned his head skyward and sighed.

'It's cold,' I said. 'Come on, let's get something to eat. Warm us up. And anyway, we'll be safer in a public place like a restaurant.'

'I don't know.'

'Can I not tempt you with some hot and sour soup? It's fucking freezing here.'

'You'll end up getting me in trouble, Jim.'

'Just come with me, Bob. Window seat if possible. I want to be able to see who's out in the street. Then you can go. I'll walk back to the NCP with you.'

He sighed. 'Fuck's sake, Jim. One hour, that's it. Understood?'

We made our way to Faulkner Street again. Bob kept looking over his shoulder. He was definitely fidgety and had good reason to be, I suppose. I knew how he felt. The night was crisp with frost. I could almost taste it in the air. Nights like this out on the streets were never good. I'd known men who had lost their lives through it. The burn of paint stripper cider or, if you were lucky, a decent vodka or whisky or rum, would help take the pain and the cold away. If you were lucky. There wasn't much of that among the nation's homeless. I knew it was becoming an epidemic. It was a fucking disgrace.

I felt a pang of hunger as we walked, which was odd for me. I'd had a roast beef sandwich earlier that Laura had made, but I was beginning to think I could really put some food away. It would be a good thing for me, no doubt. I knew it was the cold. I'd been doing a lot of walking too. My body ached, and my head hurt. I'd much rather be in bed with a shot of brandy on the bedside table. A good woman beside me would be even better.

I thought of Karen then. Karen and her new man. Her new man and my daughter.

'Here we go,' he said. 'Up the steps.'

It was warm inside and busy enough. A young Chinese girl ushered us in with two menus. Bob asked for a window table. She kindly obliged. We sat in silence for a moment and perused the menu. I ordered us two beers and kept my eye on outside. About thirty yards away, Bo Wong's dancing club lay above a restaurant at the other end. From this vantage point, I would be able to see the coppers across the other side of the street. If they rolled out, that is. For all I knew, they could have plans to stay in there all night. Wouldn't surprise me, given what Bob had said they'd gone in there for. Sex on a plate with Asian women high on heroin would be a walk in the park. Especially if they knew they were untouchable. Of course they were. They were the fucking law.

Bob was a nervous wreck. Food was the last thing on his mind, but when it came–mixed Dim Sum, hot n sour soup and a couple of special curries–he seemed to forget the evening's events pretty quickly. The food was wonderful and I got stuck in too. I was surprised at how hungry I was. Dropped a few painkillers when my head started throbbing. We knocked back three beers each during the dinner and the alcohol helped take Bob's mind off things. For a while, at least. But then the Merc pulled up outside Wong's place, and the three men we'd seen earlier in Long Legs stepped out. They went up the stairs in single file, one of the suits with a mobile pressed to his ear.

'What do you think?'

'I think we should get the fuck out of here.'

'You go. I'm gonna hang around. See what I can find.'

'I don't think that's wise, son. You've seen them tonight. It's as if that bloody Merc's never left your side–or mine. I've had enough of it, lad.'

'I'm hardly over the moon about it myself.' I asked the little waitress from earlier for the bill and Bob dug into his raincoat for his wallet and handed me fifty quid. 'Being followed, that is.'

'I'm glad to hear it. That kick to the head really has affected your senses. You know what I think, Jim.'

'Leave it?'

'Leave it,' he nodded. 'Go home, get some sleep.'

'I haven't got a home, Bob. You know that.'

'Yeah, but you're shacked up with that Laura woman, aren't you?'

'Hardly shacked up. It's not as if I'm giving her one, Bob. She's just putting me up in her sister's gaff–the one who's cut her wrists, by the way, because of Angel turning up dead– while I investigate what happened.'

'But the investigation is getting beyond your control, Jim. It's not just one dead girl, it's potentially many. And you don't know who's responsible.'

'That's what I've got to find out, Bob.'

'But you're going down a rabbit hole that's gonna give you nothing but pain, son. Trust me on this.'

'But after what you've told me, Bob–fuck's sake, I can't ignore that.'

'Well, you bloody should. Christ, lad. Are you not listening to me? You're putting your own life at risk. You think they'd give two fucks about putting a bullet in the back of your head?'

'Yeah, well, it's not as if I've got much to live for, anyway.'

'You what?'

'You heard, Bob. I'm serious. Look at me, for fuck's sake! I'm a loser. Wife's fucked off with another bloke and took my kid with her.'

'Oh, you don't know that.'

'Don't I? I saw them before.'

'You what, son?'

'Went round there, didn't I? To the in laws. *Ex* in laws.'

'And?'

'She was there.' The waitress came back with the bill, and Bob examined it. 'With another bloke. Flash car, sharp suit.'

'Are you sure it was her, son?'

'It was her, Bob. My wife. *Ex* wife. So anyway, that's it. That's what I'm saying. I couldn't give a shit if they put a bullet in my head. Because I've got fuck all as it is. Frankly, they'd be doing me a favour.'

'You really have got a death wish, haven't you?'

'You try being me. Kicked off the force, life going backwards. I mean, what the fuck am I gonna do?'

'What you're doing now. Private Investigator, Jim. But steer clear of cases like this. Do yourself a favour and get bogged down in insurance claims and shit like that. Spying on cheating husbands or something. But stay away from the fucking coppers, Jim. And the Triads. Because you don't know what you're getting yourself involved in.'

'I can imagine.'

'You can imagine nowt. Remember that. Now I believe you said you'd escort me to the bloody car park, lad. Am I right?'

It was my turn to sigh. It was going out of my way. I wanted to get closer to the action, see if I could dig up anything about Matt. And I wanted to keep a close eye on Wong's. The restaurant was a good vantage point. 'Are you sure you really need me?'

'What if they jump me like they jumped you, son? The difference is I'd be fucked.'

I grabbed my jacket from the coat stand and slung it on. 'Come on then, Grandad.'

'You'd do well to follow my example.'

'Not just yet.' We nodded at the waitress as we left the warmth. The cold hit us like a ten tonne truck. Christ, it was freezing. I sparked up on the steps. 'I want to hang around a bit longer. See what I can pick up.'

'Well, you're a bloody fool. It's freezing, for one thing. You'll die of hypo-bloody-thermia if you don't get that bullet in the back of your head. And you're really in no fit state to be carrying out surveillance, anyway. You look a bloody mess.'

'Cheers.'

'It's the truth.'

Bob sparked up a Montecristo as we walked. It was only five minutes to Oxford Road and, from there, a four hundred yard dash to the NCP. He was still anxious about being followed. He kept looking behind us. And when we reached the lights at St. Peter's Square, just opposite the Metrolink and the Library, the Merc crept up beside us again. We stood at the crossing, waiting for the green man, and we both knew there were four pairs of eyes on us. We finally crossed as it hit green. Told Bob not to panic as we reached the opposite side and headed left. There was a McDonald's up ahead and I briefly thought about ducking into it if there was any sign of a Chinese on my case. I realised as we walked that the four ex-coppers, or even Chen Longwei, had arranged this. Just drive around and put the shits up them. Maybe something like that. At least that's what I was telling myself.

'What did I tell you,' he said. 'Now do you think it's such a good idea to hang around that place?'

'If I'm gonna find out who killed her, yeah.'

'Why would you even care? I mean, it's not like you even knew her, is it?'

He was both right and wrong. I knew her, even intimately, but I didn't *know* her. I had to remind myself of that fact. I didn't know her at all.

'I feel a responsibility to Sara,' I said. 'An obligation. She's putting me up, I'm finding out what happened. That's the deal we have.'

'Except now she's on a mental health ward. How do you even know she's telling you the truth about anything?'

'Believe me, it has crossed my mind. But she's not a liar, Bob. At least I don't believe that she is. She's just ill. She's in enough of a bad place after her best mate's death. If I tell her I'm pulling out of the case, what do you think that'll do to her? I might as well sign her fucking death certificate.'

'You're a bloody drama queen, Jim.'

'*I'm* a drama queen? Bloody hell, Bob, you're the one who's spent the last two hours convinced we'll both be murdered in cold blood with a bloody Samurai sword.'

'Don't joke about this, son. Not if you really want it to bite you on the arse.'

'Listen.' I made him stop, just as we reached the McDonald's. The NCP was barely a stone's throw away on Great Bridgewater Street. I looked back and saw the Merc was gone again, heading in the opposite direction down Peter Street. It was probably going around in circles. 'I can handle this. I'm a copper, Bob.'

'Ex copper, son. And God knows how many times I've had to remind you of the fact.'

'Ex copper, granted. Which means I've seen this kind of thing before. Intimidation, Bob. I've got friends on the force too.'

'You've got nothing of the sort, lad. And you know it. That's what worries me.'

'What's the worst that can happen?'

'You find yourself in a fucking ditch by midnight tonight with a bullet in your head.'

'And you call me a drama queen...'

'I'm not joking, lad.'

'Me neither. I've got a job to do. And I intend to do it.'

'Even at the expense of your own life?'

'It won't come to that.'

'You don't know that.'

'I can handle myself, Bob.'

He laughed. 'Yeah, looks like it. Are you forgetting about your beating? Next time, they won't lay off. That was your warning, Jim.'

'You sound like you know who was responsible.'

'I know nothing of the sort.'

I attempted a reassuring smile. 'Look, I'll be careful. Okay, you're right, I should probably go and get some sleep and rest and sort my bloody head out. But I can't. Not while the chase is fresh. I smell blood.'

'You'll be smelling more where that came from,' he said 'if you don't ease off. At least for a few days. Let things die down. I don't want them thinking I'm onto them.'

'Okay, I promise I'll ease off for a few days, but only after tonight.'

'And what do you think you're gonna achieve tonight, son?'

I shrugged. Maybe nothing. Perhaps he was right. Perhaps I was wasting my time after all, chasing bent coppers down blind alleys instead of finding out who killed Angel. 'I just want to hang around for a while. See what turns up.'

He nodded, took a drag on his cigar before pointing the burning end at my chest. 'Fine.' He blew smoke into the cold night. 'But stay out of trouble, son. First sign of it, you get out of there. You understand?'

I nodded, told him I understood, and watched him turn towards the NCP. Then I turned around, sparked up, and walked back to Chinatown.

54

I found a bar hidden away down a side street, just around the corner from Wong's place. It was even better than I thought it would be, because from the little stool by the window I could see the comings and goings even more clearly. I was close enough to the door to nip out for a smoke and still be quite well hidden away in the shadows. It was a weird place. They sold noodle dishes and bottles of Japanese beer. And that was it. I guessed it was a Japanese gaff. You wouldn't even know it existed, even if you passed it. It looked like a health food shop from the outside. I got some funny looks when I stepped in. It was quiet, with some trashy psyche-pop or some such shite filtering through the speakers behind the bar. A well spoken Japanese kid served me a bottle of Asahi and a complimentary bowl of Wasabi peas. Gotta admit, I liked the place.

I took out Simon's iPhone and realised that, when there was no action on the screen, the battery had finally died. I made a mental note to get a charger for it tomorrow. I knew I needed to delve deep into what treasures the phone had to offer. I would do it soon. Instead, I took my own mobile out and dialled Laura's number. She answered on the third ring.

'Jim? Is that you?'

'It's me. Listen, I'm in a bar in Chinatown. Everything's okay, I'm just having a beer and keeping one eye on some things. I'll be back in around an hour. Everything all right there?'

'Yeah. I phoned the ward earlier. Sara's in bed. They'll have her back on her meds and she'll need close monitoring. Otherwise, they reckon she's doing okay.'

I suppose it was good news. 'And what about yourself? And Charlie?'

'He's fast asleep and I'm on the couch with a bottle of red. Watching Strictly. I swear to God, it's like Bruce bloody Forsyth's been re-animated or something.'

'Sounds like you're having fun...'

'Not really. There's nothing on telly and it's boring being on my own all the time. I'll be glad when you're back. How's the head?'

'I'll survive.'

'Yeah, well make sure you do, eh? Just be careful out there tonight. You should be back here, in bed. You been taking the painkillers?'

'Religiously.'

'Well, lay off the drink, then. It can't be doing you much good.'

Not from where I was sitting, I thought. 'I will. I'll be back soon, anyway. Just want to see if I can spot someone, that's all. Then I'll head back.'

'Just how much have you had to drink?'

'Not much. Couple of bottles.'

'You shouldn't be driving. Be careful, Jim.'

'I will, I promise. Look, I've gotta go. But I could do with your help on something tomorrow. That okay?'

'I'm planning on visiting Sara.'

'It's all right, it won't take long. We'll talk about it later.'

'Hmmm, okay. And be careful.'

'You've said that already.'

'That's because I want to drill it into your daft head.'

'I'll catch you later.'

'Bye.'

I hung up, took a long drink and kept my eye on the restaurant below Wong's. More importantly, on the side door that led to the stairs and his club above. I could picture them in there–Howe, Llewellyn, Browning and Fletcher. Perhaps others too. Getting giddy on Asian dancing girls. Arranging a private room for a half hour stint. Swilling brandy like it was tea as the whores smoked their smack and they all got their kicks dirty style. What I wouldn't do for a camera right now. I decided to come back with one on another night. Maybe next Tuesday, if this affair was anything to go by. If it was a regular thing, I guessed it wouldn't be long before they were back again.

I thought about asking the barman if he'd seen anything dodgy going on. Decided against it. There was probably something dodgy going on every night. I suspected it wasn't unusual around here. He placed another bowl of Wasabi peas in front of me and I waved the near empty bottle of Asahi. He brought back another one and I handed him a fiver.

And then there was movement. It came from the restaurant. Two faces I recognised. Bryn Llewellyn and the former Chief of West Yorkshire, Sir Michael Robert Fletcher. They'd stepped out onto the street so that Llewellyn could smoke. Both were laughing their tits off. Fletcher took out his mobile and put it to his ear. I wondered who he was calling. Watched Llewellyn pace up and down, a big grin plastered across his chops. Fletcher was laughing down the phone. Llewellyn was hanging on every word. When he finished the call, they shared a joke before Fletcher went back inside, leaving the Welshman alone on the street. I would've liked nothing more than to go over there and ask him some serious questions, but I knew it wasn't the right time. There was no sign of the other coppers. I guessed they'd be upstairs in Wong's having some Asian flesh dancing around them.

Llewellyn stubbed out his cigar on the wall, and then Fletcher returned to the street with another man. The Chinese guy with the cigarette at the bar in Long Legs. Together, they went to the little side door beside the restaurant and I watched as they made their way upstairs until they were out of view. I took a long drink and checked the time on my phone. It was coming up to quarter to eleven. I would have to make this my last one.

I sat and watched the street for another half hour, biding my time, going over the events of the evening. Seeing Karen with another man had hurt big time. It was surreal seeing her. And her father. Now that I'd broken down that wall I'd been building up, it was high time I made an appearance. Preferably when I was sober. Maybe Bob was right. I should probably back off for a few days, drift away from the scene like a ghost. Maybe try to put things right with Karen and her folks. Try to see my kid. I knew that was my priority, not chasing coppers down blind alleys. But something was afoot, and I knew it.

As I was draining the beer, a silver BMW SUV pulled up outside the restaurant. It sat idle for a minute or two and I kept my eyes peeled. This could be interesting. I could see there were two figures inside, but the glass was tinted like the Merc. Looked like they were waiting for something or someone, and it was confirmed a few short minutes later when another Chinese guy emerged from the restaurant and approached the passenger door. There was a brief conversation before the door opened, and out stepped Phil Young. They shook hands. Phil was smartly dressed in an expensive grey suit. Seemed like all the coppers got their glad rags on when they turned up for a session at Bo Wong's. Fuck's sake, Phil. The man had changed. I watched as they made their way upstairs and the BMW pulled away from the kerb and sped off away from Chinatown. My time here was done.

The Japanese barman asked if I wanted another, and I reluctantly declined. I needed to get back to Laura, but I could think of nothing else other than what was going on up those stairs. I never had Phil down for any of this. Just shows how wrong I could be about the man I once called a mate. It was a strange world, with rabbit holes everywhere. And it was getting deeper and deeper and deeper. They clearly wanted me out of the picture. Bob was right. I should listen to him more. I felt the stitches at my head beneath the Springsteen hat. I was still none the wiser about who had given me a kicking, but I had my suspects. Question was: now that they knew I wasn't hurt as bad as they thought, when was the next hit likely to happen? And from whom?

I left the bar quickly and returned to the cold of the night. I kept my head down as I walked back to the NCP. I was tired, but I didn't expect to get any sleep.

55

The NCP was deathly quiet. I took the lift to the third floor and stepped out onto the platform where I'd left the Punto. There were very few cars parked up, and I almost wondered if I was on the right level. Took a moment to get my bearings. Everything looked the same. I walked beneath the dark, low ceiling, past empty parking bays, keen to keep an eye out for anything untoward. Heard an engine roar into life from somewhere on the level above. Heard it shift up a gear as I walked on, then saw the headlights swerve into view from around the ramp at the far end. There was something familiar about that engine. Something I didn't like.

The car turned and headed towards me, its lights on full beam. Felt like a rabbit in the headlights, all right. I shielded my eyes and ducked back into the shadows beneath a giant red number 3. The Merc shot past before coming to a screeching halt about twenty yards away.

I ran out into the main concourse as it went into reverse and burned rubber. I didn't bother looking back as it screeched behind me and swerved round to face me. I fucking ran and ran, ducked to my right down a ramp and kept on running. Shit, this was all I needed. I sprinted across the concrete of level two, trying to make a split second decision about what my next move would be as it thrummed and roared from somewhere behind me. I nipped in behind a Volvo and swung around down the inner edge of the wall. The Merc swept past before screeching to a halt again somewhere up ahead.

I stopped. Frozen and out of breath. If this was it, if this was my end, how fucking ironic it was considering I nearly threw myself off a bloody car park just a few short weeks ago. It sat there and purred, taunting me. I figured if it tried to ram me, the Volvo would stand in its way and I might, just might, get a chance of finding another escape route. I looked up, left, right, all around. There was no way out. Level two filled up with exhaust fumes and the devilish red glow from the taillights illuminated my certain death.

It rolled backward, then trained its headlights on my face until I was blinded. Fuck, this was it. I couldn't move, I was trapped. Those seconds seemed to last a lifetime until I heard another engine roll its way onto this level and then I saw it come almost face to face with the Merc, which was blocking its way. Heard loud hip hop music coming from the other car, a shiny blue Audi, and could almost picture a couple of lads high on dope in the front. Nearly jumped for joy when it sounded its horn, loud. Realised I'd stopped breathing when the Merc flashed its headlights and gently manoeuvred so that it was facing away from the Audi and watched, heart in mouth, as it rolled away at a normal pace down towards the end of the concourse where it swung a right down the ramp onto level two. The Audi followed, clearly wound up and eager to get out the car park. Whoever was driving that beast didn't take kindly to being held up because it was right up the Merc's arse.

Thank fuck for that.

I shimmied out from behind the Volvo and ran on shaking pins to the edge of the parking bay at the far side. Ducked my head through the gap, out into the icy air. Looked down, relieved, when I saw the Merc pull out and take a right onto Great Bridgewater Street, followed keenly by the Audi. It was the only chance I had.

I ran back up to level three, my chest pounding, my lungs fucked. Found the Punto where I left it, parked neatly in bay 18. Got in, started her up, no fucking about this time. Put her into gear and sped out of that place faster than you could order a beef chow mien. When I reached the exit, thanking the lord for the barriers opening up, I stopped. Left or right? I took a deep breath, looked towards the direction the Merc went and put her into gear. Fuck it. You only live once, and if I was going to get anywhere with this, I needed to find out what these cunts wanted.

I turned right up Great Bridgewater Street and eased her into third as I drove on towards my fate. I told myself I was doing the right thing, but kept hearing Bob's words of caution in my head. Maybe I *was* on a death wish. Felt like I had no control over my actions. It was probably the booze. I'd be driving blind, and I had no clue if they knew I was in this thing. They'd probably laugh their bollocks off if they saw me in their rear-view mirror.

Just a short excursion would do, just a little detour to burn the adrenalin off. I rolled the window down and let the cold air wash over me. Drank that glorious air in deep. Gasped it in.

Came to a stop at the lights beside The Briton's Protection. There must've been a gig on at the Bridgewater Hall because the crowds were all crossing my path. Or it could've been the Manchester Central. Even on green, I couldn't get through. Wave after wave of pissed up, drugged up punters wandered past all laughing and singing, bottles of booze swinging between them. Several bumped into the car, and one little twat rolled across the bonnet for a laugh. He'd be laughing on the other side of his fucking face if I wasn't in such a bloody hurry. I blared the horn and revved her up, inched forwards and took a left down towards the Hacienda. Turns out my luck had run out when it came to following the Merc. It was probably a stupid idea anyway and, whichever way you looked at luck, perhaps this was a blessing in disguise.

My mobile trilled in my jacket pocket and I fumbled with the wheel as I pulled it out and answered, just as a couple of goggle eyed students thought it'd be funny to slap my roof like the little hard men they were.

'Hello?'

'Jim? Are you coming home? You said you'd be an hour.'

'I'm on my way.'

'You said you wouldn't be long.'

'I'm on my way now. Look, I got held up–look, just fuck off!'

'What?! Jim!'

'Not you, not you, it's these twats.'

'What?! What are you on about?'

'Nothing, nothing. Look, I've been a bit held up, but I'm on my way. I'll be back as soon as I can.'

She said something else then, but I dropped the phone into the passenger footwell. I finally got an inch of space and put my foot down, swerving to avoid a girl in a short skirt with a bloody tiara on her head, and took a sharp left onto Whitworth Street.

It had been a night of interesting developments. I put my foot down and willed myself to be cleansed by the cold wind and the rain it was bringing with it. With any luck, it would be a hard rain. A hard rain to cleanse my Godforsaken soul.

56

The rest of the drive went relatively smoothly apart from the police squad car that followed me for half a mile when I hit Oldham Road. I was running out of blessings to count, and I was more than thankful I wasn't pulled over. I was no doubt over the limit, and I cursed for allowing myself to get in this mess. It was a lucky escape. I got a look off the PC in the passenger seat as it overtook, and I had to focus hard on keeping the Punto going in a straight line. It seemed to work, and I was back at Sara's within fifteen minutes.

Laura was still awake, curled up on the couch with an empty bottle of Rioja perched on the carpet beside her. The TV was still on, the volume low. She said there were a few beers in the fridge she'd kept back for me. I could've kissed her right there and then. I grabbed one, flipped off the cap, drank deep. She sat up and stretched. Gave me a look and came towards me, so close I could feel her breath on my face. Her arm reached out to touch mine.

'So, where did you go?'

I told her. First about Karen, then the events at the

Midland and how we'd followed the bent coppers. I neglected to mention nearly getting mowed down in the car park. Didn't see any sense in worrying the girl.

'That must've been hard, seeing your ex like that.'

I shrugged. 'I'm over it.'

'Are you really sure about that?'

I sat down on the couch, sparked up. Blew a thick cloud into the living room. 'Charlie okay?'

'He's fast asleep. And no changing the subject, Jim Locke.'

Here we go again. Man to woman talk. 'I'm over it. She fucked off, didn't know a good thing when she had it.'

She raised her eyebrows at that, and mockingly too. Then sat down beside me. She reached out, took the Springsteen hat off and gently stroked her fingers across the stitches in the back of my head, wincing. 'Looks sore. You should probably take more painkillers.'

'I've had enough. Besides, I feel all right.'

'That'll be the drink. You'll feel it in the morning.'

I knew she was right, but for now it felt good just being here. With her. She stroked my beard, looked me in the eye, then leaned in and put her lips to mine. It was a long kiss, and I guess she needed it as much as I did. When she broke away, she said she was going to bed and took my hand.

I didn't need a second invitation.

57

Morning came quicker than I thought. Felt like I'd only had ten minutes sleep, and I still felt exhausted when the first chink of sunlight leaked through the curtains. I turned over to find Laura still sleeping, facing me with her breasts tucked beneath her arms. I stroked her hair, kissed her forehead, and got up to shower. I checked on Charlie, who was fast asleep too, still clutching his Spiderman toy beneath the duvet.

I showered, changed clothes and made a couple of coffees. By the time I'd returned to Laura, she was just about stirring from her dreams. She sat up in bed and stretched. I joined her.

'Why don't you come back to bed?'

I would've liked nothing more. 'Can't, love. Got things to do, I'm afraid.'

She stuck out her bottom lip and took a sip of coffee. 'Can't wait to have you back in here with me.'

'Tonight.'

'Hope so. So what's today?'

'I don't know. I'm gonna lie low for a day or two. I need to think about my next move. I'm gonna pay a visit to Karen's parents, though. See if I can clear the air somehow.'

'Want me to come? For some moral support?'

'Best not. It's something I need to do alone.'

She nodded. 'If you change your mind...?'

'Thanks. But I'll be okay.'

From the other bedroom, Charlie was shouting for Auntie Laura. She rolled out of bed and slung on her dressing gown. 'Better sort the wee man out. Chucky eggs all round.'

'Not for me, love.'

'Nonsense. You need to eat something. At least have some toast.'

I smiled. 'You're the boss.'

'Don't you forget it.'

We all had breakfast together with the news on the telly. Laura asked what it was I wanted her to do for me. I'd almost forgot myself.

'A couple of things.' I scooped out some boiled egg. 'I need a charger for that iPhone. Tonight, I'm gonna browse through all the content on it and I need to make some notes. Are you planning on going out today?'

'I'm going over to the hospital. I need to take Sara some clothes. And I need to nip back to my own flat for some things.'

'Can you pick me a charger up? I'll sort you out.'

She nodded. 'No problem.'

'And can you get me a notepad?'

'Your wish is my command. Anything else?'

Charlie was mithering for CBeebies, pulling at Laura's jeans. She flicked through the channels until Ben Ten came up.

'I need to book a date,' I said. 'With the agency Angel

worked for. Can you get online and find their website? Maybe book something for me?'

'So I was just a one-night stand, then?'

'Not at all. I need to speak to a girl called Sherry. She's one of the escorts. She was out the night Angel disappeared. I reckon she knows more than she's letting on, so I want to set up a meeting. Don't want her to know who she's really meeting, though.'

'So you want me to sort this out for you?'

'It'd be a help. Just check out the site for me. See what you think. If you've got time, that is.'

She nodded, took a bite of toast. 'I'm going over to hospital first. I'll drop Charlie at school then drive over, then I'll sort all this stuff this afternoon.'

'Would that be okay?'

She got up, kissed my nose. 'It'd be a pleasure.'

While Laura cleared up in the kitchen, I sparked up and got stuck into my second coffee of the morning. Tried to get my head around my visit to Frank and Maureen. It was gonna be a trying day, and I'd need to be on my best behaviour if I was to have any chance of seeing my kid. I could live with Karen having a new life, and she looked happy last night, but I had to see Nicole before I went insane.

I thought of phoning Bob too. After the Merc had tried mowing me down last night, the old guy was on my mind. I wasn't happy about the Chinese following me. And I knew it was either Bo Wong or the coppers who'd put them onto us. Perhaps both. They obviously wanted me to know, and their warnings should be enough to deter anyone. Trouble was, I wasn't just anyone. And I would not rest until all this made sense. I promised Sara–and myself–that I would find out who took Angel's life in such brutal circumstances. If they thought a beating was enough to put me off, they were wrong. They'd have to kill me first. And if last night was anything to go by, they weren't shy about that either. Bob was right. I needed to be on my toes and steer clear of trouble. It was easier said than done.

And Phil. The man had lost it, big time. No wonder he wanted me to steer clear of the case. If Phil was involved in this exclusive club business, it made sense he wanted to force me off the scent. Yet he'd fucked up big time. I thought back to the night I had my head kicked in. Was Phil in on it? After our little punch up in the Marble, I wouldn't put it past him to lose control. He could be a loose cannon. Always was. But was he a loose cannon enough to jump me? It was a possibility.

'Keep in touch.' She'd plucked Charlie's coat and hat from the hook in the hallway. 'I don't want you getting in any trouble again. And have you had your painkillers?'

'Not yet.'

She sighed, went into the kitchen and punched two from the blister pack. I downed them with the coffee, then put my jacket on. Springsteen hat, too. According to the weather girl, it was gonna be a cold one. Winter had well and truly kicked in and there was snow forecast.

'What time should I expect you back?'

'Not sure, but I don't want to be out all day. Tea time, maybe.'

'Good. Because I'm making shepherd's pie and it's got your name on it.'

'You're spoiling me.'

'It's about time someone did. Come here.' I went into her arms and we kissed, there in the kitchen with the rain battering the windows. 'Come back in one piece.'

'Which piece?'

'All of you,' she said, grabbing my balls. 'Especially these.'

58

I pulled up down Hillroyd Road, just several car spaces further down from last night. It was still fairly early, just after ten. I took a deep breath and sparked up. Sat smoking in the car with the window down and Five Live on the radio. They were talking with some politician about austerity. It was all anyone ever heard these days. The way I saw it, some things never changed. The rich just kept on getting richer and bugger the poor. It was a way of life.

Kept my eyes on Frank and Maureen's front door. There was no sign of the Audi. No sign of anyone. I'd rehearsed in my mind what I would say, but I knew that when it came to it, I'd crumble. Couldn't stop thinking about the look that would be on Frank's face. I was prepared for the worst. That's what I kept telling myself. In truth, I wasn't prepared for anything. I just knew I had to make this step. I was fearful of the most dire consequences. A complete lack of empathy on their part and the sure and certain force of complete refusal to even hear me out; to allow me access to my daughter; to the briefest of discussions with Karen. I think that's what scared me the most. For all they knew, I could be dead. For all I knew, that's what they'd been telling my daughter. And how ironic that that was almost the case.

As far as I'd known, there had been no effort to make contact on their part. It all came from me until I'd pretty much given up. In all my time in homeless shelters and soup kitchens, there was nothing. I never had a social worker or an outreach worker come to me and tell me they'd tried to make contact. Never had anyone say my ex wife and my daughter were out in the office, waiting for me. Nothing. I really was dead to them.

I finished the smoke and flicked it out the window. Turned off the radio and took another deep breath.

I opened the door, stepped out onto the pavement and locked up. Walked across the street to their front gate. Clicked it open, so familiar yet so alien, and walked slowly down the garden path. Felt like I was walking into the past. I reached the door and stopped. Took several long breaths before reaching out. Fuck it. I let the knocker go down three times and immediately thought I was making a mistake. I waited, forced myself to stay rooted to the spot. Heard thumping steps down the hallway behind that door and fixed my eyes to the space in front of me.

It opened.

It was Frank.

Standing there, mouth open, looking right into my eyeballs.

'Hello, Frank.'

He swallowed. 'Jim?'

I nodded. Felt sick. God, how I felt sick. He looked pale. I felt pale. 'Been a long time.'

He swallowed again, looked down, then back at me, then out into the street. 'You'd better come in, then.'

He pulled the door open for me and I stepped into that

familiar hallway with the familiar pictures on the walls and the mirror at the far end. The usual smell of Maureen's bloody air freshener and that strange aroma of another person's house. Frank had been cooking bacon and I could hear the sound of the telly coming from the front room. *This Morning.* I followed Frank into the living room. He hadn't changed. Got a bit thinner, which surprised me.

'Have a seat.' He grabbed the remote from his chair and turned the volume down. 'I'll do us a brew.'

I nodded. 'Cheers.'

I sat on the couch, wondering where the hell I was going to go with this next. Looked around the living room. The carpet had changed to a beige pensioner's number and there were new photographs on the wall and the mantelpiece.

Nicole.

I left the couch and had a look at my daughter, who had grown so fast since I last had her in my arms. Nicole with a dog, a Cocker Spaniel. Nicole with a swimming certificate. Nicole and her Mum. Nicole with Frank and Maureen. Yet there was something odd about Maureen.

'Here we go.' He dumped a tray with a pot of tea and a plate of digestives on the coffee table and sighed. Poured two cups from the pot. 'Have a seat, Jim. Sorry about the mess. Maureen would have a fit if she knew I was keeping it like this.'

I looked around. The place looked all right to me. I told him so. 'Where is Maureen, anyway? Out shopping, I expect.'

He sighed, put the pot down slowly and ran a hand down his face. 'No, nothing like that, son.'

'Then what?... Frank? You okay?'

He sat down, shook his head from side to side and back

again and looked me in the eye. 'She's dying, Jim. Liver cancer. She was never right after....'

Fuck. 'Shit, Frank. Oh, shit Frank, I had no idea.'

He waved it away. 'How were you to know? We didn't know where you were.'

I bit my tongue, gritted my teeth. Poor Maureen.

'She's been asking after you. You've always been on her mind since... well, since you and Karen, you know.'

I didn't know what to say. This was the woman who'd sat to my left on our wedding day, the woman who'd held Karen's hand at the birth of our daughter. The woman who used to like a good knees up at Christmas and who'd made me countless Sunday roasts, well before even Karen and I were married. And now she was dying.

'I'm sorry, Frank. I really am sorry.'

He sniffed. 'Yeah, well. We all are. We all are. Especially Maureen.'

I picked up the mug of tea and grabbed a Garibaldi. Maureen's favourite. 'How long?'

He sighed, took a sip of hot tea. 'A few months now, so they reckon. She's in Christie's but she'll be coming home soon. Got our room all sorted out for her, you know. Karen and... Karen and Chris are staying here to help out, you know.'

So that was who it was. Chris. Chris with the Audi. 'Has Karen...?'

He nodded. 'She re-married last year. Thrilled. Look, I suppose we should get down to it, son. Why are you here?'

'To sort things out, Frank.'

'To sort things out. Right. And it's taken you two bloody years to show up, has it? Too busy getting your head stuck in a bottle, is that it?'

'It's not like that, Frank.'

'Isn't it?'

'No. I tried making contact. You know I did. All I got was the phone hanging up.'

'You haven't phoned for two fucking years, lad!'

'Kind of got the impression I wasn't wanted around here.'

'Oh, you weren't. You weren't. Least of all from Karen.'

'And Nicole?'

'What about her?'

'She's my daughter, Frank.'

'Oh yeah. Didn't make a bloody appearance for her, did you?'

'How can I turn up on your doorstep when no one wanted to bloody speak to me, Frank?'

'She's your daughter, Jim. Your daughter. And you fucking abandoned her.'

'I did nothing of the sort and you know it.'

'You could've saved the marriage, lad.'

'The marriage was over the minute Karen wanted it to be over.'

'She had good reason.'

'I never had an affair, Frank. It was all lies, all of it.'

'Your drinking didn't exactly help.'

'No,' I nodded. 'No, it didn't. And I hold my hands up for that.'

'You cared more about the bottle than you did for your wife and kids.'

'That's not true.'

He laughed. Looked away, got up from his chair and walked over to the window. I put the Garibaldi back on the plate and took a sip of tea. 'Look, it's not exactly been the best two years of my life.'

'You think it has for any of us? For Nicole?'

'I never said that. Look, just hear me out will you, eh? Frank?'

'I'm listening.'

'I tried making contact, but all I got was a brick wall. Nothing. I phoned this house every sodding day and what did I get? Nothing, Frank. Nothing. Not a fucking dickie bird.'

'Is it any bloody wonder?!'

'So what exactly am I bloody guilty of?' I put my mug down and stepped up behind him. 'Being a drinker? Losing my job?'

'You could've got help.'

'I tried.'

'You could've come to me, lad!'

'Frank, you were convinced I was sleeping around! Admit it.'

'It wasn't like that.'

'You must've believed every bloody word she said!'

He turned around, teeth bared. 'She's my fucking daughter, son! Who do you think I'm gonna believe?'

'Frank, there was no affair. With anyone. You've got to believe me on that.'

'Doesn't change things. Why the hell would she say all that? Why would she leave you?'

'Someone must've been bullshitting her, Frank!'

'Oh, like who?'

'Someone on the force. Someone who wanted me out.'

'You were doing a good fucking job of that yourself!'

'The drinking wasn't affecting my job, Frank.'

'That's not what they thought, is it?!'

'It wasn't like that.'

'It affected your bloody marriage, didn't it?'

'It's not like I can fucking turn this on and off, Frank.'

'You just bloody disappeared!'

'She fucking left me, Frank! *She* left *me*!'

He was crying now and we both stood there, in that living room I knew so well. Frank was shaking and his arms went to his head and went to rip the hair from his scalp. He sank to his knees, snot and tears pouring from his face. This was the last thing I'd expected. I dropped down, reached out to put a hand on his shoulder.

'Why, Jim?' He was bawling now, his shoulders moving up and down as he sobbed. 'Why, why, why?'

'It's all right, it's all right.' I took his head and brought him to my chest. 'It's all right.'

'She's dying, son! Maureen's dying...'

'I know. I know.'

'What the hell am I going to do?!'

59

Later, when Frank had stopped the tears, we sat down again and tried to make sense of the past few years. We finished the pot of tea and tried to speak without raising our voices. I knew Frank wouldn't entirely understand, especially about the drink, but he listened as we sat there in that living room. Part of him was far away, though. His thoughts were only with Maureen. I think he could forgive me for all that had happened, not that everything was my fault. But I reckon as we talked, he softened. It wasn't the kind of meeting I'd expected at all. I thought he'd just slam the door in my face, but he didn't. I felt guilty for thinking that. Seems I didn't understand Frank's character at all. He asked what I was doing for a living. I didn't think it was a good idea to tell him the truth about that. Not yet. So I said I was just getting back on my feet, which wasn't far from the truth at all.

I watched him in that chair as I drank the tea, watched him stare off into space as I tried to explain that I was never far away, that I always phoned until I couldn't phone no more, that I'd spent months on the streets thinking of my daughter and what she was doing. He nodded in all the right places, but he wasn't entirely with me. It was a bad time for any of this.

'I want to see her, Frank,' I said. 'Nicole. Karen, too, to set things straight. But I want to see my daughter, Frank.'

He sighed. Lifted the tray with the teapot and headed into the kitchen. I followed. 'I'll speak to Karen. Just so she knows you're around. But I can't promise anything, Jim.'

'I'd appreciate just something. Please, Frank. She's my daughter and I deserve to have her in my life. She deserves me.'

He nodded. 'I know. I know. She never stops talking about you. Always wants to know when you're coming back.'

My heart sang. 'Really?'

'Really. Yes. But this is a very delicate matter, Jim. Karen's happily married again and... well, things could get complicated. Chris is a good man.'

'But he's not Nicole's Dad.'

'I know. But he's been her Dad since you've been gone. And therefore this stuff isn't easy, Jim. As I'm sure you'd understand. She's older now. She knows Chris isn't her father but...'

'I should hope so...'

'But, like I say, he has been good to her and Karen. Really, he has. So can you see how I don't want to mess any of that up? And now with Maureen...it's just a bad time, son.'

'Okay.'

He rinsed the mugs out and dumped the teapot in the sink. 'But I'll speak to Karen first. It's the best I can do for now.'

'I appreciate this. And it's good to see you.'

He nodded but said nothing, just traipsed out the

kitchen in his slippers. I followed him back to the living room where he grabbed his shoes from beside the couch.

'I need to go. Gotta go over to Christie's. I promised Maureen I'd be there by half twelve and it's ten to now.'

'Okay. How's she bearing up?'

'Not good. As you'd expect.'

'Are you gonna tell her? You know, about me?'

'I suppose so. Can't see how I can't mention it. She'll be happy about it, I think. Looks like you turned up at the right time.'

'I hope so. And I am sorry, Frank. I really am.'

He nodded, moved into the hallway to grab his coat. 'So am I, Jim. So am I.'

We were silent for a moment on the doorstep before we embraced. I'd tried to picture this moment in my mind on frosty nights hanging around the backstreets of Piccadilly. It wasn't how I'd expected it to be. With Maureen gravely ill, and Karen re-married, I'd been so caught up in it all that I'd forgotten to ask how Frank was himself. Or maybe I didn't need to ask. It was in his eyes. The man was in turmoil.

'We had some wonderful years, Jim. Some joyous years, the best of times.'

He locked the door behind him. The rain clouds were gathering again on the horizon.

'Tell her I was asking after her. I know, given the circumstances, that I might be the last person she wants news from, but still. I've a lot of respect for Maureen, Frank. You too.'

We walked down the path and Frank pointed his car keys at the Focus. The lights blinked as it unlocked.

'It's been a difficult few years, Jim, for lots of reasons, I'm sure you understand. You can call again but please, whatever you do, don't turn up unless it's the daytime, like around now. I don't want you turning up on Karen when I haven't bloody spoken to her.'

'I will. I promise.'

He nodded. 'Good. Now, I've got to go. It's been... well, it's been good to see you. I'm sorry for...'

'Don't be. I'd be the same. And it's been good to see you too. I mean that.'

He smiled, got into the car. I waved as he started her up and pulled away from the kerb and watched as he left Hillroyd Road. I looked back at the house, knowing that one day soon I would return to my daughter. One day soon, all being well.

I sat in the car for several minutes and smoked. I left the radio off this time. Checked the time on my phone. Just gone twelve. Thought about what to do for the rest of the day, keen to avoid the temptation of the pub, which would be easy after the conversation I'd just had. A simple Guinness would go down very well right now, but I knew that once the first pint went down, the rest would follow. If I was going to try to patch things up with Karen, at least enough so we were on speaking terms–enough for her to allow me access to Nicole–then I'd need to give the drink a very wide berth. Which was easier said than done.

I started her up and left. The drive back to Sara's wasn't far, but I was feeling restless. After the events of last night, I needed to speak to Bob, just to make sure he was okay. It didn't occur to me until I was in the middle of Frank and Maureen's living room that Bob could be in as much danger as I was, perhaps more so given his history with the front page. I pulled into a side street off Oldham Road, somewhere on the edge of Failsworth, and called him. No answer. Sent a text to ask him to call me back, then moved off again. I would try him again when I reached Sara's.

I thought about Laura. I was partly in a state of denial about what had happened last night. It was the perfect antidote to an anxious evening, and the sex had cleared my mind of the fact that I'd almost been mowed down by the Merc. But now it was back. Lying low for a few days was probably the right thing to do, but I was itching for more. And now that I knew Phil was getting his leg over at Bo Wong's–I wasn't certain of it, but I couldn't ignore his presence there–things were getting far more interesting.

And I wanted to know more about the girls that had gone missing. Chi Phuong was an interesting aside, and I knew there were more. If all these girls had gone missing or worse, just to keep their mouths shut, how far did it go? I needed to do some more digging around, but my face wasn't welcome in Chinatown. It worried me that, if I turned up there again, I'd end up joining the missing. I needed someone else to go digging for me. Laura? Maybe. Bob? Not a chance in hell. But there had to be someone, and someone I could trust.

If Laura came back with the charger for the iPhone–and I saw no reason she wouldn't–then I'd make the point of going nowhere until I'd been through Simon's information and made the notes I needed to make. I knew instinctively that there would be stuff buried in there that could unlock the mystery. Evidence that would lead to the killer or killers. And my feeling was that there was indeed more than one.

But it wasn't enough for me to just hang around. I was my own worst enemy when it came to being alone, no matter how trivial. There was something else I needed to do, someone I could find who I knew might help for a small fee. It was a long shot, and I didn't even know if he was alive, but it was better than nothing. Besides, he owed me one.

I got back to Sara's and had a quick cup of tea with the

lunchtime news on the TV. I wasn't watching, but I needed some background noise as I tried to think back to the last time I saw him. It was at least a year ago, but I'd heard on the grapevine that he was still around. I hoped so, because I liked him. He didn't deserve to be where he was, for all kinds of reasons. But there were all kinds of reasons, I knew, why he chose to stay there.

I smoked several cigarettes and got sidetracked by the weather forecast. It was a good job too because it looked a grim one. The snow was heading south from Scotland and they expected it to hit Manchester by two o'clock. I threw on an extra jumper and doubled up on my socks. Made another phone call to Bob and it still rang out. Which was a worry. I could only hope that he hadn't been a victim of his own prediction, that he was lying in a ditch somewhere with a bullet hole in his head. That he'd seemed certain of impending danger, and that he was adamant there were dark forces at work, told me I should be worried. If he didn't return my calls by teatime, I'd have to find him.

I locked up the house and got back in the Punto. It was just gone one. Better to be out on the case than cooped up here. Once I got to town and parked up, it would be a short walk to the place I reckoned he'd be. I could only hope he was there. If the weather was anything to go by–the clouds were heavy and battleship grey, with already a few flakes in the air–then I knew he'd be wanting to keep out of the cold. With a decent meal and a hot drink inside him, he was good company and a pleasure to be around. Without it, he was like the spawn of Satan himself. Whichever it was, I was sure he wouldn't turn down the opportunity of a twenty pound note, a packet of tobacco and a bottle of the finest cheap blend I could find.

60

I parked up again in a little spot beside the Smithfield Detox Unit. Thompson Street was desolate. I pulled the jacket tight around me and sparked up as I headed down towards Rochdale Road and Shudehill. The wind was picking up, and the few snowflakes in the air were quickly becoming a downpour.

The traffic was busy and the noise was giving me a headache. The bus station was packed with double deckers as I crossed the Metrolink tracks. Being a major terminus, there were travellers everywhere. I passed the bustle and walked down towards the Printworks and then round the back of Victoria Station towards the soup kitchen I knew down a side road, under the bridge at the Cathedral end of Deansgate.

Saw a few familiar faces–and more I didn't recognise–lingering on the cobbles outside. Thought I'd ask one or two if they'd seen him if he wasn't there inside, but my guess was that he was tucking into a pea and ham or a minestrone right about now.

I stepped up to the main door and knocked on the

glass partition that stood between me and the dining room. If you could call it that. I suppose I didn't exactly look the part with Han Lan's designer gear on, and my face had transformed since I last sat in this place with a Scotch broth, but I reckoned I could convince Lloyd, the Rasta volunteer, that he knew me if I showed him my tattoos.

He turned from the little desk beside the notice board and left his seat. 'Yeah, man. What can I do for you?'

'You don't recognise me, do you?'

He leaned forward, took a closer look. 'This is a soup kitchen, man. You a Social Worker or something?'

'It's Jim. Jim Locke?'

'Jim?'

'That's me.'

'Get outta town, man.'

'I'm serious.'

He leaned closer still, swung his dreadlocks back over his shoulders. 'Raaas, man! It is you! Well, come around here. Let me take a good look at you!'

He opened the middle door and we shook hands. Lloyd had been volunteering here for years, three days a week without fail. Sometimes he'd get his guitar out and sing as we sat and had our soup and bread roll. He used to bang on about how he was in a reggae band and used to roadie for The Smiths back in the day. He was a decent bloke, and I knew that sometimes he'd sort some of the guys out with a little bit of weed. He wasn't supposed to, of course, and he would do all the other stuff too–signposting to other services, referring us to GPs etc–but I think he liked the fact that he could palm off some of his home grown on the most deserving, if he saw fit. The man gave a shit, and everyone loved him.

'What brings you here, man? And what the fuck happened to you?'

'It's a long story. And I'll tell you one day. But I'm looking for someone. Stevie. Remember him?'

'Pony tail?'

'That's him.'

'He's in here, having a second bowl of my famous tomato. Come on through.'

I followed him down the narrow corridor, leaflets pinned to the notice boards about sexual health, alcohol detox, mental health and housing. It was all so familiar, yet strange too. It wasn't long ago I'd be hanging around here myself, deep in conversation with another man or woman who'd fallen down the cracks. We went through the double swing doors into the dining room, a smallish room just about big enough to fit a class of infant school kids in. Stevie was sitting at a table in the corner, alone, enthusiastically munching on a bread roll covered in soup. There were others too, an elderly couple sitting beside the portable heater, their thin homeless lips slurping on chicken broth. A familiar looking drunk with a heavy beard and overlong grey hair asleep on a plastic chair. In this place, they called him God, and not just because of his appearance. He was well known for speaking in tongues, at least to the voices he was hearing in his head.

'Stevie,' Lloyd said, as we approached. 'You got a visitor.'

Stevie looked up, beads of tomato soup glistening in his black beard. He looked at me and frowned.

'It's Jim. I know I look different, but I can assure you it's me.'

'Jim who?'

'Jim Locke. Ex copper.'

'Nah. I know him.'

'I'll leave you to it,' Lloyd said. 'I'll bring you some soup, Jim.'

I was going to tell him there was no need, but he was back through the doors before I could get the words out. I turned to Stevie and took the seat opposite. He was looking at me intensely, squinting and rubbing his temple before going back to the soup.

'So what happened to you? Last time I saw you was when we shared that space over behind Ho's Bakery. How long ago was that? Must be nine months.'

'Something like that.'

'So what's with all the posh gear? You've gone up the world, haven't you?'

'In some ways, I suppose. Kind of fell on my feet. The clothes aren't mine.'

He grinned, showed me brown teeth. There was a large boil on his neck and his hands were covered in dirt. His donkey jacket was covered in stains too, and the thick red jumper he wore had a gaping hole in it. His sleeping bag was the colour of phlegm and he had a bin liner beside him with more blankets in it. But his eyes shone with the colour of the sea.

'So what do you want, then?' he said, before finishing the soup and clattering the spoon back in the bowl. He wiped his mouth on his sleeve and pulled out a bent roll up from his pocket. I joined him in sparking up. 'I could do with some of those, if you don't mind...'

I handed him four cigarettes and watched him pocket them quick. 'You got time to hear me out?'

'Not as if I've got a home to go to, is it?' he laughed. 'I've got all fucking day, man. You seen Billy recently? No one's seen him for time. Rumour has it they pulled a body out of the canal last Sunday. Lot of people saying it's him.'

Billy Baldwin. Young, just seventeen, sold himself down the village and round the canals for crack money. 'No, I haven't. I've not seen anyone, Stevie.'

'I suppose not, what with that getup. So what happened? You have a fight with a set of clippers? All your fucking hair's gone, man.'

'Got a bit of help off someone I know. How are you keeping, Stevie? How's the drinking?'

'Not enough of it, I can tell you that.' He had a coughing fit then, just as Lloyd came back with a bowl of soup for me. I pushed it across the table once he'd gone. 'You don't want this?'

'It's yours.'

'Suppose you don't need it now, eh? Where're you getting your dinner these days? The fucking Hilton?'

And then the reason I was here came back in a flash. Angel missing, Angel dead. 'Not quite. But I'm off the streets. For now, at least. You getting any joy?'

'Me? Nah. Shelter down Churchill Way gives me a bed for the night sometimes. It's the best I'm gonna get at the moment.'

I knew it was true. And I knew Stevie was coming from a bad place. Gambling addiction, alcohol addiction. A life in and out of care homes. Domestic abuse. There was a rumour he'd been raped in his teens. He never spoke about it. I supposed having such a thing to contend with led to his eventual breakdown and before he knew it, he was a drinker. The worst kind. But he wasn't alone. There were a thousand like him, and more. But he had companionship on the streets. At least it was something.

'Actually, I was hoping you could help me. Just for a few nights.'

'Oh aye?'

'Yeah. There'll be something in it for you. It's a promise.'

'Something like?'

'Some cash. Fifty grams of baccy and a bottle of the good stuff.'

A smile bent across his face and he looked away. Thought I saw a tear there, but it could've been just the sores around his eyes making them water.

'For me?'

I nodded. 'For you.'

'So what do you want me to do? Where do I sign on the dotted line?' He laughed, went back to slurping his soup. 'This is turning out to be a good day. Three bowls and the promise of a drink. Can't be bad. I've got a bed for tonight as well.'

'I'm glad to hear it. It's cold out. Snowing out there.'

'I know. The past few days have been really fucking cold, man. It's bad shit out there. This place has been packed every day. Died down now. So go on. What do you want from me?'

'Just a favour. A small one. But it means you'll have to hang around Chinatown for a few nights.'

'Oh yeah?'

'Yeah. Think of it as a bit of espionage. A bit of surveillance.'

'And you chose me because...?'

'Because no one's gonna take any notice of a homeless guy in a blanket. No offence.'

'None taken.'

'Good. But I need you to come with me now. I want you to take some pictures.'

'Christ, you got one of those digital cameras? And you trust me with that?'

I shook my head. 'No, we're gonna get disposables. And

we'll do a little excursion to get some supplies for your good self. That's if you're willing to help me out here.'

He nodded, grinned. 'It's a deal.' He held his dirty hand out to shake on it. We shook. 'So when do I start?'

'Tonight?'

'I've got a bed for tonight, don't want to miss that.'

'I know, and you won't have to. Just hang around and take some pics of a few things that might be of interest to me.'

'Like what?'

'That's the fun bit.'

I filled him in on what I wanted as we walked up to Market Street. Stevie would set up camp across the street from Bo Wong's, or take a space on one of the benches at the garden beneath the arch. Anywhere as long as he had a good view. He would stay there and photograph everyone who climbed those stairs to the dancing club. And he would do this over several consecutive nights. Then he would report back to me with hopefully a couple of rolls of photographs. He seemed very keen on the idea, especially when I told him I was looking into bent coppers. He even offered to do more, should I need it.

He waited outside the Boots on Market Street while I went upstairs to the photography section and spent a tenner on a couple of basic disposable cameras. Then we walked the short distance to Tesco. Stevie insisted he walk round with me while I spent some cash on a selection of sand-wiches and pies and a bottle of coke. He was more inter-ested in the alcohol section, though. His eyes lit up when I picked out a bottle of Whyte and Mackay, that old favourite of mine. I bought him a large packet of tobacco and a bunch of rolling papers. Threw in a lighter, too. And then he was set. I left him on Market Street and handed him twenty quid and my number I'd jotted down on a scrap of paper. I was never one to shirk from a promise.

'So that's it? Just take photos?'

'That's it. For three nights. When the rolls are full, phone me. I'll meet you to pick them up.'

'Easy enough.'

'It is easy, you can just sit there and watch the world go by. But don't get ratarsed on the booze. Just chill with it. I need those photos. That's your priority.'

'Don't worry. I reckon I'll be good at this.'

'I'm sure you will.'

We parted then, and I watched him shuffle up through the crowds towards Piccadilly Gardens. He looked pleased with himself, and I was glad to help him out. And he would help me out too. Of that, I was certain.

61

I walked back to the Punto within ten minutes. Tried to get hold of Bob several times but got nothing again. I was getting worried. I was just a few steps away when my mobile rang. It was Laura.

'Got that stuff you asked for. Want me to charge it up?'

'I've got it here.'

'No, you left it here. I'll get it charging. Anything else I can do for you?'

'Just be waiting for me when I get back. That'll be enough.'

'I think I can manage that.'

'How was Sara?'

Heard a sigh on the end of the line. 'Not great, to be honest. She's been asking for you. Said she wants to speak to you about something.'

'Did she say what it was?'

'No, just that she wants you to visit.'

'I could go now.'

'Not a good idea. She's pretty tired. They've got her like a fucking zombie in there. Maybe tomorrow would be best.'

'If you think so.'

'I do. So, what time should I expect you?'

'Couple of hours, maybe. Has anyone phoned asking for me?'

'Not while I've been home, no. You expecting someone?'

'No, it's just... well, it doesn't matter.'

'You sure?'

'Yeah.'

'Well hurry up, Shepherd's pie's about to go in the oven. And I'm gonna have a look at that website you asked about before I pick Charlie up from school. You got any plans to be out tonight?'

'No, I need to dig into that iPhone. Unless something comes up, that is.'

'Well, I hope not, because I want you all to myself.'

'I bet you do.'

We left it there. I started the Punto and moved off towards Great Ancoats Street. I knew Bob lived in Didsbury, but I'd no idea where. I'd be driving around the place blind, but I had to do something to set my nerves at ease. Wherever he was, he wasn't answering his phone. I told myself there could be all kinds of reasons for that. I could only hope they hadn't got to him. Perhaps it was the paranoia coming back again. But I knew I wasn't being ridiculous. Far from it. The evidence was right before me, seen with my own eyes. As I drove down towards the Mancunian Way flyover, I glanced in the rearview and saw the Merc creeping right up my arse.

62

I came to the lights beside the PC World. The Merc pulled up right beside me in the lane to my right. I resisted the temptation to turn and give them the finger. I could feel their eyes upon me. Took a deep breath, put her into first and pulled off. I knew I had to put my foot down, but getting away from them in this shitty old thing would be nigh on impossible. Took her up to second, then third and fourth as the Merc stayed right beside me in that right-hand lane. Thought briefly about cutting down through the next exit onto Stockport Road, but my brain couldn't think fast enough. The traffic ahead was busy enough, and I was focussing hard on the car in front. I couldn't cut my speed because there was a Focus right behind me. I stayed in the left-hand lane and watched as the Merc cut in front of me. Had to brake sharply to let the bastards in. Kept my eyes drilled on the Merc's tail lights. Had a bad feeling they were gonna put the brakes on and before I knew it, I'd be going into the back of them.

I stayed behind and when I saw they were getting ready to pull off down the exit to Princess Parkway, I took a quick glance in the wing mirror and spun it into the right-hand lane. This time I did give them the finger just before they dropped down the ramp and I carried on over the flyover with a few angry horns blaring behind me. They were obviously out to warn me again and would risk not just my life but their own too. They were crazier than I thought.

I drove at a steady speed until I came to the roundabout at Chester Road. Pulled the phone out and dialled Bob again. Ringing. I took the first exit and stayed with it until I got to Stretford. Kept the phone clamped to my ear and hoped to God he'd pick up this time.

'Hello?'

Thank fuck for that. 'Bob?'

'Where are you?'

'Chester Road.'

'Do yourself a favour and get the bloody hell away from there and your arse over here. United are playing tonight and there'll be a shitload of cockneys about to pull off the M6 anytime now.'

'Where are you? Funnily enough, I was on my way over to you until a certain Mercedes appeared on the scene. And where the fuck have you been? I've been trying to get hold of you all day.'

'Oh shit.'

'What? Bob?'

'The bloody Merc. Have a guess who's just dropped my grandson off home from school.'

'You what?'

'Yeah. The lad was bloody full of himself with how bloody good the Mercedes was. Said a Chinese man offered him a lift down the road and the silly little tosspot got in.'

'Jesus.'

'Exactly. Now get here, sharpish.'

'Fucking hell, Bob...'

'Palatine Road. Meet me on the corner of Barlow Moor Road in half an hour.'

'Bob, are you okay?'

'They've been following me, Jim. And dropping my grandson off is a threat I can't ignore.'

'So what are you gonna do?'

'I can't use my car. And you shouldn't be driving that fucking Punto either.'

'They tried to mow me down last night.'

'Oh, for fuck's sake. This is worse than I thought. How the pissing hell have I got involved in all of this shite?!'

'Bob, calm down.'

'Calm down? Calm fucking down?!'

'This isn't helping.'

'They want my bloody head on a stake, lad! And yours!'

'I'll be there in half an hour.'

He hung up.

Kept my eyes peeled for the Merc as I joined the queue for bloody Old Trafford, a thousand and one Japanese tourists in United shirts. Couldn't get away quick enough. I finally turned off down a side road and headed towards Hulme and cut through the estate where the old Crescents used to be and finally made it out to the Parkway. Found my heart pounding as I drove. I was running low on fuel too. I think it was down to a combination of knowing Bob was in a state and the fact that whoever was driving the Merc seemed to want me dead. And not just me either.

I must have checked my rear-view mirror a hundred times a minute. If they'd been on Bob's case too, and had the gall to drop his grandson off, they wouldn't think twice about getting to me again. Especially since I'd given them the finger.

I bombed it down the Parkway, feeling my skin come out in beads of sweat. I couldn't shake the feeling that I was being watched. More than that–that I was being monitored. It occurred to me that my phone calls might be being picked up somehow. I knew the technology was available, and if they were tracing my phone, then they knew where I was twenty-four seven. Question was, who the hell was tracing it, if at all? I wouldn't put it past the police. Top brass had always been reluctant to put money into such surveillance, but there was a lot at stake here. This shit went deep, Bob had said. I was beginning to believe it. Angel's face came to me as I drove. Chi Phuong's too. I wondered how many victims there were. Five, six. Maybe even dozens. The stench of corruption lingered everywhere. There was a grand conspiracy just waiting to be revealed. The search for Angel's killer had plumbed new depths. And I didn't know how deep I could go.

I came to Barlow Moor Road, just beyond the edge of Southern Cemetery. Took a left at the junction and got stuck behind a bus. The traffic, I reckoned, was heavy. Weaved between cars and overtook a 111. It was backed up all the way to Wilmslow Road. There were school kids everywhere, all running for buses, swinging bags at each other, messing about in the little snow that had settled. A wind had picked up, blowing the trees up and down the road into ghoulish, blackened monsters. It was darkening quickly, and I flicked the headlights on full beam when an Armageddon sky rolled in from the north, bringing heavy snow with it. It blew in fast, cascading down across South Manchester like a storm at the end of the world. Got the wipers on full and stuck the blowers on. Flicked on the stereo and got greeted by Joy Division again from the CD player. Sparked up as the traffic rolled at a snail's pace and kept my eye out for Bob. I had a vague idea where he'd be standing, perhaps sheltered in a doorway of a hair salon or something. I knew Palatine Road wasn't far away, and I knew that, despite the cold, and like me, he'd be sweating.

Two minutes later and I spotted him, standing at the edge of the pavement, snow billowing around him as he peered out into the traffic in the wrong direction. Buzzed the horn as I pulled up beside him near the lights. He let himself in. He looked pale.

'Thank fuck you're here,' he said. 'I saw them, Jim. Had to duck into the bloody cheese shop.'

I turned the volume right down and put her into gear, steered into the traffic when a Corsa flashed me. 'When?'

'About five minutes ago. I swear to God they're gonna do something silly.'

'Where's your grandson?'

'Back with his mum.'

'You called the police?'

'Have I fuck, lad.'

'Well don't you think you should?'

'Given what I know? I don't think so, son.'

'Might be for the best.'

'No.' He seemed pretty final about it. 'But I am gonna go to the paper.'

'What!?'

He was nodding hard as he sparked up a Montecristo. 'It's time. Fuck 'em. If they want to piss about with my Grandson, I'll piss about with them.'

Jesus. Was it wise? I didn't know. Just a few days ago Bob was all against going to press about anything. Not only was he retired, he didn't want to put his life on the line. I wondered what had changed and asked him so.

'Left here.' He wound down the window, blew cigar

smoke out. I spun a left onto Palatine Road. 'It doesn't seem to make any difference. That I've kept quiet all these years, I mean. I've done nothing wrong but show my face and what do I get? Intimidation. I won't stand for it, Jim. Not anymore. Not when my Grandkids are brought into the equation.'

'Admirable, Bob, but do you think it's wise? I mean, you said so yourself. If you went to press on this, then... well, fuck, you might as well sign your own death warrant.'

'I won't be blowing it out of proportion, just a few little columns here and there.'

'About what?'

'You'll see.'

'And you think they'll let you print this stuff?'

'I'm on good terms with everyone at the paper. Editor included. The stuff I've got is gold dust.'

'Bob,' I said, as I took us through the lights at Withington, 'are you sure you've thought this through? It's easy to panic in these situations. I understand how shook up you might be about your grandson and all that, but...'

'They're not fucking about, Jim. And you of all people should know that.'

'So what will going to press do?'

'Bring it out into the open. They think they're untouchable now, watch it all crumble on tomorrow's front page.'

'Bob, I think...'

'You think nothing. They'll scarper into the woodwork faster than they can get their bloody pants down.'

'Right, so what happened to 'With great power comes great responsibility'? You've had good reason to hold back for so long–years, you said–and now you want to risk everything? I thought you valued your life, Bob.'

'I do, that's why I'm doing this now. If I don't, they'll get to me anyway, and I don't want to bow out without the truth coming out. Now's my chance.'

It was crazy talk. Yet Bob couldn't see it. I couldn't stop him from doing anything but my fear was that if all this did get out–the secrets, the lies, the corruption, the exclusive club, the dead girls–it would jeopardise my case and I'd never get to the truth about Angel's death. If he thought things were bad now, it was about to get much worse before the ink dried on tomorrow's early edition.

'Just take a deep breath, Bob. Try to think this through.'

'I have thought it through. For twenty odd bloody years, and more. I've thought of fuck all else. If they want to have a pop at me, then I want to leave this world with my conscience clear. I can't let these secrets stay hidden, Jim. This city deserves the truth, however bloody painful it may be.'

'So what happened to a quiet life, eh? What happened to that?'

'Gone already.'

'You do know that if you do this you could well end up in that ditch with a bullet in the back of your head, don't you? If you go to press, Bob, you'll have to leave Manchester. For good.'

He was shaking. Took a long drag on the Montecristo before flinging it out the window.

'I know. I've got a flight booked for two a.m. I'm going to Spain.'

63

The drive to the *Evening Chronicle* headquarters was stormy, both inside and out. Bob was almost foaming at the mouth by the time we reached Oxford Road. And yet there was a glint in his eye, a knowing certainty that what he had planned–which he wouldn't reveal in full to me–would bring a new kind of storm. It was complex, he'd said. From what he was hinting at, what I knew already would look like Disney Land next to what would come out. It scared me, seeing him like this. It was as if he'd been possessed. The snow continued to billow in, and by now it was thick enough for the wheels to go sliding beneath us. I had to wrestle with the Punto just to keep us in a straight line. The sky was heavy with golf ball sized flakes of the stuff, and vision was becoming a problem. If it got any worse, I thought I might have to abandon the car.

'You don't have to do this, Bob.' We'd just passed All Saints. 'Think of the consequences.'

'The consequences are just as bad, if not worse, if I *don't* do this, son.'

'You sound pretty certain. And on edge.'

'I couldn't be more certain.' He was gritting his teeth. 'For your sake and mine. I've got to put a stop to this madness, once and for all.'

'Bob, please, just...'

'Don't,' he said, holding his palm up. 'Just don't try to change my mind, son. It's made up.'

'But going to Spain, Bob! I mean... well... what the fuck!'

'Sheila's meeting me out there. On Saturday. We've got a place over in Gran Canaria, just a little place in a village outside San Bartolome. My daughter Isobel and the kids will follow next Wednesday.'

'But Bob...'

'Just until it dies down, that's all.'

'Making a hasty exit will have you earmarked even more.'

'But staying could mean worse. Come on, Jim. You know it makes sense.'

'And what about my case? What about Angel, Chi Phuong, all the missing bloody women from Chinatown?'

'It'll all come out, eventually. You should wash your hands of it, if you have any sense. Though I remember you seem to have lost all sense after that kick to your head. How is it, by the way?'

'I'll live.'

'That's what they all say. And by the sounds of it, last night didn't quite go your way, did it?'

'But I got away. That's all that matters.'

'But for how long, son?'

It was harsh, but he was right. Perhaps I had lost all common sense. But I was also filled with an inner resolve to find justice, whatever the risks. Though having finally contacted Frank, I knew I was playing the fool if I believed I could act alone in this. I needed allies. Bob disappearing was bad timing, to say the least. Was I mad enough to allow myself to be put in such danger? They'd almost mowed me down after all. If it wasn't for the kids in that Audi, I could be dead by now. And I wanted to see my daughter before anything happened to me. Maybe I should just walk away. Take the Punto and drive to the coast, I don't know, anything. But it was evidence that mattered. I needed it like I needed the drink, and I fucking needed a stiff one right now.

'Phone me when you're there, otherwise I'll only worry. I couldn't get hold of you today and it freaked me out. I thought...'

'You thought the worst?'

I said nothing, just focussed on the road. There must have been a smash somewhere up ahead because the traffic was virtually static. Bob was itching in his seat. I sparked up and flicked him one too.

'I can take care of myself.'

'That's not what you were saying yesterday.'

'Today's a different day.' He lit up, inhaled, blew a fog out through the window. 'Why do you think I'm going to Spain? For a laugh? No, son. This is something I've gotta do. Got no choice.'

'We can turn around right now.'

'Forget it. You can do what you bloody well like, son. But I'm out of here–until the shit dies down.'

'And what if it doesn't die down?'

'I get a nice suntan. Oh, for fuck's sake, come on!'

I hammered the horn but nothing was budging, and I was hardly surprised. Poked my head out the window, the freezing air going right through me. I felt like I was living in a fucking snow globe and some cunt had given it a good shake.

'That's it,' he said, popping the cigarette between his lips and pulling the door handle. 'I'm walking.'

'Bob!'

He slammed the door shut right there in the middle of Oxford Road and poked his head back through. 'It'll be okay.' He pointed. 'You stay out of trouble, son. Do you hear me? And take those bloody painkillers.'

'Bob, just think this through.'

'I'm not going over it again! That's final. Now if you excuse me, son, I've got an article to write. A bloody long one. And the clock's ticking.'

'Just be careful, Bob. When you're over there, I mean.'

'I'll be living it up with a big smile on my face in about ten hours. You can bank on it.'

'You better phone me.'

'I will.'

Then he pulled the hood up on his overcoat, plonked the Fedora on his head, and trudged off through the snow. I could only hope he would be okay. I knew his words were a force to be reckoned with. I just didn't expect him to want to write them anytime soon. But the pen was mightier than the sword, and I reckon he knew that more than anyone. For his sake, I hoped so.

64

I abandoned the car about an hour later when I finally got to my usual parking spot outside the Smithfield Detox Unit. I was almost tempted to bang on the doors and demand they let me in. But the pull of The Marble was stronger. It was quiet inside, just a few Posties lingering near the bar. The fire was blazing and I thought about my first encounter with Bob. Ordered two pints of Lagonda and sat down. Downed the first one and settled with the second by the fire, telling myself it would be my last. Watched the snow plummet down through the windows.

So what now? I almost couldn't wait to see the front page tomorrow, knowing it would kick up a fuss. But I also knew it could make all this shit ten times worse. I wasn't sure if my eagerness to see it should be justified, given the risks. All I could do was watch and wait. But I also had other things to do. Like Simon's phone, for one. Perhaps I was clutching at straws, believing the iPhone had all the answers. But it was one of the few things I had. There was still no sign of Matt.

But I supposed I hadn't exactly been looking. It had been easy to get caught up in the latest events. I didn't think he was involved with the Merc. I was sure that was linked to Bo Wong. But given that he was the last person to be seen with Angel, he wasn't off my radar. Far from it. With any luck, Laura had made an arrangement with Sherry from Provoke. I hoped that could lead me somewhere. But in a case like this, it was easy to go down the wrong track.

I thought about Stevie, out there in the cold of China-town. If he wasn't lying drunk somewhere instead. If he could do what I asked of him, this time tomorrow might provide more answers. At least, I hoped.

I looked around the pub. The same faces, the same smells. I was beginning to like the place a lot, perhaps too much, and I knew I had to be careful. I sipped my pint, lost in thought. Wondered what to make of my conversation with Frank. Thought about Maureen and her battle with cancer. Wondered if Frank had mentioned my visit to his wife and whether she was lying there in her hospital bed, thinking about me, the father of her granddaughter.

Nicole. I would go to her soon.

I picked up a copy of the *Guardian* that was sitting on a bench beside me. It was today's edition. I leafed through and came across a story about offshore bank accounts and the elite squirreling their cash away. And right away, Han Lan's accounts came back to me. All that money, all those millions he had in the Cayman Islands. And then his connection to Bo Wong, or rather Wong's connection to him. The police corruption. The dead girls. The missing girls. The heroin.

Heroin overdose, that'd be good. I could get you some.

Angel's words. They came back to me right then as I sat there staring out the window at nothing but drifting flecks of white. The words she spoke to me as I stood on that car park ledge.

I could get you some.

Cut your wrists, put a gun to your head. Heroin overdose, that'd be good.

I could get you some.

I felt dizzy. Downed the pint and stepped up to the bar again. Ordered a double Laphroig and knocked it back. Got another pint, a Guinness this time, and returned to the fire. Warmed my bones by those crackling flames. My head hurt, and I thought about the kicking I'd had and who might be responsible. I guessed it could be a number of people, and my cards were marked. Glanced at the door, half expecting Phil Young to walk in to finish off our little punch up.

I rolled up the paper and stuck it in my pocket. Pulled out my mobile and dialled Laura. She picked up on the first ring.

'Hello?'

'It's me.'

'Jim. You gonna be long? Have you forgotten about the shepherd's pie? It's nearly ready.'

'I'll be back soon. About an hour.'

'But I'm getting ready to dish it up.'

'Just have yours. Keep it warm or something.'

I knew she could hear the tinkling glasses behind me. 'Are you in a pub?'

I sighed. 'Yeah. For research.'

'Oh yeah? What kind of research? How many pints you can sink before you fall on your arse?'

'Not quite.'

'You can carry on back here if you want, but just get back in one piece. I don't want a repeat of the other night.'

'It won't come to that.'

'Just be careful, Jim. I mean it.'

'Have you heard anything about Sara?'

'The same. But she wants to see you. Tomorrow, if you can. And I checked out that website you were on about. Sherry, yeah?'

'That's her.'

'You have to put your contact details in and all that stuff. Might be best if we do it together. So you know what you're up against. She's pretty. Don't you go messing about...'

Jesus, what was this? We'd slept together once and I might as well be bloody married again. 'I won't. It's not that kind of date.'

'Oh shit! I've gotta go, the bloody pan's boiling over.'

'I'll see you soon.'

'An hour?'

'An hour.'

'You'd better be.'

And she hung up, leaving me with more to think about than the case.

Heroin overdose, that'd be good. I could get you some.

I savoured the Guinness like it was my last pint on Earth and thought about that day. Standing on that ledge. Angel there to rescue me, pull me right back from the brink. Angel in a freezer at the morgue. Those steps I climbed. The cold, blistering day. I could see myself tumbling to the ground at sixty miles an hour, my skull smashed as I hit the pavement. I felt the stitches at the back of my head beneath the Springsteen hat. Strange, but my head didn't feel like my own.

I drained the pint and dug in my pocket for some change as I left. The pavement was thick with snow and I went to the bus stop in the vague hope there was one due. Given the weather, I guessed I could be waiting a while. The road was black with sludge, so I supposed the conditions weren't as bad as they were across the city. There was still plenty of traffic around, though moving slowly. The air was bitter. I felt for Stevie out in this but I suspected that, if he had any sense, he'd be hiding away somewhere with the Whyte and Mackay. Though I hoped not. I needed results. And now that Bob was about to escape to warmer climes, I needed something to keep me on it and to piece each piece together.

I sparked up and wrapped the jacket around me. Thought once or twice about heading back to the pub and sitting by that fire again. It was the only place I'd really like to be right now. But then I saw the headlights of the 112 heading my way like a chariot in the dark. Paid the driver for a one-way ticket, miserable git that he was, and took a seat at the back so I could feel the warmth of the engine.

Rested my head against the glass and watched the grey, derelict tenements of Collyhurst roll by. Black curtains billowed out through smashed windows like mad witches in the night. And still the snow came, like never ending confetti. Ice formed on the glass beside me and my breath fogged the air. The bus was quiet except for a fat and lonely woman down the front and a couple of teenage lovers giggling over their smartphones. No one else was mad enough to be out in this tonight. And I felt somewhat guilty about sending Stevie out to do my dirty work. But better him than me. No one would suspect a homeless guy.

I thought about where the Merc was now, and Bob pounding away at a keyboard somewhere in the depths of the *Evening Chronicle* HQ. I only hoped he knew what he was doing. The lift home for his grandson had been a veiled threat indeed. We know where you live. We know who your grandkids are. We know what you're up to. Don't fuck with us.

I suppose if I was in his position, with the power to

change things overnight simply by writing an article, I would do the same. I'd have to do something. Was Bob desperate? I didn't think so, but he was close to it. Problem was, by writing whatever it was he was going to write, there was the potential for a dangerous can of worms to be opened.

I felt tired. Fatigued. The back of my head was throbbing, and I thought about Bob's insistence that I keep taking the painkillers. I dug around in my pockets and pulled a blister pack out. Swallowed two dry. Maybe a hot meal and a few hours' sleep was all I needed. My eyes felt heavy, and I battled to keep them open. For a few empty moments, I fell into the darkness of an exhausted nap as the bus rolled on through the winter night. Heard fireworks explode in the streets beyond the main roads and shook myself awake at the bright lights of takeaways and betting shops. If I could be half a world away, I would take it right now. The world around me was a miserable, broken down hell. Gangs of hooded youth gathered on street corners, blowing the pungent aroma of skunk into the air. Darkness and hurt lurked down every alley. Out there, a thousand babies cried into the night. No doubt a thousand mothers, too.

I shook myself awake as the bus approached my stop. I was the only passenger left. Stepped out into the freeze. The temperature had plummeted. A couple of kids were launching snowballs at each other in the terraced street beside me, but other than that, it was desolate. It was as if a new ice age had descended in a matter of hours and I was the only survivor. Although the blackened sludge had allowed the traffic to keep moving, it was icing over again, and the snow was drifting to cover up what hundreds of tyres had taken away now that the evening commute was all but over.

I steadied my stride as best I could and walked the short distance to Sara's house. There were one or two streetlamps out of action, and many of the terraces were abandoned and boarded up with metal grills. But the snow made it look like a wonderland. When I made it to the front door, thankful for not slipping on my arse, Laura was standing there waiting for me, lit up by the light from inside. I stepped over the threshold where we embraced, shared a brief kiss, and sat in the living room with the fire raging.

'I'll make you a tea. You're bloody freezing.'

'Make it a coffee? A strong one?'

She took the hint and poured a measure of brandy into the mug. I thawed out and dozed as she plated me up some shepherd's pie. Charlie was sitting on the rug in front of the fire, pushing a toy car around and making engine noises. If only I could be that innocent again. And then I thought of Nicole, perhaps sketching with coloured pencils or giving Barbie a new hairdo. Or maybe she was watching the telly with Karen or Frank as they both put on a brave face in case she picked up on just how sick Maureen really was.

'So I found that website,' she said, as she moved around the kitchen. 'Provoke, yeah?'

I nodded, feeling too tired to answer. I answered anyway. 'Yeah.'

'And you have to put your details in, you know. So I left it there because I didn't know what you wanted to do with it. I'll get online and we can check it out when you've had your tea.'

Home life. I missed it. It was where I needed to be. I smiled as she dished up and she caught my eye and gave me a wink. She brought the whole thing in on a tray and, like a good woman, urged me to dig in. The coffee was great, the brandy even better. And the shepherd's pie was the food of the Gods. It took me a while, but when I finally finished it, and Laura had insisted she wash up, I was carried away on the chair into a deep and restful sleep.

65

'So here you go. All charged and ready to go. Remember the code to unlock it?'

'Nineteen eighty-six.'

'And away you go. Now look at this. Fill in this form and then submit it with your e-mail and all that stuff. Shouldn't take too long but I suppose if you want to remain anonymous then you'll have to come up with something. I'm not that creative, I'm afraid. And why do you want to do this, anyway?'

I explained as best I could. That Sherry was a 'colleague' of Angel and might know more than she was letting on when I began this investigation. She thought I was wasting my time and said so.

'But it's another line of enquiry. She could lead me to Matt.'

'Your top suspect?'

'As good as.' I lifted the beer and swigged deep. Now that Charlie was in bed, we were free to relax on the couch with a drink and each other's company. I felt refreshed after an hour's nap and a shower. 'And yet there's still no sign of him. Not that there would be. But she might lead me to him.'

'Because he's one of her clients?'

'I think so, yeah. And even if he isn't or wasn't, I've a feeling this girl might have a few stories to tell.'

'How so?'

'I don't know, just a gut feeling, I suppose. She seems vulnerable. Easily led astray.'

'Like Angel.'

'Like Angel,' I nodded. 'I want to know her story. And hopefully find out more about Carol and some of the other clients at the same time.'

'So where are you taking her?'

'Don't know. The pub?'

She laughed. Hard. 'You've not got a clue, have you?'

'What do you mean? What's wrong with that?'

'You can't take a high-class prostitute for a pint.'

'Why not? I'm paying, aren't I?'

'She'll expect more than half a cider and a packet of crisps.'

'All right, all right, so I'll take her to a fancy restaurant or something. Whatever it takes to get information.'

'That's better. Get her well lubricated and you could be in.'

'Steady on.'

'I meant with a nice bottle of Rioja or something.'

'I know what you meant.'

'You've a one track mind.'

She was wrong, but I didn't let that get in the way of her wandering hands. I had to make a start on the booking before she got carried away. We put all the details in, making most of it up along the way. I was now one Robert Frost, solicitor, forty-eight, six foot three with a healthy bank balance. I set up a fake e-mail address and gave my mobile. I answered all the relevant security questions and even invented a whole new bogus persona on Facebook, with Laura's help. Just in case Sherry went snooping around. We both decided we had to be as convincing as possible. Laura agreed to act as my 'secretary' in case of any calls to confirm the booking and my identity. It wasn't foolproof, but I reckoned it was enough to get Sherry behind a dinner table, especially if she thought there was good money in it. I felt a bit cruel on Sherry because I liked that girl when I met her, but I had faith that once I got her to meet me, I could get what I needed out of her. I suppose I was exploiting her but I reckoned she'd be used to that. She wouldn't be getting paid, but she would get a decent meal out of it, especially if she gave me what I wanted.

'You think she'll bite?'

'I think so.'

'You seem confident.'

'I am.' I sparked up and took a long drink on the bottle. 'I think we've done enough to reel her in.'

'So where are you gonna take her?'

'No idea. Any recommendations?'

'Me?' she laughed. 'Not a bloody clue. Can't remember the last time I went for a decent meal.'

'Well, if you play your cards right, I might be able to help you there.'

'I'm gonna hold you to that, Jim Locke.'

Trouble was, now I had to find the money to take not just one, but two girls out. I wanted Laura there with me when Sherry turned up. As an observer. Just in case. She wasn't keen when I suggested it and felt she had enough on her mind without getting involved in the investigation. But she knew Angel too and wanted to get to the truth as much as her sister. And besides, someone had to pay for it. It wasn't going to be me.

'Trouble is...'

She looked at me and I could tell she knew what I was thinking. 'Oh no.' She was shaking her head and flicking ash. 'I've got no money, Jim.'

'Just a few quid, that's all.'

'You'll need more than a few quid to keep that girl happy.'

'And you as well.'

'Look, I'm not happy about hanging around like a fucking spare part.'

'I'll make it up to you, I promise. And I will pay you back.'

'Just how much do you need?'

'Don't know. Couple of hundred?'

'Jesus, Jim.'

'Look, do you want to get to the bottom of this, or what?'

'I didn't ask you to go looking for her bloody murderer, did I?'

'No, but your sister did.'

'Then ask her for the money.'

'I can't do that. She's in bloody hospital.'

'She's not mental enough to know you can't do this for free. Surely you don't do any of this for free?'

'I've never done it before. And besides, we agreed–Sara and me–that my payment was just this. She'd put me up, at least until the case was solved, and that'd be it.'

'So what about expenses?'

'What about them? I didn't think I'd need any!'

'Fuck's sake, Jim.' She had her head in her hands. I think she was almost laughing. 'You couldn't run a fucking bath, could you?'

'You what?'

She sighed. Grabbed my head and kissed me. 'Nothing. I'll get you something to keep you afloat tomorrow morning. From my ISA. But listen–I want it back, Jim Locke. And soon. So you'd better start advertising your services as a bloody private investigator on a full-time basis. That would be a good place to start.'

66

L aura went up to read Charlie a late bedtime story when we spotted him lingering at the bottom of the stairs. The child protested loudly about how much he wanted me to do it, but Laura insisted and left me to peruse Simon's iPhone. I cracked open a fresh bottle and got stuck in.

There was a lot to sift through, most of the texts rubbish and most of the e-mail plain spam. But there were more than a few text messages that caught my eye. I went into the texts he'd directly received and sent between himself and Matthew Brookes Wilkes. I suppose it could've been any other Matthew, but I reckoned it was him all right. I scrolled through, right back to the beginning of their exchanges, which took a few minutes so there must have been a fair amount of contact between the two. The first twenty or so messages were nothing much, just the usual etiquette between acquaintances. I guessed that at this point in their relationship, they didn't know each other too well. There were quick and succinct replies galore until I came across one dated seventh of September. It was sent from this iPhone.

Carol wants to know how we're getting on with Xi. Any joy? xx

And the reply from Matt, a whole day later:

There's more where that one came from. If she can hook me up with Angel, I'd be most grateful ;) Could be some sniff in it for you? x

By sniff, I guessed he meant coke. Which took me right back to Angel hiding in the bathroom, bawling. I knew she'd been getting stuck into it, and that it was a problem–that much was obvious–and I wondered where she was getting her deal from. By the looks of things, Matt was on the ball when it came to party drugs. I wasn't surprised. If he could get his hands on coke so easily, where was he getting his supply? Wong? Others? And if so, was there more than just the powder flying around? Bob had talked about heroin use among the East Asian girls that were apparently being trafficked in, so I supposed it wasn't out of the question. And this name–Xi–who was she? I was pretty certain it was nailed on to be a dancing girl, but what did Carol want with her? I could only conclude it was the obvious.

I scrolled through more, through a lot of winks and kisses and LOL's, until I came to another text barely a week later from Matt's phone to Simon's.

Great night mate–and day! I can't thank Carol enough. No worries with the coke. Got some nice MD too if you and Carl are interested? I'll see what I can do with the other stuff. Night night xx

And a cute reply from Simon:

You're welcome, big boy! LOL xxx Thanks again sweet x

Jesus, what the fuck were these two up to? So, MD. Short

for MDMA. And what other stuff could he possibly mean? More party drugs? Or perhaps the more dangerous kind?

I took the notepad Laura had bought me and scribbled it all down. I could do with finding out who this Xi was. Found the Provoke website on Laura's laptop and brought up the pics of all the escort girls on offer. It was all very professional, all very legitimate. And like Angel, my guess was that none of the girls shared their real identities. I didn't expect to find a 'Xi', and I didn't. But I did find an Asian girl by the name of Wan. Perhaps somewhat ironically, or perhaps with more than a nod and a wink, her surname was Kin. Classy.

I clicked on the contact list on Simon's phone and found the number for Matthew Brookes Wilkes. Since there were no new messages in Simon's inbox, I wondered if Matt would respond if I sent him a text myself. I opened the message icon and hovered my thumb over the little keypad.

Thinking.

Thought better of it. I needed more time and thought it would be best to see what tomorrow's front page was first. I'd sleep on it. Instead, I went into his e-mail for a closer look and browsed through online billing and statements, Facebook and Twitter notifications and all manner of other shite before I gave it up as a waste of time. The bulk of information I needed was in the texts. I went back through his contacts, feeling like a voyeur and a nosey bastard, but kept telling myself it was all for the greater good. I smiled when I came across another name I recognised. I dipped into texts both sent and received from this little individual and scrolled through to their first exchanges. Same scenario as Matthew Brookes Wilkes, all cagey and polite until this one, received to this phone on 3rd November, two days before Bonfire Night.

Simon. Any more you can throw our way? Midland's good for Bonfire night. Same as last time? Might be fireworks? Could do with something to 'spice' things up if you know what I mean...;)

And the reply from Simon:

Bryn. No problem, darling. It's in the bag. See you both at seven? I'll bring a sparkler LOL!!! xx

Fuck me, this was getting better and better. There were a few more messages between them before it all ended just over a week ago. I could only assume it had all stopped once Simon's phone had 'gone missing' and mysteriously ended up in my pocket. I wondered who this other person was that Simon was referring to. Another ex-copper? It was a strong possibility and one I wasn't ruling out.

I took a long pull on the beer as Laura's feet hit the stairs. Before she reached the bottom, my phone rang out. Asked her to grab it from my jacket pocket and she handed it to me before grabbing her own beer and crashing on the couch.

I went to answer, thinking it was probably Bob. I stopped before I hit the green button. The caller ID told me Phil Young was waiting on the line.

I let it ring out.

'Who is it?'

'Just an old friend.'

'So why didn't you answer it? Jim?'

I held my hand up and watched as a text came through, telling me I had a voicemail. I dialled it and listened, taking long drags on my smoke.

'Yeah, Jim... It's me. Phil. Look, I feel a bit of a dick about the other day, you know, and...well I just wanted to apologise for what I said and...you know, it got a bit out of hand. Listen, I'd like to make it up to you properly, mate. Give us a bell back and we can sort something out. I don't want to let this get in the way of things, you know. Hope you're okay, mate.'

He had some fucking nerve.

67

I rolled over when my phone rang. There was that faint morning light again, peeking through the gap in the curtain as dawn finally broke over the city. Laura was asleep next to me, the duvet wrapped tightly around her. Checked the alarm clock on her bedside table. 06:38. Early enough for Charlie to be getting up for school.

I reached out and picked up. It was a number I didn't recognise, and I hesitated for a moment before pushing the green button.

'Hello?'

'Jim? It's Bob. It's done.'

He sounded faint on the line, like he was far away in space or something. 'Bob?'

'It's done. I'm in Gran Canaria. You should see the weather out here. Not too hot, nowhere near cold. It's lovely. You should come out when you get a chance. Fucking hell, it's good to get away from that shithole.'

'It's done? What's done, Bob?'

'What do you bloody think, son?'

'Front page?'

I could feel him smiling down the line from a few thousand miles away. 'My last one. The rest is up to George now.'

'George who?'

'Thornley. Editor in chief.'

'He's let you run with this one, then?'

'The type of bloke who'd never turn down a scoop, Jim. Listen, it's gonna hit the shelves today. And then the shit's gonna hit as well. Big style. So be careful.'

'Well, at least you got yourself out of the way before it did, leaving me here to deal with the mess. Cheers for that.'

'Yeah, well. Sorry about that, son. Listen—be careful, Jim. Stay out of the way.'

'Not gonna be easy now you've gone and blown it wide open.'

'Any progress?'

'Some. Phil Young left me a message on my phone last night. Late on. Wants to meet me again.'

'Phil Young?'

'The guy I had the punch up with in the Marble. You remember him...'

'So? What are you gonna do?'

'Ignore him. Either that or tell him to fuck right off.'

There was a buzz on the line. It sounded like a warm breeze coming up off the ocean.

'Look, I'll phone you in a few days, just to see how things are going at your end. I'm just gonna let the story break first, weigh up the situation. Jim?'

'Okay.' I shifted myself out of bed. Laura stirred beside me and scowled, her bed hair making her look like she'd been dragged through a hedge. 'You do that.'

'You okay, Jim?'

'Yeah, yeah. It's just still early here, that's all. Just woke up.'

'Thought you sounded a bit tired. You been taking those painkillers? Look, I had to phone you early while I remembered. It's early here too, and I've only just got to the villa. Call it a wake up call.'

Was the bastard rubbing it in? He was probably standing there on his porch or something, getting stuck into a strong coffee or an equally strong wine, blowing thick cigar smoke into the warm Spanish morning.

'You could've given it another hour or two. I'm knackered. Catching up on sleep...'

'At least I bloody called, son. Listen, I've got to go. I'll call again for an update soon. If you have any problems, you can contact me. Not that I'd be able to help much from this end, but...'

'Bob. How do I get hold of you?'

'I'll call you first. No one knows where I am except for George. Be safe, lad. Speak to you soon.'

Then he was gone. I found a scrap of paper and pen and jotted down the name he'd given me.

68

I stood at the back door and sparked up while the kettle boiled and a hard rain came down to wash away the snow. The ground was sludgy as it melted and the sky was a horrible grey. It matched my mood. I brewed two coffees while Laura and Charlie rushed about the house. The kid would be late if he didn't get a move on. I dodged the porridge and orange juice, my head throbbing to the whizz, bang and wallop of bloody CBeebies. Crashed on the couch as the chaos abounded, trying to piece my head together and the bits I'd dug up from Simon's phone last night. Smoked several coffin nails and drank a second coffee as Charlie clung to my legs, thinking about what I would do with Phil's message. Should I get back to him? I doubted that would be a good idea at all. I finally got some peace when Laura left in a hurry, Charlie screaming his merry way behind her.

My head finally settled down when the noise stopped. I spent half an hour sitting in front of the breakfast news with a slice of toast and another coffee–this time with a dash of brandy, just to warm me up–and let myself wake up. Took two painkillers and freshened up with a hot shower and a change of clothes. I didn't bother shaving.

Laura came back half an hour later and did the same before powering up her laptop and checking for e-mail. We were both surprised to find a message from Sherry waiting for us.

Hi Robert. It would be a pleasure, love. Get back to me and we'll sort something! Mwah! Xx.

Laura insisted we send one back straight away, and I let her do the talking. She said she was an expert in these things, and I believed her. She sent a message suggesting dinner at Rosso. Tonight. I wasn't entirely sure I was ready for that, but she sent it anyway before I could protest. She said she wanted a night out and was actually looking forward to it. Sherry must've been lying in bed with a laptop on her belly because we got an e-mail back almost immediately. She said tonight would be fine and she'd see me there. She left her mobile. Laura made me text her to confirm. Said it would be nice and professional. I did, and made sure she knew to meet me inside, not at the door. I didn't want her to do a vanishing act before I had a chance to speak to her.

And that was it. All I had to do now was secure a table. Laura said she'd phone to book just as soon as it opened at eleven.

'Oh, before I forget.' She reached into her handbag at her feet and pulled out some cash. 'Here. Five hundred. Should keep you going, no problem. But I want it back, Jim. It's from my ISA.'

'Laura, you don't have to give me this much.'

'Yes, I do. You'll need it for tonight and probably a few more after that. You can pay me when you get the money.'

'I feel like such a shit.'

'You are,' she said, and laughed before dragging me on top of her. 'But I like it.'

69

'So, what's the plan? For today, I mean...'

'Going over to the hospital to see Sara. You coming?'

'Don't think I can stand another minute in that place,' she said, fastening her bra back on. 'God knows how Sara's able to put up with it. Well, she can't. I'll go tomorrow. You can tell her I'll be visiting in the afternoon.'

'I will. Do you know what she wants to see me about?'

'She didn't say, other than she wants to see you. That's all.'

I realised it could be anything but hoped it was connected to the case. Something important.

I spent ten minutes scraping thick snow from the Punto's windscreen and let the engine purr until it heated up enough. Laura said she'd let me know how the booking went. With any luck, we'd be all set by midday. I'd invite Sherry to join me at the table while Laura waited at the bar for her 'date' and I got stuck into crab and lobster ravioli and a bottle of Malbec.

I slung my jacket on, pocketed the money from Laura and got in the car. Flicked on the stereo–New Order–then left the street. Destination: Wythenshawe.

70

I t was a long drive. I got stuck behind a smash for twenty minutes halfway up Oldham Road. There was already an ambulance on the scene, and then a fire engine turned up to cut someone out. It brought me back down to reality right there, aware that I could go at any time. Any of us could. One minute here, one minute gone. A hard rain battered the windscreen, and the traffic slowed to a standstill. It gave me a chance to try to gather my thoughts. My head was overcrowded with everything. Sara and her cut wrists and the section under the Mental Health Act. Lord only knows what I'd find on that ward. Bob doing lunch in some Spanish cafe, safe from all the shit he was about to expose. Steve and the photos, the black Merc, the bent coppers, the missing girls, the dead girl. Phil Young, Karen and Nicole, Frank and Maureen, Laura and me. The smashed up Volvo in front of me. The stitches in my head and the beating down Dalton Alley. Tonight's meeting with Sherry. Simon and Matt, Bo Wong and Han Lan. Today's front page. The whole fucking lot.

The front page. Shit, Bob said it would all come out

today. I had to find a paper. I flicked off the music and
switched on BBC Manchester. It was 10:37 according to the
clock on the dash, so I guessed I'd just missed the news.
When the traffic finally started moving again, I got dragged
into a discussion about Feminism and pregnancy, followed
by a live phone in with the government's drug czar and the
decriminalization of cannabis. Finally switched it off when I
reached the Princess Parkway. I put my foot down when I
passed the ASDA and whacked the stereo up full for the
drive into Wythenshawe. The traffic was flowing nicely but
there was plenty on the road so it was a relief when I finally
came off at the Sharston roundabout. Now all I had to do
was find the hospital. Wythenshawe was a strange place.
Everywhere looked the same. Ended up going in the wrong
bloody direction for five minutes before I realised I was lost.
Asked a couple of hoodies for directions, but it was pointless. They either didn't understand what I was on about or
they couldn't give a fuck, and I couldn't hear them anyway
because their bloody Pitbull was barking its head off.
Almost gave it up as a lost cause until I saw the sign I
needed and followed it. Ten minutes later, head spinning
and needing a piss, I pulled up in the car park out front and
got ripped off for a one hour stay.

Laureate House was the main psychiatric unit, and I just
managed to find a toilet before I pissed myself. Laura said
her sister was on Bronte Ward, but when I asked at reception where that was, I just got a surly grunt from a woman
who reminded me of the Wicked Witch of the West.

'Up the stairs.' Nothing like a warm welcome.

Made my way up and found the main double doors were
locked. I pressed a buzzer and a nurse came out to let me in.
She was nice enough. Told her I was here to see Sara and
she smiled and showed me across the main floor. It was

busy. Got some serious stares as I stepped through. There were two heavy looking lads playing pool, one black, one Asian. The Asian kid was eyeballing me like I'd just fucked his mum or something. The black kid laughed out loud. Another lad, white, came towards me and started whispering some shit or other as he rocked from side to side. Several were sitting on a couch watching Jeremy bloody Kyle. A few hung around on a little roof garden, smoking. An older bloke was shuffling along like a doddery old fella, but he could barely be out of his forties. A woman with stains down her t-shirt and clearly no bra underneath was shouting something nasty at another guy, who just sat there blinking. The whole place gave me the fucking creeps.

'Her room's this way,' she said, and led me down a corridor beyond the main communal area. I could feel eyes boring into the back of me. 'She's just had her breakfast.'

'How is she?'

'Not too bad. A bit distracted. Are you her brother?'

'Friend.'

'She'll be glad to have a visitor.'

I would too if I had to stay in here all day. I nodded as she led me to a door with number 7 on it. She knocked on and let herself in. Sara was sitting on the bed, her bandaged wrists resting in her lap.

'Sara, you've got a visitor, love.'

She looked up, bags under her eyes, her skin pale and craggy. I didn't know what they were giving her, but she looked a mess. Her jeans had a huge coffee stain on them and her hair looked like it had gone grey overnight.

'I'll leave you to it,' she said, and closed the door behind her.

I sat down in a hospital chair. 'Sara. How are you feeling?'

She didn't look at me, just focussed on her pink slippers. Shrugged. 'I'm all right.'

But she didn't look it. I reached out to touch her knee, but she flinched and moved down the bed. Christ, this was gonna be hard work.

'Laura said you wanted to see me. So. Here I am. Everything okay in here?'

'No. The food's shit. And I can't sleep.'

'Does the medication not help?'

'It's so noisy in here at night. Loud. Tom won't let me out.'

'Tom? Who's Tom?'

'Nurse.'

I nodded. Not a clue what to say. Just a week ago, we were looking for her missing friend. She was chatty, concerned, even flirty. Now she was a completely different person. It was as if someone or something had just slipped into her brain and pulled all the personality out of her. It was fucking scary. Even worse for her.

I wasn't sure how to approach this conversation, and I'd never been on a mental health ward before. So I guessed the best way would be to carry on as normal.

'Do you remember what happened?'

She shut her eyes tight and put those bandaged arms to her face. Not the best response I would've wanted. I went to reach out again but stopped myself.

'Sara?'

'I can't!'

'Can't remember?'

'Can't talk about it. They'll kill me if I do.'

'Who? Sara?'

'They'll kill me.'

Shit, this was giving me the heebie jeebies. 'Sara, no one's going to kill you, okay? Not while I'm here.'

'They've done it before, they'll do it again.'

'Who?'

'Them.'

'Sara, I promise, no one's going to hurt you, all right? Look, I know this is hard but please...trust me on this.'

'Oh, how would you fucking know!'

'Who are they, Sara?'

'I can't.' She put those scarred hands to her ears. 'Can't, can't, can't.'

'Okay. Would it help if Laura was here? With me?'

'Laura?'

'Laura.'

'No Laura, you can't tell her! Do you hear me?!'

'All right, all right.'

'They'll kill her if you do.'

'I promise, I won't tell her.'

'They'll kill me and Angel and Laura and me.'

'Sara...'

'You can go now.'

'Sara, I've come to see you. See how you're getting on, love.'

'I'm fine. But I want to go home. I want to go home right now. Have you come to take me home, David?'

'Sara, I'm not David. It's Jim, remember? Jim Locke.'

'You've come to take me home!'

'No, Sara...' She gripped my knees then. Gripped them tight before getting to her feet and pacing up and down the room. 'Sara, come and sit down.'

'Don't tell me what to do.'

'Tell me about Angel. Tell me how you know Angel.'

'Angel's coming here soon.' She was nodding hard, her eyes darting from wall to wall. 'She told me.'

'Sara, she's...'

'Take me to Angel! Take me to her!'

'Sara, come and sit down.'

'No.'

'Sara, please.'

'Can we go now?'

'We can't go now, love. I'm sorry, but we can't.'

She clamped her ears again and jumped onto the bed, face down. She started bawling into the pillow. Biting it hard as a long drool of saliva leaked from her mouth. I went to reach out again, then stopped myself. All I wanted to do was reach out and touch her shoulder, to tell her it was gonna be all right, everything was gonna be all right, she'd be out by Christmas if she just did what the doctors said.

'Sara?'

'Leave me alone.'

'Do you want me to come another day?'

'No! Don't ever come again!'

'Sara, it's okay. I'll go now. I'll come back another time.'

'Fuck off! Fuck off! Fuck off! Just fuck off!'

I felt rooted to the spot, standing there under the fluorescent light. Bars on the window, sterile furniture and the smell of disinfectant. A half empty bowl of soggy Weetabix on the bedside table. Blood stained knickers on the floor.

I turned for the door, not wanting to leave but desperate to get away at the same time. 'Bye, Sara.'

I left her crying into the pillow.

71

S parked up as soon as I got outside and took that shit in deep. I needed nicotine and lots of it. I felt a complete shit for leaving her there. I knew she wasn't in her right mind. Far from it. In fact, she was worse than the last time I saw her, when the cuts were still fresh. I didn't know what they were giving her, but it didn't seem to be doing much good. But shit, what did I know?

Tried speaking to the nurse who'd let me onto the ward, but getting her attention was like pulling teeth. Getting anyone's attention, in fact. Spoke to a male nurse who reckoned it'd be better I speak to Rachel, whoever that was. Then his buzzer went and he was off, running down the corridor with another guy. I walked back through the communal area with the woman screeching and pool players staring. A man with a Sigmund Freud beard and his pants round his ankles staggered toward me with his arms out, and I dodged him just as the urine leaked down his leg and trickled across the floor.

My phone trilled before I made it to the car.

'Hello?'

'Jim. It's booked. Eight o'clock. Is she all right?'

'Well, not quite, but I think you should see her soon.'

'I'm going tomorrow, remember? Did you tell her?'

Bollocks. 'Shit, I forgot. Sorry, love.'

'How is she?'

'She thinks someone's out to kill her.'

'Oh no...'

'What? She said this before?'

'No, it's just... well, I hate it when she's like this. Thinks the whole world's out to get her, you know. What was she saying?'

'She thought I was there to take her home.' And I told her the rest. How I was David, not Jim. How I mustn't tell her sister anything in case they killed her. How she seems to think Angel was still with us. The tears.

There was a massive sigh on the line and I felt for the kid. She'd obviously seen all this before, but I suppose it didn't make it any easier. She kept it short and sweet and asked when I was due home. I'd never even thought about it.

'You'll have to smarten up for your date tonight. She'll be expecting it.'

'Maybe, but I just want to keep her there long enough to talk. That's the plan, anyway.'

'So?'

'Six?' It was a random number that popped into my head. 'With any luck.'

'This is exciting, seeing you in action. Sexy.'

'There won't be much to see.'

'I'll be the judge of that.'

The call ended by the time I reached the Punto. I started her up, keenly aware that I was driving the poor woman's car. The poor woman who thought they were going to kill her. Delusion or not, I wanted to know who she was talking about. Was it just her voices, tormenting her? Or did she know much more than she was letting on? I left the hospital in silence. No radio, no New Order. Just the meeting with Sara repeating over and over in my head as I left Wythenshawe.

72

Driving back down the Princess Parkway, my mobile rang again. Checked the screen as I drove. Another number I didn't recognise. It rang out, then buzzed again just as I reached Southern Cemetery. Took a left onto Barlow Moor Road and pulled up. Answered.

'Hello?'

'Hello, who's that?'

'Who's this?'

'Stevie. I'm looking for Jim Locke.'

'Stevie, it's me. Thanks for ringing back. You get any pictures?'

'Filled one roll up, no problem.'

'Good. Anything interesting?'

'A lot of blokes in suits, if you call that interesting.'

It was and I told him so. 'Where are you?'

'Just on my way to the shelter. Need to get a bed for tonight.'

He sounded drunk. No surprise there. 'Churchill Way?'

'Yeah.'

'All right, but where exactly are you, right now?'

There was a pause and a gust of wind. 'Had to walk to fucking Rusholme, didn't I? Been trying to explain to those pricks in the job centre I have no fixed abode. I mean, do I look like I've got my own gaff?'

'I'll pick you up and take you down to the shelter.'

'All right, man. Where?'

'Wait at Whitworth Park, you know it?'

'Like the back of my fucking hand, mate.' He cackled into the phone.

'I'll be there in ten minutes.'

I turned around, got back onto the Parkway, and bombed it. If Stevie had done what I asked, I could be handling some serious evidence by lunchtime. I just hoped he was cognitive enough to tell me what he saw and was able to do it all over again tonight. It would probably help if I slipped him another twenty quid for his trouble.

Ten minutes later, I parked up on Moss Lane East and stepped into Whitworth Park. He was sitting on a bench by the fountain, his coat huddled up around him and his bags at his feet. He saw me coming and grabbed his things. He wasn't as drunk as I thought, but there was something else there in his eyes.

'Jimmy,' he said, limping towards me. 'It's bloody freezing, man. You're a lifesaver. Don't think I could be arsed walking down there.'

'Have you eaten?'

'Not since last night.'

'Hungry?'

I took him to the Gemini Cafe down the road. There were a few paramedics from the MRI having a late breakfast, and the place was dotted with students and bank staff. Bought him a full English and persuaded myself to get egg on toast. I wished I hadn't. We shared a large pot of tea and took a booth in the corner.

'So tell me. What have you got?'

He reached into his bag and pulled out one of the disposable cameras. 'Filled this up,' he said, and handed it to me. 'Some right posh cunts on there. And some hard cases too.'

He probably wasn't wrong. 'How many?'

'How many what?'

'How many men did you see?'

He shrugged, dipped some toast into a runny egg. 'Don't know. Ten? Twelve, maybe.'

'What did they look like?'

'Just told you, man. Suited up. Sharp. Plenty of money. No one gave me any spare fucking change.'

'Anyone you recognise?'

He shook his head, swallowed. 'Should I?'

I supposed not. I thanked him, pocketed the camera and poured the tea. Thinking. Caught my reflection in the mirror beside us. I looked like I hadn't slept in weeks. Stevie looked even worse. Much worse, actually. He started coughing again, and it sounded like a death rattle. Wondered if he was looking after himself.

'Sounds bad, Stevie. You saw a doctor recently?'

He almost laughed. 'Nah. Just a smoker's cough, that's all.'

'I wouldn't be so sure. You spend most of your time sleeping rough.'

'Got a bed last night, didn't I?'

I almost forgot. 'Any luck with the housing?'

No reply. And to be honest, I didn't expect him to be

actively looking for a home. Not that there were any homes thanks to the wankers in government. He was the type of homeless character who liked being on the streets and off the grid. Summer wasn't too bad. Warm nights, loose talk, booze and drugs. But winter was a killer. Winter was a beast, and it showed on him. He was hungry, all right.

'So. Are you able to do it again? Tonight? Just one more night...'

He went for the egg again. 'I said I would, didn't I?'

'Good man.' I slipped him another twenty and he almost snatched it like a frog might catch a fly.

'So what do you want me to do?'

'Same again. Just fill the other camera up and we're done. I owe you one.'

He shrugged again. Even blushed. 'It's nothing, man. I mean, what else am I gonna do? It's not like I've got a woman to go home to, is it?'

'Just one other thing. About the men from last night. Did they all turn up in cars?'

'Mostly, yeah.' He stabbed a sausage like he wanted to kill it for a second time. 'A BMW, an Audi. One of those fuck off Volkswagen things. Oh, and there was a Mercedes crawling about all night as well. That was weird.'

I bet it was. 'Anyone talk to you?'

'What, other than 'Get a job, you lazy bastard'? No, not that I remember.'

I nodded. I supposed it had worked so far. There was no point in calling it a day until after the second night. Though I knew that if it went on any further than that, someone might clock what was going on. Chinatown was an unusual patch, for any homeless guy. Piccadilly, the Northern Quarter, the Shambles maybe. But not Chinatown. Tonight would be his last.

He finished up and polished off my egg on toast too. I got us another pot of tea while I tried to get to the bottom of his cough, but he was having none of it. We chatted about old times, about how we'd spend the odd night together behind Ho's bakery to keep warm. It seemed to cheer him up. I knew he had secrets even most of the others didn't know. He wasn't one for talking about himself and kept changing the subject when I asked how he was. I mean, how he was *really*.

He rolled us both a smoke and we stepped out and walked towards the Punto, cutting through Whitworth Park on the way. There was snow in the air again, just a light dusting, but it was cold enough to freeze the flame on an old sailor's Zippo. I felt a bit of a shit for asking him to do this for me, especially given the weather. But he was tough. A bit rusty around the edges, but tough. One more night would be worth it.

I drove him to the shelter on Churchill Way. With any luck, he'd be early enough to secure a bed for tonight. We shook on it and he said he'd call me again tomorrow. I promised myself I would buy him something special if he came up with the goods. I had faith in him.

I put some fuel in the Punto and drove back towards town. Almost crashed when I spotted the *Manchester Evening Chronicle* billboard outside a newsagent's on Regent Road.

EX-GMP CHIEFS IN VICE RING SCANDAL.

Christ, he wasn't pulling any punches. I pulled over, nipped into the nearest Tesco Express, and grabbed a paper. Stocked up on smokes too, and got distracted by the cool, refreshing beers in the fridge. If there was a time I needed a drink, it was now. I grabbed a large Peroni and paid the Sikh behind the counter before getting back in the Punto and finding a backstreet nearby to pop the cap and read Bob's damning verdict.

He wasn't wrong about the shit that was about to go down. I'd barely gotten through the neck and the first paragraph when I felt the hairs on the back of my neck stand up.

This was big. This was very fucking big.

73

Exclusive
FORMER GMP CHIEF AND STAFF
IN VICE COVER UP
By Robert Turner, Chief Crime Correspondent.

A *Manchester Evening Chronicle investigation, led by me, and beginning right back in 1976, can finally expose the seedy yet devastating truth that has been hidden behind the walls of Greater Manchester Police Headquarters for almost FOUR decades. And, sadly, it not only involves the GMP but at least TWO other forces that we know of. Evidence gathered by myself and my team, including colleagues at the West Yorkshire Evening Post and others, has now been handed directly to the Metropolitan Police and the International Police Force, Interpol. You can read about this expose in these pages tonight and for the next week. We at the Manchester Evening Chronicle believe the city of Manchester is owed the truth, the whole truth, and nothing but the truth. It is our moral duty to expose this outrage. Join us as we reveal just how deep this conspiracy goes, for it promises to change the face of this city's police force forever.*

74

He wasn't wrong. Jesus, this was gonna go national. I'd be surprised if it wasn't already. I switched on the radio, tuned into BBC Manchester. It was almost 12:30 and the news would be up any minute. I took a long drink and sparked up, resting the bottle between my legs. I almost didn't want to read on. But now that it was out, I wondered if Bob would be right about them crawling back into the woodwork. Just how many were involved? A quick flick through the pages told the story. I scanned page three and saw at least twenty names in bold type, including all those we'd followed into Chinatown. Former Chief of GMP, Sir David Howe; Former Assistant Chief Constable, Phillip Browning; Former Chief of North Wales, Bryn Llewellyn; Former Chief of West Yorkshire, Sir Michael Robert Fletcher.

Right now, across the city, across the *country* probably, there were thousands reading Bob's words. It would be online across the globe. They were fucked and they knew it. I read on. On pages two and three were several photographs of the men in question, all of them high-ranking officers in three different forces. On pages four and five were more photographs–all of them of missing East Asian women, the earliest case going back to 1980. Chi Phuong stared out at me. There was no photograph of Angel in these pages–yet.

75

HIGH-RANKING OFFICIALS IN
SEX TRAFFICKING
By Robert Turner, Chief Crime Correspondent.

I t is hard to imagine, except in the pages of some elaborate crime novel, just what is being exposed here in these pages. One could imagine such crimes occurring in some far-flung Communist state, perhaps. Communist Russia, North Korea... wherever. But what we don't expect is for such criminality to occur on our very own shores—and our very own doorstep. But it is—and has been for FOUR decades. Yet what we are exposing here is not some Eastern European gang operation; not gangsters or cartels... but the very organisations that are supposed to serve and protect us, especially the most vulnerable. It is with great sadness and regret that today, THREE police forces must face the full force of British Justice. Nothing less will do, because these three police forces—Greater Manchester Police, North Wales Constabulary, and West Yorkshire Police, have hidden behind a brick wall of false justice for so long. It is this very in-justice that must now be rectified, for the good of this city and others. Before *we get to the meat and bones of this most vile corruption, I ask that you brace yourself before reading on. Because scandals like this don't come around often. Thankfully. It is only when they do that we must question our collective morality. Countless women deserve justice. We owe them that. Today, the Manchester Evening Chronicle will endeavour to do just that.*

76

I slung the paper on the passenger seat and started her up. More than anything, I needed to get to Boots to process the camera film. Drained the beer and tossed it into the back as I pulled away from the main Regent Road and headed back towards town. The news came on the radio and it was the top story. Vox pops from journalists outside GMP HQ littered the airwaves. Sky, the BBC and ITV were all apparently lining up to interview the current Chief Constable, Sir Anthony George Nicholls, but had to settle for the Chief Press Officer instead. A press conference, she'd said, would be called for six o'clock tomorrow evening. That would give them enough time to come up with whatever long line of excuses they might have. By now, Bob would be kicking back with a Montecristo beside a pool, or toasting the demise of GMP top brass as he read his own, and no doubt other's words from *The Guardian* to *The Telegraph* to *The London Evening Standard*. As I listened, I shook my head in disbelief at how damaging all this was. There were coppers I knew–normal, everyday coppers– who would fall victim of their bosses' corruption. Coppers who were quick to fuck my life up. I couldn't help but laugh.

I gunned it down Deansgate and found a space on Blackfriars. Shoved a couple of quid in the meter and ran towards Market Street and the Boots I'd bought the cameras from with Stevie. Up the stairs to the photography department. A quick instruction on how to use the machine from a bored-looking assistant and five minutes later I was done. Back down through crowds of shoppers buying perfume and gift sets for Christmas until I was out the door and Ding Dong Merrily On High tromboned its way through the tunnel section of Market Street. Got accosted by a pair of Salvation Army volunteers shaking buckets in my face before I managed to get away.

The high street was hammered and buzzing. As I hit the pavement, I was surrounded by a barrage of noise. Even at this time of day, it was packed in every direction. I walked through the throng, bloody Christmas songs belting from every store. The Christmas Markets were now in full swing and there was an army of punters getting stuck into Bratwurst and German wheat beer at every turn. I was tempted to join them, but knew I had to get these photos back to Sara's sharpish. Shoved the packet in my jacket and wrapped it around me.

Weaved my way down past the M&S and stopped in my tracks as I reached St. Ann's Square. Standing there outside a jewellers on the corner was the Chinese guy who'd been smoking in Long Legs the night Bob and I stepped in to avoid the Merc. He was one of the occupants of it, I was sure; one of the bastards who'd tried to mow me down in the NCP.

I backed into the doorway of a tea emporium and tried to look casual. Stuffed the photos down my jeans and covered up the package with my shirt. Peeked out and saw him looking around. I made a quick scan of the area and saw the Bruce Lee wannabe standing on the steps outside M&S. He was carrying a copy of the *Evening Chronicle.* Bob's headline adorned the front page and the billboard he was standing next to. Seemed he was wrong about these characters retreating into the background. Whoever they were working for–and Bo Wong was my guess, even Han Lan– they'd clearly been given orders to trail me. If they'd tried to kill me once, they would do it again the first chance they got. I thought about all those involved in all this shit. With Bob's bombshell in today's paper, they'd be like a cornered and wounded animal just waiting to break from the cage. I didn't want to be within biting distance when they pounced.

I backed into the shop and tried to blend in with the old dears and the Earl Grey gift sets. Stood over near a display of tea pots and kept one eye on the window. The kid was gone. Decided I needed to be as far away from here as possible. I went to the door, peeked out into the throng again. They were both gone. I looked left, right, everywhere. I could only hope they'd not spotted me. I didn't think they had. Took a deep breath and stepped out. Picked up pace as I went left. Deansgate beckoned and the Punto was only two minutes walk away. Tried to face straight on but couldn't stop myself from looking back. I jumped when someone bumped into the back of me. The guy apologised, arms full of shopping bags. I spun around, my head throbbing. The cacophony of city traffic and crowd noise, the brass bands and the beer swilling punters in the nearby squares–it was all sending me dizzy.

Then I saw him. He was looking right at me.

Phil Young.

He was standing outside Harvey Nichols, speaking into his phone. Grinning. Our eyes met.

I swallowed, turned around, and ran.

I belted down to Deansgate and reached the crossing. Looked back, took a quick scan and saw Phil and the two Chinese guys weaving through the crowds, pushing shoppers out of the way, dodging couples and giggling teenage girls. The crossing was on red but I glanced to my right, towards the cathedral and from where the traffic was flowing towards me.

I ran out into the road, waited for a coach to pass, then several cars until I took my chance and belted it before a motorcycle came through on the outside lane. Horns scared the shit out of me and I heard a loud scream when a black cab screeched to a stop, the driver ranting and raving behind the wheel. Jumped out of his way, pushed past a group of people queuing outside the Cosmos all you can eat place, and sprinted down past the Radisson Hotel and left onto Parsonage. I could see the Punto fifty odd yards away and made the final push as I chanced a look back. Phil Young was less than twenty seconds behind me. I fumbled for the keys and kept on running, running on empty, running like my life depended on it.

PART III

77

Got in and slammed the door as Phil's boots pounded the pavement. Started her up—and for a moment it chugged and spluttered to life—and slammed on the gas. I screeched away from the kerb, gave Phil two fingers as he tried to grab the driver's door and put my foot down. Glanced in the rear-view mirror and saw him panting in the middle of the road.

Took a right and jumped a red light before spinning a hard left onto Deansgate. Took it up to third, then fourth as another set of lights approached. I could see the Merc about two hundred yards behind me. Weaved in and out of the lanes and overtook a bus. Foot down, left over Victoria Bridge, right up Chapel Street and past the MEN Arena and up to another set of lights. Glanced in the rearview again. They were getting closer. There were a lot of angry horns blaring as the Merc barged through the traffic, not giving a fuck who they bumped into either. I got stuck behind a bunch of cars and a flatbed truck as the lights switched to red. Fuck's sake, this was all I needed. I spun around, saw them coming up behind me. I had to make a decision, and quick. Left would take me onto Trinity Way and Salford beyond. Right would take me up to Cheetham Hill. I chose the latter. I pulled into the left lane beside me, shouted a big 'fuck off' to the prick in the Audi TT as I left him behind and cut down the pavement to the front of the queue. Eyeballed a couple of scaffolding workers in their flatbed truck and as soon as it went on amber, I flicked the wheel until I was in front of it and racing out into the junction. A thousand horns blared as I wrestled with the wheel and cut up an old dear in a Toyota. Took the turn at thirty and forced a hard right, gunned it up the hill and overtook a range rover, a BMW and a motorbike before cutting through another red at Cheetham Hill Road and up to forty, then fifty as I raced away down into the heart of warehouse land. The traffic ahead was thick, but I didn't let that stop me. I could smell the burn of the tyres and checked the fuel gauge. I was running low. My palms were sweating, and I gripped the wheel tight as I caught sight of the Merc getting closer. Before long it would be up my arse, big style.

Kept my foot on the floor and raced past the vehicles up ahead. There were several side streets I could easily nip down, but I couldn't be certain of dead ends. Clocked the Merc getting closer, could almost see their faces behind the darkened glass. Saw the barrel of a gun rising from somewhere in the passenger seat. I slammed on the breaks and skid into the lane of oncoming traffic as the Merc flew past. A Mini screeched to a stop before it slammed into me, and I quickly put her into gear and sped off in the direction I'd come from. Gunned it again, hitting third in seconds before swinging it left into an Industrial complex of abandoned factories. Burned down a hill beside the swanky new apartments and when I reached the bottom and the inevitable dead end I knew was coming, I finally came to a screeching halt. Ahead of me were train and tram tracks, and beside me a huge old Victorian warehouse, its windows all smashed in. I caught my breath, turned to look behind. No sign. But I knew I'd be wrong to take that as a given.

I would have to abandon the Punto.

I fumbled around, took the keys from the ignition, made sure I had the photographs and kicked the door open. I stepped out into the shadow of the old red brick buildings all around me and legged it across the street. I'd just reached the corner edge of an old textile warehouse and slipped down behind it, back against the wall. I took a peek out and was glad I did. The Merc was rolling down the hill, the Punto no doubt in their sights.

'Fuck.'

Took a quick look around. I could either scale the fence and run down towards the tracks and the River Irk, beyond which I knew was Collyhurst and Rochdale Road–or find another way, sharpish. The green land of Sandhills stood between here and relative safety, if I could get away quick enough without them spotting me. But I knew it was suicide. They'd tried to kill me already, and I didn't think they'd waste any time if they were given another chance.

So I didn't take it. I went with the first instinct that came and ran to my left, down the end wall of the warehouse and jumped a loading step, at the end of which was a metal shutter door that had been blown off in the wind. It was the perfect place for the city's homeless to doss down for the night and I knew it would be dark in there, but I squeezed in and pushed the bent metal back far enough to surround me in complete darkness.

Caught my breath again and took in stale air. I became aware I was standing on broken glass, and I flicked my lighter to see what was available. There were half inch thick shards beneath my feet that were at least a foot long. I slipped off the Springsteen hat, wrapped it around my hand and grabbed one.

I peered out through the chink of light in the metal shutter and saw the Merc crawl to the other end of the road I'd just run down. It stood, engine purring, beside the Punto. Two men emerged from the front, another from the back. All were Chinese. They were shouting in Mandarin, and I couldn't tell if they were angry at each other or at losing me. I knew I wasn't clear yet, though. Took deep breaths and kept an eye on the lead guy, the one with the cigarette. He was dressed in the same suit as the other night, extra long fag sticking from his mouth. They were all suited up. A second man pulled a gun from inside his suit jacket and together they started walking towards me, their eyes lurking in every direction until they spotted the metal door I was hiding behind.

They keenly walked towards me.

'Shit.'

I stood, flicked my lighter again so I could see through the pitch black, and scrunched across the glassy floor. The windows beside me were all smudged in grease and whiteout paint, and the whole place smelled of damp. I tried hard to not let the glass crunch beneath my boots, but it was hopeless. I knew they'd be getting closer, and I had to make a move before I found a bullet in the back of my head.

There was another door up ahead and I went for it, fumbling in the dark. I crashed into a wall and banged my knee on something solid, like iron. Christ, that fucking hurt! Inched my way down the wall, the lighter now extinguished. Water dripped onto my throbbing head as the Mandarin got louder and angrier. They were kicking the windows and pulling back the metal door, trying to find a way in while I tried to find a way out. I found a gap so dark I couldn't see my hand in front of my face. Staggered around until I felt rotting wood before me. I shouldered it hard and kicked through to the other side as a window smashed somewhere behind. I fell through, slipped on grease and almost went flying down a set of stone steps, but gripped the porcelain tiles beside me. There was one solitary flickering light bulb ahead down a corridor and I staggered down the stairs, the glass blade almost going flying from my hand.

I needed to get out of here, fast. I ran ahead, down into the belly of the building, the shadows looming behind me, the Mandarin so fucking loud and angry. I didn't look back, just kept on going, smashed through another door that had come off its hinges and found myself in a huge room. Fuck knows what they produced in this place but there was machinery everywhere sticking up from the floor, iron girders coming out of the walls, porcelain basins and chains trailing the floor. There was little light, just motes of dust clouding the air. There was a bank of windows to the left and gaps in the glass where the lead piping was bent. Water flowed from somewhere, probably a burst pipe. The walls were slimy, greasy with hundred-year-old grime.

Heard footsteps tapping on the stone in a room somewhere behind me. Heard the rats too, scurrying in a dark corner of the warehouse.

Took short breaths, held them and tiptoed over into the dark.

There were a few words in English and loud exchanges in Mandarin. Found a pile of sacks in the corner, buried myself beneath them and waited. Felt my heart pounding. My head too. Until moments later, the talking stopped and the footsteps retreated from the darkness.

I waited a long time. Fumbled for my phone and tapped in 999. Thought about it for a few seconds before deciding against it. Perhaps it would be madness. I sat there under those sacks while I thought about my next move. Soon, there was no Mandarin at all, just the sound of that drip drip drip of water and my own nightmares inside my head.

And then gunshots. Four of them. Boom. Boom. Boom. Boom.

Got myself up and stepped towards the far end of the room with the rats tip tapping in my ears. Crunched the glass as I neared the windows and rubbed the grime away. Looked out into the gloom. The sky had clouded over and there was a storm brewing. I could smell it, even in here. And then that Mandarin again. Had no fucking clue what they were saying, but they laughed it up.

The cigarette guy launched a brick through the back window and it crashed through the afternoon, down here in the silent streets of Cheetham Hill. Then something else smashed through the windscreen and minutes later I could feel the heat from the flames, even from here. I watched as the Merc powered up, the engine kicking in loud as they manoeuvred away from the dead end and gunned it up the hill, away from Sara's Punto.

I traced my way back through the empty warehouse, back through all the abandoned machinery, back through the corridor with the flickering bulb, up the stairs and through the broken glass, out into the street and stumbled back towards the car. I fell to my knees and drank in that cold afternoon air, praying for a hard rain to wash the dirt away.

The explosion almost burst my eardrums, and I felt the heat and the burn as I watched the Punto go up in flames, the black, black smoke bringing debris down with it and darkening the sky like Armageddon.

I dropped the shard of glass when I finally felt the blood leaking from my palm.

That hard rain couldn't come quick enough.

78

When it finally came, the rain came down like the spray off the ocean. It wasn't enough. I ploughed through Sand Hills, having abandoned the burning Punto, yet knowing I had to get back to Laura in one piece. I still had the photographs stuffed down my jeans. I had to make sure it stayed that way. The Merc had long since gone, and the Chinese too, though I wondered if I was being watched. Though if I was, I'd surely have a bullet in my head right now.

I occasionally turned back and saw the black smoke billowing behind me. Heard the crackle of the fire and the crack and warping of the car's metal as the sirens cut through the darkening afternoon. For a few moments I thought it might be better for everyone if I was still sitting in the driver's seat. To hell with the case, to hell with life. Then I remembered I had a reason to stick around.

I made it to Rochdale Road and jumped on a bus that smelled of piss and damp. My hand was still bloody from the shard of glass and my head felt like a balloon. I swallowed two painkillers dry and sank back in the seat and let my eyes rest. Having no transport again would make things doubly hard. It seemed everything was conspiring against me, like I was being set up to fail. And now I'd have to find a way to replace Sara's Punto. Felt like the odds were stacked against me. Wondered what fate lay ahead for me now.

I knew I was lucky to be alive. I supposed I'd never know if they knew I was hiding in that warehouse. I suppose they could've found me, and something made them want to search that place. Tried not to think about what would've happened had they done so. I'd be lying dead in a pool of blood, no doubt. Did they know I was in there? Perhaps. Probably. They sounded angry in that Mandarin. Angry at how they'd lost me, blaming each other. So they settled for the next best thing. Blow up the car.

I felt dazed on the journey back to Sara's. Dazed and bewildered. The darkness in that warehouse stayed with me, along with the smell of damp and the sound of the rats. I checked my hand. The blood was still seeping and had soaked the Springsteen hat. I suppose the painkillers would help when they finally kicked in, but it really stung right now. I wondered if I'd need stitches. Didn't seem too deep, but the glass was sharp enough to put a clean slice through my palm. It hurt like fuck. I kept the hat pressed against the wound and hoped Laura would have some bandages I could slap on.

I checked to make sure I had everything I needed. There was plenty of cash in my wallet, and my phone still seemed to be working. Smokes were all there too. Thank God for small mercies. When I got off the bus, it was the first thing on my mind. I sparked up, my bloodied fingers staining the tip, and took that shit in deep as I walked to Sara's. The rain finally came then. And the good thing was, it was hard enough for me to raise my face to the sky and let it wash over me.

79

L aura was in a state when I got back and I had to calm her down. It took a while, but she eventually stopped fussing over me when the wound had been cleaned up and the bandage was on. She wasn't impressed about her sister's car being blown up and made it clear I would have to replace it. Another reason, she'd said, for me going 'full time' as a Private Investigator. The way I felt right then, it was the furthest thing from my mind.

'I'm just glad you're still with us. This is getting very dangerous, Jim. I'm not sure this is right anymore. I mean, do you want to carry on with this? It all seems so pointless.'

I couldn't agree more. The whole thing had become much more than I expected. I lay on the couch, on Laura's insistence, and tried to blot everything from my mind. It was pointless. Tonight's date with Sherry was the last thing I wanted to do, especially now it seemed another attempt had been made on my life. Three strikes and you're out. It's funny how things change. Not so long ago, I would've welcomed it. Death. But deep down, I knew there was more for me to do as long as I was here. I knew I needed to clear

things up with Karen and my daughter. Perhaps being a PI
was the only thing that would help me get back on my feet,
give me something to live for other than my daughter. And
who knew, maybe one day I could right some wrongs, not
just for others but for myself too.

I scanned through the photographs Stevie had taken.
There were twenty-six in all and familiar faces in every one.
Phil Young, Bryn Llewellyn, Sir David Howe. Simon. All of
them. And some faces I didn't recognise too. Seems one
night was never enough for this bunch.

I savoured a long whisky, no ice. Needed something to
help calm the nerves. I fell asleep and dreamt of fire and
blood and Polaroid photographs. And when I awoke several
hours later, the dark of winter had brought a gloom with it.

I checked the clock. I had less than two hours to get
ready and meet Sherry at Rosso. Downed several pints of
water and showered. I shaved my beard off completely and
smartened up. It wasn't much to keep the bastards at bay,
but it was better than nothing. I knew I had to keep going,
and yet I wasn't entirely sure why. The faces of Angel and
Sara kept coming back to me. Chi Phuong. Bob, too. Seemed
I was living in a world that wasn't my own. Some things
never changed.

Bob's story had broken all over the place. It was on every
news bulletin from BBC to Channel Four to Sky. Seemed
things had exploded overnight. I sat in front of the TV while
I waited for Laura to finish getting ready. It was a huge
scandal and, according to some reports, this was just the tip
of the iceberg. I pictured Bob beside that pool I had in my
head, wishing I was there with him and knocking back the
sangria like it was Vimto. I only hoped he was safe out
there. He'd seemed to think it would be the best place
for him.

'How do I look?' she said, appearing beside me in a sexy black dress.

'Great.' I meant it.

'Are you ready?'

I wasn't exactly keen, but I knew I'd have to follow through with it. I couldn't back out now. And besides, I still needed to find out who had killed Angel. If I was to get any closer to the truth, I knew Sherry might have some answers. She grabbed me, adjusted my collar. 'Remember the plan?'

She nodded. 'Hang around at the bar and look out for anyone dodgy.'

'That's it. Especially anyone who looks like a copper.'

'This is gonna be fun. I always wondered what it'd be like to do a proper stakeout.'

'You'll need to be on your toes. No getting carried away with the cocktails.'

'You think it'll be all right? I mean, they seem keen on hurting you. How's the hand?'

It was murdering me. 'It's okay. Better than earlier.'

'Feel better after the nap?'

'A hundred times.'

'Good.'

But I didn't feel better about stepping out that door again. Part of me thought bringing Laura with me would prove to be disastrous, but then I knew no one involved in any of this had seen her before. She could prove to be more than useful too. I supposed I needed as many allies as I could find.

We got in a taxi and headed straight to town. Laura was getting giddy, but I kept my thoughts to myself. The last people I wanted to come across tonight were the Chinese. I knew that if they were so unfazed about blowing up the Punto, it wouldn't cross their minds to swing a sword at my head. But the devil was in the detail. Who the hell were they taking orders from? Bo Wong? Probably. I wanted nothing more than to pay him a visit to find out why. They knew I was onto them, and Bob blowing the whole thing wide open had changed everything. Yet it was Angel's killer I was out to find. I guessed it could've been any one of them. A hit had been ordered. I wanted to know what Sherry knew, if anything. And I wanted to know why Carol had given Sara and me a false number, a number that didn't even exist. What was the bitch hiding? From the texts I'd found on Simon's phone, she'd obviously been involved with one or two of Wong's girls. Perhaps girls he didn't need. And there was also the small matter of sex trafficking East Asian women, getting them high on opium and then letting a clique of bent coppers fuck them at every opportunity. Where were the missing girls? Chi Phuong and the rest? Was Angel just another statistic? The fact that she was practically living in Han Lan's apartment was enough to say she'd known a few things. Yet I knew the girl was troubled. She was unreliable. Was she killed because of what she knew? Because she was going to spill the beans? They'd shut her mouth up forever, but I was still no closer to knowing who'd carried out the murder with such callousness. Stabbed, raped, strangled. It was no way to leave the world, whatever secrets she took with her. And the scary thing was that the more I learned, the further away from the truth I got. Felt like I was falling into a black hole. And I knew the danger wasn't over. If Angel really knew more than she should have, then there were probably other girls too. Other girls who were yet to go missing.

Laura paid the driver, and we stepped out onto Spring Gardens at the top end of King Street. The night was cold and wet, with snow flurries in the air, and I'd have liked nothing more than to be in bed. As we stepped up to Rosso's main entrance, I knew that bed was a long way off.

Laura went in first to claim her table while I smoked outside. Two minutes later I followed, was greeted by a pretty girl on the counter and shown to my table by a young Moroccan waiter. Ordered a bottle of house red and sat back, perused the menu like I did this kind of thing all the time. I did once, with Karen. Right now, though, I felt like a fish out of water. I took a long look around for any sign of a familiar face, particularly one who might want to do me some harm, and relaxed a little when I was sure everything was fine–for now, at least. The waiter came back with the wine, asked me if I wanted to taste it. Told him to pour it straight in.

It was a nice place, all very opulent and busier than I thought it'd be. Glasses chinked and the conversation echoed across the marbled floor as I kept one eye on the door for Sherry. Clocked Laura on a stool at the bar and she raised a glass with a wink. She clearly thought this was just a bit of fun, and for her I supposed it would be, but I would rather have her on her guard–just in case. I didn't know what that 'just in case' would be, and thought it better not to think about it, but my nerves were ragged and I could barely think of anything else. It had been an eventful day, one in which my life had been under threat. The last thing I wanted was an evening of the same.

She turned up ten minutes later, fashionably late in a slim red dress. Clocked her straight away, and she had that dizziness about her when we first met the night Angel disappeared. I was already halfway through the bottle when she was shown to the table by our attentive waiter. Her colour changed the minute she clapped eyes on me, but she knew she couldn't turn around now. The waiter pulled out her chair, took her fake fur coat and asked if we wanted more wine. I nodded and he left. I stood for Sherry, like any Gent would do. Eyeballed her to sit down. Her reluctance was plain.

'Mr. Frost?'

I nodded. 'We meet again, Sherry. Have a seat. We've got a lot to talk about.'

'I'm not sure what you mean.'

'You know what I mean.'

'I think it's best if I just go.'

But I grabbed her arm and eyeballed her again before she could run. She stopped, tried to look away, and wrestled her wrist from my grip. She puffed out her cheeks, mouthed something under her breath and sat down. She didn't know where to look. The waiter returned with another bottle and I nodded at him to pour her a glass. She plastered a smile on and fluttered her eyelashes at him before taking a large mouthful and swallowing hard.

'So why you? And why now?'

I knew she was trying to put a brave face on it. A show of defiance, even. I took a sip of wine and got straight to the point. 'You're aware Angel's dead?'

She looked down at her napkin, took another mouthful of her drink. She either didn't know, and I'd just been the bearer of bad news, or she knew damn well, perhaps knew all along. I guessed it was the latter. Her face was expressionless. Blank.

'Murdered. Stabbed, strangled. Raped.'

'I know.'

'Terrible, isn't it?'

'It's got nothing to do with me.'

'I never said it did.'

'So why all this?'

'You were with her the night she went missing. I suppose I just want to find out what you know. About who she was with. What she was taking. And why she left that flat. I also want to know why Carol gave Sara and me a fake number. Strange, that.'

She sighed, picked up a menu, as much to hide behind rather than choose herself a starter. 'I didn't know about that.'

'About what?'

'Carol. A fake number.'

'But the other stuff. The other stuff you do know about. Because you were there, weren't you?'

There was a sob and she nodded. Dabbed her eyes with a napkin. Crocodile tears, if ever I saw them.

'I was there, yeah. Working. Doing what I do, and that's all. I don't know why she went missing or who killed her. None of us do.'

'None of us?'

'The girls. We're just as upset as anyone.'

'Because you knew her, didn't you? You knew her well.'

She nodded, dropped the menu, sniffed and dabbed her eyes again. I looked straight at her just as the waiter came back to the table and asked if we wanted to order. Asked him to give us another five minutes. Poured us both more wine. By the end of the night, I knew I'd need a stiff brandy.

'Yeah, I knew her. I've known her for years. She was a good friend. A good girl, you know. Good at her job, got on really well with everyone.'

'Did she get on well with Matt?'

'What?'

'Matthew Brookes Wilkes. She get on well with him? Because he was the last person she was seen with.'

'I think so, I... I don't know...'

'He a regular customer of the agency, Sherry? Him and his mates?'

She went to hide behind the menu again and almost deflated like a balloon. 'No one's seen him since she went missing.'

'You sure? No one's been out escorting him?'

'Positive.'

'So why do you think that is?'

She shrugged. 'Don't know. You tell me.'

She was getting cocky. 'Well, it makes me think the worst, Sherry. It makes me think he knows more than he's letting on. He was the last person to be seen with her. I've seen the CCTV footage from the Hilton. Funny how he's not turned up anywhere else, really. I thought that, being a regular user of Provoke–classy name, by the way–he'd be back soon after Sherry's disappearance. Like a concerned friend, if you like. He saw her a few times before that, didn't he? And other girls. Did you ever fuck him, Sherry?'

'Piss off.'

'That's no way to treat a customer.'

'You lied to me. You dragged me here under false pretences. How fucking dare you speak to me like that!'

'Why not? It's what you do, isn't it? That is your job?'

'It's not like that.'

'Like what?'

'How you make it sound.'

'Look. Sherry. I know that's not your real name, obviously. I don't care what you do for a living, I really don't. I couldn't give two fucks. But what I do care about is finding out who murdered Angel. Helen Shields. Your friend. Can you imagine what it's like to be raped? Strangled? Stabbed? Hit over the head with a hammer? No. Of course you can't. None of you can. So dinner's on me, just while we talk for a while. And if you don't want to be next in a long line of missing girls, it'd be a good idea to spill what you know. Now, I recommend the langoustine to start.'

Her dainty mouth twitched as she stared blankly ahead. It would be a tough conversation for the girl, and I felt for her. I didn't want to be hard on her, but sometimes, hard truths required hard questions. And I intended to dig deep before we made it to coffee and dessert.

80

The langoustine tail was stunning. For a few minutes, Sherry played with her food, anxious about where all this was going, but she must've been hungry because she finished before I did. I poured more wine and ordered another bottle, thinking that the more lubricated she got, the more likely she was to spill. And maybe I was wrong. Maybe she knew nothing. But there were secrets there behind those fluttering eyelashes. There were secrets everywhere in this case. Hard truths were often overshadowed by denial and fear and lies. With her, I guessed she felt that fear. She was vulnerable, like most of the women I'd come across these past few weeks. It was one of the common denominators in all of this. Sara, Angel. Everyone.

'Let's go back to that night,' I said. 'Angel's birthday. The night she vanished. Cast your mind back.'

'I can't remember anything.'

'Let's start at the beginning. You met us at the Thai Banana, yeah? We had a chat about holidays and stuff.'

'You told me you were in a paper business.'

'I lied.'

'Why?'

'Cover.'

'But why?'

'Just because...'

She sighed and I glanced at the bar. Saw Laura sipping a Prosecco and giving me the thumbs up.

'Why do you want to know all this? It means nothing. We went out for her birthday, everyone had a good time, she left with Matt and that's that. It's got nothing to do with me. Any of it.'

'I'm sure it hasn't but I need to get to the truth, Sherry. Lives depend on it.'

'So leave it to the police.'

That old chestnut. I dug in my jacket pocket and pulled out a rolled up *Evening Chronicle*. Handed it to her. 'You seen this? Shocking, isn't it?'

'What is it?'

'Have a read.'

She skimmed through the first page, glanced at the pictures on the others. Her mouth dropped open, then closed quickly.

'Know any of them?'

'I can't...'

'Sherry, it's okay. I'll remind you that you're not gonna get in trouble for any of this. Angel was your friend, I understand that. And I understand that you're scared. But you need to tell me what you know, however insignificant it might be. What are you scared of?'

'Nothing, it's just...'

'Come on...'

'I can't. I just can't.'

She put the paper down, pushed the chair back and said she was going to the ladies. She was halfway across the room before I could stop her making a run for it, but I supposed I underestimated her too. She headed straight for the little girls' room. I wondered if she would powder her nose or shit bricks. Maybe both. Headed over to the bar and grabbed Laura.

'Follow her,' I said. 'Don't lose her.'

'How's it all going?'

'Just follow her.'

I watched Laura head to the toilets and kept one eye on the door. The waiter came over, asked if everything was all right and if we wanted to order our main. Not yet, I said. I poured a large glass of Malbec and knocked it back. Topped up Sherry's glass too. Checked the time on the huge grand clock hanging from the ceiling at the end of the room. Just gone nine. How time flies when you're having fun. It was getting busier too. All the tables were occupied except for one. The noise was deafening, the night young. Looked around, saw lots of suits and designer dresses. Cocktails flowed, brandies sat warm and still, waiting staff shimmied between tables and the smells of garlic and fish and steak filled the air. Through the tall window on the left wall, I could see more snow and it was coming down hard. Thought about Stevie out there in Chinatown, freezing his balls off for the sake of a few photographs. Thought about Bob and his Montecristo, sitting out by the pool in thirty degree heat. I wished I was somewhere else, somewhere far away from here.

I took out Simon's iPhone and opened the dictaphone app Laura had shown me before we left. It was bordering on genius and the girl was better than I thought. She'd pre set the sensitivity and I pressed record, placing it on the table between the wine and the jug of tap water.

She came back five minutes later. Asked what had taken her so long, but she didn't reply. She drank her wine, put the empty glass down, took a deep breath and swallowed. The girl was on edge. I recognised that feeling in myself.

'I don't know much. I really don't. Do you believe me?'

I didn't believe her, but told her I did. 'Go on.'

'You have to promise me I won't get into trouble. Promise?'

'Cross my heart.'

'Please? It's important.'

'Sherry, you have my word. I promise. Those men,' I said, nodding at the paper between us, 'are the ones who are in trouble. They're fucked. You can count on it. Whatever you tell me now, I promise, will stay between us. You have my word. If it'll help find Angel's killer, you'll have done a good thing. Trust me on that.'

'I'm scared.'

'I know. But no one's gonna hurt you, Sherry. Not if you tell me the truth.'

She sniffed hard and pinched her nose. The fact that she'd done a few lines in the ladies' was written all over face. I collared the waiter and asked for more wine. At this rate, with any luck, she'd be half cut before she finished her main. I could tell the waiter was getting impatient, so I ordered the food. Lobster ravioli and prawn linguine. Breads on the side.

'She'd been living in that apartment for six months. Maybe longer. And we'd often end up there after a night out, you know...'

'Who's 'we'?'

'The girls. The clients as well.'

'So you were using it as a fuck pad.'

She blushed. 'Something like that.'

'Go on.'

She sighed, took a gulp of wine. 'Matt would bring the drugs. You know. Coke, pills, that kind of thing.'

'Anything else?'

'Not that I know of.'

'The hard stuff, maybe? Heroin, that kind of thing?'

Heroin overdose, that'd be good. I could get you some.

'I don't know anything about that.'

'How often were you using this place?'

'Most weekends. Saturday nights, mostly.'

'All night?'

'Into Sunday, yeah. Usually.'

'How many?'

'I don't know. Ten, maybe. Sometimes more.'

'Parties, then. Sex, drugs and rock n roll. Must've been fun.'

'Not always.'

I was intrigued. 'How so?'

She shifted in her seat. Looked around, I guessed to make sure no one she knew was nearby. An instinctive reaction. 'Some stuff that went on wasn't nice. Group stuff, you know. Scary.'

'In what way?'

'It's hard to talk about.'

'You'll feel better for it if you let me know. I won't judge you.'

'Some of the clients... they were really weird. They wanted things... things that weren't good to be doing. But we were getting paid for it, so we had no choice, really. And Carol was insistent we had to do this stuff if we wanted to be part of the agency, if we wanted to keep the money coming in. And we were on very good money. Thousands a night. There were always more girls willing to step in, she said. If we didn't do these things.'

'East Asian girls? Chinese, Korean, Thai...?'

She looked shocked. 'How do you know?'

'Just a hunch. But carry on. Tell me about the things they wanted you to do.'

Another sigh, another large gulp of wine. 'I can't. Just dirty stuff. Horrible things. With each other, with them.'

'Were any of the girls raped?'

She nodded.

'Did you see anything?'

'Most things. I allowed myself to be a part of it. It's easy when you're high. It almost seems normal. We're used to having sex with strangers. But there's lots of things I can't remember, and that's the truth of it.'

'Try to remember.'

'That's just it, I can't. None of us can. It's as if our memories have been wiped. A lot of the girls have bruises they can't remember getting.'

'Were any photographs taken at these nights?'

'It's possible.'

'Any faces you remember, any names that ring a bell?'

'I recognise him.'

'Who?'

'One of the men in the paper.'

'Show me, Sherry.'

'They'll hurt us if I say anything.'

'It's almost over, love. The danger's gone. You can trust me on this. Show me who you recognise.'

She opened the paper to page five. We both looked down at the photographs. She pointed to the former Chief Constable of West Yorkshire, Sir Michael Robert Fletcher.

'Who is this, Sherry? Say his name for me, love.'

'His name's Michael.' She was crying now, the tears streaming down her face. 'Michael Robert Fletcher. I saw him rape Angel. In the back bedroom. He had a knife to her throat and when he saw me his eyes were wild.'

81

The mains came. Sherry didn't bother much with hers, but my ravioli was to die for. It wasn't the food, she'd said. I guessed as much. Glanced over at Laura again. She was watching intently. Sherry left the table once more to visit the bathroom, and I only needed to look at Laura to get her to follow. She was useful, and I was glad I'd brought her along.

Sherry's revelation didn't come as a surprise. Yet I was keen to know more. I knew this was hard for her. Already, she'd made it plain she'd said more than she thought she should have, but I wanted to coax more from her.

'How long ago was this? With Angel, I mean.'

'About six months. I saw it. I was threatened by someone who wanted me to keep quiet, or else...'

'Or else what?'

'He didn't say.'

'But you can guess?'

She nodded. Sniffed. The cocaine and the booze were helping her to keep her memories–those she had–in the background, where it was safe and she could function normally. Tell herself this kind of stuff was part and parcel of her job.

'Can you describe him?'

She looked away for a moment, stared into space. 'He was Chinese. Tall-ish. Forties.'

I could see him now. The cigarette guy. The guy who'd put four bullet holes into Sara's Punto and blew it up in the silent afternoon of Cheetham Hill's warehouse district. I couldn't be sure, but I'd bet my arse on it.

'Anything else about him?'

She shook her head. 'No. I haven't seen him since.'

'What about the other girls? Any threats made to those?'

She twirled the linguine around her fork. 'Look, I'm not feeling very well. I shouldn't be talking about any of this.'

'You don't realise how much good you're gonna do by talking about it, Sherry. Believe me. Just a bit more, okay?'

She nodded reluctantly and I ordered her a Mojito. Got myself a whisky sour while I was at it. I pressed her some more while we waited for the cocktails and the waiter cleared the table.

'So. Have there been any other threats? To any of the girls?'

'Xi,' she nodded. 'From Vietnam. She's always going on about how they threatened to slit her throat, that kind of thing. And because of that, she'd do anything. And I mean anything.'

I didn't doubt it. 'You believe her?'

She shrugged, drained her wineglass. 'I suppose.'

'When you saw Angel - well, when you saw what you saw - how was Angel afterwards?'

She looked me in the eye. 'She was fine about it. It was as if it had never happened.'

'Did it happen?'

'I just told you. I saw it. I saw him holding her down, from behind, a bloody kitchen knife at her throat. She was screaming and screaming, but the next time I saw her there was nothing. She had no recollection of it.'

'Did you tell her what had happened to her?'

'Well, no. Because I didn't want to freak her out. I realised there was something weird about it all so I thought if she didn't know, if she had no memory of it -'

'Like the other girls?'

'Like the other girls, yeah–then it would be best if she never knew.'

'This other stuff, the sex stuff, the weird shit. How weird are we talking? Bondage?'

'Oh yeah. All that.'

'Strange drugs?'

'I don't know. Just pills and coke and things.'

'Like?'

'I don't know.'

'Which means you could've been taking anything.'

She shrugged again. 'I don't know...'

But I could guess. Seems the girls didn't know what the fuck they were taking, and they either didn't give a shit or couldn't remember. Probably both.

'This Xi. She talk about anything else?'

'Sometimes, though she kept herself to herself, you know. Kept a low profile. Still does.'

'Where can I find her?'

'I don't know.'

'You saw her recently?'

'No.'

The cocktails arrived and I got stuck into the whisky sour. Sherry got to playing with her straw before tossing it aside and taking the top off the drink.

'What kind of things?'

'I'm sorry?'

'What kind of things did Xi talk about? Did she say where she'd come from?'

'Vietnam.'

'Other than that. Anywhere else in this city.'

She thought for a minute. 'She said she was a dancer. You know... lap dancing stuff.'

'For who?'

'I've no idea.'

'Try to remember.'

'I don't remember her saying!'

'Okay. Okay.'

She was getting closer to freaking, and I was reluctant to get too close for comfort in case she upped and left in a hurry. I kept quiet for a moment as she sipped her drink and took a long look about the restaurant. No one I recognised. Laura was eating something at the bar and she'd gone onto bottled beer. She was my kind of girl.

'Just a few more questions and then you can go.'

She had her head in her hands. I couldn't tell if she was laughing or crying.

'Please, I don't want to talk about this anymore.'

'It won't take long. I just want to ask you about the men at these parties. These clients. You have what you'd call your 'regulars', yeah?'

'Yeah. Regular men. Occasionally women too.'

It was the men I was interested in. 'Can you remember any names? Any descriptions? Anything they talked about?'

'They talked about a lot of things. Things they told us weren't important. They'd go out onto the roof terrace and laugh about this and that. All the rooms would be occupied but there'd always be someone out on the roof terrace chatting shit, you know.'

'Like who?'

'I don't know the names.'

'This is important, Sherry.'

'I can't remember. I can't remember much.'

'What did they do for a living, Sherry? They must've had good money to pay for your services. To abuse you and your friends. To keep you quiet.'

'Stop it.'

'Because that's what they've done, Sherry.'

'Don't!'

'Give me names, love. What were their jobs? What did they look like?'

'I don't know, please will you just.... just stop.'

I stopped. For the briefest of moments. 'You can put an end to all this if you tell me what you know.'

'That *is* all I know.'

'Sherry....'

'They were bankers. Coppers, bankers, fucking.... all sorts. Architects, solicitors, fucking politicians, all sorts!'

'Good. How many coppers, Sherry?'

'I don't fucking know!'

I reached out, grabbed her arm. She flinched, but I held it there in the middle of that restaurant with the laughing and the chinking glasses and the brandy and the smells. Her eyes were wide, her pupils dilated with coke.

'Tell me...'

'One was called Bryn. Horrible, fat Welsh man.'

'Go on.'

'Someone called Phil.'

Boom.

'Go on.'

'I can't remember!' She was creased up, her dainty hands struggling to loosen the grip on her arm, her ruby red lips beginning to quiver and a bead of a tear rolling down her cheek. 'Please.... please....'

I let go, sat back. Took my phone from my jacket pocket and checked the sticker on the back where Sara had written my number. 'Here,' I said, taking a pen from an inside pocket. I grabbed a napkin from the table beside us. 'This is my number. I want you to phone me if you remember anything–anything at all. You understand?'

'They'd kill me if they found out I'd been talking...'

'Who, Sherry?'

'The guy who threatened me! The Chinese man.'

'I'm onto him already, Sherry. I promise. He'll get nowhere near you. No one will. They don't know you're here with me.'

She shook her head. 'I've got to go.'

'Okay. But don't forget. Call me if there's *anything*. Anything at all.'

She sniffed, blew her nose on a tissue from her handbag as she shoved the napkin in, then took out her business card. She wrote down her number and passed it to me, then stood, threw twenty quid on the table by way of paying for her drinks, and left. I watched as she went out into the cold night.

She hadn't finished her Mojito. I grabbed it and slung it down my neck. Followed it up with the Whisky Sour. Moments later, Laura appeared in the seat opposite with two beers. Glanced at the Moroccan waiter, who was giving me funny looks.

'Well?'

I shrugged. 'It was more than useful.'

'She was acting weird in the toilets. So, give us the juicy details.'

I flipped the business card over and found more than just a phone number.

Li Cheung, 146 Menzies Court, Miles Platting.

And that was it. Nothing more. I thought about chasing after her, but by now she'd be gone, vanished into the dark of the night.

'Drink up. It's time to go.'

82

I t was snowing again, and coming down hard, swirling around Spring Gardens with a north wind tumbling through the streets, the flakes beginning to drift and stick. It was odds on for a white Christmas this year. I thought about Nicole and whether I'd get to see her, about Karen and whether Frank had mentioned my visit - how could he not? - and about Maureen laid up in her hospital bed, the cancer eating away at every cell in her body.

Laura was hardly dressed for the weather, so when we jumped in a black cab it was a relief to get out of it. She was stumbling around all over the place in her heels, blaming the ice and the sludge, but I knew she was half pissed as well after confessing to having four espresso Martini's. Fuck knew what was in them, but they'd done the trick all right.

I checked the time. It was only just gone ten. The night was still young. Laura complained about having to go home this early and tried to lure me toward the bars down the end of Deansgate, bribing me with the promise of her bed and everything that came with it later on. But I had other things on my mind and told her as much. She was going home while I took a detour round Miles Platting way. I wanted to know why Sherry had given me Li Cheung's address, and I wanted to know who he or she was.

'But I thought that was the plan for tonight,' she protested. 'Just the meal, then home.'

'She gave me information I need to check out.'

'What kind of information?'

'Just the address of someone I need to talk to, that's all.'

'What, at this time?!'

'At this time,' I nodded. 'It'll be fine. I'll flag another cab down later.'

'Oh, Jim. Can this not wait until tomorrow?'

'He might not be there tomorrow. I've got a feeling she wanted me to check this out with some urgency, so it's better now while it's clear in my head.'

'You've had a lot to drink.'

'And so have you. Better for you to get back for a night-cap. You don't want to be out in this weather, anyway. What if you fell asleep and never woke up?'

'Would never happen.'

'I wouldn't be so sure. Look, get yourself home and I'll be back before midnight, I promise.'

'You're always making promises you can't keep, Jim Locke.'

'I mean it this time.'

She bit her lip and slid down the leather seat as the cab swung its way onto Oldham Road, leaving the city lights behind. I thought about Stevie, out there in Chinatown doing my dirty work. Poor bastard would be freezing, but I knew he wouldn't feel it as long as the Whyte and Mackay was coursing through his veins.

She clung onto me as we moved along, and I was beginning to like the girl more and more. She was funny, in a Laura kind of way. She was falling asleep as the driver kept it slow to avoid the ice. Clocked the temperature on his dashboard. -3. I wrapped the jacket around me, wondering if what I was about to do was a wise move at all given the fact that I was on the way home to that warm bed I wanted just a few hours ago. Yet I'd never been one for being sensible. Sherry hadn't given me that address for nothing.

I told the driver to pull over just as we reached the high rises of Miles Platting. They stood out there beyond Oldham Road, black as night, even the snow that billowed around them grey like ash. Most were empty, abandoned and hollowed out, their windows smashed or boarded up. Others were unoccupied except for the odd flat up above with a few sole burning lights to tell the world someone was home.

I slung him a twenty and told him where to drop Laura off. She'd sunk into the seat again and I had to drag her up. I told her I'd be back later and kissed her before I flung the door open to the winter and she slumped back in her seat. I watched as the cab pulled away, waited a moment, then crossed the road.

I knew Menzies court was down this way somewhere. It was one of the high rises set back in the heart of the estate, though I'd no idea where. I wished I'd brought the Springsteen hat with me. My ears stung with the cold and the snow seeped in through my socks. I must've been mad to think this was a good idea.

It was desolate. The faint orange glow from the lamp-posts dotted around gave the place a certain charm in a beautiful yet stark way. The tower blocks loomed around me, one of them burnt out so badly you could still smell it. And from somewhere, some distance away, came music.

Beats. No voices, no echoes, just the jungle beats of some faraway dance tune.

I stopped in the middle of a curving exit road and raised my face to the sky, let those flakes fall over me. Wondered what the fuck I was doing here and whether I'd gone mad. I took Sherry's business card from my pocket and checked what she'd written again.

Li Cheung, 146 Menzies Court, Miles Platting.

But who was he? Or she? Could it be someone who could talk, reveal more of what I wanted? Or was it the name of one of the Chinese guys from the blacked out Merc? A friend of hers? Of Xi's? Of Angel's?

I stepped on, walking down the middle of the exit road with the tower blocks looming on either side. There were six of them. I counted barely twenty flats that had lights on. That didn't mean these were the only occupied ones, but it was still fairly early–early enough for some late night TV. I'd have thought there would be more activity, at least. But nothing. Deathly quiet, and it was getting quieter still thanks to the snow. The only sound, apart from the beats in the distance, was the crunch of my own feet on the frozen ground beneath me.

Burgess Court was the first one I came across. It was abandoned and boarded up from the ground to the thirteenth floor. Steel shutters blocked every window. Further up to my right came Heywood Court, and this one was occupied. There was a burning light in the corner flat of the third floor, shining bright purple into the night, and I wondered who lay on the other side of those curtains. As I passed I saw a girl standing at the gate, hood over her head, her frail demeanour so skeletal she barely cast a shadow. She glanced up as I walked, and she was as pale as the snow falling over our heads.

'I'm looking for Menzies Court,' I said, my breath fogging the air between us. She moved her hair from her eyes, sniffed, then looked away. Charming. 'I believe it's around here somewhere...?'

But she gobbed a mouthful of green phlegm in my general direction, and I took that as a 'no'.

I wrapped the jacket around me, pushed my hands in my pockets–the wound on my right hand stinging and the bandage wet–and ploughed on, thinking this would be a good time to just put my feet forward and get this over with. At least find the place and get the fuck out of here. There was a bed calling, not to mention a few beers and a warm-hearted woman.

I found Menzies Court hidden around the back of Heywood. It was empty too, which came as a surprise, and I wondered if I was in the right place at all. Yet those beats were louder now. I looked up, the tower block before me a black scar against the grey sky. The music was coming from inside the building. Abandoned though it seemed, there must've been one or two occupied flats inside, however run down it appeared from out here. I made a quick check of Sherry's business card, just to make sure, then stepped towards the entrance through gates that had seen a hundred winters.

I hesitated before stepping across the threshold. There was a flickering halogen light somewhere down the corridor inside, and I could hear trickling water. The first floor above me was mostly boarded up except for one window. It didn't look as if anyone was inside that particular flat. You'd have to be crazy to want to stay here. There were no KEEP OUT signs, no construction going on. I could only presume the address Sherry had given me was correct. There was nothing fenced off. Nothing to tell me to stay away apart from my own beating heart and the doubt in my head. But I ignored it. There was a door hanging off its hinges, the bottom pane smashed in. Glass covered the floor on either side. It was either the housing that didn't give a toss or the few tenants who remained here, and I guessed there had to be at least a handful. Anyone could just walk in. I stepped up to the intercom and punched in the numbers. 146. Pressed 'Call' and waited.

Nothing. Nothing at all, not even a buzz. Tried it again, knowing it was pointless, then pulled the door back and slipped through the gap to the other side.

The smell hit me then. Piss and damp. Vomit. Stale booze and the threat of violence. The smell of death.

I stepped inside, that halogen light flickering. I peered down the corridor but couldn't see anyone around. It was what I expected. Spotted a lift to my right, graffiti adorning the steel doors. I stepped towards it and pressed the call button. It was out. No flashing light, no movement, no pinging sound from somewhere above. Yet I could hear those beats coming down the lift shaft, and bass with it too. And voices.

Turned towards the stairs and began to climb. The stairs were wet, and I wouldn't like to guess what with. I kept my ears keenly on the sounds coming from above. Looked back down for any sign of anyone lurking behind me with every few steps.

I reached the first floor and went through a set of double doors. There must've been a fire here at some point—seemed common around these parts—because the walls were charred black and the whole landing had that charcoal smell. It was dark on this level, so I pulled out my lighter and let the flame burn. Graffiti and glass sparkled as I stepped on down the corridor. It was a narrow space, barely

wide enough to swing a cat. I thought about turning back. In
fact, I wanted nothing more. Yet I knew there was something
more here. Something waiting up above. The drum and
bass got louder with every step. When I made it to the next
level, up another flight of stairs painted in dried vomit, I
could hear the voices getting louder too.

I wrestled with the thought of turning back. Fumbled in
my pocket and pulled out a smoke. Sparked up. Dragged
that shit in deep. Clocked the time on my mobile. 10:32. I
promised Laura I'd be home by midnight, and I intended to
keep that promise. But I needed more before I could turn
back. I moved up through another flight and found this
corridor more welcoming. The halogen lights up here were
bright and still. The flat doors all locked, just two of them
boarded up. I checked the numbers. All double digits. Forty-
Four. Forty-Six. Forty-eight. By this reckoning, 146 had to be
a few more flights up. I turned when I heard movement
behind me. The swinging door at the other end of the corridor, the door I'd just come through, creaked as it moved
back and forth. I let my breath out when the rat scurried
behind a partition wall, heading for a gap in the refuse
shoot.

'Jesus. Fuck's sake.'

I turned back and headed on, round a sharp bend at the
end of the walkway. I pushed through a heavy fire door and
ended up outside on a balcony that had been meshed off
with wire so you couldn't jump off. I guessed one or two
would be tempted in a place like this. Looked out across the
city. It was high enough up here to afford a decent view, but I
knew I needed to go higher, perhaps even to the top. The
drum and bass filtered down through the levels. It was dragging me up. I looked out, a billion snowflakes swirling
through the air. I didn't fancy the drop one bit. But I wanted

to be back out there, anonymous, flagging a cab on Oldham Road. It couldn't happen until I'd found Li Cheung.

I walked across the balcony until I came to another door. I went through it, found another set of stairs. I tried the lift again but got nothing. Then heard a shout from somewhere above me. It wasn't just a party. It was more than that. I told myself I was fucking stupid for going any further. Today had brought enough to last me a lifetime. Yet I kept going, got mesmerised by that drum and bass and what awaited me on those higher floors.

I took the next flight, stopped on the landing halfway up when I saw the drying bloodstain and the splashes along the wall. Took a final drag on the smoke and crushed it. Swallowed. Dropped down to examine the stain more closely. It was sticky. The patch was big enough to cover a square foot at least. I couldn't help but wonder whose blood this was and how it had gotten there.

I didn't like the vibes. I pulled Simon's iPhone out and took several photographs of the bloodstain. Ironic how I was using his phone to record evidence. From up above, the drum and bass was thumping. I didn't like what I was walking into, but I felt the pull of it. I pocket the iPhone and moved on. Up another level, then another, until I reached somewhere halfway. And I still hadn't found the source of the music or Li Cheung's flat.

More graffiti on this level. It was everywhere. And the whole place smelled of blood and piss. There was a foul sweetness here, and I had to find the outdoor balcony again to get some air. Felt light headed as I looked down. I'd never been one for heights. I caught my breath, cursing at how unfit I was. Out there, the city lights twinkled. And still the snow came tumbling.

Looked out to the south and thought about Sara laid up

in that mental ward. Locked in like a prisoner. Doped up to
the eyeballs on fucking anti-psychotics. Biting her pillow to
stop the tears. It reminded me of why I was here in the first
place. Angel, raped and strangled, stabbed fourteen times,
semen and blood in her anus.

Heroin overdose, that'd be good. I could get you some.

Helen Shields, the girl who had stopped me from
plunging to my death. I had to get away from the balcony
before I tried again.

Stepped back inside and heard voices and footsteps
coming down the stairs. I ducked back out into the cold,
leaving a half-inch gap so I could see who was leaving.
Moments later, two girls in miniskirts and high heels click
clacked across the polished floor. I got a look but didn't
recognise either of them. They were speaking in Mandarin.
When they were out of sight, I sneaked back in and made
my way up another flight. Had a stomach churning feeling
that I was walking into the lion's den. The thump thump
thump of the drum and bass was loud enough for me to feel
it bouncing in my chest now. And the voices were louder,
too. Shouting, laughing, screaming.

I reached the next landing and a set of double glass
doors. Lights flickered on the other side. I took a deep
breath, knowing there would be others nearby, and pushed
the door open. I came into a hallway, heard moaning
coming from the other end of the corridor. All the flat doors
down here were boarded up with plywood. I stepped down
the narrow passage slowly, the drum and bass pounding
from somewhere on the other side of the wall.

I reached the end where a dark corner invited me to step
closer. I swallowed hard as I put one foot in front of the
other.

There was a man standing, back to the wall, head

thrown back. And kneeling before him, sucking his cock, was Simon. I'd recognise those black fingernails anywhere. The man on the receiving end, a lanky guy in black eyeliner and a woman's wig, opened his eyes and lay them upon me. I backed off as he started grinning, then laughing as Simon's head went back and forth.

I turned back, almost ran in the other direction, glanced back to see them still at it, then turned another corner into the belly of the music, the beats pounding and pounding, the bass thumping across the floor beneath me. It was so loud my entire body shook. I came to a door, 146 written on it in red paint, ajar with blue flashing strobes behind it. I stepped forward, took a breath, and pushed it open.

There was a bloke lying behind it, his jeans halfway down his arse, his face contorted. He was off his head, on what I didn't know. I stepped over him, round another corner into a massive room. It wasn't a flat anymore. Everything was knocked through. I squinted through the strobes, almost fell over a pair of legs as I weaved my way through the bodies. There were tens of them, lying around. All fucked off their faces on God knows what. I looked around, saw several walls with gaping holes in them, and more rooms on the other side. There was a PA system at one end and a set of decks with no one manning them. Thick smoke rolled through the air like a pea souper, and I guessed, by the smell of it, it wasn't just weed I was breathing in but crack too.

I walked through the room, so big it was like a warehouse, and I guessed the whole level had been transformed into just that. Except this was no rave. Almost everyone was flat out, high on all kinds of shit. Women stared. One grabbed my ankle as I passed. Resisted the urge to kick her away.

There was a bank of settees against one wall, full with men and women smoking some shit or other, their heads thrown back, their faces zoned out. There was a couple fucking in the corner, she straddling him; he smoking a crack pipe. Someone grabbed my shoulder and I turned, got confronted by a Korean chick with a handful of pills resting on her tongue. She went to kiss me, rolled her tongue over my lips. I backed off, almost fell on my arse. When I looked back, she'd retreated into the darkness and all I could see were shapes. Silhouettes in the pitch black. I could barely tell if anyone was moving and the strobe was giving me a fucking headache. The drum and bass was hurting my ears. I saw people laughing and grinning, eyeballs wide. All eyes were on me. I stumbled back into the darkness. Looked around at all the crack heads lining the walls. There was a guy throwing up white puke in the corner, his girlfriend flat out on her back.

There wasn't much conversation going on, and I could see why. I crouched down to meet the gaze of a teenage girl, couldn't be any older than sixteen, her grey hoody over her head to block out the world. Raised my voice over the drum and bass and could barely hear myself.

'I'm looking for Li Cheung! Where can I find Li Cheung?'

She raised her head, spittle bubbling on her fat lips, eyes blank, pupils like black holes. 'He's..... he's.....'

Then she grinned widely and laughed as if it was the funniest thing in the world to be asked about Li fucking Cheung. I grabbed her shoulders and shook, but she just went on laughing, hard.

'Where is he? Where's Li Cheung?'

Someone grabbed me, a black guy with a spike through his nose. I turned around and he went to put a pipe between my lips, blowing down the other end. I got a blast of some shit or other while he staggered back, baring white teeth to the black room. I coughed it out when I felt my head tingle. I looked down as he backed away and saw another girl, Chinese, point towards the back of beyond.

I followed her direction and waded through the throng of fucked up people scattered all over the place. It was like a farm of arms and legs and staring eyes. Stepped over a group of girls sitting in a circle, passing a pipe back and forth. I pushed through a door that had seen better days and found myself in a room lit up in green, a bank of leather armchairs against one wall and a line of men and women lounging on them, the girls with their skirts riding up, one with nothing on below the waist at all, and all of them in pairs, cooking up heroin. Saw one or two glance at me, then slip away into opium dreams. There was a Chinese guy with his top off, his torso ripped and toned, a tourniquet around his bicep. He was about to put a needle in a young girl's vein, then looked up to see me stood at the threshold with the drum and bass behind me.

'I'm looking for Li Cheung.'

The Chinese guy grinned, his eyes creasing up. He gestured for me to come in and sit down. I took one more step and asked again.

'You found Li Cheung,' he said, the words coming out so slow it was as if he was speaking in slow motion, all the time that grin plastered across his face. 'Sit down.'

'I'd rather stand.'

He laughed, saliva bubbling on his lips like the girl in the grey hoody. 'What do you want with Li Cheung?'

'Can we go somewhere else?'

'You want something, we can do it here... right here.'

I wanted nothing more than to be out of there right now. Cheung looked right through me, eyes wide and spaced out.

He reached his arm out, the leather belt hanging from his bicep. Cocked a thumb and hitched it over his shoulder. I guessed he was indicating I go into the back room behind him. Didn't feel like following his instruction, but shit, I was here now. I wasn't leaving until I had the information I wanted.

I stepped forward as he left his seat and the girl he'd just injected, leaving his works on a little coffee table. He turned into a corridor behind him and I followed. The man was walking slowly, as if each step was an incredible effort. I kept my eyes fixed into the back of his head. We passed a room with several East Asian looking women sat around on cushions; the air filled with a sweet smoke. A few glanced at me and one hooked her finger in a 'come here' fashion, beckoning me to join the fun.

In another room to my left there were several men, black, Chinese and Pakistani, all queuing up to take turns on the Chinese girl who was bent over a settee, another black guy fucking her from behind. She was screaming. I followed Cheung down the corridor into a cool and empty room, a single light bulb flickering above. He turned as I crossed the threshold and told me to shut the door. I wasn't keen, but I did so.

'Who sent you here?' he said, collapsing into a ripped up leather Chesterfield.

'Sherry. You know her?'

He looked away, thinking. Or perhaps he'd become distracted by the heroin coursing through his blood. 'I know her. I know her.'

'A woman was killed. Angel. She seems to think you might know something about it.'

He gestured for me to sit down, though where I didn't know. Sweat beaded on his smooth chest and he fell back, his grin wider than ever. Was he taking the piss? I thought so. I didn't know what this operation was, but it didn't look pretty and by the looks of all the fucked up people in here, it was a regular occurrence. It was clear there were prostitutes everywhere. I wondered if they were here of their own accord or he was getting them so high they didn't know what day it was. Looking at him, he was so high himself I half expected him to float out of the window, if there was one.

'We're all...Angels...here....'

'What do you know of Bo Wong? And Han Lan?'

He laughed. 'Come here.'

'I asked you a question, Mr. Cheung.'

'I know of no Bo Wong. I know of no Mr. Lan.'

'But you know a girl is dead? Raped, strangled, stabbed. Murdered in cold blood.'

'I know of no Angel. But we're all angels here, Mr...?'

'Locke,' I said. 'Jim Locke.'

'You are nothing, Mr. Locke,' he said, then shouted something in Mandarin.

The drum and bass went up a notch as three Chinese guys appeared through the door behind me. I didn't recognise any of them but froze when I saw the machete emerge from the trousers of one of them.

'Escort Mr. Locke from the building.'

'I'm leaving.' I went to pass the three Chinese, but the one with the blade stood in the doorway. He stroked it down my shirt, said something in Mandarin. I went to push past him, but a fist landed on my nose, followed by a knee to my guts. I slumped to the floor, three sets of legs surrounding me, and got a boot in the jaw for my troubles. I spat blood and rolled over. Got dragged up by the collar and frog-marched back through the other rooms, thick crack smoke caking the air, the beats pounding in my chest, my head swimming. I could only hope this wasn't it, that the last thing I'd see was a fucking blade coming towards my face.

'Fuck!'

Another punch to the ribs and the room spun until I was out into the cool air of the corridor outside. Heard more of that moaning and saw Simon and the other guy still fumbling in that darkened corner, and then I went through a set of doors and was thrown down the stairs. Cracked my head on the stone steps as I reached the landing down the first flight, then turned to see two Chinese stepping down towards me. There were several half-naked girls behind them, all doped up to the eyeballs, watching and screaming as the blood poured from my head.

I scrambled to my feet and stumbled down the stairs, the breath taken out of me, the blood pouring in my eyes. I didn't look back as I went down flight after flight, but I could hear them behind me, shouting in that Mandarin, and I wondered if the cigarette man was one of them, the one who'd blown up the Punto.

I wasn't sure which level I was on but I crashed through a set of doors and found myself back on the dark corridor, all the flats boarded up, graffiti everywhere. I stumbled through the blackness, my steps echoing around me, until I found a crevice in the wall and stood in it. I could hear the voices and the footsteps beyond, the Mandarin loud and harsh in the quiet of this level. Up above, the drum and bass droned on, and beyond the glass the voices diminished. I waited there in the pitch black until I was certain they were gone, then found an entrance out onto the balcony and crashed through it. My shirt was spotted with crimson and my stomach cramped up. I drank that cold air in until I could drink it in no more. The snow pummelled down to

Earth and all I wanted to do was go with it, just float down to the frozen ground and sleep.

I pulled out a smoke and sparked up. Dragged that shit in deep. The blood from my head pooled into my eyes and I had to wipe them clean. My head felt wet and warm. I pulled out my phone and checked the time. Just gone half eleven. I thought about phoning Laura, wishing to Christ I'd followed her advice and gone home with her. Instead, I was lucky to be given the opportunity to walk out of here in one piece. And I knew I still wasn't out of the woods yet. Down below, out on the street, its engine purring, was the blacked out Merc. Seems they'd found me. I guessed Cheung, or at least one of his associates, had made the call.

'Fucking hell.'

I wanted out. I slung the smoke out into the night and ducked back inside. I could still hear the Mandarin coming from somewhere above me. Either they'd lost me or had given up bothering. I hoped it was the latter. I moved down the dark corridor and found the exit at the end. I knew I was near the ground floor, but I didn't want to come face to face with the Merc again if I could help it.

Crept down the stone stairs, looking for a weapon along the way. I could've done with a cosh, just to make me feel that bit better. Then I remembered the front doors were off their hinges. Shit, this was all I needed. They could be making their way up as I was moving down. And yet I could hear nothing but the noise from above. I knew I wasn't in my right mind. I couldn't be if I was stupid enough to think coming here was a good idea.

I stopped on the landing of level two as I emerged from the dark corridor. This one wasn't much better. The smell of piss and vomit and blood filled the air. I gagged, wiped more blood from my eyes. As I stepped slowly towards the nearest exit onto another landing, the smell of charcoal hit me, that burnt out first floor. It must have been a decent fire because the whole place was black and charred, dead smoke and dead air. Still wet with pools of water.

And then it hit me.

The place was supposed to be abandoned for a reason. The fire had made the entire building unsafe. Cheung could feasibly get away with murder–literally–if the authorities didn't know he was occupying the other floors. And why would they? Chances were, if the truth about the bent coppers really was that bad, they knew he was here all along and turned a blind eye. Keep all the drugged up wasters in one place. Dial a prostitute in exchange for their silence.

I pulled out my mobile. I knew it could be a bad move phoning the police, especially given that all eyes could be on me and my phone tapped or traced. So I went for the next best thing.

I ran back up to level three. Crashed through the doors and traced my steps. I knew there were a few flats that weren't boarded up on this level and I found one at the end– blue door, graffiti tags all over it. Tried the handle. Locked, but loosely. Went for a shoulder charge. Once, twice, then booted it wide open. Third time lucky. It swung into a pitch black room, the only light coming from a small window in the bathroom. I shut the door behind me and headed straight for it. Scrabbled around and tried to find what I needed. Nothing. At least not in here. I stood on the toilet seat and wiped the grime from the window. Peered out and saw two of the Chinese leave the Merc. They were heading straight for the gates. I went back over to the door, forced it shut. The lock was bust, but it would have to do.

Found a child's wardrobe in the small bedroom, one of those flat pack things. It was falling apart. I dragged it over to the back window and ripped a set of scabby curtains down from the rail. Rested the wardrobe at an angle next to the glass and draped the curtains over it. Just one more thing to do.

I slammed into the kitchen and went through all the cupboards. Found what I needed under the sink and thanked Christ as I grabbed it and went back to the wardrobe. I used the air freshener first, emptying the whole can over the curtains. Tossed it aside and unscrewed the cap on the turpentine. Poured half of the liquid over the curtains and the rest on the carpet. Then I stepped back into the shadows, making sure my escape route was clear. I took out a smoke, sparked up, took several long and hard drags to let the nicotine in before I flicked the cigarette onto the carpet and watched the whole shit house go up in flames.

83

I was on the phone before the flames really took hold and before I could feel the heat on my face. I backed out of the flat, back into the darkness, and headed towards the back stairs. The fire whooshed up good and I heard the window crack before my feet kicked the doors ahead of me.

'Emergency, which service do you require?'

'Fire! It's going up fast and I... I think there are people inside. Menzies court, Miles Platting.'

'Can you -?'

But I'd hung up before she could take a breath. I hesitated on the stairs before moving down into that charcoal black and raised my eyes above. I could still make out the drum and bass, could picture all the wreck heads up there. The engines would be here in minutes, even in this weather. I knew there was a station barely a mile away, near the Smithfield Detox Unit. With any luck, they'd be here before I reached the ground floor. I wrestled with my shirt and covered my mouth. The fire was going up quick and I could taste the smoke already.

I crashed onto level two and darted out onto the balcony, gasping in lungfuls of air. I was round the back of the building now, opposite side of the Merc. I peered out into the night, my eyes watery, my head bleeding, temples pounding, heart thumping. I thought about dropping down into the snow but couldn't be certain it'd cushion my fall. Scrapped the idea almost as soon as it had come. I knew I was running out of time. Fuck, this was worse than I thought. I suddenly had the terrifying realisation that I was trapped.

Went back to the exit door and pulled it open half an inch. Peeked into the darkness behind it and saw nothing. Nothing but smoke, which was now leaking through the door on the landing above. Wouldn't be long before it really kicked in, and when the flames got to this floor, I could well be fucked. This level wasn't safe as it was, and another fire could be the final straw. Then I heard voices, shouting loud. Mandarin again. Perhaps it was time I learnt Chinese.

I looked around for a weapon. Something, anything. Spotted a clay plant pot down by the back end of the balcony walkway with a rotting bush in it. Ran down and grabbed it, tossing the plant over the balcony. It was solid enough, and a crack over the head with this thing could do some damage. It was all I had and I took it. I held it over my shoulder, still peering through the gap in the door for any sign of trouble. And by now, the smoke was getting thicker. If they didn't know the building was on fire, they were either blind or stupid or both.

And then my phone went off. I pulled it out, saw the number was blocked. I ignored it, figuring it was the emergency operator on the other end, wondering why I'd hung up. But then the other sound was music to my ears. Sirens. I turned, gazed out into the milky white and saw those blue lights heading towards me. I couldn't see the fire from this side of the building, but I could only assume they could. When I turned back to the door, the smoke hit me. It was pouring through the gap, a silent killer. I couldn't breathe it in. It would be a grand mistake if I did. I took a large, desperate breath from the clean air behind me, pulled my shirt over my mouth, and made that decision I wished I'd never have to make. Dragged my jacket over my head, still gripping the plant pot, and dived back into the storm.

I couldn't hear the drum and bass anymore, just the wild crackle of the flames from above. I was running blind. It was bad enough without the fire, this darkness, but now I could barely see my hand in front of my own face. Heard a loud bang behind me but knew it would be suicide to even try looking back. Felt like my lungs were about to burst. I raised my free arm in front of me, feeling my way as best I could while the flames licked behind me and above. Heard another loud crash and stumbled. The plant pot smashed somewhere ahead. I fell over in the pitch black, the smoke reeling around me like the fog of death. Almost cried out when my free hand touched a wall. I shimmied along and fell to my side through a door that was hanging off its hinges. Took a heavy blow to my waist as I fell into a room covered in soot. Landed in a pool of water so foul I almost threw up right there. Looked up, saw a window ahead of me, grime and shit covering it from the outside. I staggered towards it and scrambled in the dark for the plant pot, launching it with one hard swing. It bounced off the glass. Lunged for it again and almost shit myself big style when I saw the flames crawling towards me through the corridor outside.

'Fuck!'

It was going badly wrong. I hammered on that glass with

everything I had. It cracked and cracked, and the heat was making it warp before my eyes. The heat I could feel on my back. Took one last plunge and screamed a big 'Fuck You!' when the bastard finally smashed and the shattering glass revealed the snowy world outside. Icy air rushed in and smoke rushed out. I quickly got rid of the broken glass at the base of the frame and hauled myself up through the window. Could I jump? Could I fuck.

I dragged that air in, blinded by the smoke and the snow and the blue flashing lights. Thought I heard voices and screaming, but it could've been coming from my own head.

I turned back. I knew there was just one more flight of stairs, and if I didn't go now, the smoke would either get me or I'd be burnt alive. I didn't want either. I covered my head and ran.

Ducked through the corridor, found my way to another exit and almost jumped down the flight of stairs. The flames had illuminated everything, but the smoke was a killer and by God, I knew it. I could feel the skin on my back beginning to blister as I ran down. Debris fell all around me and I could hear things blowing up, pipes bursting, electrics crackling. I knew I'd dodged a bullet.

When I hit the ground floor, there was no sign of the Chinese, but I could see one or two firefighters in the gloom, their torches splintering through the smoke. They were calling out to each other through their breathing apparatus and I knew that if they dragged me out there would be more questions than answers. I had to get out some other way. I ran around to the back doors and, irony of ironies, spotted a fire extinguisher fixed to the wall. I pulled it off the rack and hefted it over my shoulder.

Threw that bastard into the glass with all I had left, where it sailed through and shattered the whole thing like a

gift from God himself. I was quick to follow, eager to be out
of this rat hole; this stinking, filthy, burning mess.

Fell to my knees and rolled in the snow, grabbing hand-
fuls of it and stuffing it in my mouth like it was the sweetest
honey. It tasted like it to me. I lay on my back for precious,
precious seconds until I heard one of the firefighters out
front shouting through a loudspeaker, then staggered to my
feet, choking.

I ran. I ran into the glorious cold night, my heart beating
hard, my senses overloaded. Felt high and drunk on adren-
aline. Enough to carry me, with just one look back, into the
belly of the estate, until I could run no more.

When I finally stopped and fell to my knees, all I could
hear were the engines and the flames and the screaming.
The tower block was burning, glowing in the winter night
like an enormous funeral pyre.

Like the flames of hell itself.

84

I couldn't be sure where the Merc had gone, but I knew that if I didn't get out of here quick, off the estate and into a black cab, they'd be onto me in no time. They'd missed one opportunity, they wouldn't miss another. I couldn't take any risks in hanging around. And besides, I didn't know if the firefighters had seen me leg it away from the tower block. If they did, I could easily be nailed down as the arsonist. I'd been many things in my time, but I never thought I'd ever start a fire when I knew there were people in the building. There was a first for everything. But it worked. The Chinese wanted my head on a stake, and the only thing I could do to stop them was to keep them from getting in. Fire was the only way. I was certain I wouldn't be putting other lives at risk, though I could've fucked up badly if it all went wrong. The fire was a much needed distraction. Trouble was, I nearly killed myself in the process. Sometimes I could do the most stupid things.

I got off my knees, freezing, and ran into the night. There was no sign of any cars except for the sparse traffic on Oldham Road. No sign of the Merc. God knows what I

looked like, but I didn't feel good. I touched my head as I
ran, felt the stitches and now another cut. I didn't think it
was deep from when I banged my head on the stairwell
wall, but I knew head wounds could bleed for long enough
without even being too deep. I told myself I'd be fine as I
ran. It was times like this I needed a car. My lungs were
fucked and all I wanted to do was stop running, just stop
and go home. Stop it all, everything. I didn't need to be
involved in any of this. It was nothing to do with me. None
of it. Yet the corruption I knew–and Bob had shown–that
existed in the police force was enough to keep me going.
And even if I wanted to get out, to just walk away from all
the shit, I couldn't. I was involved, whether I liked it or not.
Trouble was, the stakes were getting higher every day. If I
wasn't careful, I could be dead myself, like Angel. She knew
things and paid the ultimate price. Her and others. I was no
closer to finding out who killed her. I could hazard a guess
at who ordered the hit, but as far as the killer was
concerned, the person who plunged the knife in, I felt I was
getting further and further from the truth. I didn't kid
myself that there couldn't be more than one. Raped, strangled, stabbed to death? It could've been a group of sick
bastards. My thoughts went back to what I saw in Cheung's
rooms. The sex, the drug use, the violence. It was dirty. Vile.
The kind of bastards who'd think nothing of getting rid of a
girl who couldn't keep her mouth shut.

I wondered what Sara knew and wasn't telling. They'll
kill me, she'd said. Did she know something too, or was it
just her delusions, the voices in her head?

I reached Oldham Road. It was black with sludge, but
the pavements were heavy with fresh snow. My boots
crunched as I jogged, out of breath, back towards Piccadilly.
I looked back into the estate and saw the black smoke

billowing from the windows, from the ground and up to level three. I could only hope no one above those floors was hurt, though by now I assumed the fire fighters were up there discovering more than flames. There'd be an investigation, especially given that the tower block was supposedly empty. I'd bet Cheung, whoever he really was, wasn't banking on a visit from the local fire brigade.

I ran, stopping and starting, until I reached Oldham Street. I got a few startled looks around the Northern Quarter, a few offers of help. But I didn't need help. I needed a drink and a strong one.

I dropped into The Castle and downed two double brandies. Bought a packet of smokes from the machine and chain-smoked several down in the back garden, my hands twitching as I lifted the coffin nails and the booze to my mouth. I checked myself in the gents. It wasn't half as bad as I thought. I washed the blood off my head, the black stains from my face and neck and hands. I took out my phone and discovered several unopened text messages. They were all from Laura, asking where the hell I was and getting more and more desperate. I found her number and pushed the green button. It took a few rings, and I almost gave up, assuming she was asleep. Then she answered.

'Jim? Where the fuck are you? Are you all right?'

'I'm fine,' I said, though by the look of my shaking hands, I didn't feel it.

'What's taking you so long? You've been gone ages. Come back....'

'I'm on the way,' I lied, though it was a half lie. I just needed the brandy to calm me the fuck down first. 'Just waiting to grab a cab.'

'Did you find that address?'

'Yeah.'

'Did you talk to him? Or her?'

'Yeah. Look, I'll explain it all later. I shouldn't be too long. Just don't worry.'

'Are you in a pub? I can hear the bloody music! Jim, where are you?'

'Yes, I'm in a pub. Just needed a drink, that's all. Look, I'll explain later.'

'You've just gone straight back to the bloody pub, haven't you? Jesus, I knew it -'

'I've done nothing of the sort. Look, I'll be back in half an hour, I promise.'

'Jim!'

But I hung up then. Dragged that shit in deep and drained the last of the brandy. I checked Simon's iPhone - the image of him going ten to the dozen over some guy's crotch firmly in my head - just to make sure I still had it. Just to make sure I had the evidence. My whole conversation with Sherry was still there on the dictaphone app. I'd been worried I might have lost it, damaged the phone in the fire, but no. It was all there. The texts, the e-mails. The photographs. Everything was in its right place. And I was standing in the very spot where I'd nicked it from the man himself.

I staggered down to Piccadilly, nearly went arse over tit on the packed down ice. There was still a bit of snow in the air, just a few flakes floating down like blossoms in a spring breeze. Got the heebie jeebies when a police squad car rolled past me at five miles an hour before picking up pace down the top end. Call me paranoid, but I think they were monitoring me. If DI Rob Robertson was on the case, and he knew I was digging around, if Phil Young was anything to go by, I wouldn't put it past him to keep tabs. The uniforms were obvious. Question was: just who else was watching me?

There were still plenty of people around. It wasn't too late, but late enough for a lot of punters to call it a night. I thought about Stevie. It crossed my mind to wander back into Chinatown, see if he was all right, but I realised it was a bloody awful idea. I'd had enough for one night. The pressure was on. I'd put myself in enough danger for one day. And besides, I guessed he probably had a bed for the night. I hoped he could deliver again on the photographs.

I joined the taxi rank queue on Portland Street and didn't have to wait long. The driver took me down Oldham Road way, and when we passed the Miles Platting estate I looked into it, saw the black smoke still billowing into the winter sky. There were three engines and several police cars down in the belly of the tower blocks. The driver was banging on about the football, but I tuned him out. I was shattered. I slumped in the seat and watched the world roll by, trying to think of how I was gonna get out of this mess and failing. Wishing I was somewhere else. Wondering if it would have been better for everyone if I'd never have got out of that tower block alive.

85

Laura was asleep when I got back, which was just as well. Trouble was, she'd crashed on the couch and I had to sneak around to avoid waking her up. I knew there'd be twenty questions as soon as she knew I was back, which was best avoided as far as I was concerned, especially given my appearance. I was still scarred, both physically and emotionally–drained. The blood stains on my shirt and the black, sooty marks on my face were a dead giveaway that I'd been up to no good. Plus, I really smelled of smoke. I supposed the truth of the night's events post Rosso would have to come out eventually, I just couldn't face it now. So I stood in the kitchen, smoking as she slept. I cracked the top off a bottle of Budvar I found in the fridge and drank it like it was my last. Followed it up with a good measure of liquid fire to help calm the nerves before I splashed a few pints of cold water over me and undressed. As I walked back through to the bedroom, she was groggily making her way upstairs.

'How long have you been back?'

'Not long.'

'How long have I been asleep?'

'A while. Come on, let's get to bed. I'm knackered.'

She didn't argue. She must've been just as tired. Five minutes later we were both asleep.

86

It was a sleep full of bad dreams. I woke, beads of sweat glistening on my skin, sometime in the early hours. I dreamt I was choking, that I couldn't breathe. Someone or some*thing* was covering my mouth and nose, forcing me to gasp for air. I finally broke the spell when I shook myself from my slumber and took in large gulping breaths, desperately grateful that I wasn't being suffocated at all and that I was here in Sara's bed, sharing it with her sister Laura, who was down deep in a dream of her own. I lay there, my chest rising and falling, feverish, my head throbbing, limbs aching. I shivered in the room's cold and turned to see the time on the alarm clock - 03:47. I'd managed a few hours, but I was fearful of drifting off again in case I didn't wake up next time. I threw the sheets off, careful not to wake Laura, who was stirring beside me, and padded downstairs into the stark electric light of the kitchen.

Downed a glass of water with two painkillers, which I'd been guilty of neglecting. Stood with my head over the sink and splashed more water over my face and caught sight of my complexion. I looked like death warmed up. Those weren't just bags under my eyes, they were suitcases. Sparked up and paced in and out of the living room. I was overcome with restlessness, a million and one thoughts racing through my brain. Sara on a mental ward, Maureen on a cancer ward. Karen, Nicole, Laura asleep. Charlie and Spiderman, Bob in Spain. Stevie and Sherry. Phil Young and all the bent coppers. Cheung, Han Lan and Bo Wong. Angel lying in a freezer. Robertson, the squad cars, the fire in Menzies Court. The smell of crack and opium, the Chinese prostitute getting fucked over a couch, Simon and the transvestite. All the things I'd seen with bloodshot eyes that didn't want to see. The article in the *Evening Chronicle* and more to come. All of it, every last fucking bit. The beating I'd took down Dalton Alley. Christmas lights and markets and the bloody songs on the radio.

I sat on the couch, one eye on Laura's laptop and not knowing why. Sat there smoking, a brandy burning my chest and my eyes blinking. It took me a while to realise I'd been shaking, and I only noticed when I dropped the smoke on the carpet and the brown liquid spilled over my fingers. I grabbed it before it burnt a hole and cringed when I saw how yellow my fingers were. Finished the smoke and stubbed it out. Downed the rest of the brandy and thought about having another. Convinced myself it was a terrible idea and carried myself back up to bed, but I knew I wouldn't sleep. Crept in beside Laura, careful not to wake her, and lay there, staring at the ceiling and trying not to think about anything but failing.

I must've drifted off again an hour or so later when my breathing fell in rhythm with her own and the first traces of dawn leaked over the horizon.

87

It had gone eleven when she finally woke me up with a coffee, sweet and black. She threw a towel at me and told me to get a shower.

'You smell. And you need a shave.'

'Morning to you too.'

She climbed on the bed and straddled me, her hair dangling in my face, her lips close to my own. 'You're a very naughty boy, Jim Locke. But I like it.'

'What have I done now?'

'Where the hell have you been? You never said last night.'

'Got caught up, that's all. It's fine.'

'I told you to phone me.'

'I did.'

'Yeah, from the pub.' She rolled off me and lay down. 'I might be daft, but I'm not stupid.'

'But I did phone you. And I'm investigating Angel's murder, in case you hadn't noticed.'

'Doesn't mean you can stay out until all hours.'

'It wasn't that late. And besides, I can handle myself. I told you that.'

'So are you gonna tell me what happened? What kept you out so long?'

'There was a fire. In a block of flats near to where I went. The fire brigade had cordoned it off and I got covered in smoke.'

'Anyone hurt?'

I hoped not. 'Don't think so. I'm sure they had it under control.'

She rolled her eyes. Said I was a shit liar. I closed mine and sipped the coffee. My head throbbed, and she made it worse when she started running her fingers over the bruise on my forehead.

'That's a nasty cut, you know. You said you'd be fine.'

'I am fine.'

'Jim...'

I put the coffee on the side table and cupped her face. 'Really. Honestly, don't worry about me.'

'I can't help it. I'm growing rather fond of you, Jim Locke.' We kissed briefly before she pulled away. 'I'm going over to the hospital. See my sister. Want to come?'

'I can't. Got plans.'

'Need a lift anywhere?'

My head felt too fuzzy to think. 'What time are you leaving?'

'About an hour. I'll make you some breakfast. In the meantime, get a shower and get that smoke smell off you.' She dived off the bed, leaving me with the coffee. 'Bacon rolls all round.'

I was going to protest that I couldn't face it, and I really felt like I couldn't, but she was already out the door. I drank the coffee, thinking about my next move as the rain drummed on the windows. There were a few things I needed to do, a few phone calls I had to make. Checked the alarm clock on the side. 11:23. It all added up to my lucky number.

88

A fter I showered and changed, I was surprised at how quickly I ate and even more surprised that I was craving another one right after I finished. Perhaps I really was getting my appetite back. Laura seemed to think so, and she looked pleased that I'd managed it no problem.

'Fish and chips tonight,' she said, as she drained a second coffee. 'It's Friday after all.'

'I'm not sure when I'll be back.'

Her smile curved into a frown. 'Please don't stay out tonight, Jim. Let's just have a night to ourselves. I'll get Charlie off to sleep early and we can have a night in front of the telly.'

I wanted nothing more and told her as much. Yet I knew that things were getting serious. It wasn't the coppers but the Chinese I was worried about. I'd come within a whisker of some serious harm yesterday, and they'd tried to mow me down the night before. But I knew I was getting closer to the truth. They knew it too. Which didn't bode well for the day ahead. All I wanted was to lie low, like Bob had advised me to do, and get as far away as possible from the whole sorry mess. But I knew I couldn't, whether I liked it or not. I was involved. I had evidence, and I knew things the authorities—in this case the Metropolitan Police and Interpol–likely didn't. I had a chance to put the whole thing to bed, once and for all. But I had to be careful not to drag Laura into it. Part of me reckoned it was a mistake to allow her out with me last night. She came in useful, if only to follow Sherry to the toilets, but I couldn't let her think she was my bloody sidekick or something. Sara had already been a victim. It was all of her own accord, but still. The risks were high. I couldn't allow for any mistakes.

'Can I not tempt you with a Chippy Tea?'

'Now we're getting somewhere.'

She laughed then, said I was a funny bugger. Said it was her shout. I promised that, whatever happened today–and I didn't expect much, which was a lie–I would be back in time for haddock and chips. Nothing would stop me. This seemed to do the trick, and we shared another kiss before getting in her car. I made sure I had everything I needed before we set off.

Laura was far from happy about Sara's Punto. Who would be? But we agreed that now would be a bad time to tell her she'd lost her car. Losing her mind must be bad enough. I asked Laura to see if she could pick up anything her sister might say about Angel's killer, however ridiculous and deluded it might sound. I hadn't forgotten her words when I visited her on that ward. *They'll kill me.* She might be mentally unstable, a danger to herself for sure, but I found it hard to ignore what she'd said. It wasn't too long ago when she and I were out looking for her missing friend, and she'd seemed more than normal then, whatever 'normal' really was. She was anxious, of course. At her wits' end. But she never said anything about herself being in danger. But why would she? Maybe she'd been in denial. Maybe she knew more–much more–than she was letting on and felt safer for keeping quiet, as if ignoring it–whatever *it* was–would make it go away. I didn't know. Seemed the more I found out, the less I knew, like an archaeological dig that brought up more questions than answers.

After Laura had finished berating me about getting her sister's car blown up, my protests falling on deaf ears, we were silent until we got closer to my destination. Laura asked where I wanted dropping off and I was unsure myself. Yet I thought a walk at least part of the way would do me some good and get some coherent thoughts running through my head again. I swallowed two painkillers with a mouthful of week old orange juice she had in the glove box just before she dropped me at the bottom end of Deansgate. I was beginning to think I was deluded myself. It was just yesterday when I'd driven away from here in Sara's Punto, the Merc on my tail. Was I mad to be coming back here, knowing that they could be lurking anywhere nearby? No doubt about it. But I doubted that was the case. I knew that whatever happened, I would be running with one eye firmly over my shoulder. Just in case.

The pavements were slippy with melting ice and sludge, the sky the colour of wet cement. It would be a good twenty-minute walk to Han Lan's pad if I got a move on, and the quicker I could get in and out of that place, the better. I felt like I had a million and one things to do and precious little time to do it in. I checked the time on my mobile. 12:47. I'd have to make a decent start before dusk settled in, just hours away.

Forced myself to avoid the nearest pub, one of those chain places, as I walked. Battled with the idea that actually, it would be okay, because they served coffee as well and that's what I was really tempted by, not the beer. But I just kept on walking and tried not to look inside at the old men and early starters. It would've been a pleasure to join them, just to let go of this sinking ship, but I knew that if I walked in, I'd never walk out again.

I'd just reached the big *Waterstones* when my phone chirped. I ducked into the bookshop doorway as the rain fell, and answered.

'Hello?'

'Jim? It's Stevie.'

'I was wondering when you'd call. Did you get any more?'

'Filled the roll up again. Some of the same faces, some others too.'

'Anyone you recognise?'

'No one I recognise, no. So where do you want to meet? I need to get my bed sorted for tonight, if I can. As soon as.'

'I'm on Deansgate. Outside Waterstones. Listen, there's a café just opposite the Kendals. I'll shout you some breakfast if you can make it there in half an hour.'

'I know it. I'll be there in twenty minutes.'

I sparked up and watched the world go by as I sheltered from the rain. I was getting close. I could feel it. Though everything felt like a total mess and I couldn't piece it back together, there were fragments that rose to the surface and floated into view. Maybe I'd never know who killed her, but I'd give it a damn good try at finding out. If nothing else, at least the other stuff was out in the open now. The lies, the secrets, the corruption. I'd love nothing more than to watch all the bent coppers squirm. Sir David Howe and Phillip Browning; Bryn Llewellyn and Sir Michael Robert Fletcher. Probably a long line of others too, and I wouldn't put it past the likes of Rob Robertson to be involved. And Phil Young. He was one of the coppers on the first set of photographs Stevie brought my way, which was telling. But still: who had killed Angel and dumped her under an arch beside the Bridgwater Canal? Who had raped and strangled her, stabbed her like she was nothing more than a piece of meat? Who had ordered the hit, if the hit had been ordered at all?

I wasn't sure what to make of Sherry and why she'd given me that address for Li Cheung. And who the hell was he, anyway? Big time dealer? Looked likely. There was no news, as far as I knew at least, about anyone being hurt in the fire. But there was time for that yet. The event itself was barely a day old. I knew I'd been lucky to get out of there in one piece, and I was the only one seriously at risk given the blaze was on the lower floors. I couldn't believe my stupidity, but it was all I had at the time.

I took the last drag and slung it into the gutter. Crossed the street and ducked into the little café I knew down the side of Kendals. I used to come here when I was a DS, and I knew it was still going. They always did decent breakfasts. Not that I needed anything. It was Stevie I was concerned about. I'd get him something to eat, question him about last night, then get the photos done before moving on, and moving on quick.

I dropped in out of the rain and was greeted by a small Italian guy. I didn't recognise him. Ordered an Americano and found an empty table in the corner. The only other customer was a construction worker on a lunch break. The little Italian had barely put the coffee down when my phone went off again. Thankfully, the radio was on loud enough to drown out our conversation. I didn't need to ask who it was on the other end of the line.

'Bob. Wish you were here?'

'Not likely, son. How are things?'

'Total shit storm, like you wouldn't believe.'

'Did it go to press?'

'You know very well it did. You've got the Internet over there, haven't you?'

'I'm lying low, Jim.' I could hear the inaudible hum of distant traffic in the background. Then a splash, as if someone, perhaps his wife or daughter or grandkid, had just dived into the pool he was sitting next to. 'I can't get to the Internet that easy around here.'

Which was bollocks. Of course he could, if he tried. 'There must be something nearby.'

'Oh, there is. There is. But seriously, Jim. I can't go anywhere, not really. I keep getting followed by this bloke whenever I go into town. So I have to send Marco to do my groceries.'

'Marco?'

'Pool attendant. Spanish. He doesn't mind, and I pay him.'

'So who is this bloke?'

'I don't know. He just keeps turning up. I've only been into town twice and both times he's been following me.'

'You're being paranoid.'

'I know paranoia, son, but this isn't it. And he's Chinese. Not many of them around here, I can tell you that. So. I've seen bits on the TV, but we don't get much. I like it like that. I need the rest. So what's happening, lad?'

I told him. About how the whole thing had blown up. SKY, BBC, ITV, the lot. It was in every newspaper in the land and he was missing out on his big scoop in a major way. He laughed, almost. He went quiet when I told him about how they'd blown Sara's Punto up, and I'd stumbled upon more than I could chew when I was directed to Li Cheung's address. How I'd almost been killed–twice.

'I thought I told you to keep your head down?'

'I can't. I'm in too deep.'

'Jesus, Jim! You'll be six foot deep before long...'

I was glad I wasn't already. But I knew there was time for that yet. 'Well, I'm not, no thanks to you.'

'What's that supposed to mean?'

'Letting all this out, then fucking off to Spain.'

He sparked up then, a Montecristo no doubt. 'You know I couldn't exactly hang around. And anyway, no one asked you to get involved in all this.'

I suppose he was both right and wrong on that score. He knew I was in it for Sara and I told him so. He asked how she was and I told him that too.

'Jesus. Do me a favour, son. It's over now. You'll never find her killer, lad. You'll probably go to your grave–and I really hope it's not an early one–without ever knowing the truth. You do know that... don't you?'

I said that I did, but I didn't believe it. Well, part of me didn't. I knew there had to be something. Something else that I'd missed. The door chinked open and in walked Stevie, looking around. I waved him over.

'Look, I've got to go. For now, at least. But call me back later. We're not done.'

'There's more to come though, Jim. The paper's far from done on this one. I just wish I could be there to see the look on their faces when they go down.'

'I don't think it'll come to that. Friends in high places, you know. You said so yourself. All part of this secret, exclusive club you were on about. Like the fucking Masons or something. Secret handshakes, all that shite. And anyway, what's stopping you? The Met are on it, Interpol too. It's in your bloody article, Bob. What have you got to lose except for a nice suntan?'

'My sanity, for one... and my life.'

'If they wanted you dead, they could've done it by now.'

'Still might.'

'Come off it, who's gonna find you in bloody Spain?'

'The Chinese guy I saw in the town. I'm not joking, son. They're onto me.'

'It's over. Your words, not mine. Phone me later. Tonight, maybe. I've got a few loose ends to tie up before I knock all of this on the head for good.'

'Okay. And be careful, Jim. Really. I'm not joking, lad.'

'Me neither. Just get your arse back to England.'

We said our goodbyes, then he rang off. I looked up to find Stevie staring at me. He was dripping with rain, his long brown hair matted with damp. He smelled like a dead animal, like something the cat might drag in. And his cough hadn't changed. He dumped his stuff down beside me–sleeping bag, rucksack, bin liners full of God knows what– and burst into a coughing fit right there. I handed him several napkins and he handed me the disposable camera. I raised my eyebrows.

'All there. Not much fun last night, but they're all there.'

'Why not?'

'Bloody freezing, that's why. I could do with a drink.'

'I'll get you some breakfast.'

I stepped up to the counter and ordered two pots of tea and a Full English with extra everything. Dug around in my pockets for some cash. Watching him sitting there, his rags and bags at his feet, made my heart bleed. He'd probably hadn't had a bath in weeks, months even. It was the least I could do, especially since Laura had given me five hundred quid to play around with. I fished out two twenties and handed them to him when I sat back down. He almost burst into tears. I poured us both a tea and watched him spoon in four sugars.

'I was there most of the night,' he said. 'Watching them come and go. Got asked to move on at one point as well.'

'And did you?'

'Did I fuck!'

I needn't have asked. Having spent several weeks on the streets with Stevie, sleeping out behind Ho's Bakery, it wasn't a surprise. My guess is he was probably three sheets to the wind as he pointed the camera. No one could tell Stevie what to do. I could smell the booze on him now. It made me want a drink myself.

The breakfast came and I watched him dive in like it was a King's feast. I let him eat while I sipped my tea and watched the rain roll down the window. Thinking. About my daughter. About Maureen. I played with the phone and thought about phoning Frank, perhaps paying a visit again. He'd warned me not to, at least until he'd spoken to Karen. But I didn't expect that to happen anytime soon, given my sudden arrival the other day and the fact that Maureen was dying. I wondered if it would be wise to try to see her before the cancer took her away for good.

'Are you all right?'

I snapped out of it. 'What?'

'You okay?'

'Yeah, just thinking, that's all.'

'Cheers for this,' he said, hair hanging down in his runny egg. He stabbed a sausage and severed it before heaping on a load of baked beans and wolfing it down. Chewing. 'I'm starving.'

'I can tell.'

'So anyway. Is that it, then? Don't need me for anything else?'

I nodded. 'That's it. And thanks for this, mate. Can't have been easy staying out there all night.'

He shook his head. 'I do it all the time. Besides, what are mates for, eh? You might have gone up in the world, but I haven't forgotten about us both kipping out that time. You've changed a lot, man. Really.'

'And how are you? You got a bed for tonight?'

'I hope so.'

'You need to get to the shelter?'

'As soon as I've had this. And listen–thanks. For the food. And the cash. It's appreciated.'

'You've done me a big favour.'

He said nothing, just nodded. Slurped his tea and took a bite of toast. I watched him until he finished, wondering if there was anything else I could do for him. I knew there wasn't. Stevie was the type of bloke who liked to live off the grid, take the rough with the smooth. Unfortunately for him–and most on the streets–it was more rough than smooth. Especially in the winter.

He finished up. We drank our tea, not saying much. He asked me what would happen to the men he'd been photographing and what they were doing in there. I told him I didn't know, and it was the truth. But after Bob's story had hit the headlines yesterday, with apparently much more to come, I expected nothing less than arrest for at least some of the coppers in the pictures he'd taken that first night. Anything less would be an outrage. But convictions? I doubted it. I was involved with the law for long enough to know they looked after their own–and that went for the judicial system as well. I wouldn't be surprised if more was to come out of all this. Cover-ups and lies, secrets and services. Dead and missing women. Drug cartels and money laundering. Bob implied all this was just the tip of the iceberg. And if the Chinese were involved, which they undoubtedly were as far as I could see, I couldn't readily see anyone who'd be willing to fuck with the Triads. Least of all me.

'I'd better get going.' He drained his tea, declining the offer of another, which I was glad about. I had work to do. He stood up, slung a bag over his shoulder. 'Been good seeing you again, man. Pop down the soup kitchen whenever you're free.'

I saw him out onto the street, gave him several smokes as a parting gesture. Shook his hand. His grip was hard, his eyes genuine. 'I'll see you around, Stevie. And thanks for your trouble. I appreciate it.'

'The pleasure's all mine,' he said, then coughed so hard I thought he was gonna bring his lungs up. He spat into the sludge at our feet as the hard rain came down again. Slung a hood over his head. Put a fist to his chest. 'Until next time.'

Then I watched him walk away down Deansgate to a life in the bottle.

89

I spent the next half hour getting the prints. Boots was a nightmare, packed with Christmas shoppers, even at this time of day. I weaved my way through the human traffic and up to the photography department. Stood in a queue to use the machine for ten minutes. Then waited a further ten while they printed. The images were grainy and poor quality. Stevie was definitely no photographer. But it was enough for what I needed. As far as evidence was concerned, these were good shots.

I wasn't too keen on standing there in the middle of the department store, flicking through the most important photographs I'd seen in years. For all I knew, I could be being watched right there. I knew it didn't take much, especially where the Chinese were concerned. It didn't take much for them–and Phil Young–to spot me on the street outside just yesterday. They could just as easily be on my case as I flicked through those prints. So I pocketed them, then made my way to one of the best little bars I knew to take a proper look.

Corbiere's, on Half Moon Street, just off St. Ann's

Square, was a hidden gem with the best jukebox in the world. I knew it was dark in there too, a little hideaway in the basement down a narrow side street and away from the crowds. I would have to be on my best behaviour if I didn't want to get sidetracked, and the combination of the best music in a pub by a country mile and half decent beer was enough to keep me there for the long haul. I kept it in my head like a mantra as I approached the bar. *Just one. Just one. Just one.*

Got myself a pint of Czech beer and took a table in the corner. *I am the Resurrection* belted out. Almost felt The Stone Roses were speaking directly to me until I realised I had the shakes. The Resurrection? I felt like death warmed up. Took a table in the far corner, grabbing *The Guardian* along the way. To the handful of punters dotted around, I had to look like I was just another regular bloke having a pint with the paper.

Slapped the paper down and pulled out the photos. Took a long drink and let it do its magic. Before I could examine the prints, my eyes were drawn to the front page. They were running a story on the GMP and West Yorkshire Police corruption. The faces of the same ex coppers Bob and I followed just a few nights ago were all over it. The accompanying article said all four had been arrested, along with several others, and were currently being held and questioned by Interpol at Scotland Yard. There was no mention of Angel's disappearance and subsequent murder, but the face of Chi Phuong stared out at me from page two like a ghost. I wondered just how far the cover up went and how deep it involved the GMP. The whole thing stank. There was no mention of any Chinese involvement either, just talk of sex trafficking with no specifics. Bob had said there was more to come. I hoped he was right. But as I took another mouthful on the pint, I wondered just how free our press was. The press conference was scheduled for six pm tonight. It would be an interesting watch.

I slung the paper aside and pulled out the photos. There were forty in all. I flicked through them one by one and saw familiar faces. Phil Young and another guy I didn't know. The Chinese restaurateur we'd seen with the coppers in the Midland Hotel, Chen Longwei, greeting a group of men as they entered Bo Wong's. Wong himself. Another guy I recognised but couldn't place the name. And then the next one.

Matt.

Matt and the other guy, Dang, both of whom I'd met the night Angel went missing and the night I'd taken a trip into hell.

Smug grins all round.

They were all in it together, all right. Probably right from the beginning.

Another one, the guy I'd hung over the roof terrace at Han Lan's. Traders one and all.

'Get you another?' The barmaid, a mixed race girl with piercings.

Just one. Just one. Just one.

I looked up, careful to cover the images on the table. 'Just one more.'

I shuffled the prints like a pack of cards in a poker game, staring into space as The Smiths kicked into *Hand in Glove*. Thought about Bob and his claim that he'd been followed in the local town. Twice, he'd said. About Sara on the mental ward. Her words. About the nightmares, Angel's face coming to me every night.

The barmaid put another pint down. I drained the first one with two painkillers and quickly got stuck into the second. Gave her a fiver and she handed me the change. I drank deep, downed it in the time it took Johnny Marr to finish up. Stuffed the photos back in my pocket and checked the time on my phone. It was nearly half-past two. If I didn't move fast, the dark would soon fall. I knew the clouds were gathering, and the wind was up.

It was just as well I left when I did, sparking up as soon as I hit fresh air. A group of suits out on a works do barged past me down the steps. From somewhere nearby, I could hear the sleigh bells ringing and *Slade* kicking in. I stepped away from Half Moon Street and on through St Ann's Square again, the Christmas Markets aglow and busy, the smell of barbecuing meat and pancakes on the breeze. Pushed through the throng as my heart beat that little bit quicker and cut through to Deansgate. I pulled the key fob from my pocket as I walked, just to make sure. Checked the code on the slip of paper I had stuffed in my jeans. I'd be there soon if I got a good pace going. I didn't know what I'd find when I arrived, but I knew there had to be something I'd missed at Han Lan's pad.

90

I kept my head down as I walked, tried to remain as invisible as possible. In a city like Manchester, it was easy enough to get away with. Ran over everything as best I could as I smoked along the way. Tried to make some coherent sense out of everything. That bit wasn't easy. Truth was, I wished I'd never met Angel. Although if I hadn't, I'd probably be dead by now. I thought about cause and effect. You know, that theory about how the beating of a butterfly's wings on one side of the world can cause a hurricane three thousand miles away–something like that. But I wondered that, if I *had* jumped that day, would Angel have found herself dead just days later or would her path have been dramatically different? Can the smallest thing really have the most massive effect? Would our fates have been different if she hadn't have grabbed me from that ledge? I'd never know, of course I wouldn't. But I wondered.

You could say the same about anything and everything then, if that was the case. You know, cause and effect, ripples through time. Whatever. It was all 'what ifs'. What if I'd never met her? What if she'd never took pity on me and took me back to Han Lan's pad? What if I hadn't have slept with her, what if she didn't go out for her birthday drinks? What if she'd never been sectioned for mania or bi-polar or whatever the fuck it was, and what if she'd never ended up a working girl? Because it all had to mean something. There had to be a purpose to it all. There had to be reasons. Existence wasn't just futile, was it?

Which got me thinking about my own purpose. If Angel *hadn't* have stopped me from jumping, my daughter would be without a Dad. My Mum, estranged though she was, would be without a son. The people who would've seen me smash to the ground at sixty miles an hour might have been traumatised for many years afterwards, which in turn could've affected *their* relationships and it would just go on and on and on, like Angel's death is doing now.

And Bob's articles. His paper's investigation over four decades. If it really went that far back, all this really was just the tip of the iceberg and I myself could easily have been dragged into it when I was on the force. Which begged the question–who else was? People I knew? People I used to call my friends? There was no doubt Phil was in the photographs, no doubt he wanted me off the case to find her killer, but he couldn't do anything about it. There was nothing illegal about being a Private Investigator. But why was he so bloody keen to keep me away and who, if anyone, had put him up to it?

Then there was the Chinese. Han Lan and his massive investments. The off shore accounts, the millions stashed away. Bo Wong running the dancing club and the dancers themselves. The heroin use, the sex trafficking. Li Cheung. The escort agency, Provoke.

The missing.

The dead.

I felt like I was trapped in some vast conspiracy, a conspiracy everyone else knew of but me. Trapped in the matrix, just like that film. Everyone watching and no way out.

Heroin overdose, that'd be good. I could get you some.

The only truth I really knew was this: I lived in a fucked up world.

With my thoughts jumbling around my brain, and my steps getting quicker with every stride - just one more drink, just one more drink - I had to snap out of it when I realised I was nearing my destination. I stopped outside the Knott Bar and thought twice. It looked more than inviting in there. I dragged myself away when I got some funny looks off a couple of women sharing a bottle of wine in the window seat.

I moved on down the canal side, the barges moored in the partially frozen water. My boots crunched through the slush as I walked past quiet bars, their gardens empty, their benches desolate. The rain had slowed to a fine spray but there was a chill in the air that gave the water a still sheen, thin plates of ice floating on the surface like gravestones.

I pushed my hands in my pockets and marched on, leaving the city behind me as I ventured deeper into the swish apartment blocks, with duplexes and penthouses on either side and the furthest beyond, away from the packed bars when summer came around. But Han Lan's apartment, I knew, was nearby, just beyond the bar with the grand piano in the window. I could see the roof terrace from where I stood, when not so long ago I paced up and down, drinking his booze and cursing the world.

I stepped towards it, keenly aware that I perhaps wasn't in my right mind. This was madness. They'd surely have this place watched at all times, and I realised right then that the place could even be occupied again. With Angel gone, who else was gonna fill the void? And then it occurred to me that that's why she was living there in the first place. As cover for whatever operation he had going. Surely he wouldn't have let Angel live there for no good reason? Not out of the goodness of his heart, if he had any goodness in it. No, it had to be for something. And I recall how Angel was guarded about the whole thing. Her circumstances. She was a girl with secrets and I knew it at the time. I knew there was something not quite right about her arrangement with the businessman.

From my vantage point, out here on the canal bank, I could see there were no lights on in the apartment. But that didn't mean anything. I took the slip of paper from my pocket and gripped the key tight as I stepped towards the gate.

I punched in the gate code and let out a breath when it clicked and rolled open. I helped it along and rolled it back behind me before it could open fully. The car park was well occupied with sporty vehicles. An Audi here, a Porsche there. There was even a Maserati over near the far end. You had to be on some very decent money to live in a place like this, and I wondered exactly how much the penthouse was worth. It was the kind of place where my face wouldn't fit, and it showed. As I stepped towards the main entrance to the complex, a couple strode out purposefully, he in an Armani suit, she in Prada. I watched as they unlocked the Porsche. They cast me a glance as we passed, and I saw them whisper something to each other as I stepped up to the intercom. I punched in the number for Han Lan's flat, thinking up an excuse on the spot in case anyone actually answered.

I waited. Nothing.

Waved the key fob at the sensor and smiled when the door clicked. I pushed it open and gently closed it behind me, then headed to the lift. Called it down and moved aside when another couple of fashionistas stepped out. We exchanged a brief 'afternoon', as if this was a usual thing and we all knew each other incredibly well, a mutual respect for the ever so fulfilling and cool lives we all lived in this swanky block. They looked back as the lift doors closed and I was moving up to the top floor before they'd even hit the car park.

The doors pinged open once more, and I walked out into the corridor. Han Lan's front door was down the bottom end, behind another partition door with a key code on it. I checked the slip of paper again and walked towards it, punching in the seven numbers and letters required before I turned the latch and finally emerged on the other side into another corridor I recognised. And here I was. There ahead of me was the front door I first crossed with Angel when she'd offered to give me a bed for the night. I put the key in the Yale lock and turned it several times until it unlatched and I put my weight upon it and pushed through.

The apartment was silent. I gently closed the solid wooden door behind me and stepped across the threshold and into the living room. The entire place was empty, and not just of people. Seems someone had had an inkling there would be others keen on seeing what was hiding in here, if anything, because all the furniture was gone. Someone had removed it all, but who? And when? It had to have been soon after I left. There was a lot of stuff to shift. I wondered who else had a set of keys.

I walked around an empty shell, checking every room, aware that since everything had been taken out - leather settee, several king -size beds, the TV and stereo system, even the giant American fridge. There had to have been someone anticipating my return to this place. It was eerie. No pictures on the walls, no house plants, nothing except for a set of wardrobes in the main bedroom, which were empty. My shoes - Han Lan's shoes - echoed around his own apartment on the parquet floor as I went from room to room, looking for nothing in particular yet hoping I'd find *something*, whatever that something was. I knew I was working on instinct, certain there would be at least something, just a tiny thing, for me to find. Something I'd missed. Yet my heart sank when I realised there was nothing. Nothing but ghosts and memories.

I didn't recall seeing a For Sale sign anywhere outside, though I could have missed it. There was no mail left anywhere. I checked the taps in both the kitchen and bathroom so there was still running water. Apart from a dirty towel left on the rack in the bathroom, there really was nothing at all except for a very large empty space.

I went over to the sliding patio doors and messed about with them until they opened and I stepped out onto the roof terrace. It was a different matter out here. I stood and sparked up, wrapping the jacket around me as I looked out across the city. The only thing missing was a large glass of scotch. I recalled how I stood here not long ago, convincing myself that Angel was still out there somewhere. That she was still alive and would turn up, that it was only a matter of time. She turned up all right.

But everything was as I'd remembered it. There were still plants lining the wall, even the lounger was still there, damp with rain. I looked around, feeling disconnected, and realised that there were a lot of cigarette butts lying at my feet. I couldn't know for sure how long they'd been there, but I couldn't recall seeing them before. To my right, the set of mini stairs which would take you right up to the roof itself stood inviting. I thought about heading up there, a mere ten feet above me, then thought better of it, especially given my head for heights. Instead, I crushed the smoke to join the other dimps at my feet and stepped back inside. One last check before I left the place for good.

Had a piss and checked the bedroom carpets for any loose edges, any places where it would be easy to stash documents or cash or anything else. But everywhere was sealed. Then my eyes fell on the attic door in the main bedroom, right above where I once lay my head. Before I could think of a way of getting up there and even getting through the damn thing, I heard movement from out in the corridor, followed by a key turning in the latch at the front door.

Seems I wasn't alone after all.

91

I went straight for the patio doors and slipped through them before the main front door could open even half an inch. Climbed the steps to the actual roof and got to my knees behind the lip of the edge. Below, I had a decent view of the roof terrace and out onto the locks. Looked around for any way out of here that didn't include going back inside. The only way was down. I was stuck. It was more than lucky I'd made it up here without being seen. Question was: who the hell was it?

I got down on my front and peered over the edge. The amount of cigarette butts on the floor wasn't lost on me. Someone must've been using the place to doss down. Or at least as some kind of hideaway. It was that kind of place– convenient. Handy for the right person or people. They weren't dossing though, as far as I could see. There was no evidence of that in any of the rooms.

And then the patio doors slid open. They stepped out onto the roof terrace as I ducked down. Phil Young and Matthew Brookes Wilkes. The bastard who'd spiked my drink. I could wring his fucking neck. I could wring both of their necks. How fucking stupid was Phil? He had a good career, once. Now he'd gone and fucked that up forever.

'So that's it,' Matt said. 'All done. Everything's out now. Good fucking job as well.'

'You sure that's the lot? What have you done with it all?'

'Wong's.'

'What, all of it?'

'All of it.'

I'd be interested to know exactly what it was they'd gotten rid of. I dug into my inside pocket and brought out Simon's iPhone. Nothing like a bit of surveillance. Opened up the camera app, careful to turn the volume down in case they heard the click. Then I pointed it and took as many photos as I could. Got their faces straight on in a few as well. This was damning evidence. I wondered if the Dictaphone app could pick up their conversation? It wasn't like I was a million miles away. I opened it up and pressed record before placing it on the ledge and ducking down behind it.

'He'll find a use for it, I'm sure,' Matt said. 'Cheung's after more, I know that much.'

'Especially after the fire last night. You hear about that?'

'Heard a few were in hospital. They reckon it was arson.'

'It was, without a doubt. Locke. They lost him inside. He probably started the fire as a distraction. I suppose it worked, smug twat that he is. Can't wait to stamp on his pissed up fucking face, I can tell you that much.'

'Did he even get out? Would be funny if he burnt himself alive.'

There was a pause while they smoked. I peered over the roof edge, watching. I have to admit; Phil's words hurt me. He wasn't the same man I knew on the force. Somewhere along the line, since I'd been pushed out, he'd lost all sense of morality. I didn't know what had happened to him. It was as if he'd been possessed by some evil demon. The guy had lost it. Just goes to show that you can't trust anyone, not even your friends.

'Good question,' Phil said. 'I don't know. Apparently, there were one or two bodies. There'll be an investigation.'

Fuck.

'Let's hope he was.'

'Not likely, knowing him. He's not that stupid. Wouldn't put himself at risk like that.'

'Well, I suppose you know him better than anyone.'

'Don't get me wrong. I'd like nothing more than to see him gone for good. Out of the way. He's the type of bloke who can dig shit up, you know. Even if he is off his face half the time. If he finds out I killed that girl, I'm fucked. So even if he isn't found dead in that tower block, Wong will make sure of it some other way. We'll find him. Take him out.'

'Sleep with the fishes...'

They laughed it up. 'Something like that. Something like that.'

Bang to fucking rights. Oh, Phil. You stupid, stupid little man.

'I suppose she had to go, though. With what she knew...'

'No doubt about it,' Phil said. 'We had some fun with her first though, eh?'

More laughter. I kept my head down. If they saw me, that would be it. No more Jim Locke. I wanted to make sure I would see my daughter again.

'Those special pills really did the trick, eh?'

'You could say that.' He was laughing. Strange how I'd never heard Phil laugh like this before. 'The way she was kicking and screaming, I'll never forget it. But it just about kept her placid enough after the first ten minutes or so. Was like giving candy to a kid after that.'

Horrible, dirty bastard. I could fucking kill him right now.

'So anyway. That's the lot?'

'That's it,' Matt said. 'As far as I know. Some for me, some for you. The rest to Wong and Chen and Cheung. They'll need to keep the girls on good form.'

'I still can't get over the fucking news. Won't be long before the Met come sniffing around. It's the last time I'll be involved in any of this. I'm lucky to still have Robertson on side.'

'You handed your notice in yet?'

'Soon. And Robertson knows it. Then after that...'

'A long holiday?'

'Somewhere fucking hot, you can bank on it.'

'I hear Hong Kong's nice this time of year....'

'Nah. Going further afield, mate. For now.'

I bet he fucking was. But he wouldn't be getting far.

'Test the water in Thailand?'

'As long as it's hot, mate, I'll be happy with Timbuck-fucking-too.'

Then I heard them step back inside. The patio door slammed shut and I was left alone on the roof in the freezing cold. I sparked up, letting what I'd just heard sink in. Pressed stop on the Dictaphone app, thought twice about listening back. It could wait. I got to my feet and paced up and down the flat roof, not really fancying dropping down to the terrace one bit. My guess was they'd been to pick something up–perhaps the last of whatever it was they'd gotten rid of–and they wouldn't be staying here long. Nevertheless, I knew I needed to be careful. One mistake and I'd be dead. No two ways about it. If they knew I was here, they could keep me here. Didn't stand much chance against two of them.

Barely two minutes later, I heard an engine fire up. Stepped towards the edge, careful not to slip and determined not to look down. But I couldn't help myself and I had to take a quick step back, both to stop myself from falling and to get out of view, because there they were and there it was. The Merc. Waiting for Phil Young to take a seat in the front.

92

I dropped onto the roof terrace when I was sure the Merc was out of sight. I could barely believe what I'd just heard, but there it was, straight from the horse's mouth. I played back their conversation, just to make sure I wasn't going mad. Paced up and down as I listened back, smoking right down to the filter and flinging it over the side before sparking up again. I needed to think on my feet, but felt like all sense and reason had vanished. I knew I needed to make a move and be quick about it. And then it hit me. I spotted a smouldering cigarette butt one of them had left behind. Couldn't be certain whose it was, but it was better than nothing. I carefully lifted it and wrapped it in a scrap of paper before burying it down the bottom of my inside pocket. DNA sampling had come a long way since I was on the force. It might just be the icing on the cake.

I turned to the patio doors and went to slide it open, but the bastards had locked it. Fuck's sake. Went to the edge, knowing it was pointless, and looked down. There was no other way, no escape route. Clocked the plant pot with the bush inside and went to drag it from the corner of the terrace. It was bloody heavy and more than good enough. Hauled the bush out, and had to work up a sweat, but it was the only option. I knew I couldn't hang around when it served its purpose. Took one last look across the city, the darkening sky threatening more rain and the night descending like a bad dream.

Then I lifted it to my chest as far as I could manage, the soil heavy as lead, and launched it through the glass. The whole thing shattered into a million pieces, just as the sirens screamed through the city beyond.

93

I left Han Lan's apartment in a hurry, knowing there would be eyes upon me from somewhere. The shattering glass was loud enough to make many a head turn, and I knew that if I didn't leave the place sharpish, I could be looking at blues and twos and staring at the wall of a holding cell in the space of half an hour.

I dropped down to the car park via the lift, trying to act as casual as possible, before leaving the grounds faster than my shadow could keep up. Having seen the Merc drive off less than five minutes ago, I'd have to be on my toes. They could be anywhere nearby. I kept my head down.

The darkening canal side was enough to keep me inconspicuous, and I kept close to the wall as I made my way past the bars and on towards Deansgate. Was more than tempted to duck into the nearest bar, now getting busier with the more eager after work drinkers, though it was still a few hours before clocking off time–but I knew it would be a mistake. I needed to be as far away from this place as possible, and I knew I wouldn't return unless I absolutely had to. I hoped it wouldn't come to that.

I reached Deansgate and headed up towards the centre of town, blending in with the Christmas shoppers as I smoked. The evidence I'd gathered was weighing on my mind. I couldn't hand it to GMP. That would be madness. And I wanted to remain anonymous, if at all possible. With the Met now involved–and better still, Interpol–I knew what I had would be damning. But I needed someone I could trust with it. No doubt Vice at the Met would find it all very interesting, but without a contact I was stumped. I needed Bob's input, and quick.

Headed up towards Albert Square. The crowds were gathering at the Christmas Markets. It was mulled wine and bratwurst all round. Enough to make my head spin. I found a space at the bar inside one of the German beer huts they put up every year. I just couldn't stop myself. It cost me a tenner for a pint, which was utterly ridiculous. Though half of that was a 'deposit' I'd apparently get back when I returned the empty pint pot. I knew one wouldn't be enough though, and I had to keep one eye on the clock.

I stood, back to the wall as the punters gathered in pairs, then groups. Friday night had started early and as the laughter and merriment gathered pace, I felt like a lemon just hanging around on my own. But I was keeping an eye out too. When I returned from the bar with a second pint, I checked the phone. There were several missed calls from a number I didn't recognise, and a text message. I opened the text. It was Laura.

I'm looking forward to tea with you later! Don't be late. Chippy tea! x x x

The quicker I got home the better, fish and chips or not. But it was the two missed calls I was more bothered about. I retrieved the number and hovered my thumb over the green call button. Thought twice. Could be anyone. As I headed outside for a smoke, phone in hand, it buzzed again. This time the caller's name flashed up. It was Frank. I took a deep breath, thought about ignoring it, then saw Maureen's translucent skin as she lay there in that bed at Christie's.

'Hello?'

'Jim?'

'Hello, Frank.' I ducked down out of the rain and backed into a spot as far away from the noise as possible. 'Can you hear me?'

'Just about. Where are you?'

'Fighting my way through the crowds,' I said, over the noise. 'Good to hear from you again!'

Even though it had only been a few days, it still felt like months since I'd seen him fall to his knees in that front room, the tears for his dying wife so raw. I knew he was calling for one of two reasons. Either he'd spoken to Karen about my unannounced visit or Maureen had taken a bad turn. I wasn't quite prepared for how it would hit me, but when it did it was as if the whole world had been sucked into some vacuum, leaving just me behind.

'She's gone,' he said, and at first I thought he meant Karen, that my ex-wife had gone to live somewhere else with her new man and taken my daughter with them. 'She's gone.'

'Frank...?'

'She wanted to see you, but it was too late. It would've been useless and she wasn't in her right mind.'

'Maureen...'

'She died less than an hour ago.' He fell apart then. Could barely get the rest of it out. But from what I heard, before the flood of tears came–and I could picture him there in some sterile hospital corridor–it was that Karen was not taking it well. And why would she? She'd just lost her mother.

And that's when the phone died, too.

94

I stood there, in the middle of the swarming crowds at Albert Square, the spell of Christmas thick in the air, the damp cold seeping through my bones, my mind empty and blank and my soul weary, and I cried. I slipped down beside one of the food huts, a hog roast bringing the punters in, and sank down to let the tears come. They came quickly. I'd always been a fan of Maureen. My mother-in-law. Forget all the jokes–she was a magnificent woman. Patient, caring, usually took my side when Karen had been pecking my head. She knew I had a tough job too. Could see how it put me under pressure sometimes. And she knew about the drink and didn't judge me for it. And now she was dead. I'd have to attend the funeral. My daughter was now without a grandma. My ex-wife without a mother.

I headed straight back to the bar and sank two more pints in a blur. The noise went up to eleven and I soon lost track of time. Found an empty seat in the corner and stared into space for a good half an hour as I nursed a hot brandy. I knew Frank would be in a mess. Karen would be numb. My daughter would be upset and confused. Tried to convince myself that they needed me. I couldn't be sure, but I suppose Frank only saw right to let me know. I didn't even know if he'd spoken to Karen. I could hardly ring him back and ask. I knew I'd have to go there in person. It was the least I could do, except I didn't want to do more harm than good.

I finally dragged myself away when I'd finished the brandy. Jumped in a black cab in a haze and left the crowds behind. Watched the rain turn to sleet as we drove through the streets. The night was still young and there were plenty of festivities already. Seemed all the offices were on work Christmas parties. I watched, not really thinking about anything, as group after group of revellers headed into the pubs and bars and restaurants, most of whom wouldn't be seen dead with each other on a night out unless it was for Christmas. It was that time of year. As we left the city centre I was reminded of what a cruel time of year it was to die.

Happy fucking Christmas.

95

Laura was full of festive cheer when I got back. I sat down and she handed me a beer. Stuck Simon's iPhone on charge, wondering about what I could do to make sure I didn't lose the evidence. I would need copies of the photos and recordings I'd taken on the Dictaphone app. I'd find a way, somehow. Thought about handing the evidence in to the paper. Who was the editor Bob had mentioned? George someone. If he phoned again this evening like I'd asked him to, I'd throw it his way. The shit I had in my possession was like a hot potato and I wanted rid of it. Get it into safer hands. I suppose I just didn't trust myself.

I drank the beer as Laura told me about her visit to Sara on the mental health ward. I was in no mood to hear it, but I let her talk. She accused me of being drunk when it became clear I wasn't listening–I guess I was just nodding my head in all the right places–and she asked what was wrong. I told her. She held me in her arms and we stayed that way for some time; her kissing my head and me gripping her tight.

She insisted I eat. I didn't feel like it but didn't want to let the girl down. She went to the local chippy while I sat and went over everything. It was something I was certainly tired of. And I supposed it was all over, anyway. I'd heard what Phil had said. He killed her. And he'd implied, though I couldn't be certain, that Rob Robertson was covering up for him. He was handing his notice in, leaving the country. I knew I had to get the evidence to the relevant people before he ran. Interpol would be best, and I would do it via the *Evening Chronicle*. It was the only way.

Found the scrap of paper with the name of the editor Bob had given me. George Thornley. Googled for a phone number and was about to call when Laura and Charlie came bursting through the door. The kid was eager to watch a Spiderman film on the telly and he was quiet as a mouse with his tea on his knee as we ate ours standing against the kitchen worktop.

I told Laura as much as I knew. She kept shaking her head between mouthfuls of battered haddock.

'A *copper*?'

I nodded. 'A copper.'

'And you knew him?'

'Used to patrol with him, back in the day.'

'Fucking hell...'

She wasn't wrong. I could barely believe it myself. Yet there it was. I would never have known he had such evil in him. As for his motives–and there was never a reason for killing someone in cold blood–someone, or even a group of individuals, had obviously corrupted him. Cover up and conspiracy went deep, as Bob had said. They thought they could hide it. But Phil's hands had been all over it. The man I'd once considered a friend was a murderer. And I'd do everything in my power to make sure he was punished for it.

I retreated upstairs to find a portable TV to watch while

Charlie was engrossed in Peter Parker and flicked on the news. The Vice corruption was all over it, and the media were demanding answers. We all wanted answers too. It was big news now, but when murder came into it, which it would when I had my way, it would explode. I knew I was sitting on evidence that would implicate tens more than those who'd already been arrested. I would take great pleasure in watching them all go down.

I sat and drank, my head empty and my heart wounded, and thought of Maureen. I thought of Karen too, of how much pain and grief she must be in. It was always hard losing someone, especially a parent, and even I was hurting when my Dad died. Even though he was a complete bastard, I still shed a tear. I suppose I'm an emotional kind of bloke, affected by funerals and endings in general, but he didn't deserve any of my tears.

The phone rang again and I picked it out from my jacket. The same number I didn't recognise. It was becoming a habit. I was in two minds about hanging up and tried to think of the consequences if I answered the damn thing. But then I thought, fuck it, and just answered. I mean, what harm could it do?

'Hello...?'

Silence on the other end, all except for a breath, then a click and the beep of a dead line.

I thought about switching off, aware that I was sweating. The number was a landline, but it wasn't one of those annoying sales calls. I could tell that much. There was someone out there listening. Someone who wanted to know if I was still around. Someone who could trace where I was. The beep carried on ringing until I hung up in my daze and shoved it in my jeans pocket.

I suddenly felt the onset of panic rising up in my limbs,

which were shaking big style. It was a sensation I couldn't control, and I sat there on the edge of the bed, the news anchor ringing in my ears, the sound of my own heartbeat pounding in my head. I swallowed and dropped the bottle of beer, where it guzzled out onto the carpet. Managed to stand up and forced myself downstairs, one step at a time and certain my legs would go from under me. I made it to the living room, gasping for breath. Laura caught me before I fell on my face, and I had to put everything I could into one deep breath at a time as she held me in her arms and breathed with me. She looked confused, concerned, and I guess I would be too if I could see myself in the mirror. It took me a while to get the word out, but I was fucked if I didn't manage it.

'Whisky.'

She seemed to understand and she left me there, twitching on the couch for what seemed like an eternity before she came back with a tumbler half filled with that sweet brown liquid. I clutched it tight, threw it back hard and felt the burn sweep away all the pain, all the anguish, all the stress until all I was left with was a sea of calm in a world of loud noise.

96

When I woke up some time later to find Laura stroking my head, I was sweating. I could feel how damp my clothes were. She said she'd run a bath for me, that I needed to relax and let it all go, that I was simply exhausted and run down and all I'd need was some good old-fashioned rest.

She helped me undress, kissed me gently as she helped me into the warm water, even washed me down with a sponge before leaving me to let the steam take the heartache from my pores. My bones ached, my head hurt. I closed my eyes, let the silence surround me. Tried to block out all the thoughts, but they just came and came again, relentless and overbearing, going round in circles in my brain, over and over and over. It was only the drink that could take them away, if just for a short while, so I could catch my breath.

I got out, dried off, found my way back into the living room. I didn't know how long I'd been sleeping, but it was dark outside. The night had descended like a black cloak over the earth. The TV was on, but there was no sound, and no sight of Laura either. Checked the clock. It was gone ten.

I could only assume she was upstairs putting Charlie to bed. I sat in the chair by the fire, the bottle of Jameson sitting on the carpet at my feet, the tumbler and a smoke in my heavy hands. I drank it down, glass after glass, and I smoked what was left in the packet, my head finally blank and my heart soothed just enough for me to be able to sit and let the silence wash over me.

The phone rang again, and I looked over at my jeans that she'd folded up. They were sitting on the end of the couch. I staggered to them, pulled the phone out. I wanted nothing more than to switch it off. I just wanted the noise to stop. I answered.

'Jim?'

Bob.

'Jim?'

'I'm here. I'm here.'

'Are you okay? You don't sound too good.'

'It's over, Bob. I know who killed her. I know it all...'

'Who, Jim?'

'Phil Young.' I let the words sink in.

'The copper?'

'The very same.' And saying it out loud made it all the more real. 'He's planning on leaving the country. There's nothing I can do now.'

I told him about the photographs and the recordings I'd made, about Li Cheung and Sherry, about all of it. The words fell from my mouth like I was spitting out broken teeth. I felt like my head would split in two right down the middle. He said nothing for a while, for what seemed like aeons, until the words I knew I needed to hear finally came.

'You have to stop him, Jim. Stop him and then it'll all be over. You have to.'

'I need to find George Thornley, Bob. I need to give this stuff to the paper.'

He very patiently gave me a telephone number and I scrawled it down as his voice echoed down the line. I struggled to hear him and it was only when I realised he was whispering that I blotted out the rest of the noise, the rain hammering on the windows. It was as if I was speaking to a dead man.

'Do it,' he said, then the line went dead.

It was the sound of that rain that finally brought me to my senses. It was a hard rain too, perhaps the hardest rain of all.

97

I sat on that number for a while, knowing that it probably wouldn't be wise to call him at this time of night. Instead, I carried on doing what I did best, pacing up and down with the bottle until Laura finally persuaded me to go to bed. Having drunk almost half the Jameson since I came back, it was no surprise to her when I passed out sometime after eleven o'clock. I awoke from a dream about Maureen in the early hours; the duvet wrapped tightly around me, the sweats and the shakes on strong. Laura slept soundly beside me, and I knew Charlie would be in a deep sleep too, so I lay there in the half light as the rain steadily sprayed the world outside and tried to ignore the racing thoughts. I thought about everything in those hours of silence, but mostly about what Phil had done to Angel and how I would stop him from getting away with it.

I must've drifted off eventually into an exhausted sleep because when I opened my eyes again, Laura was sitting there on the bed watching me.

'I'm worried about you. About your drinking. You need to get help, Jim.'

I knew it too. She was right; they were all right, they always were. I knew it was killing me and yet this was all really happening to someone else, some other me. It was as if I was on the outside looking in, watching him kill himself that little bit more with every drop of the hard stuff.

I sat up when I came round, my head feeling like it had been filled with a million angry wasps, my limbs aching, my bones battered and bruised. She'd made me a coffee and some toast, the absolute last thing I wanted. She insisted I have it and sat there watching me.

'So, that's it. It's all over. You can rest now. I don't want you going anywhere today.'

'It's not finished yet. There's still some stuff I need to do.'

'Jim.'

'It'll be done soon.'

Trouble was, I only half believed it myself. I wasn't so sure. I could only hope there wasn't anything else to contend with. My conscience kept telling me that I had to deal with Phil personally. I was the only man to do it. It was a responsibility I couldn't avoid if I tried. I mean, what are friends for if you can't tell them the truth?

98

I did the usual. Showered, changed, didn't bother to shave. Then I made the calls. I phoned Frank first, keenly aware that the man was probably as delicate as he'd ever be, but nevertheless, I needed to have this conversation whether I liked it or not. I stood in the living room as Laura lingered in the kitchen, watching as she scrubbed the dishes in the sink.

He answered after four or five rings, just when I almost bottled out and hung up.

'Frank. Listen, I just wanted to say... well, you know. I'm sorry. It came as a shock yesterday. I thought it best to leave you in peace and I wasn't gonna phone, but I just wanted you all to know that I'm sorry. I really am.'

I'd rehearsed it minutes beforehand, but it still sounded contrived and I was squirming as I spoke. I mean, who the hell am I to show any respect to my ex mother-in-law? After what I'd done, what I'd become? There was silence on the line, all except for the sound of his weepy breaths and a long, long sigh until he spoke.

'The funeral's a week on Monday. It'd be good if you can come.'

'I will,' I said, and I meant it. I almost asked if my daughter would be there, but he beat me to it.

'Nicole's staying at one of the neighbours. It'll be too much for her to really understand.'

'I suppose.'

'Thanks for ringing, Jim. Maureen will be glad you're coming. I'll let you know the details when.... when I know more.'

'Of course, Frank.'

'I'll see you then.'

And that was it. No long goodbyes, no tearful description of who was and wasn't there at her bedside as she passed away. Just the click of the call ending. I knew it wasn't my place to know the details, and I was glad about that.

I stepped out the front to smoke, suddenly eager to be in the fresh air and thankful that call was over. The next one would be less daunting, but just as important. I dug out the number Bob had given me last night. Let myself get wet standing there on the pavement. It was a personal mobile, no news desk for this one. I punched in the number and hit the call button before I could back out. It took just a moment for George Thornley to answer.

'Yes?'

'George Thornley?'

'Yes.'

'My name's Jim Locke. I'm a friend of Bob's. Bob Turner...?'

'I know who you are.' He had a gravelly voice, like he really did have stones in the back of his throat. Either that or a forty a day habit. 'And I've been expecting you to call.'

I said nothing and didn't have to. I could only assume Bob had given him the heads up.

'You know what to do. Meet me at the Kro Bar in Piccadilly Gardens. Two o'clock.'

'But how will you know...?'

'I'll see you there.'

He hung up, just like that. I stood there with the phone to my ear, listening to that dead line with the cigarette embers burning my fingers. Laura came out, asked what I was doing. I told her as briefly as I could and suggested another coffee would be just grand, just so I could get her out of the way as I made the last call. The most important one of all, the one that really mattered. I'd gone over it again and again as I lay in bed in the small hours. I knew I'd been building it up to be something more than it really was. It only needed a few paltry words. I suppose I had my reasons because things had changed between us, literally overnight. I found his number and pressed that button. Felt like I was hitting the button that would start World War Three. Felt the sweat on my palms and the heat rising as it rang. Then the line clicked and he was on the other end.

'Jim,' he said, after a pause. 'It's good to hear from you.'

I know what you did.

'I know what you did, Phil.'

I was still shaking long after I hung up.

99

I had to add a shot of Jameson to the coffee Laura had brought me, just to help calm the nerves. Because that was it now. Those six short words had sealed a fate for both of us. I knew what he did, and now he knew that I knew. Even if he tried to run, he would be caught, especially once the evidence had been handed to Interpol. Really, all I had to do was sit back and watch it all unfold. But I had my concerns. Phil had never been a man to go down without a fight. I didn't expect him to do so now, especially given the connections he had. I wanted him to know I knew he was a killer because I wanted the bastard to sweat. And come to think of it, he'd been trying to put me off him from the beginning. Tried to get me to stay off the case, got the Chinese involved. The other coppers were a part of it all too, but it was Phil who'd made the mistake of trying to throw me off the scent. He knew I'd never gotten on with Rob Robertson, and he knew I had a drink problem. He must've thought it was my weakness–and he would be right. But he made the error of believing that, just because I was a drinker, I couldn't do my job.

I felt the stitches at the back of my head from when I'd been jumped down Dalton Alley. I was now certain that it was him all along. Had he done it to get back at me after our little tiff in The Marble? Maybe, but more likely that was his first chance to do me harm. A warning. It failed. He always did have a screw loose, a few sandwiches short of a picnic. Never was that good at engaging his brain. And knowing Phil, I'd expect him to start panicking right about now. Trouble was, when a man panicked–especially Phil–he was more likely to do something unpredictable, something rash. He knew he was the caged beast this time. No excuse but to come out baring teeth.

Now would be a really good time to just go back to bed and stay there or, better still, disappear to Spain like Bob had done. Nothing would please me more. Except there were things I had to attend to before I escaped anywhere. Maureen's funeral to begin with. And I knew that I would have to deliver the news in person to Sara about Angel and why she had to die. Except that was a job I wasn't looking forward to at all. He'd killed her–*they* had killed her–because she was planning on opening her mouth. And they knew I used to be a copper. I suppose they must've known I'd spill eventually about my past to this stranger, this vulnerable sex worker. So they wanted me out of the picture as well, as quietly as possible, given the opportunity. Yet they'd missed it. His mistake was the manner of his brutality. They saw her as nothing but a commodity, even had fun with her before they'd put the knife in. If they'd have done it quietly, disposed of her body sensibly, she would still be down as a missing person and would remain so.

Just as I was draining the coffee, with Laura upstairs in her bedroom, the mobile rang again. I looked at the screen. It was Phil. I cut him off and took the battery and sim card out and slung them in the kitchen bin. Then I gathered up everything I needed to pass on to George Thornley - Simon's iPhone, Han Lan's papers and flat keys, the photographs, everything–and bagged it all up in Charlie's Spiderman satchel. With great power comes great responsibility. I'd buy the kid a new one.

100

Laura gave me a lift into town for my appointment with George. A gloom had descended over the city like a cloak. All the talk was of Christmas and the coming festivities. She said she wanted me to stay, that she wanted me here with her. She wanted us to give it a real go of things once the dust had settled and she would look after me because, she said, I needed looking after. I suppose she was right. I reckoned I did. And I liked her too. It was something I didn't want to think about just yet.

'It'll be great,' she said. 'Just us and Charlie. Sara as well, if she's out. Oh, Jim, it'll be great to have a proper family Christmas. And I do a mean dinner.'

'You're like a big kid.'

'But I just *love* Christmas! Will you think about it? I mean, where else would you go?'

She had a point. Where else indeed. I was kind of hoping Bob would be in touch and I'd wing it to stay with him in Spain.

'I'll think about it. I promise.'

'You'd better.'

She dropped me off down the bottom end of Oldham Street. We shared a kiss before she drove off, late for a hair appointment. I watched her go, then headed up through the Northern Quarter to Piccadilly Gardens, clutching the Spiderman satchel close to my chest like it was a newborn baby.

It was almost dead, with most people at work, but there were plenty of shoppers around. I headed over to the Kro Bar, the benches outside empty and very little custom inside too. I lingered outside, smoking, knowing that when George turned up he'd be coming from nearby, with the *Evening Chronicle* offices just a step away. I hadn't a clue what he looked like, nor he me I would've thought, but I kept an eye out nonetheless for the type of bloke I thought he might be. As old as Bob, I reckoned, or even older given that he was the editor. Tired and weary of the job. Perhaps a cigar smoker like Bob too.

I stubbed the smoke out and headed inside. Got myself a local ale and a Makers' Mark to chase it down. Took a table near the window so I could see the journalists coming and going from the offices across the tunnel. Checked the time. Nearly two o'clock. Took the head off the beer as the rain came again and spotted a short, balding man step up to the bar. He somehow fit the bill and I wasn't surprised when he stepped towards me with a Guinness, the lines on his face showing a guy who'd seen too much.

'Is this seat taken?' That same gravelly voice. He held his hand out. 'George Thornley. Bob's told me all about you.'

'Sit down,' I said, and he obliged. I pushed the Spiderman satchel across the table. I just couldn't wait to get rid of it. 'It's all in there.'

He nodded, took a mouthful of the Guinness. 'Damaging?'

'Oh yeah. Very. I'll let you hand it over to the relevant authorities. I'm done with it now.'

'You look like you can't wait to be rid of it.'

'That's an understatement.'

'Must be important stuff?'

'Without going into details, it is. But I'm sure you know that already.'

'I've spoken with Bob,' he nodded. 'Last night. He's told me all about it. Don't worry. We go back a long way. And I wouldn't go against anything he says. I trust him. And he trusts you. So. That's it?'

'That's it.' I took a smoke out. 'You smoke?'

'Not for me, thanks. Gave up.'

'Maybe later then,' I said, popping it back in the pack. I took a large swig of ale. 'So, what are you gonna do with it?'

'Interpol. They'll take over from here. But what are you gonna do now?'

'Nothing. Nothing I can do. That's it now. My job's done. Put my feet up and watch It's a Wonderful Life. Something like that.'

'Wish I could. A lot of work on with this story. I'm sure you understand.'

'Don't envy you. So, what else did Bob say? Did he mention when he'd be back?'

He shook his head. 'When the dust settles, I suppose. Can't blame him.'

'Did he tell you he thought he was being followed?'

Another head shake, another mouthful of Guinness. 'No. But that's Bob. Always a bit paranoid like that.'

'With good reason.'

'No doubt. Comes with the territory.'

'Are you worried?'

'Me? No. No, the Met and Interpol will sort all this out.

Nothing to do with us. The paper, I mean. We just report what's happening.'

'Took you all long enough to get round to it,' I said. 'You know. Seems like you've all been sitting on this for long enough. Why so long?'

'It's a very delicate operation. We had to wait because it would've been dangerous to go with it even a year ago.'

'So what's changed?'

'People move on. Nothing lasts forever. Let's just say it was the right time. A window of opportunity, if you like. That's all.'

'So why was it the right time?'

'Damage limitation.'

'You ever fear for your life?'

'What?'

'You ever fear for your life? You said it was dangerous.'

'It was a possibility, yes.'

'From who?'

He frowned. Took another drink. 'I've said enough, Mr Locke. Can't go any deeper than that. I hope you understand.'

I shook my head. 'Not really. But I suppose you have your reasons.'

He nodded. 'Oh yeah. And good reasons, too. Trust me on that.'

'Will it all come out one day? You know, the reasons for why it's taken so long?'

'I never say never,' he shrugged. 'Not in this job. You never know. Maybe. Possibly. It's something I don't honestly think about.'

'I suppose not. But if you don't mind me saying, you look ready to pack it in yourself.'

'What, the job?'

'The job,' I nodded. 'We all have to knock it on the head sometime.'

'As it happens,' he said, 'I'm done in a few years. Can't come quick enough.'

'I bet.'

'You can say that again.'

We were quiet for a moment. George unzipped Charlie's Spiderman satchel and peeked inside. Raised his eyebrows. 'Lot of paperwork. And what's with the phone?'

'You'll see. Don't lose it. Upload the content to your files. It's all there.'

He said nothing, just nodded and supped his pint. I did the same, swiftly followed by the bourbon. He zipped it back up and drained what was left of his Guinness. I downed that brown beauty like you wouldn't believe, finally relieved of all the baggage I'd been carrying around with me. It would remain in my head for evermore, but it was a blessing to be rid of the stuff before I went completely insane. It was done, except for one last thing.

'I know who killed Angel,' I said. 'Helen Shields. It was a man called Phil Young. A copper.'

'A copper? What, GMP?'

I nodded. 'It's all connected. They wanted her to keep her mouth shut, but it's all come out, anyway. It was a completely needless death. Poor girl didn't stand a chance.'

'I believe there are others. According to Bob, there are missing person investigations that are set to reopen once the force gets cleaned up.'

'He's probably right. There's a lot of missing Chinese women that were never accounted for. Prostitutes.'

'Who's gonna miss a prostitute...'

'Exactly. Especially a Chinese one.'

We said our goodbyes. I made a point of telling him that

I wished to remain anonymous. Less hassle that way. All I wanted was to just quietly fade into the background and get on with the rest of my life. He said he understood.

There was no point in hanging around. George said he'd be in touch if he needed me. I doubted that would be the case, but he reckoned otherwise. I watched him head back into his newsroom and he disappeared up the stairs with the Spiderman satchel under his arm. The big story was about to go nuclear. I'd make sure I was a safe distance away before it exploded.

101

I wasn't sure if he still had the flat in Hulme, but it was the best place to start. I jumped on a bus and headed out there. I was lucky to find a seat upstairs and had to fight my way through a thousand shopping bags. With Christmas just a few weeks away, there were only fourteen shopping days left. It showed. I thought about Sara and whether she'd make it out of hospital in time. I could barely remember what I was doing this time last year, and last Christmas day was a memory I must've blocked out. I couldn't recall the last time I'd had a proper Christmas. It was probably with Karen and Nicole, back when things were good. I hoped it could be happy again, one day.

The bus moved at a crawl down Portland Street. The weather wasn't helping, and the traffic was backed up all the way from the Oxford Road end. I sat and watched the world go by and thought about a past best forgotten in the force. There was a time when things were good, when it was all going right. And then it changed. I didn't want to think about any of the bad stuff - the whispers, the backstabbing, being ignored by people I considered mates - but it was there. I'd tried to ignore it. But then Phil coming on the scene had brought it all flooding back. I thought I'd left it behind me. I was wrong. And now, once I'd dealt with him one last time, I'd have to put it all behind me again. Except this time, I'd do it the right way.

By the time the bus had reached Stretford Road, the rain was coming down hard again. I dropped into the doorway of a Caribbean takeaway which stood opposite and around twenty yards away from Phil's flat–if it still *was* his flat. It was up there on the second floor, a balcony out front. It was a relatively new build. Old enough, at least, for me to remember us getting a carry out and a curry after the pub not so long ago. I waited. Smoked. Occasionally stepped aside for the odd customer, the smell of jerk chicken and curry goat wafting out into the damp air. Either he'd left in a hurry or he was still in there, pacing up and down and sweating. If he was paranoid about who was watching, I'd done my job. And he'd be right to be worried.

There was no sign of movement, but that meant nothing. He could've done a runner already, if he had any sense. Or he could be on the phone to one of his associates. Matt, perhaps. Or the Chinese. Trying to find a quick way out. I wouldn't know unless I went over there and knocked. He might not even be there at all, though I wasn't helping matters by standing around. Might even make them worse. I dragged in the last of the smoke, hoping it wouldn't be my last one, and tossed it into the gutter before stepping across the road.

I approached the door, glancing up to the second-floor window as I opened the gate to the front gardens. Thought I saw the blinds flick open, then shut again. If they did, the movement was quick. I pressed the buzzer for flat six and waited. It was answered with a click after a minute.

'Yeah?'

'Parcel for flat six–a Mr. Young...'

A sigh, then another click and the door buzzed open. Either he was completely stupid or he knew it was me. I pushed the door, stepped over the threshold. Felt like I was stepping that bit further towards my own demise. I paused, questioned whether this was a good thing to be doing at all, then thought again about what he'd done to that girl. And it occurred to me that there may have been more I didn't know about.

I took the flight of stairs one step at a time, anticipating he'd be anxious to receive the parcel straight away before making a run for it. I glanced up at the partition door, behind which I knew was Phil's flat. I could see myself stepping through that door after a session with the boys off duty, a bag of takeaway in my arms. I couldn't remember the last time I'd stepped foot in this building. So much had happened in between, most of it a foggy half memory. But it came back with every step. And just as I reached the landing, I heard a key turn in a lock behind that partition door and saw Phil step out into the narrow hallway. I stood my ground, expecting the worst, but the worst didn't come. I just saw Phil's head coming towards me and he landed it right on the bridge of my nose.

Crimson sprayed out onto the beige carpet, and the neutral, coffee coloured wall. I fell back, the pain blinding as he bolted down the stairs with a leather travel bag over his shoulder. He didn't stop to take a look at me and by the time I'd gotten back to my feet and wiped the blood from my eyes, he was down on the ground floor–he must've jumped down the flight of stairs–and crashing through the front entrance into the fading daylight.

I got to my feet, jumped down after him, and followed

through the front and out onto the street and the rain that was hammering down. I looked left, then right. For a moment I thought I'd lost him already until I saw him dart through the traffic of a side road, horns blaring. I watched him almost get hit, then he rolled across a bonnet of a BMW until he was away on the other side and running head on into the new Metropolitan University Campus and the crowd of students milling around in the gardens beyond.

I let the blood drip down my face as the hard rain belted down and ran. Found a gap in the traffic and weaved in and out before finding the other side and sprinted after him past a hundred students moving between lectures. He barged people out of the way and I was well aware all eyes were on us. The crowd made space for me as I ran, shouting for people to stop him, but no one was listening. No one wanted to get involved, and I suppose I couldn't blame them with the way I must've looked. At one time, it would've been both of us chasing a suspect for whatever reason, and now he *was* that suspect, a man with no way to go except for the traffic on the Princess Parkway. He'd have a job getting beyond that at this time of day. The dual carriageway was overloaded with vehicles at the best of times, yet that's where he was heading.

'Phil!' I yelled. It fell on deaf ears. He just ran and ran, out beyond the campus and on towards the Hulme Arch Bridge. I wasn't sure I could get that far without losing breath. By now I had a stitch and my vision was blurred from the blood and rain. I ran an arm across my face and just managed to see him jump a short fence. I knew that the embankment lay on the other side of it, and he would do well to avoid falling into the road with the speed he was going.

I caught up, my fitness totally lacking. Gone were the

days when I could chase someone *and* catch them. Yet he'd always been the fittest of both of us. Almost fell to my knees as I tried to catch my breath, but just stepped over the rail and onto the shingle and patchy grass of the embankment beside the main road. There was a steep slope and the ground was slippy beneath my feet. I'd have to be on my toes to not fall. I stood at the top, Phil in my sights below. He stood with his back to the traffic. That old friend of mine, that murderer who'd somehow lost everything I once respected him for.

'Phil!' I yelled over the traffic noise. Buses and trucks flew by, sending waves of rainwater onto the embankment. 'Come on, mate! It's over!'

'Stay back, Jim!'

'I know what you've done, Phil! It's over! I know you killed her! I know everything!'

I watched him shake his head, his clothes sticking to him as the rain pelted down. He was clutching the bag to his chest like it was the only thing in the world worth living for.

'No, Jim! Come on! What are mates for, eh?'

I eased forward, let my boots slide into the mud, and dug my heels in. Watched him take a glance behind him. He dug into a pocket, pulled out a phone. Dropped it to his feet before it went sliding down into the road. 'You can't run, Phil! It's pointless. And if you try, you won't get far. You know that! Give it up, Phil. Come with me, mate!'

'Fucking stay away from me!'

'Phil!'

'Stay away!'

'This is madness!'

And I believed it too. I edged that bit further, and by now I could see the look in his eyes. They were wide and blood-shot, with a madness only a killer could know within them.

'You killed her, Phil, and for what?!'

'No, no, no, no, no!'

'You raped her, you strangled her, and you stabbed her in cold blood.'

'Get back!'

'Just give me your hand, Phil. Come on, come with me. It'll all be all right, I promise.'

'You should've stayed away, Jim!' Several more buses went flying by, and from here I could really feel the spray and heat from the engines. 'You should've stayed away!'

'I couldn't, Phil. You know I couldn't!'

'Once a copper, always a copper...'

'What happened to you, mate?! What happened to the Phil I once knew?!'

He just shook his head again and again, that manic look in his eyes, that crazed grin on his face. In the rapidly fading light he looked half dead. His skin was pale and translucent, his arms shaking, knees buckling. This wasn't the man I once knew. He'd been corrupted, by whom I didn't know— but I could take a guess.

'One last time, Phil. I promise all this will be over as soon as you grab my hand. It doesn't have to be like this.' I shimmied down the embankment, digging my left boot into the sodden earth. Stretched out my arm and offered my hand. 'Come on, Phil!'

'It's over.' He looked up, met my gaze, the travel bag swinging from his right hand. 'It's over.'

'Just grab my hand, Phil!'

But he didn't grab my hand. He staggered back, dropped himself off the narrow kerb and stumbled into the road and the oncoming eighteen wheeler that was heading his way.

'Phil, no!'

He took one last look.

'No!'

One last grin.

'Phil!'

It hit him head on at around fifty miles per hour. The impact was all I saw, yet even then I didn't see enough. Later I would tell myself I didn't see it at all. It happened so fast that all I know now is the sound it made as his body was hammered into the ground and the screeching brakes of the cargo truck cried into the fading day, his bones smashed beneath the wheels, his skull crushed on impact, his blood spattered up the windscreen and across the wet tarmac, the life pushed from his body as quick as the heartbeat in my chest.

102

I did pretty much nothing for the next week, then in the final week before Christmas, just as I was finally getting into the festive spirit, I got some semblance of normality back and joined all the other shoppers out there and tried to find some last-minute bargains. It was an absolute nightmare, but I reckon I got there in the end. I got sidetracked several times whilst out shopping, usually when I was with Laura, and dropped into the pub frequently. Laura reckoned I deserved a break, and she was right. I sat there, usually in The Marble, occasionally elsewhere, and meditated on what had happened with the case. Angel was dead and now her killer had joined her. Interpol and The Metropolitan Police had made a further seven arrests since they buried Phil, Simon and Matt being two of which I took particular pleasure in. There was plenty more to come by the looks of things, and I watched the GMP virtually implode before my eyes. It was a force in crisis and North Wales and West Yorkshire hardly got off lightly either. As winter took a grip of the city, I sat in empty pubs and bars nursing Guinness and ale, watching it all unfold on the news. The media had gone to town on it and the whole country was up in arms. To tell you the truth, I was barely interested by the time Christmas Eve came, preferring to turn my attentions to the latest superhero films with Charlie.

There was one funeral I attended, of course. We said our final goodbyes to Maureen just over a week after Phil was killed. Karen was civil and Frank was a shadow of his former self. Karen's new partner, Chris, turned out to be a decent bloke, not half as bad as I'd imagined, and we all talked calmly and sanely in the days that followed about where I'd disappeared to and how I would get access to my daughter, eventually. It was a start. Given my ex-wife's grief for her mother, I didn't want to push her too hard. She'd had enough to contend with, but agreed that I should have a right to see Nicole. Nicole herself didn't know about any of this, which was just as well. I didn't want her to have to go through any of the heartache so soon after her grandma's passing. It had been a difficult time for everyone, and I was content to take a step back until it all settled down. It had been a long time since I'd given myself a break from anything.

I'd told Laura everything when I finally got back to the house that day. We decided it would be best to keep quiet about how Phil was killed when it came to informing Sara– she was fragile enough without having to go through that– and the last thing any of us needed was more death when Christmas was around the corner. It was supposed to be a happy time, the less morbid the better, and Laura really pulled out all the stops when it came to having a good time and stocking up on food and stuff. It was about all of us, she'd said, in the days before. Charlie, Sara, herself and me. A family Christmas, and one which we'd all remember for happy times. Subsequently, the entire affair was banned from conversation. When Sara finally came home, two days before Christmas Eve, we told her what we knew quietly and gently, and that it was all over now. No more pain, no more agony. Her wounds had healed well but the mental scars would remain forever, and it broke my heart to see her sitting there in front of the TV like a zombie, the regimen of antipsychotics and antidepressants taking all the personality from her.

We never mentioned the Punto and, thankfully, she never asked.

I'd fished out the mobile from the bin on the night I returned for good and put it back together. I'd been expecting a call from Bob, but none came, which got me worried. He'd said he'd be in touch once it had all settled down. I could understand his reasons for wishing to steer clear, but I was even more surprised he hadn't been in touch with George Thornley either. I'd called him one night when Laura was busy wrapping presents, standing outside as the snows came in again. George had said he hadn't heard from Bob since the night before he and I met in the Kro bar, but that it wasn't unusual. I begged to differ, but left it at that for the time being. Something didn't feel right, and I hadn't forgotten about what Bob had said about being followed.

It was Christmas Eve when I finally got that phone call, but it was far from what I'd been expecting. We'd just had tea–Laura had roasted a gammon joint, and I'd had several portions with a bottle of Rioja–and Charlie was so hyper about a visit from Father Christmas that we had to keep him quiet with his very own box of Heroes. The phone rang–the first time I'd heard it in weeks–and I stepped outside just as Laura was getting merry and dancing around the living room to Wizzard.

I looked up to the grey sky, the snow billowing down like a million angel feathers, and answered.

'Hello?'

There was a crackle on the other end, followed by heavy breaths and banging doors. I could hear the panic as I watched some parents from across the road bring in gift-wrapped presents from the boot of their car.

'Hello? Bob?'

'Jim!'

'Bob, where have you been? I've been expecting you to...'

'Never mind that now. Listen, I want you to do something for me.'

'Bob, what is it?'

'I haven't got time to explain, just listen!'

Shit, what new low was this? 'I'm listening.'

I waited several seconds for him to catch his breath. Heard him swallow, the panic in his voice.

'They've finally caught up with me, Jim. They've finally caught up.'

'Who, Bob?'

'Who do you bloody think, son?!'

'Woah, woah, wait a minute!'

'I need you to get in touch with George for me, there's a good lad...'

'Bob, calm down...'

'I can't calm... Oh shit. Oh fucking hell, Jim!'

'Bob!'

'Oh God!'

Then there were several gunshots before the line went dead.

I couldn't think straight after that. I called the number back several times and got a dead line. I called George Thornley straight away and told him what I'd just heard. I could almost see him turn pale on the other end. He said he'd be in touch as soon as he knew more. There was nothing more I could do.

After Charlie finally fell asleep, we helped Laura bring in the presents from the car and the next-door neighbour's. I tried to put a brave face on it but found it hard. Both Laura and Sara asked what was wrong, so I put it down to lost Christmases I couldn't remember and that I was feeling a bit run down. They left it at that and I managed a veneer of calm and festive cheer for the rest of the night, but inside I was sweating. All I could do was hope and pray, but it didn't look good.

I wished I'd persuaded him to stay in England, and I convinced myself I could've done it. When we finally got to bed, I lay there in the dark and made a wish, since that was what Christmases were for. And if God really did pull off miracles, we sure as hell needed one now.

After the chaos of Christmas morning–Charlie had us all up at five a.m.–I did the usual and was gracious and genuinely touched by the gifts I'd been given. A sweater, a pair of socks and a Laurel and Hardy biography from Laura. Something told me she wanted me to stick around. Both she and Sara were happy with what I'd chosen for them. It wasn't much but, given my lack of funds, it was enough. Neither had expected anything at all. Charlie was happy with his new Spiderman costume and insisted on wearing it. He succeeded for most of the day until Sara persuaded him to change for dinner.

It was the best Christmas dinner I'd had the fortune to eat. I thought of Stevie and all the others on the streets as I tucked in and washed it all down with a good helping of Jean Cave Armagnac for good measure.

But there was one last gift I wasn't expecting, which Laura handed me before serving up the pudding Sara had brought in flaming from the kitchen.

'Go on, then. The suspense is killing me.'

I turned it over in my hands, felt the weight. 'What is it?'

'Open it and find out,' Sara said.

I tore the paper off. I honestly didn't know whether to laugh or cry. I gave Laura a look.

'They're business cards. You know. I thought it might be a good way for you to get that money back that you owe me.'

I took one of the cards and examined it up close. I must admit, the printers had done a good job. There was a silhouetted motif of a P.I., his collars turned up and his hat tilted to the side. All very Philip Marlowe. Beneath it read the inscription:

Jim Locke: Private Investigator.

There was an e-mail address and several phone numbers, followed by the slogan:

No Crime Too Big, No Crime Too Small.

I supposed I'd be the judge of that.

ACKNOWLEDGMENTS

Huge thanks to my consultant Andrew Lowe for his encouragement and support.

Many thanks to Stuart Bache at Books Covered for the cover design.

Last but by no means least, thanks to my other half, Kel, for putting up with my expert procrastination.

ABOUT THE AUTHOR

P.F. Hughes was born in Manchester in 1976. He's worked in many jobs over the years—which has contributed strongly to his writing—and continues to work on the Jim Locke series, among other forthcoming projects.

He currently lives in Ramsbottom, somewhere between the city and the countryside, with his partner, his children and his guitar, and is currently trying to escape the real world.

Follow Paul at the social media links below, and sign up to his mailing list here for a regular newsletter: http:// eepurl.com/hpeT_f

 facebook.com/PFHughesAuthor
twitter.com/PFHughesWriter
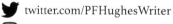 instagram.com/p.f.hughes_author